PENGUIN BOOKS

THE HEALING ART

A. N. Wilson was born in Staffordshire and grew up in Wales. His first novel, *The Sweets of Pimlico*, was awarded the John Llewelyn Rhys Memorial Prize for 1978. His other novels are *Unguarded Hours*, *Kindly Light*, *Who Was Oswald Fish?* (Penguin, 1983), *Wise Virgin* (Penguin, 1984), which received the W. H. Smith Annual Literary Award for 1983, and *Scandal* (Penguin, 1984). *The Healing Art* won the Somerset Maugham Award for 1980, the Southern Arts Literature Prize for 1980 and the Arts Council National Book Award for 1981. He has also written a study of Sir Walter Scott, *The Laird of Abbotsford*, which won the John Llewelyn Rhys Memorial Prize for 1981, and a biography of Milton. He has edited Sir Walter Scott's *Ivanhoe* for the Penguin English Library. A. N. Wilson is a Fellow of the Royal Society of Literature.

A. N. WILSON

The Healing Art

PENGUIN BOOKS

Penguin Books Ltd, Harmondsworth, Middlesex, England
Viking Penguin Inc., 40 West 23rd Street, New York, New York 10010, U.S.A.
Penguin Books Australia Ltd, Ringwood, Victoria, Australia
Penguin Books Canada Ltd, 2801 John Street, Markham, Ontario, Canada L3R 1B4
Penguin Books (N.Z.) Ltd, 182–190 Wairau Road, Auckland 10, New Zealand

First published by Martin Secker & Warburg 1980
Published in Penguin Books 1982
Reprinted 1983, 1985

Copyright © A. N. Wilson, 1980
All rights reserved

Printed and bound in Great Britain by
Cox & Wyman Ltd, Reading
Filmset in Monophoto Ehrhardt by
Northumberland Press Ltd, Gateshead, Tyne and Wear

Except in the United States of America,
this book is sold subject to the condition
that it shall not, by way of trade or otherwise,
be lent, re-sold, hired out, or otherwise circulated
without the publisher's prior consent in any form of
binding or cover other than that in which it is
published and without a similar condition
including this condition being imposed
on the subsequent purchaser

PILGRIM: God fader, shew me thyn entente: what is thys drogge and thys letuarie which passeth al the wit of Galen and of Hypocras and al thise olde clerkis?

GENIUS: Mi sone, sekest thow that salue which bindeth vp euery woorldli sore, and maketh the glad with hys gladsom spicerye and swete holsomnesse? Loue is that salue to maken the myrier then al this worldes ioies: and whoso findeth loue and drynketh hys lycour is knowynge of ioies which longen nat to this sari life but to the life of heuenes riche, of Gode, of Marie Hys Moder and of al the halwen sanctes.

A tretis of loue heuenliche
(From a manuscript in the Pottle library)

For Dorothy and Pamela, the nightmare had happened. It was over. Nothing would ever be the same. The dreadful words had been spoken. The surgeon's knife had cut into their breasts. Neither woman used the word 'cancer'. It was not even that which scared them. The shock brought with it a sense of self-loathing and emptiness which was more akin to shame than to fear; it was more like having suffered rape than being under sentence; not desexed, but mutilated. Dignity abandoned, they separately fell back on irrational faiths, awaiting what comfort these could yield.

Dorothy was a believer in modern medicine. Pamela was less sure. She trusted in luck, and the Virgin Mary and the power of prayer. But neither of them mentioned these things, as they sat in the day-room, waiting for Mr Tulloch to announce the results of their X-rays. The operations had happened six weeks before. Pamela had been discharged rather sooner than Dorothy, but now they found themselves together again for what was called 'the six-week check-up'.

'They say Swansea is very good,' said Dorothy; 'for philosophy, that is.'

She sat perched on one of the grey plastic stackable chairs, her perm gently resting against the glossy cream paintwork of the wall. Her face still had its reassuringly placid roundness, but her neck looked scraggier than Pamela remembered it, and her eyes were ringed with purplish shadows which made her seem still the invalid. They gazed out at the room from time to time, weary and frightened, but for the most part she kept them focused on her shoes. She fiddled with a white plastic handbag as she spoke, fastening and unfastening it, taking out and putting back paper handkerchieves as she explained her son's academic aspirations.

'We'd hoped he'd do something a bit more practical. Well, like medicine. But I dare say we'd all be better off if we could be a bit more philosophical.' The corners of her mouth, defiantly turned up in a smile which suggested the adjective winsome, seemed to be making the point as bravely as they could. She added a little defensively, 'Look on the bright side, that's what I say. There's a lovely hall of residence, I think they call it, and we thought the man in charge sounded very nice from Barry's description.'

'I hope he will be very happy,' said Pamela. She was a tall, thin, good-looking woman fifteen years younger than Dorothy. Thick blonde tresses were piled up on an intelligent head in a somewhat fantastic pyramid.

'Had you heard it was good? Swansea? For philosophy, I mean. I told Barry I'd ask you if I saw you again.'

'I'm afraid I don't know.'

It was hard not to sound a little crushing in reply to Dorothy's very natural assumption that Pamela, because she taught in a university, would know everything about every-where.

'They keep you waiting, though, don't they?' said Dorothy, momentarily allowing her mind to abandon Barry, and gazing rather desolately about the day-room. On the simulated teak table in front of them were some back numbers of *The Lady* and *Woman's Realm*. Beyond the intolerably jaunty curtains was a scrubby patch of lawn, parched by an unusually hot summer. It was the ninth week without rain. Beyond what had been the grass, were a row of prefabricated huts. Each of the huts was labelled with the lower-case which is now standard in every hospital: one door read 'Chest clinic', another 'Speech therapy'. Only one door remained unreformed. Directly on to the fading pinewood, an unskilled hand had some years before painted the single word.'BLOOD'.

'Mind you,' pursued Dorothy to catch and swallow up Pamela's melancholy silence, 'you mustn't grumble. I expect Mr Tulloch is very busy.'

Pamela had not thought about it. She did not feel inclined

to agree, but she said that she did, and asked Dorothy about her garden. Although they only had in common the experience of six weeks before, it had been so violent and appalling that they were inevitably drawn together by it, and felt a closeness for each other which neither could properly express. Dorothy's had been the first face that Pamela had seen when she had come round from the anaesthetic in that little ward in the previous month. Her smile had been truly sympathetic; an understanding which only a fellow-sufferer could have conveyed was contained in it. Neither of them had ever openly discussed their operations; for they were alike in their diffidence, and it had been a comfort to be in a small room, only two beds, and escape some of the unsparing confidences of the larger wards. But if discussion had been avoided, it would have been equally impossible not to allude in some way to their state; and Pamela had been moved, as well as terribly pained, by Dorothy saying one day, 'Shame, too. Worse for you, being so young and that.'

Since childhood, when churchgoing had become an obsessive occupation, Pamela had shuddered to contemplate St Agatha. *Emblem*, she remembered reading with horror in a book about saints in her father's library, *breasts on a dish*. Mr Tulloch had, in the event, been kinder than the virgin-martyr's tormentors, and only removed quite a small lump; though Dorothy had had a whole breast removed. Nevertheless, Pamela's fear and revulsion was, and remained, intense. Quite genuinely, and unlike Dorothy, she had no fear of death. But, months with a plastic bracelet reading *Pamela Cowper* on a wrist growing daily bonier and thinner, as the pain grew more intense and the nurses more jaunty and the doctors, when one saw them, more officious; while her lovely clothes hung in the wardrobe unworn, and her few friends gradually failed to keep up their regular visits; while her pretty house accumulated dust and damp and she stared and stared at the blank hospital walls, unable, eventually, to read, to pray, even to think because of the pain, and the ignominy of incontinence and bed-sores – these she dreaded, as she sat half-hearing about Dorothy's dahlias and waiting for her audience with Mr Tulloch. Her father, the Archdeacon, had

9

died in that way. She knew that she did not have the moral stamina to face such a passing herself.

Mr Tulloch, a rat-faced Scot in a white coat, strutted about X-ray, only a few yards from where the women sat, shouting at nurses whom he always addressed in the third person plural.

'They are a disgrace,' he trilled, 'a bloody disgrace. What use to a man is *that*?'

The object to which he pointed was a decomposing foetus, only aborted the previous morning. The fluid in which it had been preserved – a student nurse had actually placed it in the jar – had come from a bottle marked *formaldehyde*. A lab technician had blundered. The consultant would now be unable to conduct the tests he had hoped to do. The girl from whom the foetus had been removed would have to be lied to – like all the other patients with whom he was obliged to deal in a hurry. Her womb was in danger. Tulloch ran through the formulas in which this could be expressed – *further tests . . . I'd feel happier maybe if we could whip you in and have a bit closer look at you . . .*

He felt worn out. It was already three days since his wife had left for Argyllshire. By rights, he should have been with her now, a trout stream gurgling about his waders, the reassuring click of his reel being the only sound to disturb the natural peacefulness of the glen. But, with one colleague in the middle of a divorce, another off sick and three housemen recently left, what could a man do? At nine that morning, he had given a lecture about hysterectomy to some student midwives. He had been in the consulting room since seven minutes past ten.

'Take it away,' he said, pointing at the jar as he sipped his instant coffee from a plastic cup. 'Take the bloody thing away.'

'Where shall we put it, Mr Tulloch?'

'God! Haven't they any bloody common-sense? Aren't there any bloody dustbins in this hospital? Burn it, throw it away, get rid of it.'

A curly-headed registrar, Richard Crawford if the rectangle of plastic on his lapel told the truth, came into the room with a buff envelope and said, 'Here are the negs of those women waiting outside.'

'What women?'

'The six-week check-ups. They've just come from X-ray. You said you wanted to have a look at them.'

'Course I do. They're my bloody patients, aren't they?'

Once the fit was on, he could not have stopped himself being angry, even if it had been suggested that he tried. He grabbed the envelopes in haste and emptied the negatives on to the surface of his desk. An electric screen, designed for the purpose, was lit up, and he held the filmy grey images up to it each in turn.

'All right,' he said, quickly, tossing one down; and with another, 'all right, all right. Looks clear. Now, let's see, what have we here? Oh, Christ!'

Crawford peered over Tulloch's shoulder. A nurse came into the room and said, 'Sister wants to know when you will be ready to go down to the theatre, Mr Tulloch.'

'When I'm ready and not when she bloody well says so is the answer to that! God! Do they think I can be in two places at once? Do they think I have four pairs of hands? Do they? Who do they think I am? Look at them! They burst in here . . .'

The nurse had hurried back to the theatre sister to say that Mr Tulloch would be ten minutes.

'Are you going to tell her?'

Rage abated slightly because Crawford's face looked so young and anxious.

'Tell her what?'

The registrar picked up Pamela's envelope and refreshed his memory of her particulars.

'She's only thirty-nine.'

'It's spread so rapidly.' Horror and scientific curiosity blended in the surgeon's voice as he consulted the negative once more. 'We can't operate on that. What's the woman called?'

'Pamela Cowper. She's a don.' Crawford was still at the stage of his career when he remembered who patients were. He recalled the serene, beautiful face of Miss Cowper as she smiled at him on his ward rounds. A shame to have the tits off someone like that. The other woman, in his recollection, was a bag.

As if reading his thoughts, Mr Tulloch said, 'There's no justice in life, Rick. I'll see these women. You go down and tell that Irish bitch that I'll be in the theatre in ten minutes.'

In the day-room, Dorothy and Pamela had abandoned gardens and were discussing travel.

'I felt so guilty this year – it quite ruined Barry and George's holiday. We had been going to France. Not Normandy, we've been there. It would have been nice for Barry to have a proper break after his A's. Still, they were very good about it.'

'I'm sure they were.' Pamela more than mildly envied Dorothy her family. Nobody's holiday had been ruined by her own stay in the hospital.

'We generally go abroad most years now. Take all our own food and that, and sleep in the Dormobile. We've seen some lovely places. Italy, Spain, Florence. Did you manage to have a holiday?'

'I usually contrive to go away later in the summer,' said Pamela with a sigh, adding, and wishing she hadn't, 'after the school holidays are over, places are less crowded.'

'Well, we've had to go away in school holidays because of Barry.' She had not exactly taken offence, but there was a note of affront in her voice. 'Do you go abroad much?'

Pamela did not know of a way of saying that she disliked foreign travel – that it always ended in diarrhoea – without becoming still more offensive. She was glad – until she felt her heart leaping into her mouth – when a nurse came in at that moment and summoned Dorothy to the Presence.

It was comforting to be alone. Ever since the operation, she had felt this craving for solitude. There was no one with whom she felt on terms of sufficient intimacy to say, 'I have had a lump cut out of my breast.' In consequence, she preferred to keep the matter a secret. It had not been discovered until the beginning of the Long Vacation, so there had been no need to receive the sympathy of colleagues. She had informed the Principal by post and received a kind letter back saying that she must, if necessary, spend the next term on sick leave. There had been no need for the two of them to meet. Indeed, by the time Pamela read the reply, the Principal was on her way to Siberia to look for limestone.

So, throughout the hot summer, Pamela had guarded the secret. People at church knew that she had been in hospital with an unspecified illness. Sourpuss had visited her in hospital. He alone knew her condition and his austere, shy manner was soothing to her. There would be no danger of unseemly physical intimacies being discussed with him. Tall as a beanpole, grey, ascetic, disgruntled, he had been the perfect visitor. He had brought her the poems of George Herbert and *The Real Charlotte* in World's Classics, sensible little books that you could read in bed without your arms getting tired, and even slip into a dressing-gown pocket if you anticipated an abnormally long time on the loo. He had talked about pleasant neutral topics like botany and the Electoral Roll.

On the day she came home, he had brought her a framed watercolour sketch of a weeping ash. She had expressed gratitude, but it had given her less initial pleasure than the books, or the handkerchieves which he had presented on a later day. It seemed a vulgar extravagance to have bought a reproduction of an old painting at one of those glorified postcard shops which call themselves galleries. But looking at it again when he had gone she realized that she had been ungracious. He had meant it kindly. Who was it? Not Gainsborough; the trees in Gainsborough always had the hectic quality of cardboard about to collapse in amateur theatricals. It was too neat for Turner, and yet too mannered, not sufficiently innocent, for a Pre-Raphaelite. She wondered whether it was a reproduction of one of Ruskin's sketches, and as she peered at it through the glass, at the hand-made paper and delicate brush-strokes, she realized that it was not a reproduction at all, but the real thing.

Her displeasure when he first handed it over, had, however, registered, and he had created an atmosphere on subsequent occasions when reference to it was made which made inquiries about it difficult. She had hung it in pride of place over her chimney-piece, but talk about it was not yet forthcoming on either side.

Pamela did not exactly have men in her life. Sourpuss only touched its fringes. The only male friend in any way close to her was John Brocklehurst, whom people wrongly suspected of being her 'intended', but who was, in any case, on sabbatical leave in America until October. Normally, they had holidays in Wales together before the beginning of each term; but they had separate bedrooms. Once, at the beginning of their friendship, an alternative arrangement had presented itself. But perhaps it did not, strictly, appeal to either of them. She was glad that she had made nothing of his hint. Platonic friendships could, she had discovered, since breaking her heart and someone else's marriage over the other sort ten years earlier, be quite as adventurous, and ultimately less in danger of becoming dull. It was dullness in life that she sought to avoid, quite as much as heartbreak. It was, perhaps, above all the dullness of being ill which oppressed her and made her not want to communicate it in a letter to John. Their friendship was based on shared humour and mutual interests, and would have no place for injections and bedpans and X-rays.

Her reveries were interrupted by the return of Dorothy, whose wasted features were lit up now by a flush of pride.

'He says I'm coming on ever so well. The X-ray's quite clear.'

'Oh, my dear, I'm so glad.'

Pamela rose and for the first time in their lives the women kissed.

'I'd been so, well, frightened.'

'Of course you had.'

Dorothy was crying a little now.

'Silly, really. Mustn't grumble. It's just such a relief.'

As she held the quivering, bird-like form in her arms, Pamela felt suddenly cold, as if Dorothy's fear had communicated itself, been actually passed on to her. Over the older woman's shoulder, she saw a nurse at the door.

'Miss Cowper? Mr Tulloch will see you now, dear.'

'Shall I wait for you?' said Dorothy. 'I'm getting a taxi home. George said he'd take me, but he's funny about hospitals. Besides, he needed the car for work. You go off to work, I said. I'll be all right on my own. So it would be no trouble to wait.'

'It's very kind of you. But don't wait. I might be long, and someone is coming to collect me.'

This lie flew out rather desperately, and she hoped Dorothy's taxi would have come by the time she was slinking back to her Simca in the car park. She somehow could not face sharing a return home. She knew that, in her relief, and joy, a flood of anxiety which had hitherto been held in check was now bursting through Dorothy, but Pamela could not share it; not yet, not yet.

'Well, drop me a line and let me know how you are.' Dorothy's tone implied that she knew her place. They had exchanged addresses in the ward when Pamela was discharged, but neither of them had done anything about it. 'I'll . . .'

The nurse stood waiting impatiently.

'I'll be anxious,' Dorothy added. She sighed when Pamela left the room. For some reason she had come to love her.

Mr Tulloch looked up from his desk and smiled lugubri-ously at Pamela as she was admitted.

'Ah,' he said, 'Miss . . . er.'

'Cowper.'

'Miss Cowper. Come and sit down.'

She knew at once what he was going to say. She wished that she knew what she would say in return. It had only been such a small lump. He had said that there was a ninety per cent chance, whatever that meant, of it not spreading. But now his face told her everything.

'How am I?' she asked, to help him out.

'We've encountered some complications, I'm afraid. As I told you at the time of the operation, which was . . .' He consulted her dossier.

'The twenty-first of June,' she prompted him. Feast of the Sacred Heart.

'Ah, yes. June the twenty-first. As I told you, there might be need for some further treatment. Your condition has not quite developed along the lines we had hoped.'

He spoke as if it was her fault. She felt almost amused by the outrageous coldness of his manner.

'Complications are, of course, almost inevitable in cases of this kind.'

'Is this a complication that can be cured?'

He blinked.

'I would not be suggesting treatment, Miss Cowper, if I did not think it could be of some help.' He looked at his fingernails. He disliked clever women. Even though, at this moment, he held the trump card, he could crudely tell her – YOU ARE DYING – nevertheless, he felt a cold terror; not of death, but of Pamela herself. He knew that she could get the better of him in conversation and he was determined not to let her try. The other woman had been much more sensible; she listened to what she was told and she seemed grateful. A model patient. They weren't called patients for nothing. His mind drifted wistfully back to the dry flies and the trout streams of the highlands, as he heard her ask,

'What type of treatment had you in mind, Mr Tulloch?'

Damn the woman; as if she knew one type of treatment from another.

'As you perhaps know, we have made very great strides forward in this area in recent years, very great strides. Cases where, even five years ago, complications would have been insuperable, now, very often, have a strong chance of success.'

'A strong chance? Is that ninety per cent or less?'

'I don't find it very helpful to think of percentages,' he said. 'I had in mind a course of chemotherapy, what we call a cocktail drug treatment. What we do is whip you into a ward for a wee while and give you some injections.'

'Why do I have to have them in hospital? Couldn't I have the injections and just go home?'

'We like to keep an eye on you. The treatment can have side effects. I must warn you of that.'

'What sort of side effects?'

'Nausea, tiredness, a sort of fluey feeling. A bit of tummy

16

ache. Some people react more strongly than others. And there can be some hair loss too.'

'You mean that the drug which you are suggesting would make me bald?' There was a shrill note of rebellion in her voice. First he sliced at her breasts; now he tried to remove her hair.

'Yes,' he said bluntly. 'Hair loss can be total, I'm afraid.'

It was out of the question. She could not countenance such a thing. But she stared at him blankly, her lips quivering, and no words would come.

'What I suggest is that we whip you into one of the wards right away and start the treatment as soon as possible.'

'And if?'

'Yes.'

'If I don't have this treatment, I will die. That is what you have been trying to say to me.'

'That is not a way I like to look at it. You see, you really have no option in the matter as I see it.'

'Why not?'

'Because, as you must see yourself, if you don't have this treatment, your condition will deteriorate.'

'And I shall die.'

'Yes.'

He pursed his lips angrily. Even this, his trump card, had been snatched from him. He felt that she despised him. He in turn envied the comparative calmness with which she discussed the matter. Being professionally involved with the disease did not lessen its horror for him. On the contrary, not a day passed without its becoming more and more acute. He had his own plans prepared for the day when the condition developed in him. A wee bit of rubber tube; a drive to a lay-by on the Ring Road. Fit the tube to the exhaust, squeeze it in through the small window. Switch on the engine. Swig down the sleeping pills.

'How long do you think I will live if I don't have this treatment?' Her voice was perfectly calm now. Her large, moist, very blue eyes stared patiently at him as if he was a dim-witted undergraduate slow to construe a passage of Anglo-Saxon prose.

17

He shuffled in his chair.

'It's very difficult to say. A few months, maybe.'

She sighed, as if relieved. 'I thought you were going to say a couple of years at least.'

'I'm afraid not.'

'But, don't you see, a few months is much better than a few years ...' She had not meant to blurt it out. It seemed rather an insult to his profession to be expressing such enthusiasm for solving the Great Mystery. But the first dawnings of something like exultation were welling up inside her and she could not conceal them. So, nature was to spare her the agonizing year in the ward, with everyone pretending and getting increasingly fed up that she hovered so long. For most of her grown-up life, she had been more than half in love with easeful death, and, provided it could be easeful, she did not want to lose the opportunity of embracing it without sin. *A few months* – perhaps six, perhaps as few as three. Fear had absolutely vanished to be replaced by a sense of almost heady excitement, summoned up for her in the phrase she kept repeating inside her head, *at last, at last, at last.*

'It's my duty as your doctor to try to save your life, Miss Cowper.'

'You still haven't answered my question, Mr Tulloch. How great would my chances of survival be if I *did* have this cocktail treatment?'

'It would certainly lengthen your life. Some people have had it and gone back to leading perfectly normal lives.'

It was like the old joke – 'Doctor, doctor, when my broken arm is better will I be able to play the piano?' 'Oh, yes.' 'That's funny, I couldn't play it before.' The idea of her leading a 'normal' life almost tempted her to have a shot of the cocktail pumped into her arm at once just to study the effect. Who were these normal people? She had never met one.

'... It's difficult to be more specific,' he was still saying. 'Research in this field is making such strides forward that if we could keep you going for a year or two we might by that time have come up with an adequate solution.'

'You mean a complete cure?'

'I don't see why not.'

But, before that nebulous date, would stretch perhaps years of injections and spells in hospital; 'tummy ache' – why did they speak to people as if they were mental defectives? – baldness; and on top of all the physical miseries, one would live from disappointment to disappointment as hope gradually vanished altogether. By then, they would be prolonging one's life in misery as long as they could in the interests of research.

'I can't make up my mind all at once,' she said.

'Of course, I can't force you to live if you don't want to.' He stared for the first time into her eyes without blinking, and he tried to discern why she was behaving so stubbornly. 'But the sooner we start treatment, the longer our chances of arresting the disease will have to work.'

'I will write to you,' said Pamela, rising. She had made up her mind, but she could not entirely face telling him so, lest when she announced her decision to die with dignity the words sounded hollow, and she remained unconvinced by her own rhetoric.

She smiled, bloody condescendingly he thought, and as she left the room he began to arrange her notes and put them back in the folders with the negatives. He wondered, as he did so, how she could look so damnably healthy.

'I will write,' she said, when she reached the door.

'Good morning,' he said impatiently. In five minutes he would be in the theatre removing another breast.

– 2 –

Pamela, at the wheel of the Simca, zoomed homewards into the mid-day traffic, always heavy on a Wednesday because of the market. Late summer sunshine caught the plate-glass windows of the Polytechnic, driving mirrors of passing cars, shop fronts, as she scudded by. She drove under the ornamental foot-bridge, heavy with dark green foliage, and swooped down the hill. High summer, with a hint of fading, a promise of autumn in the air; the season had always been her favourite one. Now, with perfect timing, she would start ebbing away with the sun, and, by Christmas, if all went as she supposed, she would be gone.

She wondered when the pain would start. So far, apart from the stitches after the operation, she had felt almost none. Until it began, she would be free as a child. At last, she need no longer pretend to be interested in her work. How long was it that she had been nominally 'working' on the Middle English Alexander Romances? Nearer twenty years then ten. There was even a contract with the University Press mouldering away in a desk drawer, made when she was a promising young research fellow of twenty-two. 'Miss Cowper is going to give us the definitive work on Middle English Romances,' the Principal would say to guests at dinner. One watched the glazed expressions of boredom pass over their faces immediately. And friends in the Faculty would reproachfully ask her about it, ranging from the cheeky, 'How's Alexander?' of younger colleagues to the crabbed sadism of Professor Hovis, who had examined her thesis years before and who claimed to be 'looking forward to hearing from you, Miss Cowper'. 'Hearing' meant reading the results of her scholarship in boring periodicals, but she always took the remark deliberately and literally to mean what it said, by replying, 'You could always come to my lectures.'

There was not much danger of this. She had given up lecturing on Romance, and now gave popular, slightly jokey lectures on Dialect and Language. She had given a whole course on Australian language which Hovis had obviously found particularly offensive. She had no racial prejudice. She knew quite well that all the old truths applied: that we gave them passports and so it was our responsibility to look after them if they wanted to come here; conditions in their own country were intolerable. It was little wonder they chose to invade London, where store detectives were, on the whole, so myopic. And, just as other branches of National Life would grind to a halt without other Commonwealth immigrants – the clever hillsmen of Simla working out the intricacies of second-class postage; cheery Jamaicans telling us to mind the doors – there would be almost no one in the university apart from herself to teach *Beowulf* to the boys without the dear old Aussies with their sweaty, rough manners and their twangy old voices. Hovis, a graduate of Melbourne, a dapper, wholly anglicized little man with a sophisticated upper-class English voice, found all this hard to bear. He had even detected her humming 'Waltzing Matilda' as they paced up and down the Faculty Common Room together before lectures. It was simply not funny, unamusing; in his own term, infelicitous. For her part, the further she went with the joke, the more it seemed only one of many gloomy indications that she was in the wrong line of country. She was really rather afraid of Hovis, and dreaded his reproaches.

Medieval literature, college life, university lecturing: these were, she supposed, if viewed objectively, no more lunatic ways of earning a living than selling cars or shooting Ulstermen or sticking knives into women when they had lumps. But it had long seemed pointless enough to her. The burden of its pointlessness now fell from her shoulders. No longer, as she had been telling herself, twenty-eight more years of it until she cashed her pension. Only a few more months to go.

As she drove past Debenhams, she thought, What a mercy that this has happened in the depths of the Long Vacation. Her colleagues for the most part need never know. On house parties in Italy, or Norwegian cruises, or in remote coastal towns in Wales, Scotland, Suffolk or Devon, they were writing their books, ruining their children, falling out of love with their husbands, reading Tolstoy or collecting mineral samples. They would only begin to reassemble in five or six weeks' time, and by then, perhaps, she would be almost ready for the memorial service. A requiem in the college chapel was too much to hope for. The Principal's agnosticism would never countenance such a superstition. But Pamela decided that she could leave punitively strict instructions about the choice of hymns and insist that Hovis was not allowed to read Langland or preach a panegyric.

'Had she lived,' she imagined his professorial tones, 'we had hoped for the publication of her long-planned book . . .'

Leaving colleges behind her, she wheeled comfortingly into the street where she lived, a low-lying brick terrace, built a hundred years before for workers at the Press. Here was the only residential part of the town which had not been pulled down or increased in value beyond the means of such as she. Once an industrial slum, the world of *Jude the Obscure*, it had blossomed in recent years into a socially various neighbourhood. Old residents rubbed along with students, chic professional people, a few dons, a few Jamaican families, some orientals. There was an Indian corner-shop and a Pakistani postmaster. Some of the more fetid tenements had been replaced by modern constructions. There were new 'old people's flats'. The old church school, austerely Gothic, was boarded up until it could become a leisure centre. Children now played in the patch of green which had been created in front of the new primary school. The church clock, on what looked like a water-tower in Venetian Gothic, said one o'clock as she slammed her car door, and, while she searched for her front-door key, tubular bells in the campanile chimed the hour.

She always said that the house would be too small for more than one person, but that it suited her needs perfectly. Downstairs she had knocked into one room, papered with Morris's Willow in green. There were curtains of yellow velvet and a pale green carpet, so that the room had a summery light feel to it, with white silk lampshades and faded floral loose covers on sofa and chairs. One wall was lined with books – ecclesiastical and art history mostly. Upstairs, were five hundred or so detective stories. The rest of her library was in her room in college.

She caught sight of her face in the gilt looking-glass by the door and noted that it looked happy and well.

How unreal it all felt. How could he *know*, simply from studying a few photographs, that she was about to die? This morning

22

she had been in a low state of depressed panic. Now her mood had shot up into dizzy feelings of nonsense, as if drunk or in love. She decided to write some important letters and see how they looked. Then she would open a tin of lobster soup for lunch and eat it with Melba toast and blue cheese, followed by a cup of decaffeinated coffee. But first, she wrote to the Principal. She decided not to resign her job. She asked for sick leave. Then she wrote to Mr Tulloch to say that she had decided after long and careful thought not to take the treatment he had recommended. After writing this letter, she let down her hair and gazed at it in the glass. As she brushed it, it made a thick fuzzy halo of light, a mane of gold covering neck and shoulders and stretching down to the small of her back. *Death*, she intoned quietly, *he taketh all away, but this he cannot take*.

What about dear, solid, good John Brocklehurst? He was, in a way, her best friend even though, on the face of it, they had little in common except a host of acquaintances and the fact that they were both casualties of the nineteen-sixties, washed up by chance once more in the same university.

John's academic career, indeed his whole background, differed markedly from her own. She came from an academic dynasty: one grandfather a professor of Greek, two great-grandfathers the heads of colleges. Her father had been a parson but his intellectual promise had been unfulfilled. He had died as an archdeacon. John's people, on the other hand, had been mine-owners in the north. His father had got out of coal and started a chemical factory, subsequently absorbed by ICI. He lived on a competence as a result, but there was a ruggedness of manner which made him almost imaginable in the world of industry rather than what Hovis doubtless thought of as 'the groves of academe'. John had had difficulties to contend with, too, which prevented in his case the vegetation which had over-taken Pamela since undergraduate days. For a start, though good, his degree had not been brilliant enough to secure him the instant preferment which she had enjoyed. They had known each other since they were twenty, though their friendship had really blossomed in the first couple of years of 'research'. She had got a fellowship at that time; he had toiled on and finished the thesis and had a jobless spell before having to accept a lectureship in Canada. He had come home after a year, and been a lecturer at Nottingham for ten years before his comparatively recent return to the scenes of his undergraduate past. Had he stayed, she reflected, their friendship might have fizzled out altogether. They had been part of the same loose group of undergraduate friends and she could not clearly remember how they met. There had never been much question of an affair developing between them. She had first heard of him as the 'boyfriend' of a contemporary of hers, but this had not lasted. Gossip had it that he had proposed to another girl – playing Rosalind to his Jaques in an amateur production – but he denied this much later on when they knew each other better. After he had left for Canada and Nottingham, they had lost touch. Apparently, he married another philosopher in the same department, and she rarely heard of him.

When he returned to a fellowship at his old college at the age of thirty-five, he returned alone, and Pamela and he had renewed their acquaintance quite by chance as fellow-guests at a dinner party. They began to meet fairly regularly after that, and their first holiday together was at the end of that term. She had, naturally enough, begun to speculate about the wife, particularly since she was still wondering, at that stage of the game, what sort of 'friendship' theirs was becoming. Only recently emerging from a fairly disastrous entanglement with a married person herself, she had no wish to repeat the experience, still less – church having come into the picture – to go through the gruelling business of mentioning adultery in the confessional once more. There was, besides, everything against their friendship blossoming in a physical direction. It was not that she found him unattractive – even though by conventional standards he was too stocky to be thought impressive, and no one would call his clever bespectacled face, or his receding carroty hairline, handsome. As luck would have it, the precipice of an unhappy erotic attachment was one from which he appeared to shrink as violently as she did. It was several years

24

before he talked to her about his marriage – which had ended in his wife's suicide – and he was never eager to dwell on it much.

The undergraduate playing Jaques seemed to have anticipated the man he was to grow into by the time he was forty, habitually tossing his gingery head back with a contemptuous 'tut' at the mention of just about anything. His experience of other universities had strengthened, perhaps even created, prejudices which lay latent in the contemporary of her youth. The rather idiosyncratic socialism had been eroded by a despondent and rather romantic feeling for the past, a world-weary conviction, analogous perhaps to some of Sourpuss's bleaker moments, that everything had been finally ruined in the 'sixties. In his own field, he had lost his faith quite early on in the Logical Positivists, or what was left of them, and tried to maintain a manner of Romantic Hegelianism. 'The rest' – his term for all those with whom he disagreed – had, in common with the theologians, historians, politicians and architects, sold out to the scientists, a word he pronounced in a way which contrived to produce a 'tut' on both medial and final 't'.

All this, oddly, had not placed him on a limb, professionally or socially, in spite of his protestations that it had. His world-weariness made him, in spite of everything, appear to identify with the New Right, and his three books had been a success. In addition, he was developing a reputation as a poet and his lectures were so well attended as to lead colleagues to treat him with the nervous jealousy afforded to cult figures. Heidegger, Tolkien, Plato, even, had been names cropping up in philosophy exam papers since his return, with the inevitable clucking from hard-liners in consequence. As one remarked, they could almost have swallowed it if he had believed in God. It was his abandonment of a belief in logic which distressed them. Either way, it was no surprise that he was in demand in the States.

Pamela was baffled by his poetry because there was nobody in it, not even, really, himself. It was all about landscape, architecture and ideas, and, although she was pleased that his single volume, *Lakes*, had been so well received, she could not strictly like it. It did not convey what he was like. But this, as she recognized when talking about him to other people, was no easy thing to do. His diffidence was deep, like her own. She only knew that she grew more and more fond of him with the years and that the success of their friendship largely depended on her having no wish to pry beneath the surfaces which he chose to keep covered.

It seemed churlish not to see him one last time before the end. October, when he returned, might be too late. And yet, perhaps, by the time she got there, would it have been worth flying to America to say good-bye? She would probably be in a feeble state, perhaps even in an unseemly state, and the visit might be merely embarrassing. As she had once remarked herself, death is socially acceptable at the dinner-table – illness unpardonable. It would be difficult in this case to contrive one without the other. She tried to think what John would do in a similar plight and concluded that he would do nothing. But then, if he said nothing and then snuffed it, she would undoubtedly feel hurt, and she wanted to spare him that sense of let-down. It was difficult.

She decided to open a tin of soup and resolve the difficulty later. But she had scarcely had time to do so before the door-bell rang and the gangling, emaciated form of Sourpuss in a black shirt and tweed coat stood before her. He blinked in wonderment, the fantastic abundance of her hair draped over her shoulders resembling some beauty in a canvas of Lord Leighton. Unused to her even in so slight a state of deshabille, he said, 'This is probably an impossible time.'

His real name was Hereward Stickley, which suited him equally well, but the habit of thinking of him as Sourpuss was hard to drop. He had a short, brindled grey beard, hair to match which sprouted from the top of a sunken, thin, lop-sided face. His eyes were almost permanently screwed up behind horn-rimmed spectacles which could never decide on which part of his nose to settle. His, perhaps, was the last Anglican generation of lace and biretta men, touchy bigoted figures whose hard affected tones proclaimed the mysteries with such radiance and which concealed an ocean of kindness so effectively that almost no one would have guessed it was there. All his life he had worked in one pinnacle or another of the faith, always moving on after a purely personal row which he had elevated into an issue of principle. He had left his last job, as chaplain to some nuns in Wapping, after a violent altercation with the reverend mother about the community's catering arrangements. His last words to her had actually been, 'Even if you can't, I can tell the difference between butter and margarine', but this had since been translated into a dispute about aumbries. Pamela made jokes about him, but he was actually one of the few people that she uninhibitedly admired.

'Father, how nice, do come in,' she said. 'I was just about to eat, but you would perhaps like some coffee.'

'Only if you're making some.' His voice was, as she had often observed when dining out on his distinctiveness, pure Dover Beach – 'a melancholy long withdrawing roar'. He spoke as if nothing could really be more depressing than coffee, that making it was as pointless as drinking it; why not, his tone implied, simply cut out the middle man and pour it down the lavatory; yet, what must be, must be. Having missed luncheon, he was actually thinking how much more he would have preferred some of the fish soup and Melba toast. It smelt delicious. He wondered rather bleakly why his sister never bought fish soup. Perhaps it was expensive.

'Would you rather have soup?' she asked.

'Oh no, thanks. Some black coffee would be more than enough.'

When she was settled, and had brought in the tray of Melba toast, and bright Welsh butter, and steaming pink soup, and blue cheese to the dusty rosewood table, and given him his coffee, he asked, 'Well, how are you?' Pamela had told him after mass that morning that today was the 'six-week check-up'.

Beyond imparting this information, though, she had not yet developed a plan of campaign in relation to Sourpuss. Having been her confessor, it was perhaps only right that he should know of her state. And there was no one better fitted to receive so melancholy an intelligence. He came face to face with death in some form or another every week. But she felt shy about it. She looked up and blushed.

'They weren't all that cheerful.'

He paused and looked at the coffee. His tones when he replied were shockingly those of a real, spontaneous, secular response.

'Oh my God, how awful. I'm so sorry. Do you want to talk about it?'

It would be impossible to say No without hurting his rather acutely delicate sense of pastoral inadequacy when dealing with his social equals, so she said, 'They think I only have a few more months. But please – don't be unhappy for me.'

He slurped his black coffee. His features always appeared to be screwed up with pain, but the grimace now tightened and he looked at her over the spectacles which had now slipped down almost beyond the bottom of his nose.

'No hope at all, d'you mean?'

'Not really.'

'Are you going back into hospital?'

'Oh, father, is it very feeble of me, but I simply can't face it. Dying is one thing, and presumably one takes that in one's stride whether one likes it or not. But it would be worse than death if I had the treatment. Anyway, there's no certainty that it would work. I've watched people being treated for cancer. It's just a charade, a staving off of the inevitable.'

'But they've advised you, nevertheless, to have some more treatment.' His voice had become stern and schoolmasterly. A limp hand which even in this sultry weather looked frost-bitten hung loosely down from the arm of his chair.

'I'll get you an ash-tray,' she said.

'Not while you're eating.'

'No. I've finished, really.'

Producing Gold Flake with some relief, he shoved one into a yellowing old bone holder. When he had lit up he continued, 'Have you actually refused treatment?'

'Look,' she said suddenly, and as she spoke she took his wrist and stared into his face, 'what is the choice really? If I don't take the treatment it is a risk, and I shall probably die. If I *do* take the treatment it is a risk and I shall probably die. The only difference is that I shan't have to spend the last year of my life in hospital if I refuse to go back.'

'Is that what they said – a year?'

'Less. More coffee?'

He refused and inhaled the cigarette, peering at her closely. Silence ensued. He appeared to be on the point of saying something important, so she forestalled him by saying, 'Do you like the way I've hung that lovely picture you gave me?'

He stood up and looked at it.

'It's OK there – but the wallpaper slightly eats into it.'

'I've tried it in the hall, but I thought it would be a pity not to have it where everyone can see it. It really *is* beautiful. I can't decide who painted it. Someone suggested Birket Foster, but it's better than that.'

'Isn't it signed?'

'Not that I can see. Is it an heirloom? I feel guilty taking it off you.'

What was the point in feeling guilty? In a few months he could come back and claim it after the funeral. The thought had occurred to both of them simultaneously. He was blushing and burbling, 'No, no, I meant you to have it', while she tidied things on to the tray and took it back into the kitchen.

When she came back, she asked, 'What would you do if you were in my shoes? – about the beastly hospital?'

'I simply wouldn't have your courage, so I don't know. If we have a way of saving or prolonging our lives, I think we are bound to take it. Otherwise, it is morally no different from suicide. And yet, put as you put it, the choice would not be so easy. I just couldn't be as calm as you're being – that's all.'

'So you would do what I'm going to do.'

'Pamela, I don't know what you are going to do. I mean, I just hate the thought ...' The tide of Dover Beach ebbed and

29

then came roaring back. 'I know one thing we must do. I shall offer mass for you tomorrow. Let's have another talk soon – soon.'

She took it, when he had gone, that the one thing necessary to which he alluded was prayer. Wearily, she fingered a rosary as she rested on her bed during Woman's Hour. She had not the slightest inkling of the very specific line of action which he had in mind.

- 3 -

'Don't cry, Dol, don't cry. Whatever you do, don't blubber,' said George Higgs to his wife as they waited in casualty.

It was only ten days since Dorothy had been to the hospital for X-ray and Mr Tulloch had been so reassuring. He had asked her how she felt and she did not feel she wanted to bother him with her silly old pains in the back and neck, or her general feeling of tiredness, lassitude, depression. It seemed too bad to be bothering them again, now, with what appeared to be a broken arm. It was shame, quite as much as pain, which made her weep. It seemed so, in a way, *ungrateful* to be coming back and bothering them. She had so much wanted to be one of the doctor's success stories. They had cured the really nasty illness. The X-rays had proved that. Now she had to go and do a really stupid thing like break an arm.

It was lucky that it was a Saturday, and George at home. Barry had gone off on a hitch-hiking holiday in Italy with some of his mates. She was glad she was not being a bother to *him* and had not managed to spoil his holidays twice over. George was being very good but you could tell that he was narked. It had been such a silly thing to do, you couldn't really see how it happened. She had simply been putting a saucepan back on its shelf in the kitchen when she almost *heard* the bone crack. The pan had crashed to the floor and George had turned down the cricket in the next room and come running in to see what was the matter. He had rushed her to hospital in the Marina. He was always very good, but you could see he was narked, and she did not blame him.

'Dol,' he insisted in a whisper, 'people will see you. Here, have a blow on this.'

George was a heavily built man, a printer by trade. As Dorothy had opined a thousand times lately, he must have worked near Pamela's house. They must, Dorothy would say, have seen each other in the street any number of times. What a small world. It seemed unaccountable that someone like Pamela should live in that street. George had an old uncle who lived just round the corner. He did not even have a proper bathroom until five years ago. It wasn't where you'd expect a college person to live, not a lady. That's what she was, as Dorothy had told Vi, Barry, everyone: a real lady. George said those houses weren't healthy. Too low-lying, he said. His uncle was up in the hospital six weeks last winter with bronchitis. The air where Dorothy and George lived was clean and good. And they had a nice airy house, ever so easy to run, with metal-framed windows and nice neighbours and a view of the hills from their neat garden crammed with colour: zinnias, dahlias, gladioli. Pamela had spoken of *her* garden, but George knew those gardens. The size of a pocket-handkerchief, he said, not much more than a back yard.

He had taken out a handkerchief now – the display hankie from his top pocket, not the one Dol was using – and he mopped his brow. He had short, well-brushed, glossy hair, worn in a manner that had not changed much since army days. The thin, Enoch-style moustache conveyed similarly a military bearing. But he had none of the soldier's stiffness of manner, lolling like an old sea-lion in a state of desolate embarrassment at his wife's grief. His eyes were tired, but they tried to concentrate on objects round the room – the posters about VD, and the dangers of smoking; the piles of magazines; the pathetic, worn-out rocking-horse over which two children were squabbling – anything rather than the reproachful glances of the other patients. Anyone would think he had hit her.

'Keep you waiting, though, don't they?' she sniffed, trying to look on the bright side.

'That's my Dol.' And he regretted the reassuring tone at once for fear that it would set her off again. 'Yes,' he added hastily, 'still I dare say as they're short-staffed at weekends.' He delivered the judgement as from some professional standpoint. Dorothy took it up respectfully and said, 'Short-staffed, that would be it. Though you hear that they all work very long hours in hospital.'

The houseman in casualty removed some ball-bearings from a child's nose; stitched an ankle that had been put through a cold frame; sent a stomach-ache down to X-ray with suspected gall-stones and tipped the tramp who regularly wandered in there at ten past four every afternoon. Between patients, the young man tried, with varying degrees of success, to ignore the flirtations of a male orderly, and to run his fingers round the staff nurse's bottom. It was half past five by the time that Dorothy had been X-rayed, bandaged, put in plaster and given an appointment to return in a week's time.

'We've wasted four bloody hours in that place,' said George as he started the Marina, ignoring her tight-lipped *'Language!'*

At that moment, Highland gad-flies explored the interestingly bushy regions of Mr Tulloch's nostrils as he reclined on the bank of a loch. His wife, in brogues and headscarf, held his hand and looked at him proudly. After less than a week in Scotland, he looked a new man, his face fuller and a better colour.

'Penny for your thoughts?' he said contentedly.

'I was just thinking how well you looked and how peaceful all this is,' she said, wondering whether this was the moment to raise the question of that chair of medicine in Edinburgh.

Twenty minutes later, Hereward Stickley had finished saying evensong in the Lady chapel of the neo-Byzantine church near

32

Pamela's house. He knelt before the statue where a few votive candles guttered on a cast-iron stand.

'*Grant we beseech thee,*' he murmured in weary rapid voice, '*O Lord God, that we thy servants may enjoy perpetual health of mind and of body: and at the glorious intercession of blessed Mary ever Virgin be delivered from present sadness and have the fruition of eternal joy . . .*'

'AMEN,' said his sister, irritatingly. She usually came to say evensong with him. He looked round and glared at her.

'Still here?' he said accusingly.

She saw that there were tears in his eyes, and wondered why.

Richard Crawford and his wife lay on the grass in their garden watching the sky begin to glow with the summer evening. She was a plump pretty woman, her rather Teutonic features tanned by the weeks and weeks of hot weather.

She allowed him to put his hand into her cheesecloth blouse and to fondle her breasts as she said, 'Where would you like to be now?'

She smiled and gazed up. The few clouds in the sky were turning pink. Apart from that, she saw nothing but house martins and telephone wires.

'Here. With you.'

She kissed him.

'Where else with me?'

'France perhaps. Some nice topless beach.' He laughed. 'In Scotland perhaps' – and he burst into a not very good imitation of Tulloch's Kirkcudbrightshire voice – 'catching a few wee salmon, maybe.'

'Not with him. I wish you could forget that bloody hospital. You spend more time there than you do with me.'

'I know, damn it. I've got to be there tomorrow evening.'

'Why should you have to go in on a Sunday? You're a registrar, not a first-year clinical student.'

'Delusions of grandeur. Anyway, clinical students don't come in at weekends. We're five men short now that Tulloch's away. When he gets back we can think about our holiday.'

'All the sun will have gone by then. Oh, I've suddenly thought.'

'What?'

'Where I'd like to be.'

'Indoors?'

She laughed, and they wandered back towards the house arm in arm.

Dorothy had an early night. George brought up her supper on a tray and helped her to eat it. He shouldn't have. She wasn't an invalid; it wasn't right. She felt rather sick and could not really face even the modest meal of ham, salad and tinned peaches which he had prepared for her. He cut it all up small so she could manage it. As he took away the tray, he kissed her forehead and said, 'We've had some times together, haven't we, Dol?'

It made her want to cry when he was kind like this, and waves of guilt washed over her when he had gone. Even in the bedroom she could catch the faint whiffs of his St Bruno. He liked his pipe, but he only ever smoked it in the evenings. She wished that she was downstairs on the settee watching with him. The roar of studio laughter came up from the Morecambe and Wise show. She was fond of the tall one with glasses. You couldn't help laughing, even though some of the things he said were vulgar.

She wondered why George had said it: about their having had some times together. She supposed it was by way of apologizing for his impatience in the hospital, but the remark filled her with fear. It seemed sort of final, as if he was saying good-bye.

They *had* had times, she wasn't quarrelling with that, good times and all. She thought of how handsome he had been, when they married in 1952. He was six years her senior, but still looked a young lad; and thin, too. It had been afterwards that he started to thicken out. She remembered him standing outside the chapel, and her mother saying just after the service, 'You need some of our Dorothy's good home cooking. You look as if a strong wind'd blow you over.' And how *his* mother had taken it the wrong way and been rather shirty, somehow, ever since, even though she had lived with them for the last three years of her life; Dorothy had grown quite fond of the old woman in her last years. Sharp, she was, though. She knew how to make an atmosphere. Dorothy hated atmospheres. She did anything to avoid them. Her friend Vi said that she was a doormat to her family. But it wasn't that. She just didn't like people to be ratty. And she had been lucky. George was a good man – not like some people's husbands, always getting tiddly and running round after other women. Vi's Reg, for instance. George was a good father, too.

How lucky they were to have Barry. He *was* her life. She looked up – for some reason she was getting a stiff neck and it hurt to lift her head from the pillow – and surveyed the gallery of photographs at her bedside. Barry and his elder brother Kevin when they were toddlers. Kevin had been a lovely boy, too. But they said he wouldn't have been right if he had lived. They did everything they could for him. The hospital had been marvellous. A Doctor Rose it had been – or was it Mister Rose? She could never get it right. He was the one who did the operation. They had loved Barry all the more when they lost his brother. Meningitis. They said they could cure it now. It was marvellous what they could do. And beside that picture was Barry in the cubs. It must have been bob-a-job week 1968. She remembered how proud he had been going up and down the street in his uniform. He had cleaned a Rover. She remembered his saying it all week: Mum I've cleaned a *Rover*. Of course, they had no idea then how clever he'd turn out to be. Swansea, philosophy, his A's all lay in the future. Another photograph showed George with his arm round the boy. They were holding a football on the beach at Ventnor. That was before they got the Dormobile and started going to Spain and that. In many ways she missed Ventnor. They had got friendly with quite a few families in the boarding house, people who, like themselves, went every year. She still sent Christmas cards to some of them: the Buckleys, the Harrises, the Keegans, she listed their names quietly to herself.

Yes, they had had some times together, such happy times.

Desolately, she wondered if the happy times had come to an end – George, proud as Punch, cheering Barry on when he played football for the school; or reading his report. *He shows real aptitude* – memory still savoured the word. That was when he had started French. George had teased the lad a bit about it and tried out on him his own few words of French. But he had bought the Dormobile that year and shown them the Champs Elysées, Chartres, she didn't know what. Were they all over, these happy times, now that Barry was off to Swansea? She did not like to think of it. It gave her a cold sort of feeling. She wasn't like George, with his hobbies and his work. Apart from keeping the house nice there was nothing to occupy her any more, and the empty days without Barry stretched ahead like a nightmare.

That was what George must have meant. They *had* had some times, but they were over now, and they must think of ways of building a new life, together, without being too dependent on the lad. *You have to let them go*, that's what they said, these people on Woman's Hour and the phone-ins. Vi was always saying it, too. *You mother that boy too much, Dol.* She could be sharp, Vi, but she meant it kindly.

Suddenly, she sat up in bed, rather stiffly, so that it felt as if she had wrenched something in her back. What if they had told George something in the hospital? Was that what he meant by *We've had some times?* She miserably recited all the things that Mr Tulloch had said to her ten days before. 'You're doing very well, Mrs Higgs. I'm very pleased with you. I'm delighted to say that your X-rays are completely clear. Of course, we shall be keeping an eye on you, but for the time being it looks as if the operation has been completely successful.' 'Does that mean I'm really better?' she had asked. 'Yes,' he had said, 'you really are better.' Well, he wouldn't have lied, not a clever man like Mr Tulloch. Not when they had it on the X-ray. She was completely better. He had said so. And he wouldn't have had the chance of a word with George that afternoon in the casualty. Unless he had slipped into the waiting-room while she was having the plaster done on her wrist. It might have explained why George seemed so ratty at the hospital. He often seemed ratty when he was really just upset, like the time he said a word she couldn't repeat after his mother's first stroke.

As she lay there in solitude and the sounds of Morecambe and Wise changed to a film – a Western by the sound of it – she grew increasingly certain that George *had* heard something which he was keeping from her. There would, now she considered the matter, have been all the time in the world for Mr Tulloch to have spoken to him at the hospital – or that young doctor, a Dr Crawford. But what could they have said? Almost literally, she ached with curiosity. For some reason, it was impossible to get comfortable. Her wrist throbbed with pain, and she really *did* have a stiff neck. George must have left a window open. These summer evenings could come on nasty and cold. Vi said that *they* put one bar of the electric fire on, even though it was still August, but George derided their extravagance and said it was just plain silly.

He sat downstairs, a tin of beer and a tumbler on the coffee table in front of him; his shoes off; nylon socks plunged into the black nylon fur of the rug by the settee. The settee was 'leatherette', but comfy: beige the shop had called it. George had thought of other names for the colour but he had not expressed them. Dol liked it. She had been wanting a new, proper three-piece suite ever since that woman Vi had got one. George had wanted to know why they should 'keep up' – there was high irony in his voice as he said it – with people like that. Her husband was a foreman down at the works; not really a skilled man at all. There was something coarse about them. George would have soon put a stop to it had Dol put on half that make-up or drunk so much gin. You didn't like to see women drinking, not heavy. And he recalled with distaste Vi's orange fingers and her claw-like fingernails as long as that. It set your teeth on edge to look at them. Dol's hands were beginning to get arthritis, but they were still pretty hands, well cared for, with short, carefully manicured nails and – though she smoked the odd one – not a trace of tobacco stain. As he drew on his pipe and swilled the last of the beer into the bottom of his glass, his features were wholly concentrated in the direction of the set. He knew that it

37

was rubbish, but it took your mind off things. He had hated the casualty department. Dol took it all in her stride but he was upset by the sight of a white coat, let alone persons in pain, stitches, blood, screams. Gave you the creeps. To think, you drive past the place every day of your life, and it is going on there all the time, the screaming and the bleeding, the bustle, the white coats, the alarming smells. The air of squalor and cleanliness side by side; a worn-out rocking-horse and the smell of carbolic. Now that they were at home, and Dol properly tucked up in bed, he felt able to be shocked by it and he sucked on his pipe avidly for comfort.

Amy, the East Coast girl, who had arrived at the ranch so primly with her frills and parasol, was just beginning to melt a little when she saw that Clint had been unobtrusively kind to the half-caste Indian stable-boy. Clint still thought her a stuck-up bitch, but he was impressed by her *sang-froid* when the Indians attacked. Everyone was on the point of turning against the stable-boy after this calamity – except Amy who could see that, in spite of his Indian blood, he was on their side. Moreover, there were plenty of clues that she would be handy with a six-shooter. They put some proper rubbish on on Saturdays. Real rubbish. But you couldn't help admiring the way they did the fights.

It was a noisy bit of the film and George did not hear her at first, but it was, distinctly, Dol's voice calling out, 'George! George!'

What could she want? Just when he was settled into the film. The attackers were not Indians at all, but a gang of rustlers disguised as Indians, who hoped to poison relations between the Sioux and the local ranch-owners. He was beginning to wonder who would be on Michael Parkinson.

'George!'

'Don't get out of bed! I'm coming!' he called. He could hear her moving about now. He thought, in the manner of his *badinage* with Barry, 'We need the lad here to keep her under control.' The idea of little Dol as very naughty, rather a one, in

constant danger of stepping out of line, had run ṵ ...
of their family jokes before the lad turned so difficult.

He opened the frosted glass door of the lounge and pad ...
out to the bottom of the stairs. She was standing there on the
landing looking down at him, a scrawny, yellowing figure in
her nightdress. She had a fluffy bedroom slipper on one of her
feet. The other was red and bare, the big toe swollen and
horny, ruined long ago by the shoe fashions of the nineteen-
fifties.

'D'you want me to make a cup of tea?' he asked.

'I'll come down,' she said.

'I'm happy to bring it up, Dol my love. You stay up there
and rest yourself.'

'George,' she wailed.

'What is it, girl?' She seemed upset. It was only understandable after the long wait in the hospital. 'Is your wrist hurting
you?'

'Oh, George, if I stay in bed, will you come and sit with me?'

It reminded him of when Barry was a young boy and would
not go to sleep until you went up and stopped with him. Dol
wasn't like this, as a rule.

'Is there anything the matter?' he said. 'Shall I call the
doctor?'

'Oh no. You mustn't do that!'

'Well, I'll make you a nice cup of tea and bring it up.'

He turned to go back in the direction of the kitchen but as he
did so there was a crash and a heart-rending shriek as he
watched the thin frail figure, with its neat, white, well-permed
hair and scrawny neck, cascading, like a broken toy cast aside
by a petulant child, to the bottom of the stairs.

She something announced the expedition with the air of a strict governess who once in a while conceded the desirability of a visit to the zoo. But it had been entirely his own idea and he had pressed it on her so firmly that, even had she not been agreeable, there would have been little possibility of refusing to go. His sister, he had added, with barely concealed relief, could not manage to accompany them, it being the day for the old folks' tea. But she had provided a picnic. Cream crackers wrapped in grease-proof paper, a thermos of something boiled up from a packet; two miniature Swiss rolls covered in chocolate and wrapped in silver foil. They were asked to return the foil that evening. Miss Stickley gnomically declared that it could be 'used again'. She was a woman of few words.

Mass being early that day, seven a.m., they were able to set out after a quick cup of coffee and some toast and avoid meeting the morning traffic. They went in the Simca, Father Stickley's ancient Morris being considered insufficiently comfortable for so long a journey, but, a fact with which Pamela was not altogether reconciled, they were to share the driving. Initially, he had wanted to drive all the way, but her nerves would not have stood this. She did not want her car, like his, to bear the scars of his belief that 'bumpers are put on for a purpose'. Besides, she felt quite strong enough to drive herself.

He had raised the idea of the journey when she had gone round to tell him of a row she had had with her GP, an idle, overweight and vaguely libidinous Roman Catholic who had been the man who 'whipped' her into hospital eight weeks before with her lump. Why did the medical profession whip and pop to such a degree? Now, he had even taken the unprecedented step of calling at her house. Although the health centre was only round the corner, he had never visited her before. One got an unfailingly dusty answer if one asked the doctor to call for trivial matters like a high fever or a crippling stomach-ache and, even if one persisted in battling with the receptionists at the other end of the line and *did* insist on a visit, it would always turn out to be some more down-at-heel member of the partnership who came, and not Swynnerton-Myles himself.

He was a comparatively young man – not much older than she – but already well-shod, double-chinned, check-shirted, tweed-suited, college-tied. There was an atmosphere of claret about his breath and eyes and it was really rather a surprise to see him standing there on the doorstep. He seemed as if he had bulged from the pages of *Country Life* and did not properly belong to the sultry, dusty little street, its uncompromisingly vulgar, bright yellow corner-shop, its relentlessly cheap brick, the tiny scale of it all, its rather jaunty acceptance of life's messiness.

'Look here, can I come in,' he said, in that fruity Ampleforth voice. What was it, she had often asked Sourpuss, that made one want to punch R Cs? But Sourpuss, who in his youth would have worn a bucket on his head if it had been so decreed by the Holy Office, did not allow her to elaborate on this malice, even though it was from *him* that she had caught the trick of referring to them as 'our separated brethren'.

Swynnerton-Myles had swung his paunch through the tiny passage which served as her hall and looked round the drawing-room with smug condescension.

'Do sit down,' she had said, and his ample tweed bottom was soon smothering her poor little World's Classics Herbert on the sofa. He wriggled uncomfortably but did not move.

'Robby Tulloch has asked me to call,' he explained.

For a moment, she could not think who he meant. *Tulloch* had for some weeks been translated into *Pillock* in her own private vocabulary and she had barely considered the possibility of his having a Christian name. But, 'Oh yes', she said at length.

No tactician, Slobbering-Myles plunged straight in to a full-frontal attack.

'This is just silly. Robby is one of the finest surgeons in his

41

field. If he says you ought to have treatment, you have simply got to have treatment.'

'He gave me to understand that it was for me to decide.'

'Look here, you're bloody ill. You just aren't in a position to decide.'

'This is *my* body,' she said, not intending to sound blasphemous. 'Not Mr Tulloch's.'

'I just can't see why you are being so stubborn. We're trying to help you and you're just being ridiculous. This treatment would have been impossible five years ago.'

'So I understand. But is there any evidence that it will do anything but make my hair fall out?'

He had softened, too late, by this point and chose a kindly 'Look' instead of the abrasive 'Look here', 'Look, I know it's difficult. Do you think I like having to spell it out for you? Do you think I don't understand? It's very understandable that you should be frightened, but we are trying to help, believe me.'

'I believe you. That is, I believe you are trying to help. I don't see how a cocktail drug could help me, that's all.' She had smiled in her startled way, her large blue eyes almost bursting from her head with arrogant amusement.

'I don't know why you have adopted this destructive attitude towards chemotherapy. It has been massively researched, and it often saves or prolongs lives in perfectly reasonable comfort.'

'I'm not doubting that it works sometimes. Our Dean has had it and she looks as if she will be digging up Norse helmets for donkey's years.'

'Well then. You surely aren't doubting Robby.'

'I'm so sorry if I said anything to Mr Tulloch which sounded ungracious.'

'He just happens to be a very experienced, very distinguished man, and he quite understands your point of view. He is simply trying to help. There is no point in adopting this brave act.'

'I know that. But look at it my way. If what he said is true, and I only have a few more months, isn't it better to think of spending those few months fully alive instead of being a guinea pig for Mr Tulloch's experiments?' She ignored his

'That's just not fair' and continued, 'Either way, I take a risk. There is nothing brave about what I am doing. You are right. I *am* frightened. But unless you can guarantee me a complete cure I don't see why I shouldn't be frightened.'

He had lost his temper at this point and said that he supposed she expected doctors to work miracles.

Telling Sourpuss about it afterwards, she had admitted to being deliberately provoking. But he had merely said, 'We don't expect *doctors* to work miracles, but that is not to say that we don't expect miracles.' And it was then that he had suggested the long drive to Walsingham and back in a day, to pray at the shrine and be sprinkled with holy water at the well.

Never having been there before she had acquiesced. The heady irresponsible feeling of excitement had not altogether worn off since the Pillock broke the news, but Slobbering-Myles's visit had superimposed a sense of renewed fear. She had a strong sense, since his tactless call, of what a waste her life had been, the petty done, the undone vast.

Since her arrival in this stagnant town as a clever adolescent, she had scarcely left it except for jaunts in the British Museum and holidays never lasting more than three weeks. After an undergraduate career of easy brilliance she had sailed into a research fellowship almost at once at her own old college, and got her present job 'young'. Her twenties, coinciding with the 'sixties of the century, had been gay enough – doubts aroused by *Honest to God*, parties at which one had puffed marijuana, a succession of little affairs culminating in one big one, her own life and someone's marriage in ruins. The Alexander Romances, picked at here and there, had been gradually neglected. Then her father died, and with the little money left over, she bought her present house and found herself in the parish.

Grief (now for both parents and for all the innocent past they represented), curiosity and the love of architecture – all these things led her back inside the doors of the parish church. At first, her visits were furtive. She had stolen in when she was quite sure that it was empty and found it a potent place – somewhere that brought solace by making demands. Rather to

43

her surprise, when strolling round it one afternoon, some impulse or vestige of old habit made her genuflect to the tabernacle where the white flame burnt. It would have been hard to justify to herself in intellectual terms the direction in which her mood was leading her. But she increasingly wanted to return. Sometimes the reasons for the compulsion seemed purely sentimental; at other times, she knew that there was something much harder and more real which drew her.

Like an alcoholic who could not keep herself away from the bottle however hard she pretended it wasn't happening, she resumed the habit of going to mass. Why, she breezily said to herself, cut oneself off from obvious sources of pleasure? Smoke, processions, lace albs and Latin vestments – and as far as one could tell a different clergyman every week. Without her realizing it at the time, the parish was being amalgamated with several others, and the arrival of the new vicar, in charge of two or three similar spikey churches, made her feel safe. He was shy, uninspiring, unnoticeable. Then it was announced that the parish was to have a curate, and she felt fairly sure that this would mean the end of her brief phase of fervour. She could imagine him, fresh from a theological college, turning the altars the wrong way round and quoting from paperbacks. Missing a couple of weeks, she returned to find that the curate was apparently not yet installed. It was Christmas, and the figure in the pulpit, gaunt and furious, preached from the text *O generation of vipers*.

From then on she was hooked. Nothing was ever simple in Sourpuss's arrangements, of course. He appeared to announce some faintly different status for himself every week, increasingly less committal: from curate, he became priest-in-charge; from that to 'honorary priest'. He had, anyway, arrived, bought a house in the parish, and in effect taken the place over.

Her addiction began, like all the most important things in her life, as an elaborate sort of joke. It was nothing so crude as a desire to imitate, mock, parody the sermons. But she had formed in her mind an image of their archetypal gloominess which the reality of the thing hardly ever failed to satisfy. Yet, for all their melancholy, as she had realized from the beginning, there was

44

something about them which was compelling and in a strange manner reassuring. He was unafraid of using old-fashioned rhetorical tricks – the pregnant pause, the reconstruction of a Scriptural scene, the appeal for a decision on the part of his hearers. Intelligent beings ought, she knew, to be able to get along without artifice. But the affectations of his rhetorical manner were leading her into a recognition of things which lay deeper than life's surface. In short, he converted her. Whether or not the means of conversion were fake or real seemed wholly beside the point. His very unwillingness to be happy brought with it a joy so intense that at first it became mingled in her mind with her initial sensations of amusement.

He had seemed slightly cold at first; later she revised this superficial impression and decided that he was positively hostile. Confession to so uncompromising a figure seemed irresistible, and she was soon back in the comforting liturgical routine.

It had all ordered life splendidly for a number of years – but *how* empty that life had been when she measured it beside her contemporaries, who had appeared to cram it all in – divorce, socialism, children – on top of writing their books or shooting up the hierarchy of the Civil Service. Now that it was all hurtling to its conclusion, what did she have to show for it except some faded love-letters kept in a shoe-box and some offprints of articles published in learned journals?

Perhaps it had all been sent, or did she mean *meant*, this last phase, so that she could cram everything in before the end. She should, she now knew, have been bolder, less diffident, less satirical, more ready to face life head on, rather than obliquely and at tangents. Instead of thinking people bores, she should have Spoken Out to the few who weren't, made more friendships, in which something could be said to survive even after her death, written letters perhaps which would have been worth keeping. Now the dark end was in sight and she could not think of it as calmly as before.

She had decided that she must see John Brocklehurst before he returned in October. By then, she would probably have been dragged back into the Pillock's grasp, puffing and whimpering in some ward, bald as a coot and not fit to be seen. Her passport and injections were apparently in order (a colleague of Slobbering-Myles's had confirmed this when she went to the health centre), and she had signed a form to insure against falling into the clutches of the expensive American medical men. She had been to London and got a visa. She was to fly at the end of the week. But first, she knew, she owed this pilgrimage to Sourpuss, if only in celebration of the fact that something had, over the years, melted between them into tenderness. The religious aspect of their journey troubled her and she tried to banish it from the mind. It awakened feelings of scepticism scarcely remembered from an earlier phase of existence. But there was always landscape to enjoy on the way.

The bright ironstone of Northamptonshire gave way to the greyer colourings of the east. At Peterborough they had coffee but decided to press on without looking at the cathedral. Here Father Stickley took over the wheel.

'What I can't understand is why it has chosen *now* of all times to happen,' he said gloomily, and Pamela's heart missed a beat because she did not, at that moment, want to revert to the subject of her illness. But his mind was far away, set on the iniquitous changes that had befallen the church.

'I mean, they didn't call each other *Thou* in the last century, but they used it for God. Come to that, when I was a young man, no one called their friends *thou*; we were all you-ers. But it didn't mean we were all clamouring to *You* the Almighty. Now, these change merchants seem to think that the words are interchangeable. I should have thought there was a world of difference between them. What's your explanation?'

And she sighed with relief as she gave herself over to this endless and insoluble discussion, casting in the occasional irrelevance, such as that the Quakers addressed each other in the second person accusative – *How are thee today?* – but did they still? And then she wondered whether the sixteenth-century reformers regarded *Thou* as a more intimate term of address, whereas *you* was more formal; and for us it was the other

46

way round, so perhaps it would be truer to the spirit of the Prayer Book to adopt *you*. *Thou*, after all, simply implied that God was old and 'poetical'. But Father Stickley said that it was not a Reformation idea that God was second person singular and that the Canon of the Mass began with it – *Te igitur clementissime pater*. And so they gabbled happily on, the skies getting larger and larger above the roof of the car, the names on the signposts growing bleaker and odder: Crowland, Thorney, Adventurer's Land, Parson Drove Murrow. Father Stickley was a sensationally bad driver, and Pamela wondered whether the gear-box would survive being scrunched again as he said, 'What's wrong with the Precious Blood, I should like to know. The Prayer Book used to be full of it, but the Series have cut it all out' – or – 'Why should we drop the *Filioque* clause just to please those ignorant cranks of the East? People long to romanticize the Orthodox. I cannot see why. They have persistently encouraged ignorance and superstition among their people, and they have supported the most terrible political tyrannies in history. Yet so many Anglicans think the East is more attractive than Rome ...'

Their stomachs were both rumbling pretty noisily by the time they got to Fakenham, and Hereward had got on to Tolstoy. At almost every point, he declared, Tolstoy had been right and the Orthodox church stupid and cruel and wrong. If Tolstoy had been English, he would never have fallen out with the church, it was optimistically asserted; he would have thrown in his lot with the great Anglo-Catholic socialists like Father Lowder and Father Wainwright. It was all perfectly possible, but Pamela felt she would faint if she did not eat something, and eventually said so.

'We can have a bite at the pub when we get there,' he said.

'What about our picnic?'

'We can eat it for tea. It looked a bit meagre to me.'

Here cats, there children, here comically rustic figures with scythes dived for cover in the hedgerows of the Norfolk roads as the car went faster and faster, every jerk and scrunch giving expression to the priest's fanatical eagerness to be *there*.

Walsingham had been described so often to her, and not merely by Hereward Stickley, that Pamela approached it with some feeling of foreboding. 'The Walsingham Way' had become, in her private vocabulary, and in John's, who was agnostic, synonymous with that unmistakable and distinctive blend of homintern silliness which flourishes wherever the lace is worn. But they now used the term rather loosely and often described any male twosomes of their acquaintance as 'treading the Walsingham Way'. So much was this the case that she rather embarrassingly guffawed when Sourpuss said to her as they drove into the village, 'To think that I first trod the Walsingham Way as long ago as 1935.'

The shrine had been built, or, as they would have it, 'restored', less than five years before this momentous landmark in his spiritual development, and it had since prospered and flourished like the bay tree. For devotees, no surer proof was needed of its authenticity: here indeed was the holy well, which since medieval times had had miraculous healing powers; their devotion to the replica of the Holy House, the original of which antedated Loreto, being sufficient to justify the naming of this remote Norfolk village England's Nazareth.

Those who stayed away, and these had hitherto included Pamela herself, perhaps did so less from some English diffidence about so continental a devotion than from a sense that it all sounded a shade bogus. Whenever one heard about it from enthusiasts, it sounded more as if the whole thing had been dreamt up in order to out-spike the rest of the Church of England rather than from any supernatural prompting. There had, for instance, as far as Pamela knew, been no sightings of the BVM in Norfolk, either in the 1930s or since. But there *had* been endless acrimony and scandals associated with the place, and clergymen of Sourpuss's generation and older also spoke, in a rather creepy way, of a haunted vicarage, of presences, of poltergeists and of 'the overwhelming sense of evil which so often surrounds the holy places'.

None of these things prepared her for the sheer picture postcard prettiness of the place as they drew up in the village square, the old houses of brick and flint glowing in the sun-light. Sourpuss was quickly out of the car, stretching himself and looking twice the man.

They were soon settled by a table outside the pub with a rather good onion soup, crab sandwiches and two large gins and French.

'You are in love,' Pamela asserted. 'I can see it in your eyes that you are in love with the place.' The tension from his features had almost entirely relaxed, his eyes were ablaze, his lips moist, as much with enthusiasm as with gin.

'I've been in love with it all my adult life. I can't think of it rationally. It's been the focus and inspiration for everything. I've been here every time my life reached a crisis, and I've always left it with my difficulties resolved and my mind refreshed. The English are so terrified of beauty – not only in religious matters – in all areas of life. We think it is positively virtuous to uglify everything – ugly clothes, ugly cars, ugly new buildings, ugly poetry. But here's a place that is unashamedly pretty: that's its chief draw. It's always gone for appearances. People think that's superficiality. They don't realize that in religion as in everything else, if you look after appearances, the rest will look after itself.'

'I hadn't realized you were quite such an aesthete, father.'

'Damn it, there you go. I'm not talking about being an aes-thete. I'm talking about a fundamental principle of life.'

There was a pause. The conversation, though conducted in light-hearted tones, was becoming more serious than she had intended. He resumed more normal topics of conversation.

'They had some good relics in the shrine at one time, but I have the feeling that some modernistic wiseacre has been sorting through them. The last time I looked for the arm of St John the Baptist, for instance, I couldn't see it. They've still got bits of St Vincent, I think.'

Pamela hoped there was not going to be too much of all this sort of thing in the shrine, and, if there were, that she would not have the giggles. Given the rather solemn reason for their visit, and the kindness of Sourpuss, it would be rather a shame if she had spluttered with mirth at some pious moment. She had always believed in prayer as a generalized concept, not without Johnsonian parallel, because it concentrates the mind wonderfully. But she had never put her belief to the test by so specific a supplication as the present one. She tried to explain this as they sipped their gin.

'I don't think I'm really in the right frame of mind for all this,' she began coyly. 'I mean, I hope it won't interfere with Our Lady's healing powers if I'm not feeling exactly pious.'

'Frame of mind? I never heard of anything so ridiculous. If God had to wait for us to get into the right frame of mind, He would be unable to do anything. He takes what little scraps of faith we have and does His best with them.'

She liked this way of seeing things. She liked the way he always spoke of the Almighty in the same fashion as he viewed the hierarchy of the Labour Party. Not altogether what one would have chosen, but the best that one could hope for in the circumstances.

'The only risk involved,' he said darkly, 'is that prayer can be answered in unexpected ways.'

'How do you mean? Do you mean it might not work?'

He sniffed his gin with relish and screwed up his face into the scowl which it normally wore at home.

'This isn't a wishing-well, you know. Dear girl, how can I put it,' and he touched her hand gently with his knobbly, frosty fingers, 'God knows all our hopes. It's not a question of getting the formula right or the magic not working. When we come to a place like this He changes us, in spite of our own wills and natures.'

She looked over his head at the trees. He had never made any physical gesture towards her before, and she felt the intensity of his own hope as he spoke. He was not daring to say more. She suddenly felt shocked: not at anything *he* had done or said, but by what Tulloch, Slobbering-Myles and all the other doctors had never done. Never for a moment had they given her the impression that they wanted *her* to be better: only for their treatment to work and their theories to be proved correct. She felt suddenly, though she would have blushed to put anything so obvious into words, that it was love which healed, and not science or cleverness.

'I brought my bathing dress,' she said.

'Do you want that sandwich?'

'No, you have it.'

'There will be no time for the beach. We ought to be thinking of getting back before midnight.'

'I mean, if they want to immerse me.'

'Like our separated brethren at Lourdes!' His face relaxed again into its contented grin. 'There wouldn't be much room for you in the well here. It's about the size of a finger-bowl. Haven't I explained it? It's all perfectly simple. You simply drink some of the water while the priest makes the sign of the cross over you and then they pour some of the water in to your hands.'

'What a relief. I'd half imagined the municipal baths.'

'I only saw Lourdes once. Bernadette made them an absolute bomb, of course. I suppose they had to spend the money somehow. Besides, papists love spending money. But why a swimming-bath I can't imagine. It isn't as if she asked for one . . .'

Pamela did not have time to ask whether he meant St Bernadette or her celestial patroness, for at that moment two tittering youths passed by in tight jeans, with leather coats draped over one shoulder. They both wore white T-shirts with the motif CATHOLIC RENEWAL imprinted upon them in scarlet.

'Percy Flaming Dearmer lives again,' one was saying, interrupting the one in spectacles, who continued, 'I told her, I'm not saying mass wearing that old thing, and that's flat.'

'Maniples!' the other one shrieked. And then, turning to Sourpuss as if he was part of the conversation, he said, 'Listen sunshine, you don't mind if I steal your ash-tray, do you?'

'Very much,' he snapped. 'I was just about to use it myself.'

They hooted with merriment at this and sauntered back into the bar.

'Silly old queen,' said the one in spectacles, quite audibly.

'Impertinent bastards,' was Father Stickley's comment.

51

'Do you think they were *both* clergymen?' Pamela asked. It seemed too good to be true to have discovered a pair walking the Walsingham Way so firmly in her sense of the words.

Squeezing another Gold Flake into the holder he simply shook his head in amusement and said, 'Human kind cannot bear very much reality.'

They walked to the shrine after luncheon, and Pamela knew as soon as she saw the white stucco exterior that she need not have feared and that she was going to like it. Inside was an Aladdin's cave, with its innumerable altars and lamps and reliquaries and statues. The first thing to catch the eye as one went in was a brightly painted medieval effigy on the tomb by the door but it turned out to be a bishop who had died in the nineteen-fifties. There were several other effigies of famous spikes, including the legendary Father Tooth, who had gone to prison, if Pamela remembered rightly, for wearing the garments so much despised by the two young woofters in the pub.

The Holy House itself stood in the centre of the church. Inside, it was ablaze with candlelight, and Sourpuss left Pamela kneeling there while he went off to fetch the shrine priest. She felt mildly dashed. She had hoped he would do the sprinkling himself. Her mind drifted off in wholly impious directions; she could not avoid the disturbing impression that he was in love with her. But she managed to collect herself, and eventually the events of the last weeks and months began to fall into some kind of shape. She tried to realize the implications of her simple prayer that she should have life and, whether she liked it or not, life more abundantly. Surrendering herself to the strange atmosphere of the place and gazing up at the black Madonna in its stiff brocaded doll's clothes and golden crown, she said simply, *Thy will be done*.

The shrine priest had been prepared for their arrival. He was obviously known to Sourpuss but Pamela could not tell whether they liked each other. He was a slight, unimpressive figure, with a burbling inaudible voice and a wholly trivial face wreathed in a mirthless smile. He began to tell her in slightly more detail what she knew already about the water and the sprinkling. His grin seemed to suggest that everything he said was frightfully amusing, which it wasn't.

'They had to put up this iron railing round the well,' he explained. 'People came for cures and found themselves going away with broken legs when they fell down the steps.'

Having got over her own desire to snigger, Pamela found the clergyman tiresome. He seemed to assume that everything about the shrine was funny. This merriment of parsons is mighty offensive; and she thought how grateful she was for the tutelage of Sourpuss with his melancholy long withdrawing roar. 'I hate jokes in sermons,' he had once said to her. 'There are quite enough things in church to make you laugh without prompting from the pulpit.'

The other clergyman was only solemn for the duration of the ceremony, which began and ended rather sooner than she was ready for it. She drank the water, which was lukewarm and tasted of the washing-up liquid at the bottom of the tumbler. They had forgotten to get out a silver vessel meant for the purpose. She sprinkled herself with the water poured on her hands. He made the sign of the cross; she did so, too. A few prayers, of an inanely mariolatrous kind, were said. Then more mirthless grins and tasteless jokes.

'You can tell the chapel of the Ascension because there are a pair of feet dangling over the holy table.'

Well, it *did* look peculiar, but perhaps only one's own jokes about churchy things were acceptable; other people's never quite came off. She was glad when Sourpuss froze off his invitation to tea and said that they would soon be having to drive home.

Half an hour more or so was enough of the shrine. They found themselves being followed round by the two young woofters, who made comments about everything in rather too loud voices. Nothing seemed right for them – lamps hung too high, candlesticks not straight, frontals crooked, carpets the wrong colour. She shared none of their distaste, but the whole place, after a while, though marvellous enough in its way and somewhere to treasure in the memory, gave one the feeling of having eaten too many sweets.

'It's spoilt, of course,' sighed Father Stickley over their tea in the Knight's Gate café. 'Everywhere is. But you felt the supernatural atmosphere nevertheless?'

'Yes. Yes I did. I know it seems silly, and to undermine the whole point of our being here, but I feel a desire to live, combined with a feeling that I don't really mind how long. It's hard to explain.'

'Then don't try.'

Their hands almost brushed together as they fed the cream crackers to the seagulls and plovers in a field some seventy miles along the road for home.

Her picture of him had changed. No less remote, his single-heartedness now seemed different. They stood for some time taking in the strangeness of the moment. Her hair was loose over her shoulders, and, caught by a gentle breeze, he could just feel it touching his cheek. They stared intently westwards at the vast glowing sky, a pageant of red and gold. He seemed caught up in its blend of mystery and splendid anger and, when she stole a frightened glance in his direction, afraid lest their eyes should meet, he did not appear to notice, and continued his silent communion with the larger elements.

- 5 -

Vi's nerve was shaken by the ward. She felt that all eyes were upon her and it cramped her normal exuberance. Everyone in the beds around poor old Dorothy seemed so decrepit. One old lady had her leg hoisted too high on a pulley and kept calling out in a weird deep tone. You could not tell what she was saying; it was like an aged bird cawing in the tree-tops; and this, apart from all the staring eyes, inhibited conversation. Another old woman looked so thin and yellow that Vi thought she was dead, until she saw the eyes rolling, as she swayed to and fro on her pillow. Even the slightly younger ones looked as if they had ceased to care. Dorothy's own appearance was disgraceful: her hair not done, her eyes weak and hollow-looking, her complexion a funny waxy colour. It was alarming to see what a fortnight had done. Two weeks before, Vi had left for Torremolinos, and Dorothy really seemed on the mend. Now, it was as if she had aged ten years.

Vi, on the other hand, was in rude health and looked it. The bathroom scales said she had put on four and a half pounds, and by the look of her they had been shared fairly generously round chin, shoulders and bottom. Her cheekbones were tanned by lotion, by lamps from Boots, and by the last two weeks of Spanish sunshine. Her large arms, wobbling like jellies out of the short sleeves of her print frock, as bright as tinned salmon, rolled their way in an almost boneless extension to the long red talons at the end of her fingers.

Dorothy was, of course, older, as Vi kept telling herself, but not that much older than herself. It frightened her, to see what a broken arm (now twice broken) and a fractured collarbone could do. She gazed desolately down at the tea which the nurse had kindly brought, a brick-coloured fluid in a dark green cup. For the umpteenth time she stirred it with a plastic spoon and said,

'You'll fade away if you don't eat.'

Dorothy, prostrate in the bed, looked up at her with weak eyes and managed a smile. Vi meant to be kind, but her voice *carried* so. There were not many visitors in that ward – there never were – and Dorothy had the sense that all the other women were listening to what was being said.

'Would you like me to help you eat a bit of bread and butter?' Vi insisted.

Dorothy shook her head stubbornly and smiled distantly. Vi would not stay much longer, surely. It wasn't that Dorothy did not like Vi. You couldn't help liking Vi. Even George had once said that. Vi was one of the best. It was simply that now, Dorothy felt overwhelmed by a feeling of tiredness, an inability to think properly or to focus her mind or her eyes for more than a few minutes at a time.

'It's a disgrace, putting you in here with these old things,' Vi gassed on.

'Ssh, Vi. Don't. People will hear.'

'But it is. I mean, I wouldn't stand for it if I was you. This is like a geriatric. Well, that's what it is. I remember my nana being brought here after her stroke.'

'George says I'm better here. The nurses,' her voice sank to a hushed whisper as she saw one approach, 'are very kind. They've got more time for you here than at some of the other hospitals.'

'I can't keep track of all the hospitals in this town. But they should have sent you where you was before. You know, for your *operation*.' It was as if Dorothy might have forgotten about it. She had not let on to any other patients in this ward that she had recently had an operation. Now the nosey-parkers would call out and ask about it when Vi had gone. 'I don't like having you cooped up in here with these old darlings.'

'Tell me about your holiday,' Dorothy whispered. Vi was a one. Given half a chance, she really would have been bossing the doctors and nurses about, a thing undreamt of in Dorothy's scheme of things. Everyone came to this particular hospital for fractures. It was well known. The other hospital, where she had had the operation, did not even have a casualty department. She remembered the alarming notices in the drive to that effect.

'I've told you all about it,' said Vi, glancing up at the clock on the wall and wondering when it would be tactful to leave. 'Same as I say, as soon as Reg's stomach cleared up we had a smashing time, really smashing. The hotel had two pools – one salt water and the other, you know, like. And the sea was as blue as anything. It was really smashing.'

'Did you go to the sea much, then?'

'Well, it was a mile or so away. But the views of it were really lovely.'

'I'm sorry Reg was poorly.'

'He thought it was something he'd eaten, but you do have diarrhoea and that to start with. He wouldn't eat the tablets like I did. Seen a thing on telly as how they paralyse you from

the waist down.' She shrieked, so that even the nurse turned to
see what caused such nervous merriment. 'Chance'd be a fine
thing with Reg!'

Dorothy did not like this 'vulgar' side to Vi's talk. Of course,
she and George, in their time, had carried on like everyone
else; but never talked about it to other people. It did not seem
right.

'You'll be glad Barry's back safe and sound, though,' Vi said,
suddenly, changing the subject.

'Barry?' But the lad was in Italy. Why was Vi talking about
Barry all of a sudden? Dorothy's attention became more sharply
focused once more on Vi's loud tones.

'I *told* you. He got back last night. Well, before tea. I'm taking
him and his mate to the fair tonight.'

'But he's abroad. Naples or Spain, or . . .' It was unimaginable that the boy would have been at home for a whole day and
not been to see his mother; and now that, instead of coming to
the evening visiting hour, he would go to the fair with Vi. There
must have been some mistake. Of course, Dol had agreed with
George that Barry should not visit earlier in the summer when
she had her operation. That was all different. He had his A's still to
think about. And they did not want the lad to know too much
about the operation. But this was so different. A broken arm.

'You know,' Vi was elaborating. 'It's the last day of St Giles's
Fair tonight. You know how I never like to miss it; and,
besides, it'll do the lad good to get out and enjoy himself.'

'But why can't he come and see me?' Dorothy murmured.

'Give him a chance, Dol. He's only just got back. You
wouldn't want to stop the lad going to the fair . . .'

Vi had only half meant to tell Dol about the lad's return. It
was silly the way George wanted to keep everything a secret.
Besides, she had illogically concluded, why shouldn't the boy
be told that his mother was ill? Yet she and George and Reg
had agreed, last night in the boozer, that it would do no good
to Dorothy to look up and see Barry walking into the ward in
his present state. On the other hand, she knew that Dorothy
would not be satisfied once she knew that the boy was home.

Vi had, indeed, contemplated taking him with her on her visit that afternoon but his mate Hunk had wanted him to go to Swindon to look at a motor car. Then, since this evening was the last of the fair, it did, genuinely, seem sad to miss it by being up at the hospital. One night, they had all agreed, would not make that much difference. George could go up as usual and they could decide what to do about telling Dorothy later. It would not be nice for her. Vi wished that she had not spilt the beans, but it could not be helped. It was often better to give these things an airing.

Dorothy lay back on her pillows and closed her eyes. She was fully conscious again now, concentrating on the horror of what Vi had just said, and smarting inwardly. She could hardly believe it. Vi taking *her* Barry to St Giles's Fair. George not having *said* anything. Barry himself being prepared to come home without so much as a message to see how she was. The thought of it all revived her real, physical pain. Vi could not know how much it was hurting her. Through neck and shoulders and down to the small of her back, it stabbed away. But worse than all, there was a sinking feeling somewhere deep inside her too deep to locate. She had a sense of herself unwanted, put away, on the shelf. She kept trying to tell herself that it was only *natural*. People could not help wanting to enjoy themselves. You couldn't blame them for it. But deep waves of resentment and anger came back to conquer this reasonableness. She wondered how they *could* be enjoying themselves while she lay there. The least they could do would be to spare her the sense of their happy lives without her, not to intrude their holidays, their drinks, their visits to the fair into her lonely solitude. In short, she did not know what to think, but felt furious with Vi by the time she got up to go, an acre of quivering pink flesh smelling unpleasantly, a mixture of sweat and sun-lotion and that scent she wore.

'I'll see you again, Dolly, my love. Anything you want bringing?'

'Not really.'

'I dare say as George brings you everything you need. But

men can't think of everything. I've left a little bottle of perfume on your locker there. Is there any washing you want doing?'

Dorothy muttered something indistinct.

'You what, my love?'

'None of you care,' she spat out. 'I don't know why you bother to pretend.'

'There's no need to be like that, Dolly. Really no need.' Vi had denied herself a visit to the hairdresser's that afternoon in order to go to the hospital. Dorothy's hurtful words made her angry. Some people did not want to be helped.

'Good-bye then,' she said, trying not to snap, and she waddled off down the ward.

Tears welled up in Dorothy's eyes seeing her go. She wanted to summon her back and apologize. But it was impossible to explain. Anyway, stabs of pain once more drowned thought. She closed her eyes and tried not to think of Barry. She tried to forget that he was home, and had not come to see her or sent a message. She tried to tell herself that she had only imagined it and that Vi's tactless visit had not happened, that it had all been a bad dream.

The hospital day continued its dreary and inevitable course. The ward filled up with visitors as the afternoon progressed. The poor old groaning woman opposite, Mrs Bateman, kept calling out for a bed pan. One of the other old women was visited by a son and two grandchildren. The way they were laughing and cheering her up seemed like showing off.

Tea was over, wasn't it? She couldn't remember. The visitors had thinned off a bit. Then the orderlies began to bring in the supper trays. Dorothy tried to think what supper she had ordered at half past eight that morning. Ordering the meals was one of the few interesting features of hospital life. One did it so long in advance. Would powdered mushroom soup or fruit juice be desirable? And would one want braised liver or cheese salad? By the side of each dish on the menu there were indications of its appropriateness for certain types of diet: L for Light diet; S for Soft; that was, no teeth. She thought she had chosen no soup followed by liver and then rice pudding. She wished she

59

had chosen the jelly now, but it was too late to change things. Anyway, she did not feel hungry. If she could move without hurting herself, she would have reached up and tuned into the radio earplugs.

Through half-closed eyes, she looked down and saw the by now familiar circle of white coats and nurses' uniforms at the end of the bed and wondered how long they had been there.

'Hallo, Mrs Higgs!' the curtain was being drawn around the bed. 'Having a bit of a nap, were you? We won't disturb you for long. We just wanted you to have a word with doctor.'

She opened her eyes properly. There were about fifteen faces round the bed. What doctor? Most of them looked young enough to be her own children, with moustaches and that. There were one or two young girls with jeans under their white coats.

'You won't mind these students being here, Mrs Higgs, will you? They're all very interested in your arm.'

It was the young doctor from the *other* hospital, the one where she had had the operation. She wished it had been Mr Tulloch. She liked him. She couldn't remember this one's name. CRAW-FORD. That was it, she could read it on the plastic badge he wore. Well, she *did* mind the students being there very much. She hoped that she was not going to have to undress in front of them all. She wondered if it was possible to ask them to go away without seeming 'difficult'. She wanted to see the doctor on his own. Why, anyway, was he there? She had seen the other doctors that morning, and they had looked at her shoulder; the nurses had already changed the dressing. What did they all want now?

'How have you been feeling, Mrs Higgs?' Crawford was asking.

'Not too bad, doctor, thank you,' she whimpered, as darts of agony shot through every limb. Why was it, she wondered, that she wanted to pretend to the doctor, but not with Vi? If anything, she wanted to make Vi think she was iller than she really was.

'You'll remember that Mrs Higgs had mastectomy a couple of months back and now she has two rather nasty fractures in

60

her arm and a cracked shoulder-blade.' He spoke in a quite different tone to the students. 'Naturally, it has given rise to slight concern.' It was a bit like the voice of that man on *University Challenge*. 'Your starter for one …' She imagined the cleverer students might already start calling out what they thought was wrong with her. But why was there 'slight concern'? They had not told her about it before. It was just a badly broken arm and a funny shoulder, and that was all there was to it.

'We're naturally anxious that the radical mastectomy and the fractures should not have any connection,' he continued.

'It's quite common, isn't it,' piped up one of the students, 'for cancer to spread from the breast to the bones in the back?'

Crawford appeared not to have noticed this remark. The other students were giving the one who had spoken knowing looks, as if he should not have spoken. Crawford was adjusting her back rest, and remarking on the flowers on her locker.

Cancer? But the other doctor had said she was cured. Dorothy had never heard such cheek. She had definitely not misheard. She imagined George telling her that she had heard it wrong, but she hadn't. The doctor was pulling back the bedclothes.

'Can we just have a peep at you, Mrs Higgs?' He added, in a reassuring tone, 'It's OK, we aren't going to do anything drastic.' He helped her open the night dress to reveal her bandaged collar-bone. Dorothy felt the eyes of all the young men looking at her, seeing. She felt a mess, worse than a mess. Her mind raced in turbulent agony. Barry was back. Cancer. Vi. Spreading to the backbone. All those lads seeing parts that George had *never* seen, not even on their honeymoon.

'Mr Tulloch said I was much better,' she said, bravely.

'When was that, Mrs Higgs?'

'When I went to see him. Two or three weeks ago.'

'That's excellent.' He tried to grin. What had Tulloch been playing at? Mrs Higgs was visibly wasting away. He remembered her stumpy little legs from the time when they did the operation. Now her knees were all knobbly and one could see the shin-bones. Her complexion was yellow and sweaty, her eyes were hollow.

61

'We may have to move you back into the other hospital for a few more tests, Mrs Higgs. You know, where you were before.'

'What sort of tests?'

'You don't seem to be mending quite as fast as we thought, and it might be more comfortable for you in the old ward where you were. It's a bit less crowded, a bit airier ...'

She stared at him with a mixture of horror and contempt. Just because she was not very beautiful or very grand, he was treating her as if she was an idiot. She had heard the student's question about cancer. She knew that the place where she was before was a cancer ward. Why was he palming her off with these lies about the size of the ward and her own personal comfort?

When George came that evening, bringing a clean nightdress, Kleenex and a couple of historical romances, she was grumpy and depressed. Here was another liar. He did not mention Barry until she did.

'Oh, well, he's only just got back,' George said.

'He might have come, all the same.'

'It's not a place for a young lad,' he said.

'The woman over there had her grandchildren this afternoon,' she said. 'Only as high as that, one of them was.'

'Vi wanted to take him to the fair. They always take Barry, Reg and Vi. You know how I hate the things. They've taken him for years.'

He was embarrassed. How could he explain? The truth would be so much more hurtful than the little lies he was spinning. She in turn felt free to lie to him. When he sniffed like an old walrus and said, 'We all miss you, Dol love. How much longer then before we can expect you home again?' she said, 'Oh, quite soon, I expect.' It actually gave her some pleasure to think of how awkward he found the journey to the hospital at the other end of town.

Barry's appearance had shocked even Vi, who had two of her own to contend with. He was such a good-looking lad. Since the dawn of his adolescence, she had always been rather sweet on him. She remembered a shared holiday with Dol and George in Ventnor, and how much she loved seeing Barry in his swimming-drawers on the beach, and how she had pressed up against him in the back of the car driving home. She remembered his long lithe legs covered with quite thick hair, and how, at the age of about sixteen, downy dark hairs had begun to appear on his chest. Now, at eighteen, he looked like a real man, and before the holiday abroad he had been really handsome.

Vi blamed it on Dorothy, who had always 'mothered' the boy too much and not taken sufficient account of his real character. George was as bad. He and Dol both wanted their child to be a sort of saint. Barry did not like all that pop music like other boys, oh no. He preferred to watch boring old telly on a Saturday evening with his mum and dad. Barry had never got into trouble with the police, like some of the lads on the estate. Barry would never take anything that did not belong to him. Barry would never have a motor-bike. He did not even want one. When he was older, he would learn to drive a Marina, like George. And, of course, Barry was very clever and wanted to go to university and had passed all the exams and was off to Swansea in the autumn. But the Barry who had turned up on the estate two or three evenings before did not look like a university boy; not like Vi's picture of one, at any rate.

She wondered if he had changed suddenly, or whether, all along, his parents had been deceived by him. There was no denying that he was clever. Who was to know what he had really been doing, those evenings when George had patronizingly nodded towards her own boys, kicking footballs about the green, and said, 'You ought to get those lads to join the Boys' Brigade like our Barry'?

Her boys, of course, had left school at sixteen and got themselves jobs. Terry was on the line down the works, probably already earning more than George. Roger had unaccountably decided to become an assistant in a fishmonger's. But he liked it, and that was all that mattered. How Dorothy and George had despised these boys, crowed over them, set Barry up above them, patronized them. Now, with all his foreign languages and his A levels, Vi contemplated him. Tight glossy black trousers, with zips everywhere, a filthy shirt, with CUNT spelt out in studs on the back, and, worst of all, the hair. His head was half shaven. Only scrubs of hair remained dyed variously pale green, electric pink and blond. Round his neck he wore a razor blade on a string.

She had first set eyes on him in his new incarnation when she popped next door to see if there was anything she could do for George. It gave her quite a shock, seeing that figure in their front room, with a very clumpish shoe up on the coffee table where Dol stacked George's hobby magazines.

Her instinct was to have run out and called for the police. Then she saw that, beneath the black lipstick and the mascara, it was, unbelievably, Barry.

'Hallo, Aunty Vi,' he had said, quite meekly at first, almost as if he looked normal; so she had continued the conversation normally and asked him when he had returned from the continent, and whether he had enjoyed himself. It was then that evidences of the new Barry manifested themselves when he said that Italy was a load of nun's piss and Pope shit, an opinion apparently shared by his travelling companion, Hunk. This improbably named character had then materialized from the kitchen, arrayed more or less like Barry, only pinker as to the hair and with a fly zip open to reveal underpants with the legend GRAB ME on the front.

Hunk the Punk had been chucked out of Oundle the previous term. Oundle was a boarding school. He had since dropped out of a course on Renaissance painting at the British Institute in Florence and been loafing round Italy trying to pick up what his careers master would have called 'experience'. This meant washing up in cafés. He had met Barry at the youth hostel, a long-haired, serious, soft-spoken, rather fetching lower-class youth and they had chummed up almost at once. At first, Barry had thought that Hunk was a bit of a child. All that glue sniffing and group sex and rock music was, he considered, with a vestige of the self that he normally took on holiday with George and Dol, kid's stuff. He spoke from a position of innocence. Hunk, cleverer at disguising the limitations of his acquaintance with such areas of life, was at least able to initiate him into the delights of over-indulgence in Chianti. The rest, including the pink hair, had followed fairly naturally from there.

Vi did not know what to make of Hunk. When she asked, as nicely as possible, 'Aren't you going to introduce me to your friend, Barry?' Hunk had interposed with, 'Who's this juicy old cunt? – your mother?'

She was shocked by the cultivation of his tones. He really did sound like the sort of lad who might be up at one of the colleges. The wickedness of it seemed the more intense in someone who ought to have been a 'gentleman'.

Things really went from bad to worse after that. George had at first blustered and said that he would not have them in the house. Then they had locked him out and he had had to come round and have his supper with Reg and Vi. When he climbed in the next day, having extracted from the two boys the information that they were off to Swindon to pick up a car, it was apparent that poor old Dol's bed had been slept in. There were smudges of black make-up, God knows what else, on the sheets. A terrible mess.

It was more than George could understand that, in a funny sort of way, Vi had already made friends with the boys. They claimed that it was an accident that George had been locked out. He had, after all, forgotten his latch key, and that could not be blamed on them. They had not heard him knock because of their record player. And now Vi was insisting on taking them both to the fair. George knew that he could not begin to explain any of this to poor old Dol.

- 6 -

Mr Tulloch's tan had not faded, even though it was a month or so since his Scottish holiday. The late summer had been outstandingly fine, and his bony forehead was almost scarlet with sunburn, 'caught' on the local links, and in the garden, where he had taken to doing the lawns himself. It was not as if he was made of money. Taxes were still what he called prohibitive, whatever the Tories had done to cut them. And everything cost a fortune since they put up VAT. Having the outside of his house painted was nearly a thousand; and heating a place that size in the winter was nightmarish. He really needed a bigger salary if he was going to go on living at the level to which Gwen had grown accustomed: a new sun lounge on the back of the house, with red Italian tiles; a waste-disposer in the sink *and* Mrs Fenwick every day instead of her former twice a week; a little Renault in addition to the Jag.

There was still hope of that chair of medicine in Edinburgh; and in many ways he shared Gwen's longing to be back in Scotland. Their garden here was all very well, and of course they had done a lot to it and got it looking how they liked it. He contemplated it now from the window of his home consulting room: a nice old cedar; a row of cypressus in tubs planted by himself; neat rose-bushes and the chrysanthemums flowering in abundance. An electrically operated water-sprinkler revolved gently in the centre of the lawn, which was as velvety and weedless as a putting green. The elegant white French-style plastic-covered chairs on the patio stood out brilliantly against the fading leaves of the Boston ivy.

In the well-trimmed borders, Michaelmas daisies, thinned and cut back as much as possible, clashed with Gwen's pompom dahlias and red-hot pokers.

66

Tulloch scratched his head and considered the letter lying on the desk in front of him.

Confidential

Dear Robby,

I tried to contact you on the phone earlier but without success, so I have decided to put what I had to say in writing.

Mrs Higgs who, you will remember, came into Ward 17 in June for mastectomy was brought back six weeks later for the usual check-up and found to be clear. It was just before you went on holiday.

She is now in the Victoria Ward at the Infirmary, but I am having her moved back up the hill tomorrow for further examination, and I feel it should be a matter for you. She originally came into casualty with a broken wrist. She has since had two fractures in the same arm, and has a cracked collar-bone as the result of falling downstairs. On examining her, I have discovered that she is suffering from what would appear to be acute arthritic paralysis in her back and neck.

You will realize the reason why I am putting this back into your hands. It seems to me obvious that the X-ray did not pick up the fact, six weeks ago, that cancer had reached an advanced stage in the bone. But it would need your confirmation of this fact before we could start radiation treatment.

Yours,

Rick

P.S. I did not get the consultancy in Norwich. I have written off about another job in Southwark and once again used your name as a referee. I hope that this is OK.

Tulloch re-read the letter and rubbed his chin with his right hand. He did not understand the point of writing it. Crawford could have aired his crack-brained theories in person easily enough. God knew, Tulloch did his best to be accessible. He wondered what was so special, all of a sudden, about this case. For the last year, he had sensed Crawford's restlessness and ambition. They did not somehow get on. That bitch of a wife of his was perhaps largely responsible. She did not seem to realize that Crawford was extremely lucky to be a registrar at his age, considering his record and comparative lack of experience. And now he had the arrogance, the blind cheek, to be filling an already full week with speculations about some old woman's broken arm and arthritis.

The chair in Edinburgh, indeed, promotion of any kind, was to be claimed by Tulloch not merely on his record as an expert surgeon. His new methods were, as everyone recognized, reducing the dangers of breast cancer quite drastically. It was no longer the merely crude cutting away of flesh which doctors even ten years ago had gone in for. He was trying to develop the use of chemical treatments given to the patient in the guise of tranquillizers before and after each operation. If these were not successful, then a much fuller chemical treatment was resorted to. Crawford knew this perfectly well, which was presumably why he had thrown in the gratuitously insulting suggestion that the old biddy had radiation treatment.

Most people co-operated in Tulloch's chemotherapy. There were a few – he remembered with bitterness the maddening Miss Cowper – who held out against it. They were committing suicide. He wondered how *she* was. That was more to the point. He was certain, having examined Mrs Higgs so comparatively recently, and having checked her X-rays, that there was nothing the matter with her. Miss Cowper was another matter. If his predictions had been right, she would soon be for the high jump. He only hoped that not too many of her academic colleagues knew the name of her surgeon when they attended the funeral.

Dear Rick, [he scribbled]
    You must know perfectly well that back pains, arthritis, etc. are extremely common, particularly in women of Mrs Higgs's age.

He glanced at her notes to see what her age was. Fifty-six. Well, common enough in women of that age. He had thought her older, but he let the sentence stand.

    I am afraid that next week is chock-a-block for me.
I simply don't have time to examine all the broken arms in this city.
    Yours,
      Robby

There was a ring at the front doorbell.
'I'll answer it,' he called to Gwen.
Someone's au pair who had got herself into trouble stood on the doorstep.

- 7 -

It was still only lunch-time as Pamela boarded the inter-airport bus from Kennedy to La Guardia, even though ten hours had elapsed since she had breakfasted at Heathrow.

    New York itself she would save up until her journey home. Perhaps John would show her all the things she had promised herself she would see – the Rembrandts in the Met; the enormous episcopal cathedral of St John the Divine; the old brownstone houses on West 35th Street ... Probably, they had been pulled down long ago. The very notion of wanting to see them showed how much, for her, New York was a place of fantasy. And she was determined not to allow it to become anything else. So strongly was it a mythological backdrop to films and novels that she had enjoyed since adolescence that she could hardly think of it as a *place*. London, as a piece of physical geography, she knew only too well, even though she hardly ever went there now and associated it with the Affair. Only occasionally, on November nights, swathed in thick yellow fog, could it approximate to the image formed of it in the pages of Conan Doyle and Dickens. She was not going to let New York be spoilt for her in the same way. For her, Nero Wolfe would continue to inhabit 922, West 35th Street, even though Sherlock Holmes had long ago given way to a shop front and a photographic studio at 221b, Baker Street.

Ithaca, whither she was bound, held no place in her imagination. She had hardly devoted much thought to it, and John's letters had been curiously uncommunicative as to factual description. She was treasuring up a quantity of Ithaca jokes and quotations which she would share with him, and had been re-reading Tennyson and E. V. Rieu's *Odyssey* on the plane in readiness. The flat – apartment or whatever they called it – would, presumably, be easy enough to find, being on the campus; and John had said in more than one letter that she would always be welcome to come and stay. She was looking forward to surprising him. He hated the telephone, so she had not rung. She liked the dramatic possibilities of just dropping in, as if from the other end of town.

'I'm loving every minute,' his last letter had said, eight weeks or so before. She had taken it with her to read in hospital when she was having the operation.

I love the Americans. They all talk at the speed of steamrollers which makes one's own comparatively slow speech seem like a gabble. But they are endlessly kind and *nice*. My apartment is absurdly well equipped with a waste-disposer in the sink and two ovens, and an ice-box. But I am invited out to eat so often that I scarcely use it. My particular friends are called Sczepanik, even though they are not philosophers. Perhaps because. She once did (majored in) the History of Art from the Pyramids to Picasso. He is a professor of English and writes huge books about the Victorians. They have both been married millions of times and have teenage children.

Oh yes, and have you noticed that the Americans don't have shoes, or, come to that, *feet* in the strict sense of the word? How they manage for shoes when they come to England I can't imagine because, to judge from shoe-shops

70

here, the (male anyway) American foot is a completely different shape from mine. They never walk, except on the golf-course, which perhaps explains it. They *jog* but that only exercises the toes. Regardless of ethnic origin, all male American feet are long and elfin and thin. Isn't this extraordinary? . . .

The letter was rather crumpled and grey, she had read it so often. She got it out to read again as she waited for her plane to be called, giving every pair of shoes that passed a stealthy glance. To her untrained eye, their shoes looked exactly like ours. But John had a much sharper sense of these things.

His letters conveyed *something* of the quality of his talk and they were whetting her appetite for more. Talk with him was like talk with no one else. It was not that he – or she – was the wittiest or even the most interesting conversationalist in the world. It was not a question of that. What she had been missing, desperately, over the last six months or so was something almost too nebulous to define, but it had something to do with their unspoken rule that they would never take anything seriously.

Her flight was soon called, and she managed to gather together, or supervise the departure of, her meagre luggage. Surprisingly few people moved forward from the departure lounge for the Ithaca plane. There was an exotic-looking woman with bright turquoise shoes and a plait. There was a Negro bishop, clutching a *Christian Science Monitor*, whom Pamela hoped to sit near on the plane. There were a handful of people in sneakers and anoraks. A young family surrounded by a ludicrous quantity of carry-cots, trolleys, wheels, slings, and other baby paraphernalia. And there was her.

Maddeningly, one of the young people in anoraks sat next to the Christian Scientist bishop as soon as they boarded the plane, so she took the nearest window-seat she could find which also had some kind of a view of the prelate. In addition to the *Christian Science Monitor*, she noticed that he carried a small black volume, whether a bible or a breviary she could not be sure. She assumed on reflection he was Anglican; it would simply have been interesting to find out how high. Unfortunately, it was only by straining her neck that she could keep a steady view of him. American Methodists, of course, had bishops, too. Perhaps he was one of those. He looked far too amiable to be a papist. All papist bishops, in her experience, looked like low criminal types, the sort of faces one sees staggering out of betting shops. From where she sat, one could not see the little black volume very clearly but she wondered if it was actually an address book or a desk diary. If he were a diocesan, he was probably rather a fussy man who liked to map out his life months in advance. But he looked too sweet for that, so she went back to her original theory of thinking it was a breviary. He was un-doubtedly the spiritual sort of prelate, like the Bishop of Lewes, unable to contemplate even a short flight without dipping into the Psalter for Terce or Nones.

'Is this seat taken?'

This was asked in a gentle burr, by a balding, slightly Pick-wickian Jew in a tweed coat. He gestured towards the empty seat beside her with a rolled copy of the *New York Review of Books*.

'No,' she said, glancing away from him at once and looking out of the window. How nice it always felt to be looking down on the clouds.

'Are you from England?'

'Yes.' She could hardly reply by asking him if he was from America, since this was self-evident. So where was the con-versation to go to after that? She hated being accosted by strangers on trains, aeroplanes, buses. Why did they not just shut up and keep to themselves?

'I was in England all last year working in the British Library.'

'Really?' There was no stopping him.

'Yeah. My wife and I, we took a little apartment in Camden Town.' He said this as if it was a question.

'Oh, yes.'

'It was real, like cosy, you know, with some great neigh-bours. D'you know Julia Pleydell-Scott?'

'No.' She wished she was not being so frosty, but it was hard to see how she could possibly be expected to know some stray person in North London merely because this man had come across her during time not spent at the library. She was, moreover, bored and cross with him for being so self-evidently a don. Rather than, say, a bishop. The owner of the putative breviary had now turned to his neighbour and they were talking. She thought she detected the word 'Airflow' on his lips.

'She writes stuff for the Sunday papers. She was a neighbour; you know, a really warm, really loving person, a real haimisher mensh.'

'I know who you mean, now. She writes travel things, doesn't she?'

'That's right. So what takes you to Ithaca?'

'I've come to see a friend.'

She felt pinched, constrained, awkward, perhaps more than usual, because he seemed so very bland and relaxed, perhaps because she was faintly embarrassed by the whole expedition, and she did not want it discussed. It was not as if she was in love with John Brocklehurst, strictly. And yet, she had travelled all this way, spent all this money, because she wanted to indicate before she died, that she *did* somehow love him; that she did want to spend her last conscious, pain-free moments with him, rather than with anyone else. In an ideal world, she would have wanted to divide her time between John and Sourpuss, as she had discovered almost as soon as the plane took off at Heathrow, and she felt a great pang of regret at having left the priest behind. But life was not ideal, anything but, and she had to make her decision.

'Drink? I'm Mel, by the way,' insisted her companion.

'Pamela Cowper.' She tried to mutter the surname. It would not have been possible to leave it unspoken altogether, although this would, presumably, have been more friendly.

'Great, Pamela. I'm having a Manhattan. What'll you have?'

One couldn't ask for some medium sherry. She had forgotten what a Manhattan was, but she said that she would have one too.

73

'Great, great.' When he had given orders to the air hostess, he said, 'So you have a friend in Ithaca. I'm at Cornell, over the valley.'

'My friend is at Cornell too, as a matter of fact.'

'Oh really? At the university?'

'Yes.'

'D'you think I'd know her – him?' He grinned in the self-confident way of a man who was not used to giving up until he had extracted the information he was after.

'Almost certainly not. You see, he's only staying there a year. He's been giving some lectures and having some sabbatical.'

She hoped, rather, that her companion would *not* turn out to know John. It would be very nice, of course, in a way. But she so much wanted this time to be devoted to John and only to John that she knew she was going to be unable to enjoy incursions into their privacy by friendly outsiders.

Drinks were brought and she said, trying to be friendly, 'Would you like to look at my *Spectator* – I'd swop it for a few minutes with your *New York Review of Books*.'

'Sure,' he said, grinning. 'But tell me the name of your friend.'

'My friend?'

'Or is it some kind of a secret?' He was still grinning, a trifle cruelly, she thought, as if secret or no, he was going to get it out of her.

'No, of course it's not a secret. I just think you probably don't know him.'

'Try me.'

The grin refused to budge. She remembered reading somewhere that baring the teeth, in chimpanzees, was a sign of aggression.

'He's called John Brocklehurst.'

'You're kidding.'

'No, no.' Mel, she thought, was, if it came to that, a funny sort of name. Short for Melvyn, perhaps. There was nothing remotely incredible about a good Yorkshire name like Brocklehurst.

'Why, isn't that just *amazing*.'

74

'You don't know John?'

'Know him? Why, we have neighbouring apartments. Is John like expecting you?'

'No.' She felt foolish for confessing it. 'No, he's not as a matter of fact. I thought I'd drop in on him as a sort of surprise.'

'Oh my gosh.' Still grinning the face had become inexpressibly concerned. 'You mean like you're just calling unannounced all the way from London?'

'Term's just ended,' she tried, by way of justification.

'Do you often just fly across the Atlantic on impulse?'

'No. I've never been to America before. I thought it was about time I did.'

'Why the mad hurry? Life stretches ahead of you. Another drink?'

'No thanks.'

She could feel herself blushing. Were she an American, doubtless, she would tell him Why the great hurry, just as she felt he, at the drop of a hat, would tell her who his analyst was and how often he needed sex. Or would he? She knew already, in spite of his benignity, that Mel was someone to be reckoned with. There was, behind all the apparent casualness, a sense of control which betrayed a love of power. This was strongly conveyed to her by the timing of his bombshell. The plane had landed; they had checked out their luggage and were driving Mel's car towards the campus before he broke the news to her.

'You're not going to like this. But John isn't here.'

'Isn't here?'

Her mind instantly supplied a range of violent solutions appropriate to a transatlantic setting – a kidnapping, a street battle, a night club in Harlem, screeching Cadillacs, a chase down dusty prairie roads. Nothing she saw from the window of the Ford could have substantiated this fantasy. A townscape flitted past, a clean version of Milton Keynes, and a lush, well-planted hilly district, a sort of Brobdingnagian Surrey, spread out before them: beech and cedar against a brilliant sky. On the brow of the hill, as they approached, Victorian Gothic, as well as plate glass, caught the eye. It seemed hardly the place for any mythological episode from the violent America of her dreams.

'You'll never guess where he is.'

'Not in England?'

The last time she had summoned up the energy to drag herself to Italy, she had found notices stuck to the bare plaster of the Carmine church in Florence, where she had gone to venerate Masaccio, reading PRESTITI AL MUSEO DI VITTORIA E D'ALBERTO, LONDRA. Everywhere was the same – the Fra Angelicoes at San Marco, the putative Giottoes in the Duomo. Bang went her fresco holiday. By the time she got back, of course, the Museo di Vittoria e d'Alberto had carefully shipped the frescoes back to Italy. She had not known until that juncture that frescoes were transportable.

'No,' Mel was explaining. 'That would be too bad. No. John's gone to Mexico.'

'MEXICO!'

She felt too shocked to weep, at first, or even to be angry; it seemed so very unlikely. Los Angeles she could have imagined, if a Roman thought had struck him and he had decided he wanted to work in the Huntington Library; Boston was distinctly imaginable; but *Mexico*. In a shocked daze, she accepted Mel's spontaneous and insistent offer of hospitality before the deep sense of shame and foolishness set in.

It was impressive, she reflected much later, when she had changed, been introduced to Mel's wife Gale, and been handed yet another cocktail in the Sczepaniks' drawing-room, that they had welcomed her so without question. She tried to imagine the reaction if a visiting American bumped into, say, Hovis, on the Paddington train and expected hospitality on a similar scale. 'My dear fellow, we must meet for a little pre-prandial refreshment before the term is much older ...' She thought of the huge quantities of Americans whom she had met over the years at Faculty parties, but whom she had not invited to so much as a piece of bread and butter in her own home. If she ever had them into college, she spoke of it as if it was a chore.

Gale, dear Gale, already dear Gale, had welcomed her as if she had been a daughter.

Now, once more she was alone with Mel, while Gale fussed in the kitchen. She had fitted him into place, after a shower and a change of clothes. Melvyn T. Sczepanik, Jnr. He was in the English department here, and wrote monumentally large studies of the Victorian poets. This was alluded to when they stood by the picture window watching the sunset over the lake in the valley below.

A vast glossy volume which, had it been a cornflake packet would have been Family Size, stood on the glass table-top between them: *Algernon Charles Swinburne: The Crowning Honor* by Melvyn T. Sczepanik Jnr.

'I've been kicking my heels a little since I quit working on Swinburne,' he volunteered, gesturing with one hand towards the book, and, with the other, holding out an indigestibly icy cocktail. She wondered how much she was going to be forced to drink before she was allowed to go to bed and sleep off her journey.

'I don't know why, but I thought you worked on Tennyson.' This was something he had hinted during the car journey from the airport.

He now shrugged like a stage Frenchman, his grin becoming even broader.

'I'm in the middle of something.'

'A book?'

'Hopefully. It's still at the *re*-search stage.'

'Will it be a big book like that?' Slightly embarrassed, she waved her own glass towards the Swinburne volume.

He laughed.

'I guess you'd say it was kind of a big book. Two hundred, maybe two hundred fifty, thousand words.'

Who, she wondered, in their senses, buys such objects, let alone reads them? So bulky, so ugly, so *unnecessary*.

But she continued, 'What sort of book is it going to be?'

'It's a life, it's a critical assessment. It'll be like the Swinburne book, only bigger.'

This time the grin and the shrug appeared to concede the possibility that the subject matter scarcely merited so weighty a treatment, but that, on the other hand, these things had to be done, and he was resigned to the task.

'That *shnook* Tennyson's a tougher nut to crack than you'd think at first. Tougher than Algernon. Some of it's great, some of it's *dreck*. I'll figure out which, in time, I guess.'

'I love Tennyson.'

He appeared to bristle somewhat at this, and his brow darkened as she continued airily, 'And what better place to be writing about him?'

She gestured to the declining sun, the lake, the sports centre, the elegant, well-planted campus and the concrete skyline on the opposite side of the valley as she quoted:

> *'There lies the port: the vessel puffs her sail:*
> *There gloom the dark broad seas . . .'*

'Excuse me?'

'Ithaca.'

Pleasantries of this kind were not worth making if one had to spell them out in detail. Unfortunately, her mind was crammed with them, ready to share with John; and now, willy-nilly, she felt them bursting forth.

'Did Tennyson write about Ithaca?'

'You know, in "Ulysses" – "To follow knowledge like a sinking star", and all that. A perfect description of the academic life.'

'Uh-huh. *That* Ithaca. You had me a little worried. Have you been doing *re*-search on that particular poem? Are you some kind of a Homeric scholar? How come you have such an interest in it?'

'No, no. I'm a medievalist by trade. I just happen to like Tennyson.'

'And you mean, like, you had to check him out for medieval influences, nineteenth-century medievalism, all that stuff?'

'No. I simply read him for pleasure.'

Mel blinked at this assertion. She wished that she had never started the conversation. But the grin was returning as the realization dawned that he was in the presence not of a professional rival, merely of a harmless nut.

'For pleasure,' he repeated, not a little contemptuously. It was as if she had boasted about doing social work, or said that she cleaned drains for pleasure. 'I guess it's a long time since I read a poet for pleasure.' His voice had become much more measured in the last few minutes and it could still not bring itself to be relaxed. He spoke as if pleasure was in the same order of things as divorce or an alcohol problem; something which at some stages can be professionally unavoidable, but which was now well behind him.

'A little Wallace Stevens, a little Whitman. But that was a long time ago. I wrote an article on Whitman during my first post-doc semester. You still see it quoted in footnotes now and again.'

'I've never got on with Whitman somehow.'

'He stinks,' he agreed with a laugh and refilled her glass.

This common ground arrived at, the conversation chugged along pleasantly enough until the arrival of supper.

Gale was a rather magisterial woman whose golden hair-dye mysteriously clashed with her naturally olive complexion. She had changed into a loose kaftan and said, as she wheeled in a trolley of steaming food, 'Now would you believe it's just us?'

She began to count off the names of other members of the household – presumably children – extending her fingers with much jangling of rings and bracelets as if her right hand were playing 'This little piggy went to market' with her left. 'Paul's gone to the movies God-help-us with Maxine Fishman' – next finger – 'Billy never says where she is going or what she is doing but I just *know* she's parking with that boy Virgil Brown, and for all I know she's gotten herself raped' – next finger – 'Tom's gotten it into his head that he wants to take – would you believe – fencing lessons at the country club and like a kind-hearted dum-dum I've let him take the Chev' – next finger – 'and that leaves just us.'

'That's very nice, very intimate,' said Mel.

'I feel so guilty intruding like this ...' Pamela faltered. But with genuinely kindly hen-like noises, Gale was clucking about the trolley and getting ready the absurdly elaborate equipment which would enable them to eat. Raw onions, peppers and hunks of raw meat were being skewered into place in the indoor electric barbecue which was being constructed at the other end of the room, where a hot plate had been switched on half an hour before. Steaming rice was being kept warm there, and Greek pitta bread was warming through in the infra-red on the sideboard. After a little initial difficulty with the wall bottle-opener, Mel had uncorked the retsina and as soon as the candles were alight in their stainless-steel holders on the table, the meal was ready. It was probably nineteen hours since she had left Heathrow, but it seemed light years away. It had been foolish to drink so much on her first night in a strange country. The hot oil and the peppers and the retsina would have been unwise even had she been in rude health. In her present state of exhaustion, they were too much. At first she thought that she was going to burst into tears. To have come all this way only to find that John was in Mexico – still no real explanation of this from the Sczepaniks – was too great a shock to absorb at first. The horror of it all overwhelmed her now, as Gale held out a steaming plate of rice to her and said, 'Watch out for the little red bastards. They're chillies.'

They were the last words she remembered being spoken before the room swam, and she fell backwards into oblivion.

She awoke with the knowledge that she was exceedingly ill, but she could not remember where she was. The bedroom was unfamiliar. In the shadows, she could only make out the vague outlines of dressing-table, fitted wardrobes, a bookcase. She heaved herself out of bed in search of a loo, and found one *en suite* beyond the door next to her bed. She wondered where she was, and what time it was. Then the previous night came back to her: Mel and Gale, the barbecue supper; John in Mexico; she in New York State, where she did not know a soul.

The apartment whirred peacefully about her, vaguely electric noises, reminiscent somehow of Mel's voice.

Flushing the loo, and switching on the light over the bathroom mirror, she peered at her face and was shocked by its emaciated worn expression. The certainty dawned on her at once that she was approaching The End. She felt sick; she felt weak; pain of an indefinable kind had begun to shoot through her body, coupled with a nauseating self-hatred. How *could* she have been so foolish? What would have been more likely than that John would have decided to see some other part of the continent before coming home? She would not have predicted anything so extreme as Mexico; but in principle the idea was obvious. A single transatlantic telephone call would have saved all this fuss. No it wouldn't. She would have just assumed that he was 'out'. Whether inevitable or not, the present muddle was intolerable. The poor Sczepaniks now had a dying woman on their hands. 'What – in our house?' She imagined Gale saying it, only she wouldn't, she was too nice. Pamela thought with a pang that she would never see England again. She felt that she would do anything for one last glimpse of the Thames. She missed Sourpuss. She could even have done with some of her nice colleagues with whom she somehow never got on; anything rather than this over-warm, amiable, pappy environment in which she already felt so alien.

For I am a stranger with thee: and a sojourner, as all my fathers were, she thought, wondering at the same time, as she gazed at the gushing blue waters swirling round the pan, whether she had wiped herself properly.

She crept back into the bedroom desolately and lay on the bed, exhausted now, but unable to sleep. She was at least well enough to walk. The only thing to do was to fly straight home. When the rest of the household stirred itself, she would find out the times of planes back to La Guardia and be at Heathrow by nightfall. Even if it killed her, especially if it killed her, this was the obvious thing to do.

She felt too agitated to concentrate on anything for more than a few seconds at a time and muttered Hail Maries to calm herself. Then the real shock came.

There was a figure standing at the end of her bed.

In the shadows, she could make out a cropped head of hair, a thick jersey, perhaps jeans. She could smell the cigarettes on his breath. He looked tall and young. Where had he come from? What was he doing there?

This was all that she needed. It was in its way predictable. She had not been in America for twenty-four hours and already she was about to be raped. Redoubling the prayers under her breath she tried to pretend to herself that she was dreaming.

But when she opened her eyes again, the figure was still standing there. He was closer to the bed now, and she saw through half-open eyes that he had begun to undo his trousers.

She wanted to scream her head off, but all that came out was a faint squeak, and she was surprised when a female voice said, 'Are you awake? I didn't mean to scare you.'

She reached out for the bedside lamp and blinked at the brightness of the room. It was larger than she had guessed in the dark. She was lying in the end of an L-shape. In the main body of the room there was another divan.

Standing before her was a tall, androgynous figure with short dark hair, rosy burnished cheeks and enormous dark watery eyes. The upper half of her body was swathed in a sloppy Peruvian jersey. Blue denims had fallen to the region of her knees.

'Mel left a note in the hall to say there was someone in this room,' she explained. 'That's my bed. I didn't want to wake you up.'

She continued to undress in a leisurely way as she spoke. She was not wearing much – a T-shirt, drawers, white socks, tennis shoes. Pamela gazed at her in bewilderment.

'You look sleepy,' she continued. 'I can find my own way to bed if you want to put out the light.'

Pamela fell asleep instantly after this, her mind strangely and instantly at peace as she contemplated this final piece of fantasy.

How long she was asleep she did not know, but daylight was forcing its way through the double-glazing when she next awoke, and she lay for some time trying to piece together the various happenings of the previous night. She still felt very ill. She remained cruelly certain that the last phase had been entered, but she had felt less immediately lonely since the intrusion of her strange companion. She looked over at the bed where the girl had slept. It was made and empty.

'Holy Mary Mother of God,' she said aloud, 'Pray for us sinners now and at the hour of our death. AMEN.'

She thought of her day in Walsingham with Sourpuss: of the extent of her own superficiality which it had revealed to her. For whatever reasons of desperation, Sourpuss's faith was real and hers, she now felt, was not. It no more occurred to her that you could cure cancer by praying at a well than you could do so by keeping your fingers crossed or touching wood. Although he had said to her, 'Dear girl, this isn't a wishing-well,' she could not logically see the distinction he was trying to draw. He had taken her there for a cure, and the only sign of Our Lady's prayer being efficacious would be, surely, if a cure happened. A grand wishing-well, perhaps; a holy place; a beautiful, hilarious piece of magic; but still, a wishing-well. Religion had consoled her at so many phases of existence, soothed broken-hearted moods; elevated moods of physicality and self-hatred; provided the perfect antidote to all those years devoted to promiscuity. Everything in her temperament responded to it. She loved its mental word-pictures, its intellectual world. She felt more at home reading Thomas Aquinas than she did 'the masters of modern thought', with whom she never had got on. She was quite happy to speak *as if* God existed. But she did not, fundamentally, deep down, imagine that He ever actually *did* anything. This troubled her. It was not a new thought, but it was returning to her with renewed force. She would be more honest, in a bleak Cambridgey sort of way, if she recognized that this was a complete test of faith which she failed to respond to, and which she could not understand; to admit that she could not believe in miracles or the power of prayer, as she had sometimes supposed. As a moral force, as an aesthetic delight (and what was wrong with that?), as a personal presence, even, she could imagine God; but not as an effective force in the physical universe. She thought of Him as some clever old fellow of All Souls. Someone who had started something perfectly brilliant in their youth, but now preferred to be left alone in worlds of unapproachable light, and not to be bothered with requests to repeat the trick.

How often she had mocked the absurdity of modernist theologians who wanted to take all the miraculous elements out of the New Testament. They were dimwits, of course, and they deserved to be mocked. Since the New Testament was written by people who believed in wonders, there was no virtue in trying to accommodate it to the sceptical requirements of a prosaic age. But there was no denying, either, that deep inside herself, even though she stood up Sunday by Sunday and listened to the Gospel in Sourpuss's church, she did not believe in a God who could feed the five thousand, or walk on water or bring the dead back to life.

When clergymen wrote this lack of belief into articles or books she seized delightedly on their inconsistencies. Either they believe or they don't. Will they please say which. If they don't believe in the raising of Lazarus, they ought to resign their livings and their chairs and refuse to say the creed, like the honest agnostic clergymen of the last century ... It was so easy to say. But in many ways she was like them, only less honest. Catholic forms of belief, of a seemly Anglican character, had seen her through a series of emotional crises and disasters. She wanted to be able to live with herself, and *be* herself, and religion of all things enabled her to do this. Nothing else had worked as well. But it remained an unthought religion on so many levels; and an unbelieved religion. And this was to be her punishment, to die in an alien land, cut off from people who knew her, cut off from the reassuring presence of Sourpuss at the deathbed. Her body shook with tears as she contemplated it. She had never felt so weak, or so alone, or so terrified.

The door of the bedroom opened and the androgynous form reappeared, dressed in a coarse shirt of dark blue wool and tight pale grey corduroy trousers.

'Are you awake?'

Pamela murmured a reply.

'You sure slept a long time. Mel and Gale are just crazy not putting you to bed as soon as you arrived. Jet lag can be *dangerous*.'

She spoke with a low serious voice. Pamela wondered who she was. A child of one of her hosts, evidently; but which? She did not look like either of them. She seemed like a very tall boy of about fourteen, but perhaps she was twenty.

'What time is it?' Pamela asked.

'The day after tomorrow.'

'No . . .' she wailed.

'Say, it's not as bad as that.'

The girl came forward and sat on the bed. She had taken Pamela's hand and was stroking it affectionately.

Pamela's whole body shook now, and she let out low little moans as she allowed herself to be petted and cuddled by her protectress, and pressed her cheek into the coarse weave of the girl's chemise.

'You'll feel better when you've had some coffee.'

'Oh, but I won't, I won't.'

'There! You will, you will!'

'You don't understand.'

'I understand,' she said, with the assurance of youth. Pamela was sitting up by now and being held firmly in the girl's arms. They conversed gazing over one another's shoulders, a physical arrangement which had much of the anonymity of the confessional, and perhaps loosened their tongues.

'I'm very ill,' Pamela gasped. 'I must not stay any longer.'

'O K, so jet lag fouls you up. If you want, I'll call a doctor.'

'You are being so kind. I . . .'

'*Please* stop crying. Here,' she produced a Kleenex from her sleeve and made Pamela blow her nose on it. Then she chucked her under the chin and gazed into her eyes. 'I'm Billy,' she said.

'Hallo, Billy.'

'That's better.'

They laughed.

'I'm being silly,' Pamela smiled. Throughout the summer,

85

she had kept her dignity. She had cried a little, quietly, in the ward, after the operation; but she had hoped that Dorothy had not seen it. Since then, there had been no tears. Exhaustion drew them forth now; but, as she realized almost at once, there was more to it than that. She had a sudden illogical certainty that it had been worth the whole wild-goose chase after John in order to have met Billy; that hers was a face that she had been waiting to see since time out of mind, a last taste of beauty before they finally wheeled her off to the cancer ward to die.

'Your parents have been so kind.'

'My WHAT?' There was high-pitched incredulity in her response.

'Mel and Gale.'

'They aren't my *parents*.'

Her large cherry lips spread into a smile revealing almost ludicrously immaculate dentistry.

'No,' she continued, launching at once into the endlessly extensible autobiography that almost any American young person could provide, 'My mother, she's in California, in LA. I haven't seen her since I was just a kid. My father – she left my father and me in New York.'

'Here?'

'No. In Scarsdale. Then we moved into New York City. My father always liked New York. He was Irish. He was brought up in a house in the Bronx. My grandmother still lived there until she died. It was near the zoo. Dad and I used to go see her on Sunday mornings . . . I love New York.'

'Why did you leave it?'

'After my father split up with Gale we reckoned it was time to move on. They were still good friends. She only married him just to get in out of the rain after her first marriage bust up. Then she met Mel.' She sighed.

'And your father?'

'He died three years ago. A coronary thrombosis. He was fifty-one. My mother did not even reply to the letter when I wrote and told her. Gale has been marvellous. This place isn't exactly home, but they mean to be, well, kind.'

'What's wrong with it, Billy?'

'Have you got ten years and I'll tell you what's wrong with Cornell and what's wrong with Ithaca, and what's wrong with this whole, goddammed lousy continent.'

Mel had made a joke, or whatever it was, along similar lines yesterday evening, but now something made Pamela's eyes fill with tears again and she felt her lower lip trembling.

'Hey, what've I said?'

'Billy, I'm very ill. I mustn't stay here. I can't explain how I know I am so ill. I should never have come here. It has all been the most terrible mistake. I wanted to see John, you see, and tell him how ill I was and then ...'

Billy blushed and turned aside, unable to follow the sentence.

'I'll fix you that coffee,' she said. 'Then we can figure out what to do. I could call up Hart – Hart Erlstein. He's *my* analyst. I mean, if you felt you were just cracking up ... I don't know.'

The absurdity of the suggestion brought relief and Pamela smiled. 'I don't want an analyst. I'm not ill in that way: or if I am, it's too late to do anything about it.'

'You mean you've got a pain?'

'Billy, dear, come here again and hold my hand.'

The girl sat sideways on the bed and smiled at her.

'I don't know why I'm confiding in you, or boring you, or what, exactly, has come over me. The whole thing feels like a dream, a piece of terrifying fantasy. But I am dying. I want you to know that. It is why I came here. I came here because my doctors in England told me that I only had a few more months to live and I wanted to see John before I died.'

'Then, are you and John ... ?'

'John and I are old friends. He is my oldest friend. The person I like and trust – almost – most in the world. That is why I came here. It was foolish. It would have been better not to say anything. Not to have come. But it is essential, now that I have come, that I should not be a burden on Mel and Gale. So will you help me? I might be entering the last phase of my illness. In fact, I am fairly sure that I am. Do you understand, my dear? I can't possibly stay here in the circumstances. You must help to get me moved into hospital.'

'I'll fix that coffee,' said Billy. 'We both need it.'

- 8 -

Hunk the Punk – his real name was Martin Seymour – had, in the event, only stayed a few days. He had wanted to give the town a look-over before deciding whether to try the college entrance exams in November. If he had decided in its favour, this would have meant a term at a crammer's in Hampstead. As it was, he concluded, after a brief survey of one or two colleges and the paperback bookshop, that the town had little to offer, and that a university career was not for him.

Such an approach to academic questions seemed almost as esoteric and outrageous as his hair and clothes, and certainly far less approachable. Thrown back on himself without the stimulus of Hunk's example, Barry began to feel rather idiotic. The very short hair had been bad enough. He had hacked most of it off himself with nail-scissors and watched as Hunk cast the thick brown tresses into the fetid waters of the Arno. Then had come the shaving and the dyeing. The bald patches were beginning to grow again now, though, and by the time he went to Swansea in a month's time, it would be respectable enough.

His dad had settled down since Hunk's departure. This was a relief. At first, Barry had thought he would blow his top. They had not meant to lock him out; leastways, Barry had not meant to. Hunk claimed that he had bolted the back door to keep out burglars, and, when challenged, he merely made improper suggestions about Dad keeping late hours with Aunty Vi next door. But inside, Barry felt painfully unhappy and guilty about hurting his father; and about his mother being up at the hospital. Yet, in spite of himself, this made him want to hurt them all the more.

'Your mother just can't understand why you won't go and see her,' George complained at breakfast.

'I would go if you'd let me.'

'Looking like that? Don't be daft. It'd kill her.'

'Don't say that, Dad. Don't say that.'

'I can say what I like, can't I?' George resumed the angry old walrus expression. He hated breakfasts not cooked by old Dol. He had never learnt to fry eggs properly. They either broke in the pan or they went all leathery and hard. In consequence, he was in a foul temper most mornings.

'I still think I should go and see her,' the boy insisted.

'If you walk into that ward with pink hair, that's it. You can pack your bags and leave this house.'

Thanks for nothing, Barry thought. Thanks for bleeding nothing, silly old fart. How could two people contrive to exist in such a way that they made you feel guilty all the time, whether you were with them, whether you weren't? That's what his parents did. He did not enjoy their company any more. Perhaps that was no one's fault. Perhaps it was theirs as much as his. They had always expected him to be just a toy grown-up, eating picnics out of tupperware and watching the Black and White Minstrels on the telly. He had had a bellyful. He wanted to be independent, even if the price he paid for it was looking daft with pink hair.

For all that, he wanted to see his mum. It hurt him terribly to think of her lying alone in that ward with no one to talk to at visiting times. He determined that he would go up to the hospital while his father was at work.

George shook his head and looked at the boy. What a disgrace. What a disappointment. You scrimp and save to give him everything nice: foreign holidays, books, clothes; and then, at the time when you most need him, he does this. Of course, it was Dol he blamed. She had always spoilt the lad. Ever since the elder lad died, she had *spoilt Barry*. He said the words over slowly and deliberately inside his head. University. Uni-bloody-versity. Uni-sodding-versity. Uni-effing-versity. George liked swearing privately to himself. And since Dol had been in hospital he had even been allowing himself the luxury of swearing aloud. It was like smoking in bed, the sort of thing he would not dream of doing with the wife around. A lad like that going off to read philosophy at a university. We must be bleeding mad, spending taxpayers' money on that sort of thing.

'I shall expect you to wash up before you go out, my lad,' he snapped, expertly rolling one of his own and lighting up.

Barry murmured and stirred his cornflakes.

'I spoke,' said George pompously.

'I heard you. I'll do the washing-up.'

'Properly.'

Barry continued to stir his flakes.

'I said properly. God almighty, if you was younger I'd put you over my knee and wallop you.'

Barry smiled as 'camp' as he could and said, 'That would be nice, sweetheart.'

George stared at him uncomprehendingly and waddled into the hall for his cap and his car keys.

When he heard the front door slam, and the engine of the Marina being coaxed to start, Barry stretched his arms. It felt like having a sack of potatoes lifted from his shoulders whenever his father left the house. He cleared the table in a desultory way and half washed up the dirty crockery. His father's eggy plate, with its rubbery old white half-eaten on the side, he left for Aunty Vi to deal with when she came round. She was being quite good, washing, shopping and that. Barry felt sorry that Hunk had been so rude to her. She had recovered remarkably well; even, in a strange sort of way, struck up a friendship with the boy and called him Martin. It had never occurred to Barry that Hunk was not his proper name. Vi soon had him jabbering away about this boarding school he'd been at – she knew about it, even knew young men who had been there – and his parents, business people from Newport Pagnell. It was extraordinary what Vi got out of people. All the same, he wished that Hunk had not called her a juicy old cunt.

Probably, Barry reflected, she was. She and Reg seemed to be go-ers, still. They behaved and looked years younger than his own parents. They were more fun than his own parents, too; even though George liked to speak slightingly of them because Reg was down at 'the works' and Vi was a college servant.

'I wouldn't let you go making beds and skivvying for a lot of kids, Dol, my old love,' he would say. There had, indeed, once been a question of Dol going to help Vi out with her 'staircase'. Dol had obviously liked the idea. She said it would take her out, and you felt she meant 'of herself' as much as 'of the house'.

But Barry was glad his mother had not gone. He liked hearing Aunty Vi's stories about her 'boys'. Two or three of the gentlemen on her staircase were dons and wrote books. She even looked after Sir Jorrocks Monteith, whose history of the reign of William and Mary had been required reading for A levels. He had decided to read philosophy though. One of his teachers had read them an essay by A. J. Ayer. Hegelian, the teacher said it was; or was it Existentialist? Anyway, Barry had liked its pugnacious, iconoclastic tone.

When Aunty Vi came in later that morning, having done her stint of bedmaking and cleaning at the college, he put it to her that he was going to visit his mother.

'Your dad won't be very pleased.'

'Just because of my hair?'

'He says you've changed since you went to Italy.'

'I wish *he'd* changed.'

'Give him a chance, Barry. He's had ever such a hard time of it, your mum being so ill and that.'

She lit an Embassy while she washed up the frying-pan and the cigarette danced on her lips as she spoke.

'I think you're right to want to go, though. Your mum's getting ever so depressed since they sent her back to the other hospital again. Panicky, you know. Your dad's just trying not to think of the implications.'

'What implications?'

She turned to him compassionately and removed the fag from her mouth. In spite of his appearance, he was as naive as the rest of them. Her work had taught her that young men of eighteen or twenty are very often little more than children. It was something to do with staying on at school. Her own boys seemed much more grown-up.

It was a *shame* Barry cutting off all that lovely thick dark hair.

'You could dress a bit smarter,' she said, 'and I don't know what to do about the hair. I don't really.'

'You're a sport, Aunty Vi,' he said, coming up behind her and pecking her on the cheek.

She enjoyed, in many ways, the new image. The voice was like her favourite female impersonator on the telly. She found all that sort of thing very amusing. She had been right all along, of course. Dol *mothered* the boy too much.

'P'raps I'll have my hair done before I go up the hospital,' he lisped, now parodying himself.

'If they could dye it black it wouldn't be so bad,' she said. 'It *was* silly, wasn't it? I wonder what made you do it.'

He wondered why he did not mind *her* being quite outspoken about his appearance, even though he felt himself boiling with rage if he even sensed his father looking in his direction.

'And put some more normal trousers on, there's a duck,' she added. 'All those zips'll give Dol a rare old fright.'

'I'll put on some jeans,' he assented.

Ten minutes or so later, in a lumberjack's shirt, blue jeans and an anorak, he looked quite respectable. He pinched one of Vi's cigs and set off on the bus for the centre of town.

He decided to go to one of those poncey places where they blow-dry you and some little poof tries to persuade you to have it permed. His few visits to places like this in the past had been his highest form of dissipation. He felt a sense of excitement which was almost erotic in its intensity as he pushed through the varnished Scandinavian oak doors of the parlour.

They kept him waiting ages. It was quite a big place, unisex, where most of the girls still had variations of the Afro. One of them helped him into his short-sleeved little overall (it had a white and brown floral pattern to match the coffee cups) and she led him over to a slightly older girl chewing gum. It embarrassed him when he actually saw his face in the glass. The very strong lights showed up the hacked scalp, and the rather spotty complexion. He would have done anything to have it all restored to its original colour.

'Trouble is,' said the older Afro girl, chewing her spearmint and addressing his reflection in the mirror, 'there's not much to go on, see what I mean,' and she picked up the few remaining inches left on one side of his head. 'Still – see what we can do, eh?' And she laughed condescendingly and went to discuss the technicalities of the matter with one of the young men. While she had been stroking his hair, Barry had felt inflamed with longing for her. He was in that dizzy condition where any smooth, stroking finger, any round firm bottom, any laughing moist eyes could reduce him to a state of aching desire. It was unfair, he thought, to have so much sex stored up inside you, more than you could ever find an outlet for.

He scanned the pile of magazines for anything to feed his lust and ended up with the problem page of one of the women's weeklies.

Whenever he touches me I go all cold and stiff. I just curl up inside. He says that if I don't go with him, he doesn't want to know me any more. But I do not want to lose him and I love him very much. Yet I think we ought to wait until we're married.

Reply. If he will not respect your wishes over this, perhaps he is not the marvellous man you thought he was when you fell in love with him! But I am worried by your saying that you curl up inside whenever he touches you. Perhaps you both ought to sit down and have a frank serious talk. Who knows, he is probably feeling a bit upset about it all himself!!

The letters and advice poured out all over the page. There was a picture of the lady who wrote the answers at the top. She had silvery hair that looked like a wig.

Barry knew what he would do to a girl who said that she did not want to have it, and he sweated under his little slip as he contemplated her screams. It was the girl who had washed his hair. She wanted to wait, did she? Well, he would show her. He would give it to her, long and hard.

And so the thoughts vibrated and churned through his head until the slightly older girl, who had inflamed him originally, returned and said, 'Right! Dark brown, didn't we say?' And with foul-smelling fluids and deft movements of the fingers, she had soon set to work, a little trolley of instruments and papers at her side, a boy acolyte in attendance.

'Lots of kids come in here with this,' she said, still chewing in a patronizing way. 'The bright colours look all right for a couple of weeks and then you want to go back to something a bit more normal. I'm always doing it,' she continued.

He grunted in reply, half listening. With the other half of his mind he was slowly unpeeling her skin-tight denims.

Her voice meandered on.

'What are you doing this evening?' he eventually blurted out. He could see himself saying it in the glass and he watched his cheeks burning crimson.

She blinked back and smiled self-confidently as if she had not heard.

'There!' she said, putting the finishing touches to one side of the head and moving round to the other. He would not have the courage to ask again. He wished Hunk was there. They could both take her out. Do some of the really interesting things Hunk sometimes talked of doing.

'You're cheeky, aren't you?' she smiled, running her finger round the back of his ear. 'Haven't you got a girlfriend of your own then?'

'Which one were you thinking of, then? There are so many.' But his blushes were betraying him.

'What were you thinking of doing?'

'See a film, go to a disco, it would be up to you.' His voice had sunk into tones of seriousness. Perhaps she wanted him to plead with her. Perhaps she was one of those. He had read about them in sex magazines. They wanted to tread all over you with high-heeled boots.

'OK,' she drawled, 'where shall I meet you?'

'At the Wimpy'; he could hardly believe his ears.

'Half past six?'

'All right.'

She half smacked the back of his head and minced off to fetch a drier. Barry wondered what could have possessed her to accept his invitation.

For all her expertise, there was not much that she could do to the hair. After it was dried, it was a rather coppery auburn brown. He decided to tell his mother that he had got oil stuck into it while sunbathing on an Italian beach. As a result, he had had to have quantities of it shaved off.

'Six-thirty, then,' said the girl.

'Outside the Wimpy or in?'

'Ooh, inside, I should think.'

He paid at the desk, his heart thumping about. Now that it appeared as a possibility in prospect, the evening with the girl seemed different. He felt no less consumed with lust. But he also felt a purely social fear that they would not find enough to say to one another; that the evening would turn out to be a disaster.

Wandering out into the street, he surveyed his whole appearance in the shop windows. She had not done a bad job. In his anorak and jeans he looked quite pretty. He turned his profile to its best angle while he waited for the bus.

The hospital was a little way out of the town, up the hill in the direction of London. Barry sat on top of the bus so that he could smoke, about halfway down the gangway so that he could survey any passenger who got on or off. The bus proceeded fairly slowly. The streets were still crammed with coaches and tourists. Barry stared about, as if drunk, in a haze of lust. It was terrible, the way these fits descended; and yet, he cherished them, savoured the images they produced in his mind. He could switch them on and off almost at will – on anyway – like flicking the pages of a dirty magazine. Nowhere seemed inappropriate.

Nothing could really distract him from his concentration. Lighting a cigarette, he gave himself over to a fantasy about Rena's boots. Rena she was called. He had had to read it over her mirror. She had asked his name.

He imagined her wearing nothing but the boots, as she dug the heels of them into his shoulder-blades. He wished he had bought some more of the acne cream and hoped she would not mind, or notice how spotty his back was.

Behind him, two old women, bound in the direction of the hospital also, lugubriously discussed the man they were going to visit.

'It's like a tube what they ram up 'is nose,' one was saying. 'Helps him breathe easier, see.'

'Wonderful what they can do, isn't it?'

'Like I say, it goes up 'is nose and down into 'is system. Takes some of the pressure off 'is insides. 'E can't swaller proper, see, not since they cut that bit out of his gullet. That's where the cancer had got, see, into his gullet . . .'

He tried to concentrate on his fantasy, but the words shook him out of it and he felt goose-flesh creeping all over his body. He had never set foot in a hospital. When his elder brother had died, he had been too young. And ever since, his parents had 'spared' him the experience. He was frightened of what he would see there. He felt a mixture of guilt and fear, and his cowardice increased the feeling of guilt. He realized that he should have brought something to give his mother. A bunch of flowers. Something like that.

'Course, they 'ad to cut the tubes out of his gullet to stop it spreading, like.'

'That's right.'

They might have been discussing how to truss the Sunday joint for all it seemed to worry the old bags. It sent Barry into a cold sweat. Were the doctors cutting bits off his mum? He knew she had had 'an operation' earlier in the summer, but neither she nor his dad would tell him what it was. And Aunty Vi was fairly uncommunicative about it, too. Now, she had broken her arm rather badly and done something to a shoulder.

They had merely moved her back to this place to be more 'comfortable'. That's what his dad had said. Vi had seen 'implications' in it, but Barry could not imagine what they were. Until that moment, in fact, he had not even begun to consider the matter. The summer had been such a full one: leaving school, which he hated; wondering if he could really face going to a university simply in order to please his parents; acquiescing in the notion because he could not think of anything else he wanted to do more; tentative, very clumsy overtures in the direction of alcohol and sex.

They had kept him on such a tight rein that, until he went off (the first holiday on his own, unless you counted Boys' Brigade camps) to the continent, he had no thought of his parents but how to escape. His mother's being ill meant, initially, no more to him than that he would not have to have another of their bloody holidays in the Dormobile; every moment supervised; all their food brought with them in the tupperware and tins. Being, in effect, an only child had enabled him, compelled him, to develop the habit of withdrawing entirely into his own thoughts, and not noticing much what his parents were up to. It was the only way not to go bloody mad. If he noticed too much, he became almost helpless with seething anger and frustration. He remembered the holiday in France the previous year. His parents had thought it would be so good for him, with his A level French coming up. He had learnt all the French he wanted, of course, in the language laboratory at school. You never got a chance to talk much French with Dol and George around anyway. They had spent almost two weeks in the Loire valley and then driven home. Between fussing about the next meal, and endlessly checking the oil, and cruising along at forty-five so as not to waste petrol, and reading guide books borrowed from the public library, they had seen all manner of landscape and architecture which, in someone else's company, he might have enjoyed. Chateaux, cathedrals, towns and valleys blurred into one, as he thought of the holiday, which he had devoted largely to masturbation, and flattening shandy tins with the heel of his shoe.

About hating his father, he felt no compunction. He was a self-important, silly old fart, who had been imposing his view of things, and his way of doing things, on his boy ever since Barry could remember. The only anger he felt with Dol, though, was that she put up with the old bugger and, by her obsequious, simpering attitude towards him, actually made him worse.

'I feel ever so guilty, letting you both down,' she had wailed, when it became clear that their holiday together that year was to be called off. Barry had felt such a glow of relief that he had not given the actual illness much thought.

The bus was stopping now. Over tree-tops, he could see the sprawling makeshift hospital buildings, a collection of Nissen huts and air-raid shelters put up to house wounded Canadian soldiers at the end of the war, and never since abandoned.

The two old women were wobbling down the stairs now. He saw that they had left the bunch of flowers they had with them, some very bright marigolds. Thinking fast, he flung his anorak over the flowers and picked them up.

'Well, there's a nice thing,' he heard one of them saying, 'I must have left me flowers in the Co-op.'

'No, no,' the other persisted, 'you had them with you when you was sitting upstairs. I'll go back up and get them.'

And the driver, a bad-tempered Bengali, began to expostulate with them, pointing out that he did not intend to wait all day while they searched for a bunch of flowers.

While the row was in progress, Barry set off down the winding road towards the hospital buildings.

It was a positive maze, the hospital. It took him ages to find the way in. The porter at 'Reception' was quite a Colonel Blimp, with a white moustache and pop-out eyes and a very class voice. He wore his uniform as if he was an equerry at Buckingham Palace and he took more interest in Barry than seemed altogether necessary.

'Now, young fella-me-lad,' he said, putting an arm round Barry's shoulder. 'What can we do for you, eh?'

'I've come to see my mother – Mrs Higgs – she's in Ward 17, I think.'

'And brought her a lovely bunch of marigolds by the look of it. That's the stuff. Now, you come along here with me and we'll see where she is, eh?'

Without releasing the arm, he led the way behind the desk.

'Sit 'ee down, young fella-me-lad, sit-ee down.' He consulted a wall chart and then looked at a ledger, shooting back lecherous glances in the boy's direction.

'Ward 17, Ward 17, where are we? Yes, that's right. Mrs Higgs, Ward 17. Now, do you know the way, or would you like me to show you?'

'I think I can find the way, thank you.'

'You want to go up the ramp, through the floppy doors at the end of the corridor, up the stairs, turn left and it's third on your right. Got that?'

'I'll find my way.'

He felt himself being watched as he wandered off in the direction indicated.

'Any time, laddy, any time!' called the porter.

He went wrong a number of times, and had to be directed by nurses and orderlies, but eventually he came to the right ward. He was tingling with fear by now. The hospital had a strange smell. He hated the trolleys everywhere; the wheelchairs; the human wrecks being trundled about in their pyjamas; the jaunty, asexual nurses.

When he reached the door of the ward, he wondered whether or not to turn back. It was full of women, old bags, most of them; and it was very crowded. He had been given to understand that they had brought her here to be more comfortable. God knew what the other hospital was like. There was an unpleasant smell in the warm atmosphere; a mixture of pee, flowers, decomposing fruit and sweat. His mother was quite near the sister's office.

He hardly recognized her at first. She was leaning back, her eyes closed, her head on the pillow. Her hair was unwashed and straggly, her face much thinner and yellower than when he had last seen her. In her sleep, she was masticating and smacking her chops as if she was an old lady of about eighty.

The only familiar things were the smell of her soap, and the Jean Plaidy novel on the locker; things which he noticed as he approached the bed.

She opened her eyes when he touched her hand.

'Hallo, mum.'

'Who is it?'

His heart leapt a beat. He suddenly wondered if she had gone nutty.

'It's me, mum.'

She opened her eyes wider and then beamed with delight. No, she was sane all right.

'I was asleep. You look different. You've done something to your hair.'

Her voice sounded frail, as if it was coming from far away. He was just about to start on his preposterous explanation: the sticky lump of oil on the Italian beach, the necessity of shaving his head, when she added:

'I like it like that. It suits you better than having it long. Better for all this hot weather, too.'

He gawped. He would never have expected this response. At home, she was so ditheringly in awe of his father's opinions, that she never expressed herself independently. It seemed inconceivable that she should have a taste for the punk mode.

'Aren't you going to give me a kiss?' she whispered.

He leant over and kissed her. Her face smelt of bread and butter.

'Yes,' she said. 'It's more like a crew-cut, isn't it. Your father had his hair like that when he came out of the army. I like to see the shape of a man's head.'

'I've brought you some flowers.'

'See if you can find some water for them. A nurse will help you. They're lovely, Barry pet, really lovely.'

He went off in search of a nurse. There was no one in the sister's office and he had to walk round the corner to a little kitchen, where a staff nurse was gossiping with an orderly.

'Can I have a vase for these?'

'All right, my love.'

And while they were filling the little plastic vase, he was full of relief and excitement that everything was all right with his mother. He thought of the parts of his Italian holiday that she would like hearing about. He remembered so much more of it than any holiday he had ever had with her. He carried the marigolds carefully, like a child of seven on Mothering Sunday.

When he got back to the ward he had lost his bearings, and he could not see his mother's bed at first. Then he realized that they had drawn the curtains round it. There were a number of voices coming from inside it. He hovered awkwardly.

After what seemed like ten minutes, the curtains were drawn back, and there was a curly-headed doctor, thirty-five perhaps, with a red face and big brown eyes, standing there with the sister and another doctor in a white coat.

'Barry, this is Doctor Crawford – or is it Mr Crawford? This is my son, Barry.'

They nodded at each other cautiously.

'Barry's just got back from abroad,' Dorothy prattled. 'He's going up to University in October, aren't you, Barry?' He felt as if he was being stabbed, she was embarrassing him so much. 'He's just been arranging me some nice flowers. He's a good boy, isn't he?'

'They're lovely,' said Crawford, looking at Barry gravely. He couldn't have known they were pinched, could he? Why was he staring, all solemn? 'We're just going to take your mum along the corridor for a few blood-tests, Barry,' he explained. 'I'm sorry if you've only just arrived.'

'Oh, Barry can come back later, doctor.' It was just like her attitude to George: always anxious to please, over-zealous to eliminate any impression that she might be awkward. 'As I say, I'm feeling ever so much better.'

'Good, good,' said Crawford uneasily.

He appeared to be sizing Barry up: not as the old roué at the door had done, but seeing how gullible the boy was. 'These checks are purely routine,' he tried. 'But if you could come back later ...'

They were already disconnecting the brake on Dorothy's bed and wheeling her in the direction of the door.

'Barry will come back this evening, won't you, pet? He'll come with his father.' She was addressing her remarks to the doctor. She seemed quite triumphant; almost, in a lugubrious way, to be enjoying the attentions of the nurses and the young man with curly hair.

'Well, it's a bit difficult this evening,' he began.

But she was through the door by then and being wheeled down the corridor.

- 9 -

From one of the windows in the Goddess's diadems, Pamela gazed, enraptured and entranced by the view. Nothing could have prepared her for the brightness of New York: everywhere energy, movement, light on water. The size, the sheer vibrance of it all was something that no number of photographs could suggest. High up on Liberty Island, moreover, the air was bracing and felt clean. The guide book said that they could see fifteen miles. It looked more like a hundred: windows and water glistened in the sunlight which beat down on a thousand fantastic towers.

'Isn't it crazy; you live your whole life in a city and you never get to seeing spots like this.' Billy touched Pamela's hand as she spoke. The little holiday was being an enormous success.

'I'm exactly the same about London. I've never been to the Tower, or St Paul's Cathedral.'

'When I come to Europe, you must show me round.'

'I'll show you everywhere.'

They smiled into each other's faces.

That morning, before Billy was awake, Pamela had got up, and dressed, and ordered a cab to take her to church. They had a spacious, airy, twin-bedded room in a ridiculously large hotel overlooking the Pan Am building. Leaving the girl with her head still recumbent on the pillow, she had murmured,

> 'There lies the thing we love, with all its errors,
> And all its charms, like death without its terrors.'

Not exactly a Haidee, Billy. Pamela herself was scarcely Don Juan. But the girl seemed to have brought with her peculiar blessings, which it was still too soon to appreciate or understand. Everything had happened so fast. Pamela had no sooner awoken from her jet lag in Ithaca than she had found herself telling Billy of her condition, speaking in fairly open terms, which she would have abhorred at home, about her expectancy of life. And then, Billy had shown such surprising commonsense. She, together with Gale, had arranged for Pamela to be rushed into hospital. By evening, she had been put on the body scanner and tested with a thoroughness which would have been almost impossible in England. And then that extraordinary interview with the nice handsome Dream Boat of a doctor. He had a ludicrous, Ivy League handsomeness, yellow down on brown arms, bright blue eyes, regular very white teeth that looked too clean to be real.

DREAM BOAT: *Well Miss Cowper* (which he pronounced as if the first syllable were *cow* and not *coo*), *you're fine, just fine.*
PAMELA: *I'm certainly feeling much more comfortable.*
(The hospital was disgracefully, magnificently better than the collection of huts in England where she had had her operation.)
DREAM BOAT: *It's natural, after an operation of the kind you had a month or so back, that you should be a little anxious, a little fearful maybe.*
(He pronounced *little* like the compiler of the Greek lexicon, the father of Alice in Wonderland. He was *gloriously* bronze and handsome.)
PAMELA (memory now supplied a little mood music; some glycerin drops in the corner of each eye): *But I was told by my doctor in England that I have only a few more months ...*
DREAM BOAT: *A few months to live? But that's ridiculous. Were you examined on a full body scanner like the one we have here?*

(*Full body scanner* seemed to take on laughably sensuous implications.)

PAMELA: *But I was examined by one of the top surgeons in the field.* (Why so sniffy? Why the sudden urge to defend the dreadful Pillock? But she had done so. A certain brand-loyalty, no doubt, a desire to Buy British even if it killed her.)

DREAM BOAT: *I can assure you, Miss Cowper, that there is absolutely nothing wrong with you. I have examined you, and the senior surgeon in this hospital had a look at your print-outs. He is also a top man in the field. Believe me, if there was something that needed doing, we'd do it.*

(Distant strains of 'The Star-Spangled Banner'.)

PAMELA: *I would rather know the truth, doctor. I'm not afraid of being told that I am dying, you know.*

DREAM BOAT: *What more can I say to convince you, Miss Cowper? There is nothing at all wrong with you. You have been suffering from a Liddell Jet Lag. That's Arl.*

Well could she have been poor Alice Liddell, caught up in that donnish Victorian fantasy which had always scared her so much as a child. (She had had nightmares for weeks after being made to learn 'The Walrus and the Carpenter' at primary school.) Life had happened at the speed of the Looking Glass Country. Three days after that conversation with the Dream Boat, she had said good-bye to Mel and Gale – forever as far as she could guess – and was in New York. There was no possibility of getting hold of John in Mexico. A short holiday with Billy and then home. That was what she planned.

But she had a secret intention, secret certainly so far from Billy, which she realized first thing that morning when the cab was summoned. More famous churches – St Thomas's on 53rd Street, or the Cathedral of St John the Divine, would not have been to the purpose. Nor would any (more readily accessible) papist conventicle quite do. St Mary the Virgin was the church she had heard of as suitable for spikes, and its dedication made her journey inevitable.

She was late for mass, which was being celebrated in a side chapel by a rather distinguished looking woman of about fifty.

Pamela did not mind; she had not come, specifically, to hear mass. She made her way purposefully to the statue of the large, rather impressive Madonna and determined to worry the matter through with a few decades of the beads.

The Dream Boat's reassuring message could not sink in at once. The more she remembered it, rehearsed it in her mind, the less real the episode became, so that memory had already made a complete film out of it, with credits in bright yellow, a dying nun in the next bed, all the usual tricks of hospital melodrama. In turn, it made the Pillock's prognostications seem unreal too. And, crazy as it now seemed, the only real thing about the whole summer, apart from books read, and a few letters from John, had been her poor old religion. Sourpuss, and not the doctors, had been a help, with his mixture of theatrical melancholy and touching desperate optimism.

What, then, if it did not seem too dignified, too scientific a way to think of it, what were the facts?

Fact One: She was operated on and had a lump removed in late June.

Fact Two: Six weeks later, her surgeon told her that the X-rays made it quite clear to him that she had a very short time to live; perhaps as little as two months.

Fact Three: She was prayed for, and sprinkled, at the shrine of Our Lady of Walsingham.

Fact Four: She left for America, not feeling very well, and arrived quite certain that she was on the point of death.

Fact Five: Billy burst into her dreams, her sleep and then her waking life, beautiful and improbable as some nut-brown glossy angel, and arranged for her to be seen at the local hospital.

Finally had come the announcement that she was cured.

She had not realized, until she heard the news, how much she had accepted the idea of her own death. And now the idea of life flooded back as something wonderfully refreshing, young, hopeful. Billy was so pretty, so energetic, so amusing, that she would have perhaps brought this feeling to anyone meeting her for the first time. But to Pamela, she brought peculiar benediction, something which could not be explained solely by her youthful exuberance. Now, partly (or was it chiefly?) owing to Billy, Pamela wanted to *live*. She felt ashamed of her earlier, ready acceptance of death; ashamed, too, of the sluggish, cynical idle way of life that she had been having before. It had all been so self-contained and inward-looking. Suddenly, life blossomed again. She felt a sort of bubbling inside her, the kind of excitement felt as a child at the approach of a birthday party.

And yet, and yet, could it really be? In the cool of the early morning church, quietly telling her beads, she gazed up at the rather quizzical face of the Madonna and wondered. A line from Laurel and Hardy suggested itself: *Here's another fine mess you've gotten me into*. Yet it might be, who knew, Her way of showing that RCs were not the only pebbles on the beach as far as She was concerned, with their dreadful Lourdes and Knock and Fatima. Why not the Walsingham Way for a change with some irritating but benign poofter sploshing holy water about like scent in a boudoir? Much more fun. And just as likely, when one came to think, as the vulgar make-believe that Rome went in for. *Think*, Pamela almost said aloud to the expressionless statue, of the razmatazz that would be made if Sourpuss were a Roman Candle. Letters to the Vicar General. The whole embarrassing story of the lump in her breast and the Pillock's 'negs' read out to some ecclesiastical court. Prurient visits from apostolic delegates and devil's advocates. And, as like as not, if they decided that it was an attested miracle, they would try to make it the responsibility not only of Her, but of one of their own jumped-up and rather unconvincing 'saints' – some brave but misguided Elizabethan terrorist like Edmund Campion; or one of their pathetic little nut-case saints like Thérèse of Lisieux. *Thank God*, she really did say aloud; *thank God, thank God*.

But what was she thanking Him for? For Billy. For Sourpuss. For the fact that in some way the Pillock had been proved wrong. For what the Prayer Book so richly called *newness of life*. She stopped telling her beads and sank her head in her hands, remaining on her knees in front of the statue for half an hour, rapt in silence and wonder.

This feeling had continued, deep down, throughout a lovely day with Billy. It being so fine, they had taken the ferry after an early brunch in Battery Park, and now gazed together from the heights of the Statue of Liberty out over the sea towards the Verrazano Bridge.

'You are making me so happy,' Pamela heard herself saying as the girl continued to hold her hand.

She wanted, desperately, to talk to someone of what was on her mind, but she was not sure that Billy was an appropriate sharer of the secret. Yet, such a quick intimacy had sprung up between them that she already felt they knew each other well enough to talk of things which she would normally only have been able to murmur about incoherently with Sourpuss.

'I still can't get over the way you just flew over like that without consulting John, without finding out –' The girl was beaming with admiration. Already the absurdity of Pamela's journey had swollen, in their conversation, to the proportions of myth. 'And then, meeting Mel on the plane. It was just fantastic.'

'Dear Billy,' she began, interrupting the flow and staring into those large brown eyes. 'There has been something on my mind ever since the hospital.'

'Look here, you're OK. You're OK, d'you hear me. You're not to go, like, getting hung up over this cancer bit. You're clean, like the man said.'

'I know, but you don't seem to realize . . .'

'Your doctor back in England screwed it up, that's all. Everyone knows English doctors are a load of crap.'

'He's Scotch.'

'Scotch, English, what's the difference?'

'Loads. I agree he's probably wholly incompetent. But you see, there's something else I haven't told you about, and it's been on my mind.'

The top of the Statue of Liberty was an odd place to be embarking on what proved to be a long and really rather involved argument about religion and the Virgin Mary in particular. Different parties of tourists came and went, ooh'd and ah'd and gasped at the view, while Pamela and Billy, a light wind blowing in their faces, discussed the issue with all the enthusiasm of the medieval schoolmen.

'Who is this miracle-worker anyway – Sourpuss? How come he has a name like that?'

'He hasn't. I call him that – well, I don't, but I think of him as that. Not all the time. His name's Hereward Stickley.'

'And he's some kind of a saint like Padre Pio, right?'

'No. He's a rather fidgety, irascible sort of person, but since you haven't been to England I can't explain him to you. Perhaps I couldn't even if you had met him. But he is a very important person in my life, and we are fond of each other. I think that's the thing I've discovered since leaving him behind.'

'And you're claiming he's worked a miracle? Jeez . . .'

'I'm not claiming anything, dearest Billy. I'm just trying to work out what has happened.'

And she tried to explain the peculiarity of the day in Walsingham, how intensely she felt a growing sense of Hereward's personality on the journey home; of how she had been frightened by the thought that he was in love with her; had even begun to wonder whether she was not in love with him herself. (No, don't ask her to explain.) And Billy had been sensible and said no, one could not explain falling in love, because it was much too intense and peculiar and never happened (or almost never) with people one would have chosen. And then, returning to the subject of the 'miracle', Billy had said, 'Surely if you had been cured then and there at the shrine you'd have felt something – I mean you would have *known* that you were cured.'

'I'm not so sure. Many people think that religion is a matter of feeling. But the reason why I came to like Hereward so much in the first place was the sense I had in his church that it was something much bigger, something easier and yet more solid than feeling. I remember one Corpus Christi he preached about the mass and said that the Lord had not left us instructions about the state of our heart. He had not said *this feel*, or even *this believe* but simply *this do*, and that it was the doing which involved us in the divine event; even if, at the actual moment of doing, our minds were distracted. Well, when I went to Walsingham I was afraid that I was in quite the wrong frame of mind. He told me I was being ridiculously scrupulous, and I think he was right. I mean, if it was a miracle, there is no reason to imagine it was dependent on any feeling of mine.'

'OK. But what's the reason for supposing it was a miracle at all? You've already admitted your surgeon was a dum-dum.'

'He had the negatives. He was certain.'

'The more stupid he was, the more certain he would have been he was right. Perhaps,' Billy scratched her head. 'I don't know. Frankly I just don't believe in miracles. I didn't know any intelligent person believed in them.'

'You see, it's not just the fact that my illness has disappeared. I know this sounds as if I'm contradicting what I said about *feeling*, but I really do feel quite different.'

'How come?'

'Well, on the side of life. Happy. You can't imagine what a grumpy old thing I'd become in the last few years. When they told me I only had a few more months to live, you know, I felt almost relieved. Apart from the terror of the illness itself, I was *glad*. I did not have anything left to live for. Everything feels quite different now.'

'It's the wonderfully clean New York air.' The girl was already trying to catch some of Pamela's relentless ironies.

'It's no worse than the Thames Valley, I can assure you. And up here's lovely. Oh, it's partly you, I know that.'

'That makes you want to be alive?'

And they gazed into one another's faces. Pamela's eyes filled with tears at Billy's youthfulness and good looks, the high flush on the cheekbones, the boyish fringe of slightly lank dark hair, the very oval jaw and firm chin, the slightest down on the upper lip increasing the look of the darling of the upper fourth in a boys' boarding school. Billy, in turn, was moved by the delight and love in the eyes of Pamela; the softness of her complexion, the firmness, yet fleshiness of the face, the very piercing, rather mocking bright blue eyes.

It was years since Pamela had jumped in so fast out of her depth with another person. When their lips met, their kiss was slight and gentle, but both of them shivered with its power. The moment was soon gone because Billy resumed:

'I don't think I can swallow the cult of Mary. That's all.'

'Why ever not?' Pamela's tone was that of the outraged hostess whose guest had claimed to find caterpillars in the salad. 'What's wrong with Her?'

'She's OK, I guess. It's the idea of her. The idea that all women should be aspiring towards the ideal of obedience, motherhood: that's their highest moment of glory. That's a sick idea.'

'Motherhood *is* many people's highest moment of glory,' said Pamela, thinking for a moment of Dorothy Higgs and wondering how she was. She could see that by some standards Dorothy's immolation to her son – Brian, was he called? – was perhaps unhealthy. But the woman had *chosen* to feel like that, presumably. 'And besides, Mary is an ideal of virginity, too.'

'Big deal. Either way, women aren't allowed to enjoy sex. Either they're way up on the pedestal as the pure virgin, or they're sausage machines to have babies with. Very elevated. Very dignified. And the cult of Mary has fostered that idea right through the centuries: that our greatest call is to be obedient, subservient, down-trodden . . .'

Pamela, who did not feel subservient, and had never been obedient in her life, wondered how to reply.

'And another thing,' Billy poured it all out, 'why is God always *male* for Chrissakes?'

'It's just a way of speaking, isn't it?'

'And is it just a way of speaking to think of Jesus as male?'

'Well, I suppose he had to be one or the other. Most people are, so it would have looked rather odd if He had been a sort of Tiresias. I don't see that it affects matters much. I mean, He could just as easily have been a woman.'

'It might not worry you, but it would worry a lot of pigs in the church, right? It would probably worry your Sourpuss.'

'Yes. But it would worry Sourpuss to have a little girl singing in the choir or a woman serving at the altar. What worries him doesn't have anything to do with it. It was just a fifty-fifty chance that Christ was born a man.'

'And you're saying that most priests would agree with you?'

'Not necessarily. But I don't get all my religion from priests, thank God.' She remembered a very unhelpful little pamphlet which Father Stickley had purchased in huge numbers and left at the back of his church, called *Why the Christian Priesthood Is Male*. She generally found little booklets rather boring and had not read it. It all seemed rather illiterate and hysterical. 'Mind you,' she said to Billy, 'if it upset people, I think one ought to be gentle to their feelings.'

'But you still can't deny that the majority of *male* Christians think of God as male.'

'Yes, but it doesn't mean they are right or wrong. How they think is up to them, surely.'

'But it's their religion you believe in. Can't you see that?'

'No. It's my religion. I probably agree with them in all essential things – about the sacraments and the historicity of the Gospels and the existence of God. But it's left to us to make up our own minds about how we think of these things, what pictures we find helpful.'

And so the argument rambled on, Billy trying to persuade Pamela that it was beneath her dignity to be taking part in any such masculine fantasy as Virgin-worship; and Pamela trying to sort out the sense from the nonsense and wondering why she felt so terribly strongly about it.

'I'm sorry,' Billy said at last. 'I didn't mean to be rude about your beliefs. I just . . .'

How could Pamela explain that such conversations did not hurt her in the least. Or that, for all her spikery, there would always be a part of herself which found it impossible to shake off the freedoms of scepticism?

'I would prefer it if it wasn't a miracle,' she said deliberately. 'Can you see that? I hate the whole idea of it being a miracle.'

'I don't,' Billy announced suddenly.

'Why?'

'Need you ask?'

They went down in the elevator, and in the cafeteria at the bottom they drank iced tea while they waited for the ferry.

'I wish you weren't flying back at the end of the week.'

'I have to.'

Silently they were both wondering if they would ever meet again after the week came to an end.

'It was lovely up there,' Pamela added, awkwardly. 'Have you seen *Saboteur*?'

Billy hadn't.

'It has this wonderful final scene at the top of the Statue of Liberty . . .' Her voice faded away. Nothing was more boring than going over the plots of films.

'Pamela, I think you are meant to have come here. In some crazy way I can't figure out, I really believe we are meant to have met.'

'I feel that too.'

She ran her fingers through the girl's hair and stroked her forehead.

'You see, I haven't been able to tell Gale, but in a few weeks it's going to become impossible.'

What was the girl talking about?

'Pamela, is John an important person in your life?'

'Very,' she responded lightly.

Yes, friendship was the most important thing in her life.

'I mean, are you two lovers, or . . .' Billy's voice trailed away, unable to think of a convincing alternative.

'John and I are . . .' she paused, 'close.' She did not know what inspired her to draw this coy cloak of mystery over things.

'He said, like, he didn't have a regular mistress back home.'

'John said *that to you*?'

It seemed wildly improbable. Until that moment, the implications of John and Billy inhabiting neighbouring apartments had not dawned on her. In so far as she had given the matter any thought, she perhaps imagined them nodding on the stairs. Nothing more. Billy had in a superlative degree what John called 'spontaneous overflow', the feature, he said, that he had been most dreading about the American young. Although infatuated with it at the moment, Pamela could see what he meant. There were ways in which it could be greatly embarrassing. This discussion of relationships, for instance: so overt, that it destroyed the reality under discussion, which must always be more delicate and tenuous than could easily be conveyed by words. Was so-and-so important to you? Was your relationship with them deep, shallow, very deep, important, unimportant . . . Billy must be fantasizing. John, in no circumstances that she could imagine, would have confided in a young girl the state of play about bed in England.

It was almost literally unthinkable.

'I thought when you came out, so eager to see him, that he must have been just lying. I mean, a girl – a woman,' she unflatteringly corrected herself '– just doesn't fly the Atlantic, God help us, in order to see a *friend*. Not,' she added insult to injury, 'not a mature woman.'

'Why ever not? That is precisely what I did do.'

'But you admit he is a special kind of friend.'

'Are you trying to tell me that something happened between you and John?' she asked, steadily, gently, trying not to suggest either outrage, jealousy or prurient curiosity.

'Dammit, we had an affair.'

This was shrieked, so that people at neighbouring tables turned to stare.

'It's time we went,' said Pamela.

They boarded the ferry and resumed the conversation when the boat was moving.

'It was fouling us both up, I guess. He felt guilty perhaps, hung up about sex in general. I dunno. I was more experienced than he imagined I would be. Then he got somehow mad when he found that out. I dunno. We were just wrong for each other.'

'And how' was the vulgarism which came to mind, but Pamela did not use it. 'So he went to Mexico?' she prompted. 'To allow you to get over it all.'

'Uh-huh.'

'And you feel pretty cut up about it and you're missing him?'

'Pamela, I don't know. I don't know what I feel any more. I just assumed you and John were, well, you know, Christ, like.'

Really, Pamela thought with a sudden donnish petulance. The Americans were too inarticulate to live. She felt herself breathing heavily and her heart was pounding. She wished that Billy had not told her. It was hurting much more than she would ever have guessed, and she could not tell why. Was she jealous of Billy having been to bed with John? Or of John for having been to bed with Billy? Or of both of them, for at least having had an *experience*, while she moped and was ill and thought about theology? Or was it merely an extension of the feeling of irritation which is almost inevitable when two friends strike up an independent *tendresse*?

Billy had lit a cigarette and was gazing away from Pamela out across the water. Her eyes were full of tears which she brushed away as inconspicuously as she could, with the back of her hand.

'Try not to,' Pamela suggested, adding with perhaps unnecessary consciousness of how good the English must always appear on such occasions, 'Have a blow on this.' It was a large snuff handkerchief, one of the ones which Father Stickley had brought to the hospital with the poems of George Herbert. It compared rather favourably with the Kleenex which Pamela had been given to blow in, that first night in Mel's apartment.

The girl blew noisily and they sat in silence until they got back to Manhattan. They returned to the hotel without saying a word, and it was only when they got back to their room that Pamela said, 'I wish you had not said all this.'

'I guess it was a mistake. I thought it would make things a bit clearer. I need help, Pamela. I thought you'd be sympathetic.'

Pamela looked at her. They were both more self-composed now that the awfulness of the shared news had sunk in as far as such things can sink.

'John is a very secret person, Billy. I suppose I know him almost as well as anyone': she wondered now whether this was

114

true, but she did not want to deny herself the pleasure of saying it – 'and there are some things we just never discuss. I quite thought, for instance, that when I came over here to tell him about my illness, we would never actually get round to talking about it.'

'You mean he's squeamish.'

'It's not so much that. He's one of those men who has a terror of obviousness. I think that's it. We would have got on as well as ever – had he been here. We would have looked at a few pictures, had a few meals together, seen a few films, and I would have gone home and snuffed it. He would, I assume, have understood. But he would have much, much preferred that to a frank, open discussion of the whole question. Do you see what I am getting at?'

'No.'

There was a kind of desperate mirth about Billy as she lit up yet another cigarette.

'All I am saying is that you probably feel very left out, very cheated by John. But he is a basically kind person.' She paused and considered the proposition. She believed it was true. 'I should say a very kind person,' she added. 'But he can't give expression to what he feels, and he hates "scenes". So what he has done – whatever it is – has probably hurt you much more than he would have meant it to. He would not want to hurt anyone. He would have preferred it, if *you* had left *him* and gone off to Mexico and said nothing.'

'Pamela, are you crazy? I dare say you do know John better than I do. I only went to bed with him' – there was no sarcasm in her voice. 'Frankly, I'm not all that interested in speculations about his character.'

'Now you're being lofty. It's impossible not to be interested in John's character. He's the most mysterious person in the world.'

Billy had come merely to regard him as 'difficult' in the sense that some books are 'difficult', and also in the sense of cussed. You could not get near him. His secret, if he had one, was too well guarded. This, in time, had come to bore her deeply. She had been bitterly upset about his departure to Mexico; by all the painfulness of the way the affair ended. But she had never gone in for analysis of the characters of her lovers.

'I'm truly not interested in John's character,' she said, her voice faltering on the edge of tears once more. It had become very high-pitched and childish. Pamela rose and put down her crochet. She moved over to Billy's bed and put her hand on the girl's forehead.

'What's the matter, then? I don't like to see you so unhappy.'

'Goddammit, haven't you guessed? I'm having a baby.'

The tears simply poured. Billy drew back the corners of her mouth, like a child pretending that it was not happening. The effect was a grotesque lachrymose smirk, which made Pamela want to hold her in her arms very tight.

The inevitable questions would come later: how long? how sure? what to do? who to tell? Now they held each other, their breasts squeezed, their hearts beating together.

Thousands of miles away, Hereward Stickley intoned: *Remember O most gracious Virgin Mary, that never was it known that any one who fled to thy protection, implored thy help, or sought thy intercession was left unaided. Inspired with this confidence, I fly unto thee, O Virgin of virgins, my Mother: to thee do I come, before thee I stand, sinful and sorrowful: O mother of the Word Incarnate, despise not my petitions, but in thy mercy hear and answer me.*

- IO -

'You really had no right! No right at all!'

Tulloch was beside himself with rage. Crawford, though brick-red in countenance, still spoke in quite low, deliberate tones.

'I was merely doing my duty,' he said solemnly.

'And it's your duty to interfere with my patients, I suppose.'

'Oh, come off it, Robby. You're quite happy to let me look after them when you want to be off on holiday. It just happened that Mrs Higgs broke her arm while you were away. It's natural that I should take an interest in the case. Damn it, it's our duty to save life.'

Tulloch looked up at the young prig with a sneer.

'If she's as ill as you think she is, there's not much life left to save.'

'I still think we should conduct a biopsy to make sure.'

'And if she's riddled with it?'

'That will be that.'

'Where does that leave us?' Tulloch fumbled with a biro on his table-top and tried not to meet Crawford's gaze. This was the moment the young bastard had been waiting for. Ever since he had come to that hospital three years before he had been waiting to catch Tulloch out.

'You mean,' he said, slowly, sadistically, 'where does it leave *you*, Robby?'

'I don't know what you mean.'

'You know damn well what I mean.'

There was a bit too much melodrama about the way he spat this through his teeth.

'If she proves to be very ill – critically ill,' Tulloch corrected himself, already speaking as if to a committee of inquiry, 'then that is very disturbing. But we all know that there is no infallible way of diagnosing the extent of this bloody disease. If it's got into the bone as you suggest, that would not necessarily have shown up in her chest X-rays two or three months back. I don't know what the case is that you are trying to prove, but,' he shrugged. The balance of power had shifted to him. He now knew how the case would appear if Crawford were ever fool enough to make any complaints. It was moreover what Tulloch believed to be true. It was quite impossible in cases like this to be sure.

'I am simply trying to get at the truth.'

'Are you?'

Crawford threw up his hands in despair.

'Anyone would think I was accusing you of deliberately killing the old bag off.'

Tulloch looked at his fingernails and did not reply.

'I mean, you said yourself, it's impossible to be sure one way or the other.'

'Why you are taking such an interest in this particular case is what puzzles me.'

Tulloch knew quite well that spread of cancer from the breast to the spine was this young man's specialist subject of research. He had a bee in his bonnet about it. Moreover, Crawford wanted to supplant Tulloch's own indiscriminate use of Adliamycin D with an entirely new chemical treatment which had been tried, not, to Tulloch's mind, with any notable success, in California.

'If that woman dies, it will be our fault.'

'Now you're talking like a first-year clinical student,' snapped Tulloch. 'You know perfectly well that if we took that line about every old woman who died in our hospitals we should just despair.'

'Mrs Higgs is not old,' Crawford protested. 'She is fifty-six. The same age as you are, Robby.'

'And she's had a cracked collar-bone and a couple of breaks in her arm, and a pain in her back; and I dare say she's been a bloody nuisance to the nurses, whimpering and crying and moaning all the time. And for that reason, we ought to treat her as a special case, according to you, and cut her open at great expense to the Health Service and worry her family sick when all that's wrong with her is that she has outlived her usefulness.'

'I beg your pardon?'

'You see it again and again. Particularly with women who have got no jobs. Their children grow up; their husbands are no longer interested in them; they have lost their looks. The only thing left to them is illness. Otherwise no one would take any notice of them at all. Oh, I'm not saying they aren't really ill. They develop real symptoms. But there's nothing we can do to save them. It's their families who ought to save them. Not us.'

Crawford disliked Tulloch's little speeches about psycho-somatic illness. They were too pat, too vulgar, too self-congratulatory. What was more important, Crawford knew that he was losing the argument. He had come to Tulloch convinced that he would have a showdown. The more he contemplated it, the more certain he became that Dorothy Higgs showed all the symptoms of advanced cancer. Like so many of the cases he had studied for his thesis, the cancer was, he felt sure, spreading in classic fashion down the bone marrow and into her limbs. She was riddled with it. That was why she had broken three bones in the space of forty-eight hours. He was sure it would happen again. This meant, very clearly, that Tulloch had wrongly diagnosed her condition when, at her check-up a few months before, he had pronounced her to be clear. Sometimes, of course, this was the kindest thing to say to someone in an inoperable condition. That was what Crawford assumed Tulloch would claim had been his policy in this case. Instead, he stubbornly insisted that he had not been lying. And this could only mean that he had been mistaken.

There were so many mornings like the one when Mrs Higgs came for her check-up that Crawford could not remember it at all clearly. All such mornings were the same: Robby raging; nurses scampering out of his way like rabbits escaping the fog-lights of a Jaguar. Then there would have been operations to be performed; the wards to be gone round; and probably several other people to 'clear' from X-ray. The nightmarish possibility was, of course, that Robby, in his fury and hurry, had muddled Mrs Higgs's negatives up with someone else's. While she languished in greater and greater pain, Robby was perhaps already pumping Adliamycin into someone's system, with all the horrendous side-effects of nausea, hair loss and general weakening of the system. Crawford had begun to suspect that the drug itself, while killing off cancer in the affected areas, killed off quite a lot else as well; that the effects of the drug could conceivably be stronger, crueller and faster working than the chaotic progress of the disease itself.

But with Robby Tulloch in a stubborn mood, not even conceding the necessity of further investigation of Mrs Higgs, he was not going to admit having made such a mistake. And, most certainly, if he could, he would be keeping any such unfortunate patient's notes well hidden from Crawford in the future.

'What do you suggest we do with Mrs Higgs then, Robby?'

'What were the results of her latest X-ray?'

'Well, the wrist seems to have healed. Just about. There is still some nasty swelling round the collar-bone.'

'How many more beds in this hospital are you taking up with broken arms?' he asked quizzically.

'None, but . . .'

'Then we have nothing for it but to send the old biddy home.' He had ignored Crawford's disturbing observation about her age. In his mind, Mrs Higgs was antique.

'Tell her GP to keep an eye on her. Who is he?'

'Rupert Swynnerton-Myles.'

'He's a very good physician. Let's sit back and see what happens. We can give her some exercise at the orthopaedic hospital if she's having back trouble. I see no reason, as I said before, why Mrs Higgs should be singled out for special treatment.'

- II -

The placard on the up platform announced welcome to the home of pressed steel. There was the usual Gadarene rush in the tunnel crossing the line to the exit, and, with two heavy new suitcases, John Brocklehurst did not compete. By the time he reached the rank there was a queue of about a dozen people and not a taxi in sight.

Red with the Mexican sun, he surveyed the damp English scene with delight. It was wonderful, the way this town kept its secrets. Beyond the canal, and a few warehouses, he could make out the Venetian water-tower of that church where Pamela was so fond of going. It was, from where he stood, the most impressive architectural monument in sight. A row of scruffy Edwardian shops; a lumpy hotel insultingly aping a classical manner; a railway bridge; the most hideous of all office blocks, a cube of black glass: these were the campanile's only rivals for the eye's attention. The delicacy of pinnacles and spires, the grandeur of domes, the ingenuity of buttresses, the proportions of quadrangles, now intimate, now superb, for which the town was more noted in the imagination of travellers, were kept sensibly hidden from view.

He was glad to be back. It was not only, as he would hasten to tell Pamela, the predominance of the Romish cult; though that side of things had been fairly ghastly. Never, he felt sure, would Pamela mention the Virgin Mother again if she had witnessed the Mexican mode of venerating Her. Nor was it even the ugliness of the antiquities, the tedium of the pyramids, the inadequacy of the cinemas, the unpalatability of the oily, peppery food. He could not put his finger on it, but the whole country had a dreary provincial feeling about it, not diminished by the enthusiasm everywhere displayed, in bars, hotels, posters and street corners, for the game of soccer. Moreover, the Mexicans had all shouted their heads off from dawn till dawn, and this, combined with the heat, had brought on migraines. The sheer colourlessness and drabness of the present scene brought peace to the soul. Reassuringly, he felt himself already beginning a slight cold. He even quite looked forward to seeing his colleagues again, who would be clambering out of their mothballs in preparation for the new academic year. He tried to guess who would be the first figure that he would encounter in the quadrangle. Perhaps it would be poor old Nigel Garfield, dubbed unaccountably *Hovis* by Pamela; had she spotted him, little lower than an angel, in some tea-shop's inglenook? Or did he resemble an actor in some now discontinued advertisement for bread? John could not remember. He was, anyway, a ripe example of self-parodying donnishness.

'You find us all much the same, my dear fellow, innocently pushing back the frontiers of knowledge from our cloistered haunts while you have gadded hither and thither across the Herring Pond. Still, let it be said, these Yanks are very excellent fellows . . .'

Or perhaps he would bump into the Chaplain, smugly arrayed in cassock and bands, believing himself to be Dean Swift, but looking for all the world like a draper's assistant in fancy dress. In *his* voice, the regional tones had been scarcely transformed. Hovis, who specialized in vowel sounds, would have had little difficulty in identifying those of the West Midlands. But the lilt and sway, professorial rather than clerical, hinted at the direction in which the Chaplain's ambitions lay.

A few cabs had come and gone by now, and John shuffled towards the head of the queue, imagining further meetings: fruity historians, scientists in anoraks, economists sidling out of sports cars with cigars in their mouths all rose in an etherial picture before his mind's eye until he found himself at the head of the queue, and giving directions to the next driver who came along.

It would, above all, be good to see Pamela again. She was the person he had most often and most actively missed in his year away. Even in Mexico, where his mind had teemed with other distractions, he had found himself dreaming of Pamela. Her companionship had provided what, after the collapse of his marriage, he had imagined he would never find again: a shared language, a privately inhabited linguistic world, surest sign of a bond between souls. The laughter and the sense of security which it brought – all the nameless things one meant by another person's charm, which might only be felt by a few of their closest intimates and might be quite incomprehensible to the outside observer – all this was too precious to be lost. For this reason, if he could identify a single reason at all for so tenuous and fraily governable an area of consciousness, he had held himself back from initiating a love affair. It seemed to be mutually understood between them that this was how things stood, this was what they wanted. Sex, initially the most beguiling factor in any human encounter, so fast, in his experience, became the most boring. And when that was discarded, it was merely luck if there was anything left but tatters of the more readily analysable elements of the friendship. This had happened, long before, in Nottingham. What an end to a marriage! Nothing had been said, because neither he nor his wife would have been capable of saying it – even if they knew what it was to say. It had all been perfectly English. They might have gone on for another thirty years, never asking, never saying; separate beds; then separate bedrooms; then separate worlds. But they would still have been invited out to the same dinner parties, had the same friends, gone on holiday together. Then, he had come home one evening to find the note, archly worded, and coyly placed beneath the empty pill bottle. She was still breathing, considerately stretched out on a li-lo in the garage to avoid the awkwardness of getting a stiff down the stairs. He had waited until the breathing stopped before he rang up for an ambulance.

Sex being unwilling to go away, despite its obvious power to damage anyone it touched, he had since kept it as casual as possible, saving it up, if he could, for moments when he was away from the home territory and unlikely to be mixed up with anyone on an emotional level. It was ages since he had been as badly stung as by Billy.

The girl had been so teasingly provocative ever since he had arrived at Cornell, running about the place in little more than loose jersey and tights, picking bits of grass out of his hair during a picnic, luring him to a campus dance. Mad, and bad and dangerous to know, all right. One felt drunk in her presence. Normally very diffident, he had found himself plunging in at the deep end with her. One got high on her company as on a drug. Besides, when she came back to his apartment one night after a film, it was plainly what she was expecting. It would have been as churlish, as unnatural, to refuse as not to offer her a chair to sit on or something to drink.

Since his marital disaster, it was the first casual encounter which had been repeated often enough to become an arrangement. She was an inventive, teasing and apparently insatiable companion, and his appetite increased by what it fed on. Perhaps all American girls, since what Pamela called The Tablet had become so readily available, were similarly wild. But there was a kind of manic animal intensity about Billy which made it impossible not to become hooked. Until 'well in' he had not realized any of its possible implications: that at some stage of the game 'falling in love' might be involved; that eventually emotional demands would be made to which he could not conceivably rise.

It had been on their umpteenth time together one afternoon that the awful truth had dawned. Her squeals had ceased to be cries of pleasure, and there were tears running down her cheeks as she said, 'You don't love me at all. I'm just your fucking sex kitten.'

A funny sort of joke, perhaps, but surely it could not be anything else; and then the chill had entered his heart as he had realized that a joke was what it was not, and that in her view they were indulging in a love affair.

He had tried the old ploy, early on, of warning her that any such language could not be used with him; that life had emptied the words of meaning for him; that she must never think of sex with him as anything more than sex: something you liked doing with some people more than with others, just as you might have a favourite partner in tennis or chess. It was not, he had been almost professorial in his insistence on the point, it was not a reliable guide to human compatibility. The sociological reasons for pretending that it was had been obvious enough in their historical context. Since the advent of sure and effective means of controlling birth, such strictures no longer applied. One should rid the mind of any notion that sex and companionship of a deeper level went together. So he had prosed on their very first evening, as she lay curled up like a sleek dark animal in his arms and introduced him to practices which he would have hitherto thought outré.

But she, of course, had not listened; and perhaps neither of them believed what he was saying in any case. The infatuation threatened to drown them both, and he saw the hell which inevitably stretched ahead if it did. This time, he realized, it would be he who wrote the note, and she who found the empty pill bottle, she who was left frozen, brittle, broken and guilty by the experience. Anything would be better than that. He had therefore packed his bags six weeks before he need have done, confided in Mel that he was off, left grateful messages for Gale, who had been endlessly hospitable and kind, and flown off to Mexico City. He had left no message for Billy.

The obvious way of killing sexual infatuation, in his limited experience, was to get oneself a sprinkling of very strong experiences of the same order to obliterate the painful memories. It was no good thinking to distract oneself by reading, or looking at architecture or visiting friends. One had to fight fire with fire.

Either the red-light district of Mexico City was less good than any of its equivalents sampled in other parts of the world, or he struck it in a season when all the real professionals were watching the football. Or perhaps he was simply unlucky and in the wrong mood. The tarts seemed too lazy to move; one made all the going oneself. One of them was too idle even to switch off the television; it was curiously hard to concentrate on the act of shame with a loud, latinate sports commentary bawling away at the end of the bed. He had arrived in England feeling sexually disgruntled, and this necessitated breaking the journey in London before catching the train home, to call in at a joint he used regularly.

He would now suffer the usual three weeks of agony wondering if symptoms would appear.

While his mind throbbed with these confusing thoughts, the taxi traced its way through the familiar streets. Returning home after a year, their familiarity hit him afresh. So many layers of experience were associated with every corner and stone that he saw that it was like coming upon the photograph of a parent.

He wondered if Pamela was back in town. There were two weeks to go before Full Term. There might even be the chance of one of their little holidays in Wales. If not, jaunts in the Simca to Berkshire pubs, or evenings in her peculiar little drawing-room watching the Sony and eating take-away curry. He resolved to ring her up when he had taken a bath and unpacked.

The Luxicar had swung through the high Gothic gate. John glimpsed the bespectacled, bowler-hatted, dignified figure of Ramsden. Holding a telephone to his ear, he waved a lordly greeting as the car parked by the lawn.

When the taxi went away, John stood for a while surveying the college: the row of pinnacles on the chapel roof; the brown bell-tower almost dark in the mist. The lawns were deserted. Croquet hoops had been removed in readiness for the winter. The last of the conferands had departed. The undergraduates were yet to appear. There was an almost eerie stillness in the air, only broken by the distant chiming of the quarter hour.

'I can manage,' he said, when Ramsden appeared and offered to carry his bags.

'Welcome home, sir.'

He had wanted to take in the full poignant melancholy of the scene alone. He wondered, almost like a contrite philanderer returning to a loving wife, how he could have so forgotten the sheer majestic beauty of the place.

'You've picked up a bit of sun, sir. We've had it nice here, too, until the last few days. Too good to last, I suppose, sir.'

Ramsden's humorous tone insisted that it be complied with.

'This weather's all right. How have things been, Ramsden?'

'Oh, they'll start settling down now you're back, eh, sir? Doesn't do to stay away too long. You can't trust 'em not to get up to mischief while you're away.' Exaggerated facial distortions accompanied these observations, stage directions which demanded that the remarks be accepted in a spirit of banter.

'I don't believe it with you around, Ramsden.' John's own tones took up the cry, so that he almost felt inclined to nudge and wink. 'You keep us all in good order.'

'Are you sure you can manage those cases, sir?' Ramsden pursued, now half serious.

But John, still switched on to the earlier mode, said, 'Do I look as decrepit as that?' and started to hump them towards the further gateway that led towards the Garden Quadrangle.

The whole place, he reflected, insisted upon putting on this elaborate pantomime; not, as he had once supposed, for the sake of the outside observer, but for its own amusement. College porters doffed their bowler hats and quipped in grotesquely obsequious jokes with dons who were equally determined that the show should go on according to their own egocentric variations of academic eccentricity. Over-playing the parts, either in the privacy of common rooms or in the public rituals of the university as a whole, did not diminish their seriousness. The architecture itself happily collaborated in the routine, medieval gargoyles sniggering in perpetuity at the charades enacted beneath in cloister and staircase.

Returning after a period of exile brought the timid sense that he was not quite yet in the swing, and that a period of readjustment would be necessary before he could acclimatize to the roles assigned him in the drama of the place. It was nothing so crude as resuming affectations which had been discarded for the sake of not drawing attention to himself in the States. If anything, his 'Englishness', whatever that was, was more pronounced, certainly more gleefully appreciated, at Mel and Gale's table than it could ever hope to be in analogous households here. Or was his sense of uneasiness simply based on the instinctive reaction, that returning to any academic institution, even to one which was nominally home, awoke inevitable memories of the first day at boarding school? Perhaps it was more akin to the fluttering of a canary which, having spent a few agitated hours asserting its independence among the telegraph poles, returned to the reassuring perch, the looking glass, the old expected routines of trilling and balancing, but was unable to avoid a moment's terror as the door of its cage was locked once more.

Liking the simile, he whistled to himself, an absurd mixture of pleasure and trepidation. His tubby form, amply filling the square shoulders of a lightweight suit cut on an American model, was the reverse of birdlike. He was a stone fatter than when he went away. During the last twelve months, he had only consumed the proliferations of tasteless steak out of politeness. The excellent bread – fresh from authentic bakeries, Italian, Greek or French – had been the sole form of nourishment which he actually felt inclined to eat. It had added flesh, inevitably. He felt red-faced and gross and in need of a drink. Sweat stood out on the high forehead and matted his scrubs of gingery hair.

The Chaplain, lurking in the Bursary on the opposite side of the quadrangle, stared through the window with a little sigh and paused for a moment in a catalogue of domestic woes which he had hoped might be rectified during the Long Vacation. If he had told the Bursar once about the faulty cistern in his bathroom, he plaintively asserted, he had told him twenty times. Moreover, flecks of paint from the redecorated skirting-board were discernible on his carpet. *His*, he had repeated, carpet. And, with the winter coming on, he could really not be expected to do his work heated only by a gas fire, defective in several ways, and an electric radiator. College, he had said, preferring to discard the definite article when referring to that institution, really ought to wake up to the realities of life and install central heating on the staircases. He would mention it, he averred, at Governing Body.

It was some relief to the Bursar when his clerical colleague observed wearily, 'There goes John Brocklehurst.'

'He's very red in the face,' said the Bursar.

'And corpulent.'

'Too much good food in California, or wherever it was.' The Bursar was glad to have dropped the subject of radiators.

'He's one of those people,' said the Chaplain, 'who will just go off pop at any minute. Now what else was I going to ask you? Oh, yes. About the electric sockets in my bedroom . . .'

Brocklehurst's 'set' was altogether less palatial than the Chaplain's. He had been put there when appointed to his fellow-ship, and, having accumulated all manner of belongings during the intervening ten years, been too lazy to move out. But he felt that conditions in a place like this were almost by definition spartan. He, for instance, had to cross a landing to his bath-room, shared with another fellow, and, having no taste for querulousness, he never went over for extended conversations with the administrative staff about plumbing or heating or paint-work. The room which he now entered was, therefore, shabby but home-like. The gurgle of the gas fire, ineffectual as a source of heat, brought compensatory reassurances, a sense of belonging.

It was all so familiar to him, that it did not initially strike him as odd that someone had lit the fire. Two massive glass-fronted Victorian book-cases dominated the two sides of the room where there were no windows and housed the bulk of his library. The rest, neater and more dustless than when he had left it, lay in piles around the skirting-boards, spilling over into fitted shelves in the bedroom. There was a grandfather clock, and a roll-top secretary in one corner, now closed and locked and polished, slumbering like some chestnut-coloured armadillo. In the centre of the room, a capacious writing table lay uncharacteristically bare; but someone had arranged pens, boxes of drawing-pins, blotter, broken tobacco-pipes and ash-trays into neat little rows and propped up between book-ends works of reference which normally lay higgledy-piggledy: a University handbook; *Examination Decrees and Regulations*; portable dictionaries of English, French, Russian and Latin; a Coronation Bible whose pristine binding made clear that it was seldom consulted.

The only picture on the walls was a portrait of his great-grandfather, a bearded merchant in a black frock coat, prosperous, rubicund, no nonsense. He was flanked on either side by eighteenth-century maps of the West Riding.

The whole scene needed to be absorbed slowly, both the room, and its slight neatening and rearrangement. This was his canary's cage; this the visible expression of the personality he had chosen to present – no, rather, found himself presenting – to colleagues, friends and pupils. There was something a little dogged about its scrupulously old-fashioned appearance which brought a moment of shock, as if he had slightly hoped, in his memory of the room, of his persona here, that some concessions might have been made to the march of time. His great-grandfather looked more at home than he himself felt. Resisting trendiness was one thing; being imprisoned in the quaint quite another.

The unmistakable smell of polish from an aerosol spray which lingered and glistened not only on the mahogany and walnut veneer but also in the brown velvet of the long curtains and the plum red of the carpets confirmed that a servant had been round very lately. It was mysterious how the true professionals gave the impression of always sensing one's return, like wary domestic animals. It was not, he had become convinced, the result of any sixth sense; merely the consequence of endless hovering about and gossiping with the other staircase staff while they kept an eye out for comings and goings in their own domains. The spluttering fire had probably been switched on during his conversation with Ramsden; certainly the room did not feel aired.

A yellow duster appearing to move by itself along the top of his half-closed bedroom door showed that finishing touches were still being put to the room. When the door actually opened, to reveal Vi shaking the duster all over the carpet, and then stuffing it into her white house-coat, he felt so pleased to see her that he could almost have hugged her.

Perhaps because she was a woman – and there were still few enough about – perhaps because of a near greatness of character with which he romantically inclined to imbue her, Vi did not fit strictly into the pantomimic aspects of college living. It was not that she showed any aversion to self-parody or self-advertisement; but the role she chose to adopt was one of riotous commonsense, a deliberate standing back from the spectacle, a cocky assertion of independence. This took the form, most obviously, of regaling John with narratives of life on her estate, and the doings of her family and neighbours. The world outside was her province.

'Hallo there, stranger!' she called cheerily. 'You've brought some nice weather with you as usual.'

Drizzle was appearing on the window-panes as she drew the curtains.

'Evening, Vi.'

'I put your fire on. I'm just nipping off home now, but I'll be down in the morning. I've given your furniture a bit of an old polish. You'll soon have it in a nice mess though, won't you?'

'I hope so.'

'You're looking very well. Had a nice time?'

'It's good to be back.'

'I should like to go to America. Reg and me went to Spain this summer. It was really glorious. But I said to him, I wouldn't mind going to some of the places Mr Brocklehurst's seeing. He pulls my leg, Reg, says I've got my eye on you.' Gales of laughter implied the preposterousness of the suggestion, but John could imagine it being rather nice – 'but I want to go. Manhattan' – she clicked her fingers as if about to break into a dance routine – 'Los Angeles, New York. Must be wonderful.' She gave the back of the chair where she leant a rudimentary flick with the duster and sang, 'Give my regards to Broadway.'

'I didn't travel about all that much, but I went down to Mexico.'

'That must have been smashing. You should have had me with you to help you with the lingo. The waiter in our hotel said you wouldn't know I wasn't Spanish from my accent. Reg had bought one of those records. You know, you teach yourself.'

'I've tried the German one.'

'I wouldn't try that,' she shuddered. She spoke as if it was like an experiment with dangerous drugs. 'Reg doesn't like the Germans. Says it isn't right their being so rich after all the things they done in the war. Funny that, isn't it, I mean the way some people go on minding. Now me, I can't abide nursing grudges. I have to let bygones be bygones. And it isn't as if they was all against the Jews. Still, I mustn't keep you. You'll want to settle in and unpack. I've got to catch a bus and go up and see my neighbour. She's been having such a time. One illness after the next. First, well in June it would have been – or was it July, never mind, she had to go into hospital for, you know, an operation.' She pulled a face to indicate that John was not to ask what sort of an operation. 'Then she started breaking bones, see. First her wrist and then she'd no sooner come home from the hospital than she fell down the stairs and broke all the way up the arm and into the shoulder. It was more of a fracture, the doctors said, but if you ask me she broke it. She's been ever so good, but I think,' she added with the contradictoriness always implicit in the English language, 'I think she's pretty bad. If you ask me she's got cancer.'

John picked a pipe from the rack on his mantelpiece and began to play with it. The very word *cancer* disconcerted him. He tried to think of ways to shut Vi up. On the face of it, there was nothing surprising that a neighbour of hers had been ill. It was impossible to pretend to any personal sympathy. Yet the spectacle which her narrative conjured up chilled and terrified him.

'Shame, too, with her lad just starting at college. Swansea he's going to. Philosophy he's going to study, I think it was. You're philosophy, aren't you?'

'Yes. Yes. I am.' In a desperate way, he even wondered whether to pause and analyse her last sentence, dwell on its syntactical oddity, compare it with sentences such as *L'état, c'est moi; Cogito ergo sum* or, a favourite joke of Pamela's, *I am the Immaculate Conception*. But all he could manage was, 'Yes. I am philosophy.'

'Well, of course his dad, George, he's worried sick about poor old Dol – worried and yet he's still not quite admitting it to himself, you know what I mean, and I don't know how it is but when men worry they start quarrelling with each other – it's the same down at the works, that's why they keep having all these strikes if you ask me – they're *worried*, frightened almost, it makes them edgy, you know – and it's been a pretty rotten start for the lad, having to go off to college with all that hanging over him – in fact I don't know how he'd have managed if he hadn't made friends with this nice girl – Rena she's called – who works at that posh hairdresser's opposite the ABC Cinema.'

'Is that what used to be the Regal?' Anything to take the

conversation as far away as possible from that illness, the very name of which struck fear and weakness into his soul.

'That would be it. The Regal. But, as I say, even though Rena's been ever so good, poor old Dol hasn't got any better. Barry, well he's only a kid – I think they are till they've had a job; these ones are –' she waved an arm in the direction of the window – 'just a kid, and he thinks his mum will be better just as soon as she gets the movement back in her arm. But there's her bad back as well and all, and I mean, you can see she's just wasting away and what I can't understand is why the doctors don't do more; I mean, with all those letters after their names and their difficult writing why can't they see what's wrong with her? But they just keep driving her up to the Orthopaedic for exercises like in that swimming pool they have there. But goodness me, if I was George I'd have a thing or two to say. He's too much in awe if you ask me. Some people are. Says they know what they're doing. Understandable. I mean, he can't really face it himself, I suppose; probably doesn't realize how much they're all kidding themselves. We all do, don't we, kid ourselves?'

'Oh dear,' John said, 'what a sad story.' He tried to brush it immediately to the borders of his consciousness, but Vi had a sort of *presence* and her narratives on this score, however chaotically thrown together, had a way of remaining in the mind. 'Her arms,' she added as a final flourish, 'are as thin as that.' And she curled thumb and forefinger together to make a tiny circle. 'I must be going anyway, else Reg will be jumping to conclusions. He's never easy when he knows you're around. Looks at me real old-fashioned when I say as I've been having a bit of an old natter with Mr Brocklehurst.'

Grateful that humour had been resumed, John laughed with nervous hilarity and said, 'We'd make a great team, you and I.'

'Get away with you.' And, still talking as she made her way down the stairs, 'I've made your bed up with clean sheets, but don't go smoking in bed, if you don't mind, else you'll set the whole building on fire one of these days. We don't want to go disturbing the poor old wood-worms . . .'

Smoking meditatively, John sat by the fire until the room was dark.

- 12 -

Pamela had been back for about a fortnight by the time that John returned from Mexico City. For her, the return to familiar surroundings after a so much shorter period had the effect of making the American interlude unreal. Mel, Gale, The Dream Boat, Billy, the Virgin Mary: so much, in so little time, had changed the complexion of life. The changes were so radical that the actual elongation of existence itself seemed the slightest of them. For, the next day, Billy was to arrive, and with her newness of life in almost every sense of that rich term.

The plans had been worked out during sleepless conversations in the hotel bedroom those last three nights in New York. Billy's initial reaction had been to believe that 'disposing' of the baby was the first problem. But for Pamela, as they talked, the whole thing took on a different colouring. There was no need, much, to have all the old arguments about the sanctity of human life, the rights of the unborn child and other metaphysical imponderables. She was not, in general, bigoted on the subject. She could not believe in all circumstances that this operation was wrong, as the Candles insisted. But she felt strongly that it was wrong in this case. The obvious solution, she had at last persuaded Billy, was that she should come to England, live with her in her little town house until the baby was born, and see what happened after that.

Any number of motives could be discerned for her wanting this to happen. She was not too fussed by motives. Of course she longed to see – perhaps even to possess – a child of John Brocklehurst's. Equally, she had an intense desire to cement her friendship with Billy. Her mind raced ahead to a future together, perhaps in a country house where they could bring up John's child slightly aloof from the vulgar gaze.

Why did not matter. She had a complete conviction that this was what she must do, that it was for this that her life had been spared. Yet where to begin in explaining all this to anyone else? . . . Would it mean an end to her friendship with John? This was unthinkable. But, by the time John was out of his bath and ringing her number, she was sitting in Hereward Stickley's smoky little parlour. Where to start any conversation with him took some sorting out; but conversation of a kind had begun. He sat grimacing behind billows of cigarette fumes, his face contorted into its habitually strained mask, suggesting grief, outrage, sarcastic mirth or perhaps merely the suppressed desire to cough.

'But is your tiny house,' he spat the word out, 'big enough for you and a baby and this girl, whatever her name is.'

She had told him Billy's name a thousand times.

'Well, if it isn't, I shall buy a bigger one. There's one round the corner for sale that I thought I might go and look at. It's two storeys higher than mine and it has a nice little walled garden where the child could romp or toddle or whatever it is children like doing.'

He smirked, half in disapproval, half in admiration.

'You have no idea what they're like,' he exclaimed.

'Nor has anyone who's not had one. People go on having them all the same.'

'That's different.'

'Why?'

'Because they're born as a result of, you know.'

'But presumably this one will be born as a result of You Know. I mean it's not a case of parthenogenesis. She admits that she knows who the father is.'

'And she's told you?'

'Yes.' Pamela felt herself blushing. 'It's an old friend of mine as a matter of fact.'

'An old friend of *yours*? In *America*?'

135

'He was there on sabbatical leave. If you must know, it's John Brocklehurst.'

'Not the one I call your fat friend?'

Why, tonight of all nights, was Sourpuss being so deliberately cussed? He knew perfectly well who John was. She had more than once tried to combine them as dinner guests. They did not like one another. She accepted this. But there was really no need for all this silliness. It was like his apparent inability to remember Billy's name.

'You know John,' she said quietly. 'It's all been the most ghastly shock, if you must know. I still can't quite take it all in. To become so fond of a person in such a short space of time, and then to find out that she had been the mistress of one's best friend ... And then to find out, on top of that, that he had behaved shabbily, cruelly ...'

'Let me top you up.' They were drinking a cheap whisky. She accepted his offer of something to smoke.

'This is all awful,' said the priest at last, allowing the smoke to pour from his nostrils. 'Quite awful. I'm not altogether sure you've done the right thing.'

'Nor am I. Well, I am in one way, as I told you. But in another, I just don't know. I mean, why should Billy want to come and live with me? She hardly knows me: and what would be the point of it all if it broke my friendship with John? It's just ...' She stared hopelessly at the bars of his electric fire.

'It's just that you love her very very much,' he said surprisingly.

She stared up at him and for a moment the facial muscles behind his spectacles relaxed and she saw the humorous, much younger face which had flickered into view during their drive to Walsingham.

'That's true, isn't it?' he asked, screwing up his eyes once more.

'Yes,' she admitted. 'Yes, it is.'

Their silence again seemed prolonged.

'Well, when you're in love you can't really tell whether what you're doing is right or wrong. Morality just doesn't come into it. You're merely guided by compulsion. If you weren't, you wouldn't be in love. Afterwards, if there is an afterwards, you wake up and start to live with the consequences of where your compulsion has led you.'

The contortions of his sentence seemed to be doing duty for his face which was relaxing once more into a smile.

'What do you mean by afterwards?' she asked.

'Oh, I mean, if you fall out of love or if love turns into something else – coldness or enmity or friendship or simple affection. The trouble is, once it's vanished, you can't understand how you can have been so disloyal to all the other things in your life – your friends and your job and your religion, or whatever else it might be. But it's all very real at the time.'

He sipped quietly.

She wanted to tell him that she was soothed by what he said but no words adequately expressed her feelings. 'I think that's true,' she murmured, 'only, you see, I now feel for the first time in ages that there is a real purpose to life. I have long ago given up interest in academic research, as you know. And although I like my college and my teaching and my little house, they aren't reasons for living. But this *is*: and the baby as well . . .'

'I know, I know.'

'Of course it perhaps won't work out. But I've got to try. You do see that, don't you?'

'You know that I understand perfectly.'

'I hope you do. I so want you to understand. You've been – well, a great help. You know that.'

'It's odd that we have become friends,' he said abruptly. It sounded as if he had been preparing the line all evening and now threw it out at random to see how she would respond. 'If, that is,' he added, with equally rehearsed flourishes, 'you think that we have blossomed into friends.'

'Well, of course we have.' But there had been a faltering in her voice, a moment of hesitation before she spoke which plunged them both into silence. She could have kicked herself for not speaking sooner. Of course she was *devoted* to him. How could he doubt it? But because of that flicker of silence he would now be nursing the paranoid certainty that she did not particularly like him at all.

'Pamela,' he said, moistening his lips with the whisky once again. 'Where on earth does religion fit into all this?'

All, she felt tempted to ask, what? Into her life in general, or into the peculiar little dark hole of embarrassment into which their conversation had cascaded during the previous few moments? Did he mean, how did religion affect her feelings for him? Or her love for Billy? Or her friendship with John? Or was he at last reverting to what must surely be his chief interest in the whole story, the miracle business? The latter suggestion was the one that she pursued.

'Do you think that a healing miracle has happened?' she asked.

'Are you going to give me any alternative answers?' he ventured with a smirk. This was all to the good. The dark hole, or cloud, seemed to have been passed over.

'Well, it could simply have been a blunder by the Pillock or Slobbering-Myles.'

'Do these doctors really have these frightful appellations or is it your own mean nickname?'

'Mean nicknames.'

'How awful you are!' There was such delight in his voice. 'I dare say that you have some perfectly dreadful name for me when my back is turned.'

She tried to mutter, 'Oh nonsense,' but he was in full theological swing.

'Do you remember, our day in Norfolk, that I said we weren't going to a wishing-well? You weren't really satisfied. Either we were expecting the magic to happen or we weren't. And if we weren't, it was all a kind of pious sham.'

'*Oh Christian religion, Oh Christian religion,*' she began in her Stevie Smith voice.

'Exactly. And of course that was not what either of us meant at all.'

'*That was not what I meant at all.*'

He waved her to stop. She had this way of bombarding him with flippant quotations.

'The point is, we were praying for a miracle. Nothing else could have saved you. We were agreed on that. But a miracle is different from a magic trick. It comes about through prayer, not through hoping for the best or keeping your fingers crossed. And the point about it all, surely, is that it is a way of releasing divine grace into the human scene in a way which normally, through the general awkwardness of things, isn't possible.'

'But how would it differ from a magic trick?'

'A magic trick exists for itself. We can applaud it, think how clever or gifted or mysterious the performer of it. But once done, it is finished. The rabbit has come out of the hat, the ace of spades has mysteriously risen to the top of the pack, the toad has turned into a handsome prince . . .'

'Or the handsome prince into a toad,' she felt bound to put in.

'Never mind Mr Brocklehurst for the present.'

She scowled furiously but she was already coming rather to enjoy his passionate jealousy of anyone dear to her. Perhaps it was the whisky, the smoke, the warmth and intimacy of the room. Perhaps it was the extraordinary sensation of having the melancholy long withdrawing roar displayed on such a domestic scale. For he was in full flight, as he continued his explanation.

'You know much more Greek than I do. You know they are always called *signs* in the New Testament, not tricks, not even miracles, but signs. It is because of what they stand for, what they signify, that our faith is sustained by them.'

He peered at her longingly.

'To tell the truth, father, my faith has never been in more of a muddle than it is at the moment.'

He allowed a decent silence to elapse, but he had been ready for the confession. 'Is that surprising?' he asked. 'After all, your faith has never had such a test. You wittily said yourself that when you realized that you were cured you said what people are supposed to say when they discover they are ill: Why should it happen to *me*? Misfortune does not try one's faith. It's perfectly easy to dismiss as bad luck. And we are educated from youth up not to be moaners and groaners.' His voice and manner suggested a fine disregard for any such education he had received himself. 'But it is much more worrying to imagine that God has actually decided to declare Himself unambiguously in our own lives. It is more than worrying. It is positively embarrassing.'

She smiled at him, perhaps for the first time, with real warmth. She loved the way his hair fluffed up at the back, and the way that his lips were perpetually moist.

'It's such a help, your being so kind and understanding. Imagine what it would have been like if you had been a Roman Candle and . . .'

'Don't start riding that hobbyhorse. It wouldn't have made any difference. It is the same God that they worship, you know. Or perhaps you hadn't noticed.'

'No, I hadn't.'

'Well it shows how ignorant you are,' he said with an air of finality. 'But seriously –' for the homily was not yet complete, 'it would be a worry if you did not find it difficult to believe that God had spared you for some singular purpose. Why you, when people are dying like flies all around us? It would be the most unendurable, unimaginable egotism to be able to *accept* it without qualms.'

'I suppose you're right.'

'I know I'm right. *And whence is this to me, that the Mother of my Lord should come to me?* That's all you're feeling. All right, so you are over-excited and in love and a lot of other things. But bafflement, bewilderment, are perfectly proper emotions.'

The sermon was over. The evening could resume its normal gentle course. Pamela lit up one of her own and said, 'Isn't it odd – I'd never have been sitting here, talking about love, death, God knows what, if I hadn't gone into hospital during the summer.'

'Wouldn't you?'

'I mean, it's one of the nice things the summer has brought about, our friendship. I felt you were so shy at first.'

'I was. I am.'

'I don't mean of me or of women or anything like that. I thought you probably had some rather firm old line about not making friends with parishioners. Lots of clergymen do, I know.'

'You must know that I *do* have such a rule,' he said. 'Normally, I would never dream of entertaining a member of the congregation; particularly not when my sister is away; particularly not,' he hesitated, 'a young woman.'

'Come off it.'

'I mean it. I have been a priest for thirty-odd years and I never in all that time had an experience like this evening . . .'

'I meant come off it, I'm not young,' she said, gulping a little, for the import of what he said was hard to absorb at first. Her importance in his life was slow to dawn, even though it was she who raised the subject. It had never occurred to her so strongly that the reason she had initially tried to make a joke of him, affected his locutions, given him a nickname, repeated his mannerisms to friends, was that she was so much in awe of him, and that this awe sprang almost entirely from personal attraction. It was scarcely religious at all.

'You are young,' he continued. 'Young enough, practically, to be my daughter.'

'I'm thirty-nine,' she announced despondently, as if the hills were scarcely older.

'And I'm fifty-nine,' he said. 'So what I say is true. Not,' he added, 'as if it makes a blind bit of difference.'

Difference, she wondered, to *what*? It was time to leave.

'I still don't feel that I've told you the half of what I'd meant to say, but if I stay any longer I shall fall asleep or become drunk.'

He smiled indulgently and squeezed her arm.

'It's been a lovely evening,' he said, 'a really lovely evening.'

- *13* -

'Up!' called the physiotherapist through cupped hands; 'and *down*. Good! Now, we'll try that again.'

Strains of light music accompanied the movements of the figures in the pool. Arthritic hips, cracked femurs, dislocated shoulders, fractured, paralysed, pained and contorted limbs swayed gingerly in the blue chlorinated waters.

They said it helped to do the exercises with a lot of other people. Dorothy had felt shy at first, but the nurses at the Orthopaedic were very kind, and, after the first few sessions, a sense of community had developed among the bathers. It was fascinating, the people you met afterwards over coffee. One of the broken ankles was a judge; she had read his name in the papers. The worst arthritic hip was a Sir, and a professor at one of the colleges. A paralysed left leg had been a foreman down at the works before his stroke, and knew Reg. The broken collar-bone was a nice lady about Dorothy's age who was a buyer for Debenhams. At first, she really had thought it was the Prime Minister. Well, they *did* get all sorts there, and she looked just like, the same hair-do and everything.

The doctors said that Dorothy was doing very well. They had given her pills to increase her appetite. She had been shy, the first couple of times in the pool, about exhibiting her skinny little limbs to the rest of the company. She used to have such lovely legs. Now, it no longer seemed to matter. Everyone's body, for the hour they spent together in the hospital, became a sort of shared joke. The judge, ever so friendly, prodded his pot-belly in a way which made you laugh; you had to; it wasn't vulgar, somehow. The collar-bone lady twitted the 'physio', as she chose to call her, about working them all too hard. They had come to be called 'Pat's galley slaves'. Pat was the physiotherapist. She was really called Miss Watson, but she asked them all to call her

Pat. Quite a young girl she was, but my goodness she knew her job.

It was true that she was rough.

'I came here for treatment,' the prof. had said, 'and all I have had is a bad case of assault and battery.'

But she was kind with it. And since taking the pills that the doctors had prescribed, Dorothy found that she was putting on a bit of weight again. It was funny, because she was not eating more. She felt sick most of the time. But these new pills made her feel delightfully muzzy in the head and had, as George observed, 'put a bit of flesh back in her face'.

Vi had said they made her look 'puffy'. She had tried to ignore the taunt. Vi did not mean to be tactless. She had been kindness itself since the illness started. And so, since Barry first brought her round, had Rena.

Dorothy did not know what had got into George the last few months. Vi said it was because he could not help being worried. But he had been ever so ratty somehow. *Hard* on Barry. Dorothy, of course, had not met his friend Martin, the one he had met in Italy, with, apparently, a hair-style and that. The language George used to describe the boy made you shudder. But Vi had liked him well enough, and said a lot of college boys went in for these styles nowadays, punk or whatever it was. If it seemed harmless to Vi, Dorothy was satisfied. She regarded her neighbour, quite justly, as something of an authority on the changing fashions of youth. After all, she practically mothered about twelve young men a year – well, young men and women now, apparently. Dorothy hated all these words like *poof* and *homo*. She supposed that George had picked them up in the army. But there was really no call to be insulting Barry and his friends with them. Vi said that a lot of youngsters had a *phase*. It was only natural. Dorothy herself still formed passionate attachments to her own sex. There was nothing *funny* about it. She would never have wanted *that*. But people like Pamela, for instance, the young lady with whom she had shared a ward earlier in the summer. It made you feel happy to be near them – their kind smiles, their lovely hair and soft skins. You could never feel like that about a

143

man. Seeing George sitting in the kitchen of a morning, with a stubbly doubly chin (as Vi called it) and a string vest, made Dorothy wonder why she ever wanted a man in her life at all. But the thought never lasted long. She knew that George was a bit of a stick. But, the habit of more than half a life-time, she felt deeply and warmly attached to him, even with his moods.

Why he had to make all this fuss about Rena, though, was beyond her. Either he was attacking the boy for his punk friends from Italy or he was making dark hints about what he got up to with his hairdresser girlfriend.

Dorothy's friendship with the girl had blossomed in the last two or three weeks, in spite of George's grumbling. She had been kind and good and companionable – helping Vi with the shopping and now, most kindly, driving Dorothy to the Orthopaedic in her Mini, inherited from her mum who had died the previous year. She was a bit older than Barry, twenty-six. George said 'they always are'. Dorothy did not know what he meant; age did not make all that much difference. Rena had brought round her set of equipment one evening after Barry had gone off to college, and given her the most lovely perm and blow-dry. She had felt a different woman since. George had been foul about it – mocked the very faint touches of blue that Rena had put in the rinse – and asked what was wrong with his Marina for driving Dol up to the Orthopaedic. Nothing, of course, was *wrong* with the Marina. He always kept it in the most perfect working order: tinkered with it most Saturday afternoons; polished it twice a week; said it needed it, the Dormobile being in the garage. The point was, he could not miss work every Tuesday and Thursday for the next however many weeks it would be, just to take Dorothy for her session at the pool. And, besides, she preferred a little feminine companionship on these occasions. George got so nervy going to the hospital, he started to swear and crunch the gears, and she got so on edge that it undid half the point of the treatment. Rena could not take her on Tuesdays, of course; on those days, the ambulance came round to collect her. But on Thursdays, she told the hospital that she had her own transport.

During these reveries, Dorothy had been raising her legs in the water to the time of the music, making swimming movements with her arms, and finally, the rituals complete, she had steeled herself to the agonizing business of being hoisted out of the water by a nurse and wrapped in a lovely big bath towel.

'They need a crane on this job,' quipped the foreman. Sensation not yet having returned to his limbs since the stroke, he was the only one who could speak during these operations. For most of them, it was scarcely endurable. But coffee, chat, the drive home lay ahead.

When they were dressed and nibbling biscuits, Dorothy found herself next to the Buyer and started to tell her about Barry's career at Swansea.

'He's been ever so good about writing,' she said.

'You wait,' said Mrs Thatcher. 'They soon stop feeling home-sick.'

But, not to be deflated, Dorothy was looking in her handbag and producing an already crumpled and much-read missive from South Wales.

'*Some of the lectures are rather boring,*' she read, '*but going to them gives you the chance to meet people.* Well, that's nice.' Since her illness, she had begun to regret bitterly that she had not met more people, been more social. Ever since their family tragedy, the loss of Barry's brother, they had lived too cocooned from the world, not mixed enough. Vi had been right. They *had* tried to shelter the boy too much. She felt thrilled to think of him broadening his social horizons at philosophy lectures in South Wales. '*I have written my first essay. It was about the problem of knowledge.* George said what *was* the problem of knowledge – why wasn't he learning something useful? But I'd say knowledge was a problem, wouldn't you? I can never hold things in my head for more than five minutes at a time. How people like my neighbour can learn languages is beyond me.'

The Buyer looked as if she wanted to dissent from this frank confession of mental incompetence, but did not know how to do so without implying superiority. She produced a powder puff and made some rather savage little dabs at the side of her nose while she said, 'Go on. I'm enjoying it.'

'*I wish you could see my room. It was a bit bare at first, but I've brightened it up with some posters of Kate Bush!!!* George said he hoped he didn't use drawing-pins else they'd be throwing him out on his ear but I'm sure they're used to young lads liking something a bit bright. Kate Bush is an actress,' she glossed for the Buyer's benefit. '*Perhaps one weekend soon when Mum's a bit better you'd like to drive up and see me, only don't come on a Friday because there's a disco in the hall of residence.*'

'Is that all?' asked the Buyer after a decent pause.

'It's a lovely letter,' said Dorothy firmly. '*Give my love to Aunty Vi and Uncle Reg and look after yourselves. Lots of love, Barry.*'

She gave every word its full weight and then brought the coffee to her lips with quavering hand. She wished she was not all of a shake so much of the time.

'Wendy, that's my daughter who's living in Andover, is expecting!' announced the Buyer, not to be outdone.

'Oh, that's lovely!' It seemed only lately, from the Buyer's previous accounts, that the girl had got married. How fast things happened. 'I'm ever so looking forward to Barry getting married and having grandchildren and that,' she said generously.

But the commercial or competitive spirit was triumphant in her interlocutor, and she felt bound to say, 'Of course, Heather, Wendy's elder sister, has two of her own now. I'm just glad that Wendy's catching up. I think she felt a bit out of things.'

'When is the baby due?' Dorothy innocently inquired.

'Oh, not for ages yet of course. I'm just very glad.'

So. It *had* been an embarrassment. But Dorothy covered it up as fast as possible with, 'You'll be making all the little darling's blankets and booties and pram-coats.'

'Pram-coats –! My dear, it's all baby-gro's now. Wendy wouldn't look at anything I'd made even if I had the time. No, I shall just give her a cheque and let her choose what she wants at Mothercare.'

Dorothy had not heard about the abolition of pram-coats. She found it inordinately depressing.

'Surely,' she said, 'you can make a shawl, or some little booties.'

'I found with Heather that nothing I made was ever really used. These modern girls are more practical than we were.'

Would Rena, Dorothy wondered, discard specially knitted garments if she were to become a daughter-in-law? It was an aspect of life that she had never thought about before. Of course, she had *seen* the Mothercare shops everywhere. But it had never crossed her mind that they were making grandmothers superfluous. She sighed at the unhappy way life had of pushing her to one side and making her feel unwanted.

Rena was waiting, though, with her little motor car. She had been to do some shopping while Dorothy was at the pool, and when she had shuffled into the front seat, Dorothy found that a little bunch of anemones was being pressed into her hand.

'Here,' said Rena.

'What are these for, then?' She was delighted.

'Being a good girl,' said Rena and she squeezed her hand.

She was a bright-faced little thing without much feature; but art had made up where nature had failed to supply: thick brown artificial curls, like some Renaissance Bacchus; dabs of blusher on each little cheekbone; a thin, small mouth filled out with some moist-looking scarlet lipstick. Behind the mascara the eyes were smiling with kindness and affection. It was strange, the feeling that had grown up between the two women. That first night, Rena had gone out with Barry almost with the aim of punishing him for his cheek. She could tell that he was impressionable and sexually inexperienced. But somehow, over their Wimpy, they had got talking. He was at a loose end because his friend Martin had gone away and he had not yet started at college; and because his mother was ill. And she was at a loose end because she had just had a bust-up with Kev, her steady, and because, since her mother's demise, she was bored with putting up with so much of her father's depression and doing so many of the chores which could equally have been done by her brothers. Barry's loose ends met her loose ends and the evening had been a success. When she heard that Dorothy was in hospital, she insisted on driving straight up there after their Wimpy and sitting in the car park for half an hour while he popped in and saw her. It was reassuring, for him, that she thought there was nothing smart or clever about not visiting the sick. He had come out complaining about his dad, but they both felt the better for it. The evening was still young, and they had danced it away to the insistent thumping of the disco.

There were several other evenings like this. She had not fully predicted the beguiling way in which Barry would admit to being a bit of a poof. It quite turned her on. One night in the disco, she found that the hot, bouncy atmosphere of the place suddenly failed to match her mood: its smoking, its gyrating, its shouting, its wiggling, its bumping and gesturing. She was surprised at herself. She loved dancing and enjoyed showing off to the fellas. On this occasion, instead, after only a short time on the dance floor, she put her arms round his shoulders and yelled into his ear. 'Why not let's go somewhere a bit quieter – you know, back to your place or something?'

They had taken their time about getting there. The Mini was being serviced, so they stood by the bus stop, locked in such absorbing embrace that they missed the first Number Eight to come along, caught a Number One and then walked from the roundabout, pausing every now and again to rub noses or to transfer each other's chewing gum from mouth to mouth. Yet, once down the cul-de-sac, the sight of his dad's gleaming Marina seemed to dampen Barry's ardour. He began to mutter about his father, explain that his mum was home now. Rena did not know what to make of all this. It was true that when the old gent appeared, carpet-slippered, braces, pipe, he had been rather churlish.

'What do you want to be bringing visitors here for at this time of night?' he had asked. 'Have you no consideration? Don't you realize your mother is ill?'

But, rather surprisingly, Dorothy herself had appeared at the door of the lounge in a pink dressing-gown, and said she wasn't as ill as all that, and would like to say hallo to Barry's friend.

Rena had liked Dorothy at once. She was not intrusive, like some boys' mums. She asked about the disco, and tried to get Rena to explain what the dance movements were. She remembered George trying to jive at the old Palais. She had liked a nice jive herself. Now her neighbour, Vi, she could jive like nobody's business.

From dance to hair seemed a small step and before anyone could stop them, both women had settled down to talk to each other. George, protesting that he had an early start to make in the morning, took himself off to bed. Barry was sent into the kitchen to make tea. Dorothy began to explain about her bad back. Rena explained about her dad's bad back, and her mother's various illnesses and their bereavement.

It had all progressed from there: so that, by the time Barry had gone away to Swansea, it was really Dorothy that Rena kept coming to see. The little bunch of anemones seemed an appropriately modest expression of what had happened over the last few weeks, but Dorothy's eyes filled with tears as she looked at them.

'I must put them in water,' said Dorothy, as soon as the car was on the road. It was not a long drive to the estate.

'How about going home, putting the flowers in some water, and me making you your dinner; and then we could drive out to look at the autumn tints. It's turned ever so nice again now, and the trees are really lovely.'

'It's my favourite time of year,' said Dorothy wistfully. She loved the idea of a drive, but the session at the pool had exhausted her. She did not want to let the girl down, and it would be boring for her to spend her afternoon off just sitting indoors. It had turned into a glorious golden day: trees thick masses of orange, brown and yellow; thick clear white clouds high in a bright blue sky. But she felt the pain returning and she only wanted to take a pill and lie down.

'I won't need much dinner,' she said. 'Just a bit of cheese.'

'They said as you ought to eat,' said Rena.

But she was no bully, unlike Vi, and when they got home, they only pecked at some cottage cheese and shared an apple. The drive in the country could wait till next time.

'There'll be plenty more nice days like this,' said Dorothy.

- 14 -

'No man would ever see the point of doing this.'

'This?'

'Lying in bed all afternoon combing one another's hair,' said Billy. She murmured with pleasure as Pamela ran the tortoiseshell over and over through the short fine strands of her dark mop.

'So you're glad you came.'

'What do *you* think?'

And she turned her face upwards to be kissed once more.

'What are we going to do about John?' Pamela asked quietly.

'Do we have to do anything?'

'I so wish we didn't. He'll be back at any moment if he isn't already. It's going to be an obvious shock for him, isn't it?'

It was a scene which would have delighted the Venetian masters: Pamela, long, white and splendid in her nakedness, her thick golden hair falling over shoulders and breasts like a magnificent fur cape; Billy, curled up in her arms like an Indian boy or like Adonis in the arms of Venus. Her well-proportioned body was brown and dusky and smooth. A rich paisley counterpane lay crumpled at their feet, and down one side of the bed, spreading out a sort of peacock's tail of turquoise on the floor, stretched Pamela's Chinese silk dressing-gown. The walls of the bedroom were a deep red, hung with eighteenth-century prints of the Roman Campagna.

Outside the window, the street diminished into another; but the rows and rows of mean nineteenth-century terraced houses, as if to match the hint of Mediterranean luxury behind the gap in those velvet curtains, threw up the campanile of the church, whose clock said twenty past four.

'This isn't New York,' Pamela explained. 'It's in effect a village. It is simply not possible to avoid people. Besides, I don't want to avoid John.'

'I wish you did.'

'Why?'

'Because I feel sure it will spoil everything when he knows that I'm here.'

'Leave him to me.'

'Oh, Pamela, you will look after me, won't you?' And once more the girl moved on top of her lover and felt the comfort of the linen sheets being pulled over her head.

As the church clock struck a quarter to five, Pamela asked, 'Is it the baby that worries you? About John, I mean?'

'Uh-huh. But that's just for openers. It's the baby; it's me, I guess; it's him, it's you. It's my *knowing* what he's meant to be like over here. I had just no idea until you told me that he had this thing about *discretion*. You wouldn't have guessed it back home.'

'He's obsessively discreet. I've known him ages now, and although it's perfectly obvious that he *does* need women – for sex, I mean – I've hardly ever heard who they are. He likes to keep them in quite separate compartments of his life. There was a bit of talk during his first year back here about a pupil. She went down though with "nervous trouble" and it was never very clear what had happened. You would never see him walking about with girlfriends arm in arm or anything like that.'

'Well, he didn't walk arm in arm with me, now you mention it. It was the most you could do to hold hands with him in the drive-in movies. But back home, when the door closed, oh Jeez . . .'

'I can imagine,' a little sigh accompanied the remark, 'or can I? When we were research students together – he was older than I was, of course, but we overlapped – it was all different. In his way, he was pretty blatant.'

'Always women?'

'Always. Of course, I've wondered that about John. One must, inevitably, about a man; particularly about a man who keeps his sex life so organized.'

'Does he?'

'I think he does.'

'It wasn't very organized with me. I'm not so sure he just wasn't very very frustrated when he met me. What makes you think sex had played any part in his life since his marriage broke up? A lot of men just get desexed by that experience. Mel had to have sex therapy for six months after his second divorce.'

'It's possible,' said Pamela.

'I don't see what other explanations there can be. John isn't gay – or you say so. And he doesn't appear to have any women in his life.'

'There are always whores,' ventured Pamela.

'Oh my God!'

'Does it shock you? Someone has to use them or they'd go out of business, poor old things. I don't see why John shouldn't use a bit of his spare cash . . .'

'Oh, but it's so *degrading* . . .'

'To him or to them?'

'Both. And just think – oh my sweet ass, you don't think he's gotten VD?'

'Darling, how should I know? It's not the sort of thing we ever talk about. Probably you're right and I'm wrong. He has probably led a life of abstemious rectitude for the last ten years or whatever it is until he met you. It would be understandable enough.'

'What would?'

'Departing from the straight and narrow for you, my sweet, adorable girl.'

Hereward Stickley was in the sacristy, jangling the bell for evensong at twenty-five past five by the time they stirred themselves again.

'I'll go and make some tea,' announced Pamela, standing by the bed and stretching her arms in the air. 'You lie here. You ought to spend at least two days in bed after your flight. You don't want to be as ill as I was.'

'I'm very, very sleepy.'

'Well, sleep, my pet. I'll bring up something later.'

Pamela surveyed her own elegance in the glass for a moment before she slipped on the turquoise dressing-gown and the pink ballet shoes which she used for bedroom slippers. She was halfway down the narrow staircase when the doorbell rang. She did not think to ask her caller to wait. Her mind was so drunk with happiness that she did not think at all. She merely flung open the door and gulped to see John Brocklehurst standing there in his cycle clips.

'Having a bath?' he said. 'I tried to phone you up but you seem to have been out for the last couple of days.'

'Come in,' she said. 'I was just about to make some tea.'

'I've been riding my bike,' he said. 'It needed oiling. Hadn't been used for a year.'

'Where did you go?'

'Berkshire Downs.'

He looked almost fat, and rather touchingly sweaty. He went in for these long rides on his bicycle when he was having a bout of slimming.

'Welcome back,' she said, and kissed him on the cheek.

'Wondered if you were going to say that. I've been in Mexico.'

She in turn wondered whether to say that she knew; how much, indeed, that she knew. It was hard to assess whether it would be worth explaining the whole ludicrous history of her Long Vacation. It was one thing to say to Billy that the truth must be told. It was quite another, when face to face with her old friend, to know whether it was worth saying anything. Their friendship had been sustained, she now realized, as she fiddled with the electric kettle, and he sat on her kitchen chair, by all the things which they had *not* said to each other, quite as much as by the things which they had said. Sensing that the atmosphere needed a slight thaw, he began a very detailed account of his Mexican holiday, the pyramids, the mountains, the churches, the hotels, the food. She liked his long narratives. The Lapsang was infusing by the time he had finished.

'Will you excuse me, John, for a moment. I'm just going to get dressed. No, really, don't move. I'll be down in a moment. Have a read of our parish magazine.'

She tossed it across to him and carried a brimming breakfast cup from the room with a slice of stale seedcake in the saucer. Billy was asleep when she got to the bedroom. She pulled up the bedclothes and tucked the child up with a kiss. Then she hastily dressed: thick green tights, a cream-coloured woollen blouse and a brown tweed suit with a pleated skirt. She should have put her hair up but it took half an hour to plait it in the style which she had lately adopted.

'Sorry to keep you waiting.'

'You've left your tea upstairs.'

'No I haven't. This is mine.'

She smiled at him awkwardly.

'I suppose this is the best moment to tell you because she's asleep. I've got a guest upstairs who's a friend of yours.'

'Oh yes?' He smiled good humouredly. 'No, don't tell me, let me guess.' He named the Principal of her college; the wife of Professor Hovis; one or two other joke characters in their shared gallery of grotesques.

'It's all rather awkward,' she spluttered. 'But you are bound to know sooner or later. It's Billy.'

Only the faintest flicker of shock registered in his facial expression.

'I thought you said it was a woman.'

'Billy MacNamara, John.'

'Oh, yes,' he said. 'Nice girl. Mel's step-daughter. I told you about Mel in my letters?' He was eyeing her closely as he spoke now, but she tried not to give away any clues. 'What on earth's she doing here?'

'She's staying with me.'

'You said. But I don't get. I hadn't realized you were friends.'

'It's all a terribly long story. I went to stay with Mel and Gale.'

'With Mel and Gale. You're kidding.' He even managed to

154

reproduce Mel's extraordinary shrug and grin. 'You mean, like, my old friend Mel. Gee, was this because of some *re*search you were doing?'

Tears of laughter welled up. She shook. 'He really did ask me that.'

'Maybe a liddle checking out of the twennieth-cenyury campus navvle; maybe a liddle Woman's Studies.' He swayed from side to side with Yiddish enthusiasm. 'Did you get Gale to fix you some of her borsch, or maybe her strogonoff, followed by bilberry strudel and sour cream?'

'Believe it or not,' she said, when mirth had subsided, and he showed signs of resuming his own persona, 'I went to see you. But you'd left for Mexico.'

'Had a wasted trip then, didn't you?' It was now his turn to laugh. 'Why didn't you phone up beforehand? We could have had a lovely time. I bored myself silly in Mexico.'

'It was just an impulse.' She realized that there was not going to be the slightest possibility of talking about her illness with him; still less about her Cure. The whole thing was at once too bizarre and too sordid. Perhaps it would never be mentioned. Now there was really no reason why it should be, and it was really the least of their problems.

'And the chick just invited herself to stay?' he helped her out. He was the master of the conversation. 'How long for?'

'It's fairly indefinite at the moment.'

'That's a bit much, isn't it? You're always pointedly saying that there's only room in this house for one person.'

Now was the moment, if she had the courage, when she could say that there would need eventually to be room for three; to talk about the baby. But the moment passed. She was suddenly seized by doubt. It was not that she doubted the wisdom of telling him that he was going to be a father. Few friendships could survive such assaults. It was that she suddenly doubted whether Billy were telling the truth.

'Where will she go once term starts?' he asked.

'I'm on leave.'

'Really? And are you going to spend it here?'

'I haven't decided.'

'Leaving things a bit late, aren't you?' He had pulled his glasses down on to the end of his nose and hunched his shoulders in order to become Hovis. 'We may hope, perhaps, that Christmas will see the completion of some of Miss Cowper's valuable investigations into the Medieval Alexander.'

'Don't.'

'Anyway,' he said, standing up and pushing his spectacles back onto his nose. 'What I was coming round to suggest was that you came for the guest night on Sunday.'

'This Sunday?'

'First day of term. We could go to evensong first and then hit the big time over the *boeuf en daube* with Hovis.'

'It would be lovely.' She meant it, but it did not sound as if she meant it.

'Good. Lovely cup of tea.' He put it down on the oilcloth with finality and made for the front door. 'Come to my room about six.'

She stood by the front door watching the red rear light of his bicycle flicker out of sight up the street. Her doubt, as she stood there, was dispelled. She was quite certain that *he* knew that *she* knew and that he was playing his cards close to his chest in the hope that the difficulty would just go away. She felt more painfully torn in her allegiances than she would have believed possible. If it were any other girl, it would not have mattered. She would never have known. Her friendship with him would have remained unimpaired.

She had forgotten, in the interval which had elapsed since last seeing him, how deeply conversation with John differed from talk with anyone else. However much she liked other colleagues and friends, and however quick they were on the uptake, there was always a fuzzy edge to their talk, a need to explain things or express them in terms which she would not have chosen if she was expressing them to herself. John and she, on the other hand, inhabited so much the same linguistic world, shared each other's conversational shorthand, knew the furniture of each other's minds so well that, although it was almost persistently light-hearted, it felt more like communion than conversation. This was quite largely because there were such deep reticences in them both. They each had secrets to guard, and they respected each other's silences. It was far from being all gabble and shared confidences. But the psalmist's definition of good conversation – *Thou understandest my thoughts long before* – most certainly held true for them.

Perhaps all along, she thought aimlessly, they had loved one another more deeply than their conversations allowed them to admit. Perhaps even now, her adoration of Billy, and her desire for Billy's baby, were manifestations of her desire for unattainable intimacies with John. The thought nagged her as she ate soup and turned the pages of Ruskin in a desultory way. After the ten o'clock news on the little white Sony, she had a bath and slipped on her nightdress, before climbing back into bed beside the sleeping girl.

Which woke first, neither of them knew. They lay together, nuzzled into each other's arms, in a state of half sleep until they finally opened their eyes and heard the campanile's tubular bells strike ten. Through the chink in the curtains, sunshine fell down in brilliant beams on to the end of their bed.

'Breakfast?' Pamela asked. 'You haven't eaten properly for hours.'

'I'm famished. Just let me go to the bathroom, then I'll answer your question.'

While she was gone, Pamela got herself up and went downstairs. There was no very interesting post. Since she was officially on leave, they had started to forward her letters from college, so that every weekday morning for the next eight weeks would bring the minutes of meetings she had not attended, requests for references from the prospective employers of pupils she could scarcely remember; invitations to join insurance schemes or to purchase unnecessary academic volumes from Wisconsin and Illinois; or to drink sherry with graduates; or to give money to appeals.

She scrambled eggs, buttered toast and spread it with anchovy

157

paste, fried some chipolatas, decanted some black cherries from a tin, and warmed some croissants in the oven while she made the coffee. Billy was sitting up in bed, washed, smiling, more radiantly lovely than ever when Pamela brought in the tray.

They were both so hungry that they fell on the feast like animals and did not speak until they had reached the stage of nibbling the French pastries and sipping their second or third cup of coffee.

'I'm so excited,' said Billy. 'What are we going to do today?'

'Well, with this marvellous Indian summer, perhaps we should go north and search for a palace.'

The girl was looking at her as if she was speaking Hindustani.

'That was such a lovely breakfast.'

'I'm glad you aren't suffering from morning sickness.'

'I was doing. Just lately, it seems to have gone away.'

'John called —' she tried to make it sound as casual as possible. 'While you were asleep.'

'*Here?* John came *here?*'

'He often does. That was what I was trying to talk to you about yesterday but we were both so tired.'

'I like it when you're feeling tired,' the girl said, resting her head on Pamela's lap.

'So do I.'

And they kissed each other for the umpteenth time that morning.

'Did you — well, like have it out with him.'

'Have what out?'

'Well, did you tell him about us?'

'Having things out with John is impossible. I don't know how much he surmised about your being here — as far as my feelings for you go, I mean. He obviously realized that I had been told about him and you.'

'The baby and everything?'

'The baby will come as a great shock,' Pamela said authoritatively. 'He simply looked sheepish — he was trying to size up how frank — indiscreet — you'd been; just in spelling out the thrilling details of your affair with him. He'll be completely thrown when he hears about the baby.'

'Pamela,' said the girl suddenly, intensely, 'I can't go through with this thing; you know I can't.'

'Haven't we discussed all that before?'

'Not properly we haven't. Don't you see? We might just about, the three of us, make out some way, some how, with the knowledge that I've had an affair with you both. But no way is John going to take my having an illegitimate baby that is his. No way.'

Pamela allowed the odious expression to pass. Now was not a time for an English lesson.

'Look, it's nothing to do with him. He hasn't had the decency to find out if there's anything he can do to help. Why should he take the life of our child.'

The possessive seemed an odd one but it had slipped out to tell its own story.

'*Our* child? It's my child, and John doesn't even know that I'm pregnant, Goddammit. If you're so keen to have one of John's bastards round the place why not go and get him raunchy – it's easy enough, believe me – or at least, it was for me – maybe it wouldn't . . .'

'Come, now, we aren't going to have a row.'

'I am not having a row.'

'Then turn the volume down a bit.'

'Excuse me?'

'Stop squealing, my pet. I can't bear the noise.'

They stared at each other desperately.

'This is just going to tear us apart – all three of us, right?'

'No. It just needs a little careful handling, that's all.'

'Careful handling. My GOD! You English people think that every single bloody problem in this world can be solved by carefulness and politeness and speaking quietly and not losing your head.'

'Most problems can.'

'You'll be quoting Kipling's "If" at me next.'

'If the formulas suggested in that poem were reliable, it would certainly be the end of all our problems.'

'How come?'

'You'd be a *man*, my son.' Her voice sank to a wonderful contralto on the word *man* and they were friends again.

When their laughter and kissing had subsided, Billy asked in what she was trying to make a faintly more English and sensible voice, 'OK. So let's work from there. What would we do if we were men?'

'Smell horrible.'

'No.' She gave a poke to Pamela's navel which hurt. 'What would we do *really* if we were in this predicament, but at the same time, impossibly, we were men?'

'I know one thing we would not even think of doing.'

'Telling the truth?'

'Right.'

'So, what would be the little white lie that we would tell? We're both friends of John, and he's a jolly good bloke, and probably belongs to the same club as we do and is a friend of all the people we most look up to and admire.'

'So we don't want to offend him by saying that there is going to be an addition to the family.'

'Definitely not.' Pamela's firmness was decided. And then for a moment she spoke more earnestly and said, 'What's wrong with that approach? He's never going to ASK. No man would, for fear of getting the answer he was dreading. He'll just hope it is the fruit of some other union.'

'And when he counts back on his fingers, isn't he going to come to the two or three weeks when he did nothing but bang me in every position in the book.'

'Yes, but how's he to know you didn't have another chap?'

Billy looked at her timidly and blushed.

'What kind of a girl do you think I am, for Chrissakes?'

'We both know perfectly well what kind of a girl you are,' she squeezed one of Billy's nipples as she spoke. 'But even the most big-headed of chaps can be persuaded to imagine that his girl has been having it off with someone else on the sly. Look at Othello.'

'He was black. All black men exude sexual conceit.'

'I thought Americans were meant to be liberal.'

'I am. It just happens to be true. I can't see John as Othello. Anyway, when would I have had the time?'

'It was really as full-time as that?'

'Perhaps not *full* time. Some days I went down to play tennis at the country club and he worked in the library. I guess I went for a drive or two with Virgil Brown – he's my boyfriend. Gale always said we went parking, I suppose ...'

'Parking?'

'You know, like you pull up on the verge and switch off the headlights, and maybe kiss a little.'

'Nothing more than kiss?'

'Maybe a little heavy petting. But I don't want to involve Virgil in all this. He's only halfway through law school.'

'But was he – is he – your lover?' Pamela tried to keep a note of shock from her voice.

'Not at the right time.'

'Oh, *really*.' Impatience took over. 'You're impossible. Why not say it was Virgil? Say it was *anyone*.'

She slipped off the side of the bed and moved to the dressing-table to plait her hair as she spoke.

'Let's go and see a palace,' she said, abandoning the awfulness of the questions before them, and beginning to explain which palace she meant and where it was, and how, though she had walked a thousand times in the surrounding park, it was years since she had been inside.

'Shall we take a picnic?'

'No. It's on the edge of a nice little town. We'll have lunch in a pub.'

Pamela wore a pale blue tweedy dress, tightly waisted, full-skirted, and trimmed at the neck with lace; over this, partly for extra warmth, she wore a sleeveless gown of black velvet, open at the front, and a necklace of turquoise beads and Indian silver. Billy wore a black jumper, dungarees of grey corduroy and a leather flying jacket. Outside, while Pamela fiddled in her handbag for the keys of the Simca, Billy said, 'All these houses are so *tiny*.'

'And until quite recently, people brought up huge families in them,' said Pamela, as if to make some kind of point. 'It isn't locked your side.'

They were soon gliding northwards out of the town, Gothic villas of the 'nineties giving place to the white stucco of more modest twentieth-century domestic aspirations.

'The trees are certainly in their autumn beauty today,' remarked Pamela approvingly, 'and that,' she added, braking with some violence, 'is where Hovis lives.' She indicated a neat white house, no different from any of the others. Billy had already heard a good deal of this obsession. 'And there, if I'm not mistaken, is his Sheila, cleaning the windows. Oops!' The car shot off again with a jerk. 'I think she saw me staring in.'

She sang lightly as she changed gear and whizzed north after the roundabout:

> '*Snick goes the shearer,*
> *Snick, snick, snick!*
> *Wide are his blows, and his hands move quick.*
> *The ringer looks around,*
> *But he's missed it by a blow,*
> *And curses the old snagger*
> *With his blue-bellied Joe.*'

'I don't understand the song,' said Billy.

'It's sung by the shearers. You got paid for shearing the sheep quickly, and obviously if you had one which was blue-bellied and half-shorn already you were a lucky snagger.'

'What's so funny about being Australian?'

'Being any nationality has comical potential, doesn't it?'

She had a terrible sinking feeling when Billy asked for jokes to be explained. All the joy which their love had brought with it seemed to vanish as one prosed one's way through attempts to analyse chance remarks. 'You'd see,' she said, 'if you met Hovis.'

'I don't need to now, really, do I?'

'It's worth doing. He terrifies me. I think.'

The grey crumbly wall of the park now stretched along the left-hand side of the road. Beyond, paddock and meadow stripped of elms could be glimpsed spinning past. Before long, they reached the town. A gateway led through a splendid vista of vanishing trees towards the palace. But they drove on to the traffic lights and traversed the serpentine main street which dozed in an autumnal glow. Shops and inns, the houses and the church, varied, handsome, self-possessed, stood back behind the yellowing plane trees.

'This street's just the right width,' Pamela said. 'You can see things in proportion on either side and yet it's not too grand.'

At the end though, turning the corner after lunch in a pub, they entered the park itself and here was grandeur on an unashamed scale, so that Billy could only hold her breath and stare as the car drove slowly, to give perfect views of Capability Brown's landscape, slopes, lakes, bridge and trees all so perfect that it was hard to believe it was really there.

'It must have taken such confidence in the future to have planted all that out,' said Pamela. 'They would never have seen it like this. It must have taken a hundred years to grow to look as they intended it.'

'And there's the palace. Boy, it really *is* a palace!'

In spite of a lifetime in New York, it was the stupendous size of it all which overwhelmed Billy. When Pamela told her that there was still a Duke who actually lived there, she assumed that this was yet another of her friend's impenetrable escapades into comedy. Once inside, she was less sure. Grandiose wonder was multiplied upon wonder; marble, gilt, stucco, glass; painted ceilings, sculpted cornices, staircases and chimney-pieces of the most abandoned extravagance and absurdity. It was no mere whim, it was an actual emotional necessity which prompted Pamela to suggest they eventually tore themselves away from these architectural meringues and explored the grounds. 'We could look at bird tables in the "Garden Centre", for instance.'

It was an odd time of the year to be visiting a 'garden centre': too soon to buy bulbs, too late for any bedding plants except perhaps wallflowers. But the place had its own tedious fascination; one went, Pamela explained, partly in order to see what one did *not* want to buy, partly as a change from the flamboyance of Vanbrugh's interiors. Concrete and plastic urns, trellises and pagodas of fibre-glass; jars of 'Cotswold' honey and expensive jams were all on sale, as well as the plants, the seed packets, the gardening gloves, the bird tables and the shiny black sacks of fertilizer and bedding soil. It was enough to beguile twenty minutes or so before they went home for tea.

Billy trailed round like a child happy to have a hand to hold, but otherwise bored by its surroundings. She was arrested by Pamela's palm suddenly pressing into her own, and by her whispering, 'Did I ever tell you about Dorothy? Dorothy Higgs?'

'Oh, my gosh! Is this going to be another grisly confession?' There was perhaps an element of seriousness in her tone. 'We certainly can pick some crazy places . . .'

'Don't be absurd. Dorothy Higgs was in hospital with me earlier in the summer. You know, when I had my horrible "do". Hers was much worse. Then they told her she was better. But I didn't recognize her at first. She looks twenty years older.'

'Where?' Billy remembered that Pamela had mentioned Dorothy a good deal during their early conversations in New York. She had produced the name, for instance, as someone who had happily immolated herself in the role of wife and mother.

At the end of a row of cacti and indoor plants, a spindly old lady stood, pointing with quavering fingers to a fuschia in a tub. It was too far away to hear what passed between them; she was accompanied by a young woman, presumably a daughter, a cheap-looking girl in the modern mould whose cleanliness and elaborate make-up Billy found an aphrodisiac.

'I *must* go and speak to her,' said Pamela. 'I don't know whether she's seen us.' But this was only announced when she had weighed in her mind how to avoid Dorothy's glance and had become fairly certain that she had failed to do so. She thought that Dorothy was explaining in lowered tones to her companion – a niece? She had never mentioned a daughter – who Pamela was.

'I was just saying, it's a small world, isn't it?' Dorothy said, with evident lack of self-consciousness about having talked of Pamela and Billy.

Pamela, on the other hand, felt the need to concoct a fiction that no analogous colloquy had taken place at their end of the hothouse and said, 'Billy, this is Mrs Higgs, a friend of mine.'

'Hi. I'm Billy.'

'Rena's been meaning to drive me out here for weeks but the weather's not been so good, has it? Still, mustn't grumble 'cause it's lovely today. Real Indian summer. St Luke's summer we used to call it.' In her excitement, Dorothy forgot to make introductions and Rena smirked shyly.

'We were just going to have some tea,' said Pamela. 'Would you like to join us?' She suggested it with an enforced brightness which could hardly disguise the anguish on her face. Dorothy felt the bright sapphire of the young woman's eyes running her up and down and noticing the disgraceful waste which the weeks had effected. The pills had not really worked. The puffiness had faded. In the ward where Pamela had first seen her face smiling across at her, the cheeks had been round, almost plump. There was now something unnaturally angular about the whole face. No amount of pink powder could disguise the deathly yellow of the complexion or the gaping hollows around the eyes. Her beige skirt looked baggy; the spindly little legs beneath it were no more than sticks; and the white cardigan dropped from bony shoulders so expansively that it had had to be turned up three or four times at the cuffs. Only the eyes retained any sort of animation, and they stared as if from far away, imploring Pamela not to notice, not to look, not to comment.

'There's a place,' Pamela continued, 'just outside the park, which does a lovely tea.'

'That'd be nice,' said the girl who appeared to be chewing gum.

'So long as we can be home by five,' said Dorothy jumpily. 'George'll be wanting his tea when he gets in.' She was feeling overpoweringly tired and nauseated. She was afraid there would be scones, cream, jam, cakes; things for which, only six months before, she had an appetite which was scarcely controllable, but which now filled her with dread. 'So,' she added, 'perhaps just a quick cup. It'd be nice to have a chat, like.'

She could not walk fast back to their cars, and her arm was in a sling. An awkward silence fell as she crept along, holding on to Rena, and when the pairs were separated and driving in convoy out of the great park gates, none of them spoke. They were each desperately wondering how the next half hour would be got through. A chat would of course be nice. But what would they all chat *about*?

To Rena, the couple encountered were simply odd. She could not place them in any social category that she had ever known about. The tall woman with the bun thing was in a nebulous way formidable. Her relentlessly upper-class gabble made it unthinkable that one could have a chat with her, or anything like it.

For Billy, following behind in the passenger seat of the Simca, the matter was simply a bore. She was shocked by how ill the old woman looked and she could see that, in the circumstances, some kind of extended social encounter was inevitable. But she felt out of place and foreign. Pamela's accent had been hard enough to get used to at first, but Dorothy's was almost incomprehensible.

Dorothy, in the passenger seat of the Mini ahead, realized that they had not met since the day of the 'six-week check-up'. Presumably, Pamela's, like her own, had been 'clear'. Younger people, of course, did find it easier to get over illnesses. She rather wished it could have been just the two of them. She had always felt shy in gatherings which outnumbered three; and now she found it hard to think of anything except her own bodily sensations.

166

Pamela was frantically rehearsing in her mind topics of conversation which would not relate to their shared illness. Barry was the son's name and he would by now be up at a university, but which one she had forgotten. Would it seem hurtful to show that one had forgotten by asking? Or would it provide a helpful, neutral topic to break the ice? What else? Well, there was gardening, and the weather, and programmes on television. They must be punctilious about Dorothy's desire to keep the party short.

When they had parked, and crossed the golden street to the tea-shop, and settled themselves in a corner by the window, Dorothy was relieved that no one appeared to be hungry. Just a pot for four and biscuits were ordered. She tried to avert her gaze from two retired married couples from the Black Country at the next table who were wolfing scones with a kind of bestial fervour. The way they licked their fingers and piled jam upon cream sponge made you want to be ill.

'Billy is over here from America,' said Pamela, handing round the sugar bowl.

'New York?' Dorothy asked.

'Yes,' said Billy.

And that, mysteriously, was that conversation finished with. The silence threatened to come back. Pamela found herself shaking her wrist watch.

'This is quieter for you, then,' Dorothy added at length. 'How are you liking it?'

'It's simply beautiful,' said Billy, her ear adjusting slightly better to the rhythms of Dorothy's speech. 'That palace was simply beautiful.'

Pamela felt herself dreadfully ashamed on Billy's behalf. She wished she would say something surprising, intelligent or unpredictable; failing that, something friendly, warm, approachable.

'Pamela will be showing you all the colleges and that, I expect,' said Dorothy. 'There's such a lot to see.'

Pamela, who had rather thought *not* too many of the colleges, and even less of That, did not respond much to this suggestion but at last plunged in with questions about Barry. Dorothy gulped rather alarmingly and appeared to be silenced by the inquiry. She had put her hand to her mouth and said, 'Excuse me.' It was a terrible, electrifying moment. She knew that she had herself under control. She was not actually going to be sick. It was simply that, in her present condition, she got a lot of 'wind' and it was so powerful that it sometimes took her breath away and made speech impossible.

'He's doing ever so well,' she said eventually. 'But,' she added archly, 'you had better ask Rena.'

Rena had already begun to feel embarrassed by the memory of her few evenings spent with Barry. It was Dorothy that she liked, not the boy. She was hoping that the term would sort out the position to everyone's satisfaction, and without embarrassment. He would be bound to make a Welsh friend who could take her place; and he would scarcely object if she continued from time to time taking his mother out for drives.

'He sounds as if he's getting on all right.' She did not want to say much.

'It's *very* hard work,' Dorothy insisted. 'He's finding he can keep up, of course. He's a clever lad, as you know. But they certainly keep him at it. What was it he had to write an essay on the other week?'

Uninterested, Rena could not remember.

'George said it was all Double Dutch to him,' she tried to make a rather mirthless joke out of it. 'I don't know what I'd do if I had to write an essay, I'm sure.'

Her tea was largely untasted in front of her.

'I've been having a bad old time since I saw you,' she eventually blurted out. Pamela flinched. Should she say how ill Dorothy looked? Of course not. There can never be any justification for telling someone they look ill. It can only cause pain. On the other hand, something more than a grunt of assent was needed. She could not, alas, provide it.

'I've broken this arm, as you can see, and my back's been playing up. Made me really tottery on my pins for some reason. You probably noticed. Rena here's been marvellous, haven't you, my love?'

168

'I like *doing* it,' said Rena. She had by now taken a dislike both to the snooty lady and to the American transvestite and she was longing to get Dorothy back into the Mini.

'The doctors say I'm all right,' Dorothy went on, 'but it's tiring, you know. Tiring.'

The thread of conversation seemed to evaporate at this point in all four round the table. It was an eternity before the waitress brought the bill. Pamela agreed that breaking limbs must be very tiring. She had broken an ankle once and found it exhausting. And, as Dorothy added, it is not so much the pain as the feeling tired. Exhausted, Pamela had agreed. Too tired to sleep. And also, Dorothy had suggested, sort of floppy, like you did not feel up to doing anything much. There were all manner of jobs about the house which needed doing but she could not get down to them. Her neighbours had been marvellous. Vi said she ought to learn to relax more. But you can't sit in a chair all day long.

This merciful truth was eventually demonstrated when they all rose to go. None, perhaps, had spent a more embarrassing hour in the last month; yet none of them would have known a way of avoiding it.

As Dorothy said, when she had settled in the passenger seat and Rena started the engine, 'You've got to be sociable.'

Pamela sat for a while in silence before starting up the engine. She watched Rena back the yellow Mini into the main stream of traffic and jerk off to the right. Then she let out a low sigh.

'That was *terrible*,' Billy said.

'Awful. I'm so sorry, darling, but once the idea had been raised there was no way of getting out of it. Poor Dorothy.'

'You don't get that way by breaking an arm,' said Billy.

'Of course you don't. It is all so horrific that I can't bear to think about it.'

'About?'

'In an odd way, it makes me feel like a murderer.'

'Don't be ridiculous. You aren't responsible for her being that way.'

'What way?'

169

'Anorexic. I used to be like that until I'd had treatment.'

'Billy, you can't know what she was like, even a few months ago. What is it, four months now? She was almost plump. There was something like life and colour in her face. She is obviously *dying*. That is what I mean by saying that I feel like a murderer.'

'But that's plain superstitious. You can't really imagine that the Virgin Mary is saving your life and taking Dorothy's instead.'

Pamela started the engine and did not reply until they were on the open road again. The evening traffic was so heavy that she decided not to follow the straight route home. They found themselves soon enough in deep country, and she drew up on a slight eminence so that they could look down on a meadow where willows shed their leaves on a meandering stream.

'I'm not parking in your sense of the word, my angel, but the traffic is so hellish, and I feel I must just stop and think. It'll be dark soon. You realize what's happened, don't you?'

'Are you feeling OK?' Billy reached out and touched her. The colour had faded from Pamela's face and she looked stricken, as if about to weep.

'There has been the most terrible mistake. Don't you see? I went to the hospital on the same day as that poor woman. They told her that she was perfectly all right. They told me that I was dying. That I would only live a few months if I did not accept treatment. It all seemed mad. I felt frightened, run down. But I did not feel *ill*. I did not have any pain ... And all the time, *she* did. It was *she* who was dying, it was she who only had a few more months, it was she who needed prayers and magic, not me.'

'But that's *crazy*. Who do you have looking after you in these hospitals of yours? Some kind of dum-dum who can't tell the difference between a woman who is *dying* for Chrissakes,' her voice rose to a high squeal at this point, 'and someone who is perfectly healthy?'

'I told you he was a pillock'; perhaps humour, even of so strained a kind, would reduce the volume. 'He really is. He is an appalling little man.'

'But how do you make a mistake like that?'

'By trying to do ten things at once. You'd think that a specialist gynaecologist, or whatever the Pillock is, would lead a leisured, learned existence, only seeing a few patients. But even when he was telling me that my life was over, you could see that he could scarcely wait to get me out of the room before he was rushing off to give a lecture or perform another operation. On top of which, of course, he has a huge private clientele for his wretched abortions.'

'He does?'

'It doesn't bear thinking about, the number of girls who pass through his hands. I'm sure he never asks them proper questions, or finds out whether they really need an abortion or not. He simply whisks them in – or whips or pops them in as he would put it – and by the time they have changed their minds it is too late. The whole operation is over. He is busy slicing away at someone else's womb or breast. It is horrifying.'

'Some of those girls might actually *want* abortions.'

But Billy would have to pursue these reflections in silence. Their egoisms now ran along parallel lines, and there was little to connect them. Pamela could not stop herself speaking.

'Do you realize what would have happened had I taken that man's advice? I would have started to take the vile treatments he was prescribing. I would probably have lost weight; I would have felt sick all the time. I would have been bald . . .'

'You're prejudiced against him simply because he does abortions. Damn it, you *are* like the Catholics, whatever you may say.'

'Darling, you aren't listening. I might have been bald. Just because the Pillock had made a mistake.'

Rena and Dorothy fought their way through the rush hour and took a more direct route home.

'She's ever so nice,' Dorothy said, thinking of Pamela. 'A real lady.'

'Yeah.' Rena chewed. She had been stuck behind a lorry for the last ten minutes and was longing for a chance to overtake. Moreover, she could not even pretend that she liked Pamela.

Not even in retrospect. If the truth were known, she had been frightened by her.

'Would you believe it, she's living in one of those poky little houses down behind the Press? I expect she's spent a lot on it, mind. Vi says they're becoming fashionable down there now; but I wouldn't want to live there. Some of the houses don't even have proper bathrooms.'

'Enjoy yourself, then?' said Rena, turning to her momentarily and smiling.

'It was a lovely afternoon, thanks, dear, really lovely. I wish we hadn't spent so long over tea, though. George will be anxious if we're out long. He told me this morning before he left for work, not to go overdoing things. Still, we can look after ourselves, can't we?'

'I'll look after you,' the girl said. She had now turned to Dorothy to look at her intently and lovingly. Thoughts passed through her mind of her own mother, of the last year of her life, of the misery which grew day by day as the truth had dawned on them all that this was an illness which she would not pull through; and then, worst of all, the callous impatience which had set in, when they were all actually longing for her to die ...

'You're wonderful,' Dorothy said. 'I don't know what I'd've done without you and Vi these last few weeks, I don't really. Still, they say "a friend in need", don't they?'

The social embarrassment of the tea party faded away and both women relaxed into the happy state where it no longer mattered if what one said was inconsequential and uninteresting. Dorothy felt tired and what she had taken to calling her funny old pain shot up and down her spine sometimes mild, sometimes strong, but never breaking out to that pitch of intensity she had known earlier in the hospital.

Her face smiled, in spite of her back. It was such a piece of luck to have found Rena. She was not everyone's cup of tea. George grumbled about her make-up, but that was what young people did wear nowadays.

172

'A lot of lads need an older woman,' Vi had said. 'Makes them feel more secure. Not that he hasn't had enough mothering from you, Dol, my old love, but he's probably been spoilt by it, know what I mean?'

It was all a lot of nonsense. Vi *did* speak nonsense much of the time. No one could have *too much* love in the world. If Barry found yet more love from Rena, that was all to the good. Dorothy felt pleased for him. Pleased, not, as she would have expected, jealous or anxious. Simply pleased.

'Get on with it,' said Rena petulantly. She smiled back at Dorothy to reassure her the cross words had been addressed to the lorry-driver in front. The Mini could wait no longer. She swerved the steering wheel violently and moved up into third gear. The headlights ahead were flashing; someone was blowing a horn; but it all happened in a matter of seconds. The Mini smashed into the front of another lorry driving at speed. It buckled and the little car was instantly crushed. Too late, the lorry jerked from its path, lashing the little car once more with its hinder parts, like a dragon swishing its tail. The Mini rolled over two or three times and burst into flames.

No one else was hurt. By the time that the police vans were sounding their sirens, and the road had been blocked off, Rena's moment of horror had blanked out into unconsciousness. She had seen Dorothy flung against the roof of the car, hurled half through the windscreen, and then slumped hideously backwards again, her neck broken, blood everywhere. This was her last sight. Rena herself died in the ambulance on the way to hospital.

'And anyway,' Pamela was saying, 'I feel that something ought to be *said*.'

'If he's as devious as you think he is, the Pillock isn't going to admit making a mistake.'

'Perhaps not.'

'I'm sure not.'

'People ought not to be allowed to get away with these things. That's the point.'

They were on the road for home now, as dusk fell. The traffic seemed to have got no better and they were held up in a long queue by a policeman obstructing the traffic.

'There's been an accident I guess.' Billy averted her gaze.

Neither of them could have seen much as they drove past. One was dimly aware of glass and moisture on the surface of the road, but it was getting dark. The burnt-out car, blackened and bashed up, lay on its side by the verge, smoke still coming from its wreckage.

'Horrible,' Pamela said. She did not realize that her mood could have become blacker, but the accident, suggesting the ubiquity of human misery and disaster, made a cold chill run through her breast.

'I wonder what it's like to be burned up,' Billy morbidly said. 'I used to have this thing when I was a kid about Joan of Arc. I read everything I could lay my hands on about her. I was just fascinated by someone who had actually been *burned alive* . . . Still, it's not a very cheerful subject, is it?'

'Not really.'

'Why not sing one of your ridiculous songs?' Billy suggested. She felt the heavy descent of Pamela's mood and was alarmed by it.

They had 'Waltzing Matilda' and 'I'll sing a hymn to Mary' and 'Snick goes the shearer' once more. But then Pamela's strangely cultivated tones began to hum airs from old music-hall songs, learnt from a favourite gramophone record.

> *I was wed at nine o'clock today,*
> *My husband Jimmy in a lovely way,*
> *We drove down to Brighton for a month to stay,*
> *So we travelled in a motor-car.*
> *Off we started at a rare old speed,*
> *Knocked down a policeman but we took no heed,*
> *Others tried to follow but we kept the lead*
> *It was lovely in a motor-car.*
> *But going down a country hill,*

We saw a great big wall:
Tried to put the brake on,
But it would not brake at all!
My poor Jim's got a broken leg,
And the 'ump as well, I'm sure;
And I've had a lively time myself,
I'm a sight you never saw:
All through riding in a motor,
Riding in a motor-car:
I've lost no end of things,
Don't know where I are.
Punctured a tyre and it all caught fire,
It's a thing I shan't forget:
My poor Jim's got a broken limb,
So I 'aven't 'ad me 'oneymoon yet.

'It sounds vaguely obscene,' said Billy with delight. She laid her head on Pamela's shoulder and they drove home in a new mood of strangely discovered contentment.

- 15 -

Hereward – she was bidden to think of him so now – came to his front door wearing a Clydella shirt, purple knitted tie, brown corduroy trousers and a pair of decomposing tartan slippers. She supposed she must often have seen him in mufti before. He usually wore it on his 'day off'. But it altered his appearance subtly and radically. As he led the way through the study and into the sitting room, where smokeless fuel glowed in the grate, she found herself wondering whether she would guess his profession, had she met him dressed as he was now, in a public neutral place for the first time. She might have taken him for a rather terrifying master in a boarding school. The

English master, perhaps; the sort who liked striking radical attitudes (the beard), but who was relentlessly strict (the hair, the eyes, the mouth) and valued the discipline of learning to declaim (the voice) Milton or Wordsworth. But surely, as one listened to the voice a little, one would begin to suspect at the very least a clerical past. There was something inescapably sacerdotal about him. It was not really in his case a physical thing. With some clergymen, you had the impression that they were always filing and scrubbing their nails in preparation for handling the Most Holy. But his raw bony fingers were reassuringly grubby. They looked as if he had the habit of nervously fidgeting with the contents of the overloaded ash-trays which littered every surface in his house. Some clergymen, similarly, always looked as if they had just had a haircut; his hair on the other hand, though never markedly long, had evidently not been in the hands of the professionals for years. It stuck out at odd angles and was obviously hacked with nail scissors when need arose.

Indeed, it was one of his contributions to economic theory that if every Englishman cut his own hair, sending the price of the barber's bill he would have paid to Africa, the problem of starvation would be solved. African starvation, Pamela always wanted to reply; then the Africans would have to start sending money to all the starving English barbers. But it was not a subject on which he admitted any kind of foolery.

'Ah, Pamela, dear, I was just thinking of you.'

'Is your sister back?'

'She got back the day before yesterday. She is having a lie-down at the moment. Did you want to see her?'

'No, no. I just wondered.'

'To tell the truth,' he lowered his voice and lit a cigarette, 'things are a little difficult at the moment.'

'I'm so sorry.' She had so much to say to him that she was not particularly interested in the difficulties of Miss Stickley. What strange reversals of spirit she had experienced: a few months before, when the Stickleys were still figures of legend to her, and she would not have dreamed of swanning in and out of their house, she would have been fascinated by this indiscretion. *How* were things difficult? Now, she could not care less.

'It's nearly tea-time,' he said. 'I was going to have it in the garage, but perhaps we should have it in the kitchen.'

'Are you having difficulties with the Morris Traveller?'

'Why do you ask?'

'It seems odd to want to take tea in the garage.'

'Come and sit down,' he said, drawing out a kitchen chair.

'I've had the most awful experience,' Pamela prattled on. 'Do you remember that when I was in hospital there was a rather nice woman there called Dorothy Higgs? She was the only other bed in the ward.'

'I remember.' He was burning to communicate *his* news to her, and the cause of the difficulties with his sister.

'Billy and I drove out in the country the other day and we met Dorothy in the Garden Centre.'

'I've been driving in the country, too. There's something I want to tell you about it.'

'It was awful,' she said, ignoring his eagerness; indeed, not noticing it. 'She looked so dreadfully ill. It came to me quite clearly that there has been the most horrifying mistake. I feel it is rather terrible to be saying all this to you. You've been so kind and so helpful, and we have become such friends.'

'Yes,' he said in a leisurely way, 'we have.' He went to close the kitchen door and indicated with exaggerated movements of the eyebrows that there was trouble aloft not unconnected with this fact.

She failed to catch the signal.

'It was her we should have been praying for, not me.'

'Sorry. Who?'

'Dorothy. I was absolutely sure as soon as I saw her. The doctor made a mistake when he examined both of us ...' Her voice was earnest, low, serious; its seriousness at last arrested him and he began to listen.

177

'They made a mistake. They told me that I was dying, and they told her she was perfectly all right. But it was the other way around.'

'And you saw her at His Grace's Cactus Centre?' Hereward affected to despise everything about the aristocracy.

'She was having a day out, as I was.'

'She was well enough to drive a car, then?'

'Hereward' – there! naturally, and without strain, except the strain of anger, she had used the name – 'it was *awful*. She was being driven by a young girl. A niece I think it must have been. She looked more ill than I can describe. She had no flesh on her bones. Her skin was a sort of bright yellow colour. Something had gone terribly badly wrong.'

'Different people take shorter or longer times to get over illnesses.'

'She was not getting over anything. It is appalling. They have made a mistake and they ought to be told.'

'But she must have a doctor looking after her.'

'A *doctor*? Those people are killers.'

'Come, that's rather an exaggeration. It's like your bee about our separated brethren.'

'It is *not* a bee. Don't you understand, you idiotic man; that woman is DYING, the doctors have made a MISTAKE. Just think what would have happened if they had continued to treat me. I would be bald by now.'

He screwed up his eyes and surveyed her bleakly.

'Would you really?' There was an acute note of grief in his voice.

'I know it's hard for you to accept after our visit to the Shrine and everything. It meant a lot to you to think that I had been healed by Our Lady, and all that. But I hadn't. I had nothing wrong with me.'

'That's rather a big claim for any fallen creature to make.'

'Oh, don't be so pompous. You know perfectly well what I mean.'

She felt so strongly about it all that she scarcely noticed the

178

intimacy implied by her anger with him: by her insults, her impatience.

Tea was made and he put it on a tray. He looked up at the closed door of the kitchen over the top of his spectacles and thought better of taking the tea things into the garage. 'Let's just have it here,' he said. He still nursed hopes of telling her *his* news.

'I'm sorry,' she said, sitting down and touching his tweedy sleeve. Life with Billy had made her enormously more demonstrative. She even found herself pawing the milkman these days.

He brought his hand down on to hers and sandwiched her fingers between the tweed and his palm.

'If they have made a mistake,' he said slowly, shutting his eyes and allowing the implications of it to sink in slowly, and more deeply into his mind, 'that is terrible. Quite terrible. But how can we possibly know? How long was it you spent with her?'

'A couple of hours.' She was not going to be made to admit that her impression was superficial. She saw no reason on this occasion to be strictly accurate.

'I imagine her doctor sees her every week.'

'Why? Mine doesn't.'

'Hardly surprising, since whenever they come near you they get their heads bitten off. Have you really not been to see Swynnerton-Myles? You *promised* me.'

'I've been so busy since I got back.'

'Go. There's a good girl.'

He withdrew his hands and began to pour out the tea into rather ugly mugs.

'You mean, there's nothing you think we can do?'

'Well, if what you say is true, then you will have to let your doctors know that your tests in America show that you have been completely cured.'

'I suppose that's right.'

'They are hardly going to take your word seriously unless you do that. You should make an appointment at the hospital, and then, when you see Mr Tulloch, you will have the chance to voice this other anxiety. And you can always drop in on Dorothy Higgs casually and find out if your suspicions remain the same. After all, you did not see her for a very long time, by the sound of it.'

She smiled.

'But did you?' he continued.

'You so long for it all to have been a miracle, don't you, Hereward? Why can't you accept that it is all a muddle, not part of a plan, just a series of flukes and accidents?'

'So long as you are alive, and well, and reasonably happy, I don't much mind why that is so. We have already talked endlessly about the nature of what happened – or, as you believe, did not happen – at the shrine. My belief, as you know, is this: If you went there with cancer and came away healed, but that healing did not register in your heart as a divine event, then no "miracle" of importance took place at all. You might as well have been using a lucky charm to get rid of warts. But if you went there and offered yourself unreservedly – never mind your particular frame of mind at the time – to God, then God will have taken that offering and opened to you the channels of His Grace in whatever funny ways He intends. Don't ask me what ways. Don't ask me why I believe all this to be the case. But . . .'

'You think I've changed since Walsingham, don't you?'

'You obviously have.'

'If you were listening to my confession you'd realize that I haven't changed for the better.'

'We agreed that I should not hear your confessions any more.'

She had accepted this without difficulty. Their relationship no longer allowed for the necessary anonymity of the confessional. 'I'm just a machine,' he had said to her once through the grille. 'It's not me you are speaking to. It's God. I'm just a machine through which you talk to God.' But he was anything but a machine now, and she would have been unable to say things to him in that odd setting without reflecting on the thoughts which were passing through his head.

'I know we agreed all that, and it's obviously right. But I am not behaving like someone who has been touched by divine grace.'

'As I say,' he repeated, 'I am not your confessor any more.' He glanced nervously at the kitchen door. Then he added, 'I've been out in the country, as I told you.'

'Where did you go?'

'Oh, Berkshire.'

She wondered if, like John Brocklehurst, he had gone on a bicycle. However he had been propelled – and it was hard to imagine the old Traveller managing the steeper parts of the downs in anything but bottom gear – the expedition had obviously been in some way agitating.

He was making the funny little grunts which she remembered from earlier colloquies when whatever they were discussing had been painful – a non-verbalized sound which approximated to *Mm-ya, mm-ya, mm-ya.*

'Was it nice in Berkshire?' She was teasing him now, but only in order to help him Speak Out.

'Mm-ya, mm-ya, mm-ya, yes of course, absolutely lovely. Look here, I've been helping out in this parish five years now and I've told the Bishop that it's time they found someone else. No, mm-ya, mm-ya, don't interrupt.' He was in the swing at last, and the prepared speech was flowing with something like the fluency and certainty with which he could speak of less personal matters – purgatory, women priests, what did or did not constitute a state of grace. 'He's offered me the living of the most beautiful little parish you ever saw.'

'In the country? But surely not your sort of thing at all?'

'I was born in the country. I don't see why I shouldn't live there.'

'But won't the church be all Matins and Elevation of the Plate and people in tweed declaiming from Eagles?'

'I like that sort of religion.' There was no trace of this fondness in the splendid performances he stage-managed in his present showplace. 'One can have enough of High Jinks, you know.'

181

'I didn't realize that you could.'

'I'm not happy here – mm-ya, mm-ya – that's the point. You see, I'm no longer suitable here.'

'No longer suitable? But everyone *loves* you. Even the Eastern grocers call you "father".'

He blushed and smiled guilelessly.

'Hardly the point, I'm afraid. I must go to avoid – mm-ya, mm-ya. Scandal is too strong a word. Upsetting people. I'm going to get out before there's talk. I've known it happen to friends of mine. Even the nicest parishes can suddenly blow up in your face without very careful watching.'

Oh, good heavens, she thought (and just when she had made up her mind that he really *wasn't*), the poor old thing *has* been treading the Walsingham Way and some nasty little man has threatened to squeal.

'Stay, do,' she said. 'No one really minds these things nowadays. We'd all stick by you, you know. I would, I know.'

'Stick by me? There's never been any question of your not sticking by me. Can't you see? That's what I'm trying to make abundantly and crystal clear.' He gestured with frantic little stabs of the cigarette-holder.

'I'm getting lost. You want to retire to the country because you think you ought to?'

'Yes. I don't want to put the parochial church council here in an embarrassing position. It would be hard for them. They have placed great trust in me, treated me more or less as if I was the vicar, let me run my own show . . .'

She sipped her tea rather desperately. It was one of those conversations which made her feel terribly afraid that she must have fallen asleep in the middle and missed something vital. First it was a parish in the country; now the idea of not letting people down. But *what* was he talking about? She had a strong sense that he was about to propose marriage and did not know whether the kindest thing would be to help him to say it and then, as politely as possible, to turn him down – or whether to try to change the subject. Anything to get the agony over.

'Lovely little church,' he had started again. 'Norman porch, the remains of a doom on the chancel arch, a crusader buried in the lady chapel ... And there's a marvellous rectory; one of the few that they haven't sold off. Not far from Wantage, a beautiful bit of country. I think the change will do me good. The trouble is,' he said, and pointed to the ceiling without adding another word. Instead, he lit another cigarette and stirred his tea.

'Your sister?' Pamela managed to ask.

'Sssh!'

'Your sister,' she whispered, 'does not like the idea of living in the country?'

'It's the last thing in a series of impossible disagreements,' he whispered.

'What about?'

'The trouble is, we can't very well go out in the street and talk about it.' One might almost have believed, given the air of conspiracy, that the kitchen was actually bugged.

'Besides,' Pamela agreed, 'it's getting a bit dark for a walk.'

'Is it?' Hope returned to his voice. 'Perhaps we could risk it, then. I really don't like talking in the house like this.'

She was asked not to talk as she collected her things from the hall, and she became increasingly puzzled as she stood waiting for her host in the shadows by the coat-stand. Eventually, a lavatory flushed and he emerged in a long black clerical cloak and a beret.

'Right,' he whispered, and they stepped out into the dusk.

The canal glowed with the reflected light of the factory windows as they walked along the towpath without saying anything. Then, the darkness giving him confidence, he began again.

'My sister says there has been "talk",' he spat out contemptuously. 'I thought it was a tasteless joke at first. But now I believe her. Mrs Dickson – you know her? The plump little woman who is assistant sacristan when Rodney is away? – said to my sister the other day that "before long there would be bells".'

'Bells?'

'Well, that was what I said. But you see, people *will* talk and

I don't want to make people anxious. They've never had a married priest in this parish.' There was an appalling hush as he allowed the words to sink in. Only the sound of their shoes squelching in the muddy footpath.

'And,' he added, 'I hope they never will. I don't want to upset them. Ever since I've done parish work, I've been steering people through disasters. In Liverpool, it was the Blitz; in Polperro, it was the issue of the Church of South India which made them all want to go over to Rome; in Leeds, it was Methodist reunion; for my nuns in Wapping, it was Series III; and here, we've survived the crisis of the Ladies. What's the point of taking a lot of trouble to spare people from all these threats to happiness if one then goes and *upsets* them? It wouldn't be fair to *them* if there was a lot of gossip.'

'Don't you think you're over-reacting?' She thought she understood his drift, but much remained unclear. It was all mildly horrifying.

'No,' he spoke carefully, 'I don't think that I am. It's terrible when there is gossip in a parish.'

'Isn't there always gossip in a parish?'

'About me?' he replied, quick as a flash. 'What have you heard?'

'Nothing. I was speaking generally. Look, hadn't you better be more specific? I'm rather lost.'

'Perhaps I had. There's been gossip about you and me.'

'I thought that was what you were driving at. But since it's quite unfounded, I don't see why you should take any notice of it.'

'That sounds very wise, but it is actually very foolish,' he said firmly. 'It's all very well to say that we should take no notice. But people are, in a way, entitled to gossip. We *do* see a lot of each other.'

'We can always stop, if you'd like.'

He was mm-ya-mm-ya-ing again.

'I mean,' she said, 'if you are afraid of your reputation.'

'It sounds very insulting to you, put like that. Of course, it is lovely, seeing so much of you. There's nothing wrong with

184

it. We haven't behaved irresponsibly. I know all that. But there *is* something in the gossip, isn't there?'

Since the only gossip mentioned related to wedding-bells, Pamela once more wondered whether she had missed some crucial part of the conversation. Had he actually proposed to her, had she even, in some roundabout way, accepted, without her quite noticing? Was the marriage, as it said in the papers, arranged, and would it shortly take place? Bizarre as it all seemed, there *were* things that she would like worse. A combination of fear and joy took hold of her as they paced along beside the dark waters.

'I'm very fond of you, as you know,' the now complete darkness allowed him to say. She could not make out his features; only the reflection of a street lamp on the bridge which they were now approaching glinted in his spectacles.

'I thought our friendship was so nice,' she said. 'It makes me feel very irresponsible to think of it hurting you so much.'

'It doesn't hurt me at all.'

'No, but it's sad if my dropping in at your house makes you feel that you ought to leave, go and live in the country ... Has your sister been very difficult about it?'

He exhaled sadly. 'Poor Frideswide has been impossible.'

'She'll be all right,' Pamela insisted. 'The country air will do her good.' It seemed settled, this country parish business. She might as well accept it bravely. She would, she realized with a pang, miss him rather terribly. But there was no way of telling him this. It would be painful; more a cause of confusion and bitterness than of pleasure.

'She's not coming to the country' – was it a wail, or a cry of triumph? 'She has a little flat, as you probably know, in Fulham. She is going back to live there whatever happens. I don't blame her. She has only been living with me since I left Wapping. I am very grateful to her. It is nothing to do with incompatibility of character or anything like that. It is fundamentally a religious issue. She had no sympathy with the way I was doing things here.'

Goodness knew how the domestic frictions of Hereward's

household were soon to be translated into an issue of principle; how Frideswide's joyless cooking and bad temper were to be viewed as part of a wider question – a dispute about genuflections, an argument about the placing of flower-vases on the gradine.

'I don't blame Frideswide. Not at all. She doesn't want to live stuck out in the country. She can't drive. She wouldn't have any friends there. It's all perfectly understandable.'

'So you'll be rather stuck?'

'I'll manage. I'm said to cook a very plausible fish pie.'

They took the little footpath up by the bridge and continued their walk along the road, turning back in the direction of the parish, south-west.

'If your sister doesn't want to go to the country, wouldn't it be more sensible to stay on here? I can always promise not to call any more, if that is the difficulty.'

'I wouldn't want you to promise that,' he said.

They could see each other's faces now as they ambled past the cinema and the Indian restaurants. The lights brought a return of diffidence.

'I just seem to cause trouble wherever I go,' Pamela blurted out after a period of silence. 'I've practically killed Dorothy –'

'Now, that is absurd.'

'I have. If they had not got her muddled up with me, they would have started treating her.'

'We don't know that's true. And if it is, by no stretch of the imagination can it be thought of as your fault. As I said earlier, you must find out.'

'I will. I will. But don't you see? I am a bringer of chaos. Look at the way I've blundered over Billy.'

'I thought things were going so well?'

'I don't know.'

'Not well?'

'It just *feels* a muddle. I don't know whether it's a good thing or not. I just wish I hadn't chosen to fall in love with the discarded mistress of my best friend. It makes things awkward. And now this – you moving house to get away from your bells.'

'Ah!' he said. 'Bells. Who knows?'

If there was any more to reveal on the subject, it remained unexplored that evening. They had reached the corner of Pamela's street and, with only half-spoken agreement, parted by the kerb. As she sat in the gloomy solitude of her sitting-room five minutes later, not bothering to turn on the lamp, she could hear poor Hereward ringing the tocsin for evensong.

<h1 style="text-align:center">- 16 -</h1>

It was, in the nature of things, inevitable that they would bump into each other if they left it much longer; but Billy dreaded the embarrassment of any chance encounter. The only thing to do was to anticipate the fates and visit John herself.

She had decided to do so several days before plucking up the courage to act on her decision. Then, Pamela sailing out, as she had a way of doing, calling only 'Hereward!' by way of explanation of where she was going or when she would be back, Billy realized that she had a few hours of her own to play with.

Life with Pamela had been so different from anything she had expected. Initially, Billy had been overwhelmed by it; not so much by the intensity with which the 'affair' had blown up – intensity was the air she breathed; she had grown so used to creating its atmosphere wherever she went that she was un-aware that others lived at a less fevered pitch when she was not around – as by the foreignness of it all. Since the first intense week, life had simmered down to a point where the two women could feel the distance between them rather acutely. It was, surely, embarrassment which made Pamela slip out all the time, and leave the girl on her own. Billy had not been introduced to many friends – although they had chatted to people met on street corners, and even had a cup of tea with one of the dons at Pamela's college, who happened to be in the pub one morning when they were there.

There appeared to be a whole world which Pamela took for

granted and which remained strange to her new companion. She began to master the names of its inhabitants, learnt at second-hand. Sourpuss, now Hereward, and the whole baffling wonderland of ecclesiastical life, formed one considerable part of it. She had only met the old boy once, buying stamps in the post office, a slightly ravaged, mad-looking man, hugely tall in a filthy soutane. It was hard to see why he had been a figure of comedy in Pamela's eyes or, for that matter, a figure to be taken seriously, which now appeared to be the line. He was merely odd, impenetrable. Billy was not used to laughing at people, still less at people one professed to admire. She did not get the hang.

The huge catalogue of university friends and colleagues remained an undiscovered country: Hovis, the Principal, the Senior Tutor; all figures described to her in this baffling, half-serious way. She wanted, if only to start with, something a little more straightforward. An explanation of their real names, who they were, what they did, where they fitted into Pamela's scheme of things. Moreover, she wanted some coherent explanation of the way the university worked; indeed, where it was. She had been shown the colleges, or some of them; she had been taken to an old library and innumerable churches. But they had still not visited the university itself. Pamela said there wasn't one; but what was this supposed to mean? Everyone had heard of it. It must, if only for that reason, be *there*.

John's college had not, of course, formed a part of their itinerary. She made her way there earnestly in the last of the light, guided by a little map picked up in a bookshop that morning. The streets were full of young people thronging in and out of colleges. They were all dressed extraordinarily; only one in ten like a college kid in the States. Girls could be seen in coats and skirts; there were even some in hats. Young men in ties, obviously too young to be professors, must, *incredibly*, be students. Not all, of course, were dressed in this way. There were a good sprinkling of people in jeans and sneakers. But, at the opposite end of the pole, one passed young men in fancy dress: gowns fluttered, winged collars pressed their starched points into adolescent throats; watch chains slinked from waistcoat pockets. Between these two extremes lay a middle ground of extraordinary sartorial self-confidence.

She passed the famous emperors' heads, now clean and new, staring disapprovingly across traffic jams to the bookshop. She turned a corner and walked under a replica of the Venetian Bridge of Sighs. She recognized it as this: her father had been fond of Italy. The tiny serpentine street turned two abrupt bends and she found herself face to face with a medieval gateway, above it a mouldering statue of the Madonna being adored on the one hand by a bishop and on the other by the Angel of the Annunciation who looked as though he had been caught peering through a keyhole, and was perched elaborately on one knee. Billy wondered what it was about this arrangement of stone figures, and the Madonna in particular, which seemed to echo a feeling she had about Pamela. Could it be the lofty, yet indistinct features of the central figure? It was not that Pamela's features were physically indistinct; indeed, they were beautiful to the point of oddness. But, in the statue's case, the absence of any discernible facial *expression* (one only *felt* she was smirking) seemed to suggest an unwillingness to give anything away. Not that the secretiveness was furtive; she and the prelate were in the secret already, took it as a matter of course. Only the poor angel Gabriel (not caught peeping – he had surely just genuflected on a drawing-pin) whose shoulder, upturned hand and quizzical face all expressed puzzled astonishment, was not to be told: the others took it all so much for granted, they did not even see that explanations were necessary.

There was a little door in the gateway, and, bowing her head, she crept inside, her heart now beating fervently beneath her jersey. She was beginning to feel it was unwise to be wearing jeans, given the expected expansion of her person, but she felt that on the day she ceased to do so, some private battle with life would have been lost.

A man in a bowler hat appeared as soon as she was inside. From his smart navy-blue suit and dark tie, she took him to be a man of business, or perhaps a lawyer: up from London, surely, and, like herself, lost. It was a surprise when he appeared to be a sharer in the secret, and not a stranger and sojourner like herself; for he said, 'Can I help you, laddie?'

'I'm coming to see someone.'

She wiggled her hips slightly to denote femininity. He appeared unembarrassed by the mistake – if such it had been; he seemed at once distant and lascivious.

'Very good, madam,' and he touched his bowler hat with an absurd wink.

'Do you live here?'

'Me, madam? Oh, no. Don't blame me, I only work here.' He was laughing – at her? What was funny? What did he mean – he *only* worked here?

'Would you know where John Brocklehurst lived?'

'Mr Brocklehurst? Certainly, madam. You'll be wanting the Garden Quad, madam. Staircase 16. Through the arch straight ahead of you, turn right, and it's fifth on the right. Mr Brocklehurst's rooms are on the first floor.'

'I just walk through there?'

'That's right madam. Straight through.' He had become ingratiating since she mentioned John's name. She set off across the wide quadrangle, crossing as she did so the pretty circle of grass, as the porter had indicated. It was a shock when he bellowed after her 'MADAM!' in sergeant-major tones.

'Excuse me?' She stood innocently wondering what he wanted. Had she dropped her purse? No. It was still suspended from her shoulder. What then?

'Keep off the grass if you don't mind, madam.' He was smiling now in a way which displayed total self-confident dominion over her and over the territory for which he was responsible.

'*Excuse* me!'

She felt as if she had taken a pork chop into a synagogue, and she crept off the velvety turf as if it were a minefield which might at any moment explode. Her mentor beamed amiably; now he raised his hat. He liked to make visitors feel at ease. She felt so confused that she had completely forgotten his directions about how to get to John's room, but she felt too frightened to go back and ask him to repeat them. He might tell her that women were not allowed into the college wearing trousers.

Gothic gave way to Classical. The quadrangle which he had indicated opened out into an elegant T-shape, flanked by curvaceous Georgian cast-iron, beyond which was a walled garden. A mass of Michælmas daisies and chrysanthemums, brown against thick grey stone, filled the huge herbaceous border. In the middle of the lawn, trees towered towards the darkening sky on an artificial mound.

To her relief, there were names at each doorway, and she crept along, fearful of infringing any more esoteric regulations, until she came to the appropriate list. 1. DR JONES. 2. SIR J. MONTEITH. 3. TRAIN, M. F. 4. MR BROCKLEHURST. 5. BLUNDY, S. T. 6. KOMINSKI, F. X. Even the names, spindly white Roman capitals painted on a black background, appeared to occupy their own baffling categories. When, if ever, could Blundy, S. T., hope to become Mr Blundy? And could Kominski ever dream of becoming Sir F. X.? It was rather a surprise when a ravishing girl in a dark blue donkey-jacket – Train, M. F., as it happened – scuttled down the stairs and out into the quadrangle, interrupting these musings. These regions, then, nightmarishly bristling with taboos and mysteries, had been penetrated by women. This brought reassurance of a kind. So did Vi's voice, shrieking 'Red sails in the sunset' as she cleaned Sir Jorrocks Monteith's lavatory. But Billy's heart thumped as she began her tremulous ascent of the creaking, uncarpeted stairs.

She knew that she was about to encounter a John whom she had never known. In the States, she now believed, he was being, according to his own lights, uninhibited. It was hard to call back their few passionate weeks together in the face of all that had occurred since. He had fled because he had not wanted involvement; did not want the affair to become a love affair; did not want her to have any claims upon him. She had been through that one with men before; it was not uniquely English. Pamela, Billy thought, romanticized this desire of John's to keep himself unspotted from the world. Plenty of people had 'tragic' lives and were able to muddle through in spite of them. So OK, his wife – it was news to Billy that he had been married – had fouled him up; so he was broken by the experience; so she had killed herself. OK. But had he not – she enjoyed the cruelty of the speculation – been all his life looking for an excuse to dignify his desire to treat women like whores? He had said – and meant it as a compliment – that there had never been another girl, for ages, with whom he had allowed things to go on so long before breaking them off. He had wanted to seem mad and bad and dangerous to know. He had implied that she would be hurt, dreadfully, if she continued to throw in her lot with him. But it was he who had run away to Mexico the night after these words. The escape would have been effective, had it not been for the peculiar chance of Pamela's crossing the Atlantic. Billy felt almost sorry for him, *almost*, as she knocked on his door. It was hard luck, she could see that, her turning up again like a bad penny. She had tried to be blasé about him to Pamela. Yet there lingered within her a fascination which was not wholly spiritual, a fascination with John himself. He had been a delicious lover.

'Hallo! Come in!' She could hear his voice from far inside the room. Cautiously, she tried the doorknob. It felt so wobbly that it might come off in her hand, and it appeared to turn the wrong way. She had to push, and eventually fell into a room which she found heavily furnished, panelled, a filmset for a nineteenth-century costume drama.

John's voice came from a corner by the fireplace, where gas blazed, and a standard lamp shone dimly over a low-slung leather armchair. The subdued browns and yellows of the room, its only brightness the hissing Edwardian false teeth in the gas fire, had the tones of a canvas by Rembrandt. She could scarcely see him at first. He had a telephone receiver to his ear.

'No. No,' he was saying. 'Just a pupil, I expect.' He looked up to see which pupil it was.

His manner of registering shock, if he felt it, was different from what Billy's would have been. There were no raised voices, not even raised eyebrows. He peered myopically and pushed his spectacles up and down the bridge of his nose; he blushed, very slightly – or was it heat from the fire? He waved, and indicated the lumpy sofa.

'I wasn't on the syllabus reform committee,' he said, 'so no one can blame me ... Yes, whatever that means ... Just someone trying to be clever, I suppose ... They do, rather, don't they? Right.' With great abruptness, he had put down the receiver without apparently saying good-bye.

'Back in the swing,' he said. 'As you can see. Faculty business. I spent the whole of this afternoon at a Governing Body meeting. Tomorrow I'm on the Library Committee. On top of that I've got twelve hours teaching this term. Cup of tea?'

'I ... I ...'

'I've just made one.'

'Oh, thank you.'

'No?'

'Yes please.'

'Or would you rather have a drink?'

She accepted the tea. It was as if she had just walked out of the room for five minutes to go to the lavatory, rather than been thrown over in a painful emotional way three months before, and crossed the Atlantic pregnant.

'Been here long?' he asked. He came and sat by her on the sofa. She was aware once again of why she had fallen for him in the first place. He was too short, too plump, too facially idiosyncratic ever to be thought handsome. But he was in the highest degree physically reassuring.

'I'm staying with Pamela,' she managed to say.

'She said.'

'I met her back home.'

'I don't know what prompted her to fly all that way without phoning me up. She isn't usually impulsive.' He paused and slurped his mug of tea. 'No. That's wrong. She is always impulsive.'

'I'd say so.'

'Like it – do you – this place?'

It was as if he was interviewing a schoolboy for a scholarship.

'Yeah. It's great.'

'This part of the college was built in the eighteenth century.' He was putting on one of his funny voices. The guided tour. Why? 'Over there, you see the garden. No you don't, it's too dark. What –' he suddenly reverted to his own gruff tones and drew the curtains – 'what are you doing here, anyway?'

'Oh, John, I'm sorry.'

He came and sat beside her again. He could see the pupils quivering in her large moist eyes. He could smell the wonderful freshness of her soap. A nervous tremble rose and fell on her silky white throat. He had stretched out on the sofa and drawn her down on top of him, running his fingers through her hair and saying, 'I've always liked the back of your neck.'

'You haven't known it always.'

'Oh yes I have.'

'I had to come.' She whispered in his ear. 'I know it's messing you up. I know I'm not wanted. I just had to come.'

Not much was said for the next quarter of an hour. Almost nostalgically, almost in spite of themselves, their bodies moved into the familiar rituals. It was only afterwards that she was able to say, 'I'm pregnant.'

He did not reply at first. Her face pressed against his shoulder and she could not see his expression; could not even tell whether he had heard.

Then he said, 'Thought you might be.'

'What are we going to do?'

'What do you want to do?'

'Pamela's like talked me into keeping the baby. She wants me to live with her, and we'd bring it up together.'

'What do you think?'

'Oh, John, when I was back home and heard I was pregnant I just assumed I should, well, like, get rid of it. It seemed just awful. *You* wouldn't want to have a baby. I couldn't cope on my own. The whole thing seemed one big mess. And then, the way Pamela talked, I thought perhaps it would be kind of nice. And now I'm here, I'm just' – her voice sank to a low whisper – 'just so frightened.'

He squeezed her and stared at the ceiling.

'We ought to get dressed,' he said.

The garments which, in the preceding half hour, had been scattered on the hearth rug were retrieved, and they clothed themselves again with what dignity the room allowed.

'Thank you,' Billy said.

'What for?'

'Thank you for not saying that I was a fool to have come here.'

He looked back at her with sudden kindness before putting his spectacles back on his nose.

'Perhaps you were,' he said.

'I just felt I had to.'

He walked about the room like a man in a trance. Eventually he picked up a pipe and a tobacco pouch, perched himself on an upright chair by the window and devoted himself to lighting up.

'Everything – I said – that last night – was true,' he said deliberately, between puffs.

'But why does it have to be? Just because you've had some bad times with women doesn't mean you can never . . .'

'You don't understand,' he said. 'There's no point in talking about it.'

'Dammit, we are talking about it. OK. So you don't want a baby. I understand that. I'm not threatening you. I just feel I have a right to know why you ran away.'

'Because you *feel* you have a right does not mean that you really do have one.' He smoked disconsolately in silence.

She wondered how much he had surmised of Pamela, or her, of his own nature. He never appeared to be interested or to ask questions. Had Pamela told him about her illness, or about the miraculous cure; did he know that she and Pamela were having (just about) an affair. Was it because of him that there was in the last few days an almost imperceptible cooling between the two women? There was no way of knowing, but almost certainly not. She believed Pamela when she said that nothing had been said about his own affair with the girl. This, besides, was all something of an irrelevance. The baby was on both their minds. It was perhaps impertinent to be meditating upon human character.

'Why do you never want to *discuss* these things?' she wailed.

'Like what?'

'Like why we behave as we do. Like why you are so god-damned terrified of women.'

'It's only worth discussing things one knows something about, surely?'

'I won't eat you if you say that you are gay.'

'What would be the point in saying it? It doesn't happen to be true.'

'*I* am.'

'So you've often said.'

'Now, that interests me. Why do I want to go to bed with girls? It's different from sleeping with men.'

'Obviously.'

'Yet I want to do both.'

'It's not so unusual.'

'I guess it's all something to do with my mother, my father's marriages, some longing for security. Has it ever occurred to you that you and Pamela are old enough to be my parents?'

'No. I haven't had the chance to give the matter much thought. You see, I didn't know you knew Pamela until a few days ago.'

'Do you think I intuited Pamela?'

'I thought you met her at Cornell?'

'Do you think I wanted all this to happen, somewhere deep down, somewhere unconscious, that I really programmed the whole thing, set it up? So I could have, like, parents I never had before?'

'It's an interesting theory.'

'Pamela says you are her best friend.'

He smoked as if he had not heard the remark.

'Are you in love with Pamela?' she persisted. 'Are you in love and afraid to say so? I sometimes think she's a little in love with you.'

It was like talking to a brick wall. The lover of only a few minutes before had turned into a stiff little man in a sports coat and cavalry twill trousers, sucking desperately at a pipe.

'You seem to think that all human relations can be plotted and explained,' he said at length, with great precision, as if afraid that she would miss a point. 'But they aren't like that most of the time. Please don't think I am trying to be off-putting, but you are very young.'

'Christ!' her voice rose to a scream. 'Is that all you can say?'

'No, of course it isn't. But let's stop fantasizing, shall we?'

'I'm not fantasizing. I am simply trying to find out where I stand with you people.'

'People?' he looked round the room, as if for a crowd.

'You and Pamela. I sometimes feel as if I've walked into some kind of trap and you aren't going to tell me which way to move until I'm firmly in and you've gotten the ropes firmly tied round me. Then you'll just take me and dump me and get on with your own very funny, very ironic, very sophisticated lives and heave just one huge sigh of relief that I'm not embarrassing you, for Godsakes, by trying to find out the truth.'

'It's all perfectly understandable that you are upset. And there is no reason at all why you should understand me. I can't speak for anyone else.'

'Not Pamela?'

'I'd rather leave her out of all this, if you don't mind.'

'She's *in* it, Goddammit, can't you see?'

'The point at issue is you.' He turned to her with a smile which tried to melt.

'I'm having a drink,' he added, 'even if you aren't.'

'OK. I'll join you.'

He poured whisky into two tumblers and squirted soda up to the top. His hand trembled a little as he drank. She did not really want to drink and gulped too much in consequence.

'I'm sorry,' she said. 'I don't mean to be embarrassing.'

'There's really no need to keep saying it.'

'But I *do* feel sorry.'

'Have you seen a doctor?'

'I saw one back home. He just assumed I wanted an abortion.'

'And he assumed right, really, didn't he?'

She put her glass on the table by the fireside and ran across the room to where he stood, stiff as a ramrod by the door.

'Oh, look after me,' she said, burying her face in his neck. 'Please, please look after me.'

- 17 -

Tulloch, Crawford concluded, had become impossible. One expected a degree of autocratic behaviour, but of late his irascibility was out of control. He refused to see reason. He might at least, the young man thought feebly, do his own dirty work.

The girl under discussion had arrived from nowhere, more accurately from the United States, and Tulloch was insisting that she be dealt with at once. There was no explanation for this. Tulloch had arranged a private bed for one night. He would supervise the initial stages to make sure it was all going smoothly. Then it would be in Crawford's hands.

'Leaving things a bit late, aren't we?' Crawford had asked.

'Are you telling me my job?'

'I'm not telling you anything. I was asking. If she says it might be *five* months . . .'

'She's mistaken. Evidently mistaken. I would not do this if I did not consider it was absolutely necessary. *Absolutely* necessary.'

'There'll be a hell of a stink if the anti-abortion lobby get to hear about it.'

'There is no reason why anyone should get to hear about the private affairs of my patients. I've given it as my opinion that it is completely necessary to terminate this pregnancy.'

'For medical reasons?'

'Look, Rick, I'm getting rather fed up with your questioning my motives at every turn. Everything I do in this bloody hospital is for medical reasons. If you don't like them you know what to

198

do. But I'm damned if I'm going to have your snide imputations interrupting and interfering with everything that I do.'

She had paid him. Or someone had put up the money. Someone who mattered. Someone Tulloch thought mattered. It was as clear as day. Crawford had spoken to the girl. She had said it was at least five months. Then, when Tulloch came back she had changed her mind and said she was not sure. Crawford had briefly examined her. Blood pressure normal; no previous record of bad health; excitable, perhaps, but in no danger of going bonkers. Tulloch had been bought and he was not going to admit the fact. Moreover, he was expecting Crawford and the nurses to stand by and be a part of it.

Crawford had been applying for jobs all summer and autumn. Cardiff, Bart's, Glasgow. He had even asked for his old job back in Birmingham. Nothing doing. He suspected that Tulloch was fouling the pitch with lukewarm references. Why, he could not imagine, since they had come to hate the sight of each other and Tulloch would surely be glad to see the back of the young man.

If he could have got out of it, this particular operation, he would have done. But it was not that easy. It was all right for the people who opted out altogether, the Catholics who did not countenance it under any circumstances. But it was all less clear-cut than that for Crawford. There were some cases where it was obviously necessary, obviously the right thing for everyone concerned. Perhaps this was such a case: not for strictly medical reasons, obviously, but there was no knowing what nightmares were going to be avoided as a result of the operation. But why did Tulloch not come clean? It was mere casuistry to say that in this case there was no reason for believing it had gone beyond twenty weeks. If he could not be sure about a thing like that then he ought not to be doing his job. Further, it was sheer hypocrisy to pretend that he feared 'complications' would develop if the pregnancy were allowed to continue. But it all had to be done. His wife had accused him of moral cowardice. They had started to have rows all the time about Tulloch. But the plain truth was that unless he in some sense kept on the right side of the man, his career was effectively blocked.

Tulloch came into the room as he thought of these things.

'I've got ten minutes and no more,' he snapped.

Tulloch hated the way that Crawford stood around with his hands in his pockets, as if he had all the time in the world. He hated his long hair, not very clean, curling over the collar of his white coat. It was, he was afraid, true, as he had written so often during the summer (his arm was tired with all the references he had written), that Crawford was, in the final analysis, unreliable. God knows, he would be only too glad if the young bastard buggered off to Leicester or wherever the last consultancy post had been vacant. But the truth was the truth. Moreover, Tulloch felt a twinge of jealousy in recent months for anyone who seemed eligible for anything. He had no wish for Crawford to advance in his career, since it had been made so clear to him, after he had failed to get the Edinburgh chair, that he had reached the peak of his own career.

The fools who had turned Tulloch down did not realize that what he missed in individual academic achievement he made up for in range. There were not many aspects of the field of obstetrics and gynaecology which had passed him by. Breast cancer, fertility, the menopause, premature labour, unwanted pregnancy; he had dabbled in them all. They all connected up, all questions relating to the (to him) slightly distasteful subject he had chosen: the female body.

'Right,' he said. He and Crawford had been breathing heavily at each other. 'She's waiting for us I believe.'

Billy, in an operating gown, lay on the table as they entered the theatre and looked up apprehensively as they entered. Crawford blushed.

'It's OK,' he said. 'Nothing to worry about.'

'What's that drip doing there?' Tulloch asked the midwife, and without waiting for an answer moved it a few inches to the left.

'That's better,' he said. 'Now we can see what we are doing. Seen one of these before?' He almost smiled at Billy, and indicated the machine to which she had been connected. A flattened rubber tube had been connected to her wrist at one end.

A needle on a dial darted about on the other. She was terrified of Tulloch. She began to wish that she was not there. She knew that if she had stayed and talked to Pamela she would have been talked out of it. But things were hopeless. She could not face having the baby, and that was that. John had not given her much time to decide. Two days after seeing him, she had her appointment at the hospital, and found that a bed in a little ward was awaiting her. There was no worry about the money. He had taken care of that. He would try to come up and see her when the whole thing was over, but she was not to bank on it.

Pamela was to know nothing of it. They were both agreed. Any story could be concocted – a miscarriage, a mistaken pregnancy; anything but the truth. Billy had not been able to face Pamela when she had packed her overnight bag. Luckily, Pamela was out more and more. When it wasn't Hereward, it was the library. Billy had scribbled a note to say that she was going to London and might, if she was too late for the last train, stay over a night or two.

She did not allow herself to speculate what Pamela would say of this. She had not been off on her own before since arriving in England. She hoped that Pamela's preoccupation with the priest would be of a nature to distract her from Billy's where-abouts.

There she lay, strapped to the machine.

'It's measuring the contractions,' Tulloch said. 'It looks as if it's going quite well.' He twiddled a few things above her head and appeared to be adjusting the equipment with the dials on it. 'I think she can take a wee bit more,' he added to the midwife. 'I'll just wait till the next one.'

They were coming more strongly and more frequently now, hard spasms of pain, like cramp, spreading across her body and seeming to tear at her belly. The machine brought on labour. They used it for inducing the births of children at a later stage of the game. But it served in the present case as well.

Billy was having her forehead wiped by the midwife.

'She's doing OK,' said Mr Tulloch. Their eyes met momen-tarily, doctor and patient, and he added, 'Hallo, there,' realizing that he had omitted to greet her. He was damned if he could remember her name. 'I'll leave you to it,' he said, adding, to the younger doctor, 'It's more or less time for her injection now.'

After the injection, she did not feel much more pain, although the strange spasms still shook her body with increased violence until she was asleep.

The bloody thing was wrenched from her. When the nurse thrust her rubber glove into the formaldehyde there was a muted very faint splash, like a moorhen stirring in water, which plunged the whole room into stillness, broken only by the whirring of electrical machinery.

- 18 -

Auntie Joyce, Dol's married sister from Hartlepool, had departed that morning with her husband, the Post Office engineer. A few cousins, and quite a lot of neighbours, considering, had been to the funeral. Now the little house was given the chance to assert her absence, so that George and Barry, weighed down by the shock, felt momentarily drawn together.

George still felt angry, though, with that bloody girl and her car. What right had she to be taking Dol in a Mini if she did not know how to drive the bloody thing? But other emotions gave him the ability to be silent: respect for Barry's joint sense of loss; pity for the girl's father and brothers; simple, sorrowful bewilderment that life could turn so poisonously and so suddenly sad. Barry had Swansea to go back to. For George, there was nothing. Six years older than Dol, it had never occurred to him that he would have to live without her. Cold premonitions, when he had had them during the past few months, had always been smothered in that general sense of optimism of which married people learn the habit, the belief that things will turn out all right really.

Barry was being very good, making up beds, taking sheets to the launderette, manipulating frozen meals in and out of the oven, and trying to do some of the housework. But he would be gone by the end of the week. Vi, too, was being good. She had done baking and ironing and tried to be soothing. Reg was not to be blamed for failing to see that playing his cassette recordings of Hawaiian music had not been quite the thing to do over the funeral baked meats. As for Vi, she was really too upset herself to be of much consolation. George tried not to notice it, again, but he was becoming more than ever conscious of how down-right *vulgar* the woman was: the nail varnish, the swear-words, the cigarettes. It made him more aware than anything of Dol's mysterious absence from the scene. She had been such a decorous person: quiet, wifely, respectable; a good mother to his children.

The drug of television did not do much to lighten the gloom, but George was watching everything, slumped like a sick mastiff on the settee as the brightly coloured images danced and flickered on the screen. Vi found him like this, while Barry was upstairs endeavouring to have half an hour with a book.

'Reg is going down the darts this evening,' she said. 'Why don't you and Barry go with him?'

'I'd rather stay in.'.

'It won't do to mope here all the while, George my old love'; but she added, 'just as you like, though.'

'Yes.' He did not take his eyes off the screen: football, politics, soap opera; *Baggypants and the Nitwits*; the Open University: which was it? He was not really noticing.

'I've made a shepherd's pie. It's in the oven. Barry can cook some frozen peas to go with it,' she said, looking round for an ash-tray.

'Right.'

'You can open a tin of peaches or something for your sweet.'

'Thanks, Vi.'

'Seems funny without her, though, doesn't it?' Already, the wedding photo on the mantelpiece, Dol in a new hat and coat bought cost price at Webbers (where she had worked as an assistant until 1955) seemed to belong to the mists of a vanished age.

'It'll take some getting used to, that's all.' He was trying to adopt his sensible voice, the one which told women that *he* at least had a head on his shoulders and was not going to flap.

'I bought you a bit more tobacco,' she said. 'Barry said as how you was running out.'

'I'll pay you for it,' he said, diverting his eyes for a second or two from the set.

'No. Don't bother. It's a little present.'

'I don't need . . .' What was the use?

'You keep it,' she said, putting the St Bruno on the coffee table before him. 'Barry upstairs?'

George nodded.

'Tell him I popped in, then. I've got to go. It's the first big dinner of term.'

'Oh yes?'

'With any luck I'll be away by half past nine, quarter to ten. Like me to pop in on my way home?'

'Don't bother. Thanks all the same, Vi. I think I'll have an early bed. I feel rather tired, you know.'

'I'm sure you do. You need a bit of a rest. You ought to have a holiday. Go and see Barry when he goes back to Wales. Bit of sea air. That'd be nice.'

'We'll see,' said George. His face had sunk into even gloomier folds. He felt for his new tobacco and opened the tin with a coin, his eyes now fixed, moist and concentrated, on the television set.

Vi checked her face in the hall mirror and then walked down to the bus stop at the roundabout. She could still scarcely believe that it had all happened. A young girl's life senselessly cut short. Dol no longer there to be chatted to . . . Now they would never know the truth about Dol's illness. Had George ever realized? Not properly. Now, the full painful process of such recognition was something he need never make.

She heaved herself on to the bus and was lost in a blanket of sorrow until, with automatic step, she found herself walking into

204

the college pantry. The jokes, the banter, would get her through the evening.

'You're a bit late,' said the butler. 'Been on the bottle then have you?'

'You're one to talk!' And her shrill automatic laughter drowned her own sensations.

Owing to staff problems, they now had women serving at the High Table. Vi had preferred waiting on the undergraduates. You could have a bit of a laugh with them and spill soup down their necks if they got cheeky. Serving the nobs always made her a bit nervous, even though she knew from the ones on her staircase that they were the same as anyone else when you got to know them.

The vast dark medieval hall was so high that you could hardly see the ceiling at night. Lamps and candles blazed on the tables, electric light lit up some of the portraits; but these were only golden pockets in a general blackness.

There was to be cold to start with, bits of ham wrapped round slices of melon, so there was nothing to do except stand to one side until the first course was over. She was waiting and ready as the dons made their way into the hall, so she had a chance to observe them.

The Warden came first, a weird-looking man, beetroot-faced, six foot three and bald as an egg. The servants on the whole liked him. He was benign and generous and always made a point of coming to their Christmas or retiring parties. In Vi's view, a real gentleman. He had been something high up in the previous government; not in the Cabinet, but behind the scenes. His wife was a nice woman, too, quite ordinary, or so people who worked in the lodgings always said. She, of course, was not at the dinner.

The other fellows came trooping in with their guests. Vi saw Mr Brocklehurst with the guest he often brought to these occasions, a tall woman in thick turquoise velvet and blonde hair piled up in a bun. Vi wondered why they never married. It must be lonely for a man living all on his own in a college. She could not imagine putting up with such conditions: no stair-carpet, the toilet half a mile from his bedroom; cold draughts, gloomy uncomfortable furniture, nothing of the homely. She liked him. He gave her a kind smile as he showed his guest to her seat.

'You sit there,' said John, 'next to Garfield.'

There had been a scramble, as so often, to avoid being placed near Sir Jorrocks Monteith. Thirty people milled round at one end of the table, playing a desperate sort of musical chairs in order to be at the Warden's end. Pamela stuck fast between John and Hovis.

'Ah,' said the Professor, 'an unexpected pleasure.'

As the guests pulled themselves together and accepted the unsatisfactoriness of their placement, the Sub-Warden knocked the table with a hammer and grace was said by a scholar in the main body of the hall. The undergraduates said AMEN but this was not said, by convention, at the High Table. Pamela thought she saw the lips of the Chaplain moving, but he was saying to the Bursar, on his left, 'Thank you for being so prompt with the gas men. It turned out, in the event, to be the tap, not the meter.' Then there was a screech of chairs and they were off.

No one passed anything. Pamela was still waiting for pepper when Hovis, having downed his Parma ham in one mouthful and swilled it down with Chablis said, 'You have, I trust, spent a profitable vacation?'

'I went to America.'

'To visit young Brocklehurst?'

'No, no.' She felt foolish to have disclosed the fact to Hovis. But it was something to talk about, something to take his mind off her work.

'Which part did you go to?'

'I was mostly in New York.'

'And doubtless you made abundant use of the Pierpont Morgan? They look after you extraordinarily well, these Yanks. I'm extraordinarily fond of them.' He prosed for a while about air conditioning.

Vi had moved into action, whisking away plates before the last guests had abandoned any hope of getting the fruit from their under-ripe melon. Warm plates were rattled under their noses, but the braised beef was being eaten, the claret glasses being refilled, at Sir Jorrocks's end of the table before the meat reached the Warden.

'The choir was in pretty awful voice tonight,' John said, when vegetables had eventually come.

'I thought they were lovely.'

'But the setting was hideous.'

They always had this debate after evensong. Pamela had a taste for the more modern, shrieky type of Magnificat. For John, art stopped short with S. S. Wesley, anyway as far as church music was concerned.

'You haven't seen Billy, have you?' She thought that she would slip this in as casually as possible over the meal, to avoid embarrassing conversation later in his room.

'Why do you ask?'

'She's gone away for a couple of nights, that's all. I wondered why.'

'We can't very well talk about it at table. I'll tell you afterwards.'

This was so tantalizing that she found herself distracted from the meal, only listening with half an ear while Hovis discussed the inadequacy of a recent volume of the Early English Text Society until the ice-cream came, and Vi was taking Sir Jorrocks his nightly rice pudding. The old man was in good voice, silencing the whole of the end of the table where he sat with accounts of the treatment he was receiving for his arthritic hip. He was still bellowing raucously as they processed out.

'I said to the doctor – this isn't treatment: it's a bad case of assault and battery. Still, mustn't talk too loud, but if you ask me, the Warden isn't walking too well lately . . .'

Vi was not doing coffee in the common-room. She decided to linger for a cigarette with the butler and then catch an early bus home. They'd managed to get dinner over in almost record time.

Gowns were removed, dons and guests adjourned into a high-proportioned eighteenth-century panelled room and sat in a semi-circle round the fireplace. The marginally absurd ceremonies of such evenings always delighted Pamela: the junior fellow moving about like a footman with plates of fruit and chocolates and Oliver biscuits; the port railway scuttling its way up and down across the hearth; cigars and cigarettes held at the ready, to be lit up when the drinks – Sauternes and claret as well as port – had circulated twice.

John, by nature unritualistic, was always embarrassed by the whole procedure. He could not make himself forget the possibilities of social disaster afforded by such occasions, rather than noticing the pleasure that might be given to the guests. His memory was full of ladies who had failed to pass the decanters round and thereby excited the fury of those who wanted to smoke; of young women fainting; or of guileless figures up from London, bored stiff, who had got up to leave before the Warden.

Pamela's feeling was that no one minded – few even noticed – such solecisms; that there was something reassuring about social gatherings in which almost every moment was covered by external rules of etiquette and that once one had achieved a rough mastery of how the thing worked, it was actually more relaxing than 'casual' occasions, where everyone sat round wondering what would happen next. As she liked to quote,

> When the World's great Scorer
> Writes a mark against your name,
> He'll ask, not if you won or lost,
> But how you played the Game.

– a tag from some framed verses which an uncle, a headmaster of Uppingham, had always kept on his study wall.

Lost then, in sheer enjoyment of the scene before her, candlelight glistening on silver and mahogany, thirty or so red faces that had drunk too much, she did not much notice her neighbours round the fireside. John had put her to sit beside a retired professor of philosophy, who liked good-looking young women so long as they listened to his monologues without interruption. The repertoire was fairly limited, and once one had dined with him half a dozen times it was possible to give him only half an ear because one knew what was coming next. His obsessions were Trollope, Peacock, the non-existence of God and the continuing existence of the class system. This evening, in benign mood, he was on Trollope.

'Do you know how many novels Trollope wrote?'

This was merely the catechism, the limbering up before the monologue began.

'About seventy, I imagine.'

'Not a bad guess. Sixty-seven full-length novels. Most people think about twenty. I reckon I have read them all at least twice, and the political novels three or four times. How many words would you say were in an average Trollope novel – *The Claverings*, let's say?'

'Eighty thousand?'

'Oh, more, much more. More like a hundred thousand, I would say. Less in the short ones, of course, like *Rachel Ray* or *Doctor Wortle's School*.'

'Let's say a hundred thousand.'

'Probably more, but it's a good round number. That's, let me see, seven million four hundred thousand words; plus, as I say, the ones I have read more often. Then there's the *Autobiography*, not very long; and the other non-fiction. I bet you didn't know he wrote a book about Thackeray. I should think I've read twenty million words by Trollope. At least twenty million . . .'

It was relaxing to discuss literature in these terms. Pamela used to imagine exam papers in which all the answers could be reduced to the formula of multiple choice, as she believed happened in chemistry. *Tick one of the following:* King Lear *contains a) forty characters; b) twelve characters; c) one hundred and twenty-five characters.* (A trick question for those who had forgotten about the hundred knights.) Or: *The Book of the Duchesse is a) 1334 lines long; b) 7900 lines long; c) 2569 lines long.*

'I've calculated that Trollope wrote a little over ten times as much as Peacock,' her companion was saying; 'half as much again as Sir Walter Scott, but marginally less than St Augustine, who was a Christian and therefore by definition very boring.'

She no longer rose to these baits; no longer even pointed out that Sir Walter Scott was a Christian, too. The Emeritus

Professor's atheism lacked the old fireworks which had made him famous. His tired old arguments now seemed merely ageing, the intellectual equivalent of crows' feet round the eyes of a film star or false timing in a tap dancer. No one was shocked; no one really cared. The objects of his opprobrium – Father d'Arcy, C. S. Lewis, Joad – had all slipped from the scene, leaving him shadow-boxing.

Perhaps disturbed by the pathos of this fact, Pamela turned from her companion to see who was seated on her left. A cadaverous figure was removing the skin of a banana with a knife and fork. He seemed intent on the job. His eyes did not shift from the plate and he did not appear to be making much effort in the direction of conversation. He was seated well back and he was perhaps a yard or two from the nearest candelabra, so that one was not much aware of his appearance; only of distant candlelight glistening in his spectacles, and catching the hairs of his wrists as he dealt with the banana skin. It was so surprising to see him there that Pamela felt she must be mistaken. It was, after all, several months since they had met. But she at last felt emboldened to say,

'It is Mr Tulloch, isn't it?'

He smiled awkwardly.

'Yes, yes, indeed. Have we met before?'

'My name's Pamela Cowper.'

'Ah, yes.' It was hard to tell whether he recognized her or not. He was clearly not a man to clutter his brain with patients' names. On the other hand, she thought he might at least remember her face.

'Whose guest are you?' she asked bluntly. It was slightly unimaginable to her that anyone should elect to spend an evening with the Pillock, but some physiologist had felt it his duty to do so.

'Ah, me, you mean. No, I'm here off my own steam. I have dining rights here on a Sunday, you know.'

The college was full of these people who, for one reason or another, were encouraged to use the place as a club. Sunday was most often the night for them, and there was always a sprinkling of parsons, headmasters and others dining if she came on that particular night.

'Quite nippy,' he remarked, after a pause. She was not altogether sure whether the remark was addressed to her. They had sat so long without saying anything that she had already turned half an ear back to the Emeritus Professor, actually hazarding a guess, wrongly – 'Fifteen!' – for how many of Trollope's heroines get divorced.

'Would you like to move nearer the fire?' Pamela asked, not without malice.

'No, no, it's lovely and warm in here,' Tulloch assured her. 'I meant, the weather has become in general nippy.'

'As you see,' Pamela felt bold to continue, 'I'm still here.'

'Yes, yes.' He appeared to see no significance in what she said.

'I have an appointment to come and see you. Your secretary said that you would be booked up for a fortnight. But since you're here...'

'This is hardly the place for a consultation,' he said. 'If that's what you meant.' She passed him the Sauternes, which he handed on at once, but he refilled his glass with claret when the decanter came round.

'I don't think I need a consultation,' she said. 'As you can see, I am alive; and, as it happens, I have never felt better in my life.'

'I'm very glad to hear it. In that case, what was it you wanted to see me about?'

'You had rather expected me to be dead by now, if you remember.'

He stared and then switched on an expression of benignity.

'What was the name again?'

'Cowper. Pamela Cowper.'

It was impossible to add that he must remember her perfectly well but her tone did as much to suggest it.

'Ah, I remember you now. Of course I do. Well, as I can say, I can hardly discuss your case here and now. But we simply never know, do we?'

'You don't, evidently.'

'I'm very glad you are feeling OK. I'll look forward to seeing you in my consulting room if you've made an appointment.'

'Mr Tulloch, I am perfectly well.' Her voice had sunk to a furious whisper; she was actually spitting with rage. 'If I had taken your treatment I would have gone BALD and I don't know what else would have happened to me. After you said I only had a few more months, I went to America. I was examined there in a huge new hospital and they told me that there was absolutely nothing the matter with me.'

'I never said you weren't entitled to a second opinion. If I thought you were very ill, it would have been irresponsible for me not to recommend treatment. Now, wouldn't it?'

'I'm not saying that. I just think you might be a little more careful. You came to your diagnosis by examining some negatives. Now, if those negatives showed someone very ill, and it wasn't me, it follows that you were looking at the wrong ones. There must be someone walking about who really is about to die, and whom you have said is perfectly all right.'

'No doctor ever makes a diagnosis on the basis of X-ray alone,' he said, trying to generalize the subject and keep the thing on an almost plausible level for after-dinner conversation. 'As for the idea of someone casually muddling up negatives as important as that, it is quite out of the question. If you don't mind my saying so,' he had become very red, and the veins were projecting from his bony forehead, 'I regard the suggestion as highly offensive.'

'*You* find it offensive? What do you think I feel? What about the poor woman's family – they'll find it offensive when they discover that you have failed to treat their mother or their sister or their aunt...'

'This really isn't the place,' he spluttered, 'as I said before... And if I were you, Miss Cowper, I should be very careful before I started to impugn the professional conduct and standards of someone like myself, who, if I may say so...'

'Professional standards!' She spoke aloud.

'What are you talking about?' asked the Emeritus Professor.

'Medical ethics,' said Pamela, trying to recover herself.

'Ah, with Tulloch, yes. There's a good doctor in *Ralph the Heir* and another in *Ayala's Angel* if memory serves me rightly. And then there is *Doctor Thorne* itself. I never quite like the Barsetshire ones, though – the ecclesiastical ones, I should say. So many insufferable clergymen.'

'Surely you can't call Mr Harding insufferable.'

'Oh, quite insufferable. A moral coward of the most despicable kind. Trollope is brilliant, of course, at showing that Christianity is fundamentally immoral. Look at Archdeacon Grantly.'

'My father was an archdeacon. Not one like Grantly.' In her mind's eye she saw his saintly, silver head poring over Agatha Christie or the Greek Testament in that ghastly hospital ward. 'He was much more like Mr Harding,' she said seriously. Then, to rescue the poor Professor, she said, 'What about Mr Arabin, or that rather manly dean in *Is he Popenjoy*?'

'Exactly . . .'

The Warden had risen; some people were already drifting into the neighbouring common-room for more coffee, or whisky and soda. The Emeritus Professor also rose to his feet, silken hands dramatically held to a furrowed brow as he searched for the name of a character momentarily forgotten from *The Three Clerks*.

By the time Pamela looked round, Tulloch was gone.

John, who had been entertaining the Senior Tutor's guest, a South African physicist, now rejoined Pamela and asked if she would like to spend the rest of the evening there or in his room.

'Oh, in your room. We can play the gramophone.'

'OK.'

They wandered down the spiral staircase and out across the quad, which was hung with a heavy mist.

'I'm so angry that I shan't be able to speak for a few moments,' she said.

'What's eating you? Charlie been laying into the Trinity again?'

'No, no. It was Trollope tonight. He was being perfectly good and nice. And besides, I never mind it when he lays into the

Trinity. It all has a nice old-fashioned ring, and they can surely look after themselves; or should one say He can look after Himself?'

'You should know.'

'That poisonous little man, though. I didn't know he had dining rights in this place. You can certainly pick them, can't you?'

'What's all this then?' A mock cockney had been assumed. 'Who's been getting up the wrong side of you then?'

'That wretched little man Tulloch.'

'Old Robby Tulloch? What's he been doing to upset you, then? Did he eat your banana?'

'I don't like bananas.'

'Robby does. Always puts one in his pocket to eat in the car on the way home.'

They had reached John's room now. The gas fire had been on all day and there was an agreeable fug.

'What's it to be,' he asked, surveying his records, 'Scott Joplin, Mozart, Gregorian chant, Handel . . .'

'Got any Katchaturian?'

'At three a.m. I was walking the floor and listening to Katchaturian in a tractor factory. He called it a violin concerto. I called it a loose fan belt and the hell with it.'

She did not respond. There was a time when they had enjoyed capping each other's quotations.

'Course I haven't got Katchaturian,' he continued. 'Got a bit of Brahms, though.'

'Anything swirling and defiant.'

They never listened to the music, unless there was a song with funny words. It just provided a sort of blotting paper for talk; which was peculiar, because they both professed to loathe muzak in public places on the grounds that if the music was worth playing it should be something more than in the background.

'Good man, Robby Tulloch.' John was pouring malt whisky into glasses.

Pamela knew that the moment had come when she would

have to tell John the whole story of her summer vacation. Perhaps if they were able to talk there would be some chance of salvaging their friendship from the wreckage. But other feelings fought for predominance. Jealousy was uppermost. It seemed outrageous that he should appear to know where Billy was. And she felt angry with him for speaking so warmly of the Pillock.

'Aren't you going to tell me where Billy is?'

'What?'

'At dinner you said we'd talk afterwards.'

'Do we really need to?'

She felt flummoxed. She only had a limited amount of spirit for this conversation and his stalling tactics broke her nerve. They listened to Brahms swirling for a bit and as they did so her mind went back over the dinner searching for nice things to say about it.

'Your Warden's a sweety.'

'What sort of sweety?'

'Oh, an old-fashioned chocolate liqueur, I think.'

'How about the others – the Chaplain is, I suppose, really a soft centre. Jorrocks Monteith is a too-good-to-hurry mint.'

'Your Bursar is an extra strong mint, perhaps. And Hovis is something fruity – but nutty as well. A fruit and nut case, I suppose.'

'What about the Emeritus?'

'Oh, a sweet you can eat between meals without spoiling your appetite. Or should that be your astronomer? What,' she added in a tone which she hoped would shift the conversation to things she actually wanted to discuss – 'What about us?'

'Oh, we're both crystallized fruits, surely.'

'It's ghastly that all this has happened,' she began again, 'but don't you think we should try and talk about things a bit? I love Billy – don't you understand? I adore and love her.'

'Where does that get you?' He was still trying to keep the thing on an abrasive level of humour. He sucked noisily on his pipe and looked at the fire.

'I used to wish I knew what was going on inside that head of yours. Now I am glad not to know.'

215

'I'm not sure I know myself.'

'That's easy enough to say. You know, I've never been so struck, as during the past few months, by the appalling futility of our lives. I almost wonder whether it's not *us* that are the trouble, whether we aren't bad for each other. No, don't protest; for once in a while I want to try to be serious. Look at all those people at dinner. All Sorts, you might say, if not actually Fruit and Nut. But in a peculiar sort of way, most of them are sincere. Most people outside academic life would think it was fairly insane to live like that – day in, day out, tutorials, dinners, research into subjects that no one – a handful of people perhaps – cares about. But there is a sort of purity about it. They on the whole believe in what they are doing. They on the whole...'

'This is ludicrous. Jorrocks Monteith has never "helped" anyone in his life, since he helped the college to build a new library floor in 1927 and was mysteriously elected to a life fellowship. I very much doubt whether any young person has ever been "helped" by a tutorial from anyone. They are largely content to get up...'

'All right. Let us assume that I am being highly sentimental about the others. But what about us? Here am I – forty nearly – it's my job to teach and analyse the use of the English language – heaven help us! – and I can never bring myself to say what I mean.'

'Perhaps that's because you don't mean anything much of the time.'

'That's horrid.'

'No it isn't. You always say yourself that deep down you are superficial. Where's your sense of humour?'

'Damn my sense of humour. Why should I never be allowed to be serious?'

'Because if the present conversation is anything to go by, being serious makes you embarrassing and boring.'

So it had come to this: abuse and raised voices between friends who prided themselves on being decorous and civilized.

'What are *you* up to?' she resumed, biting a lip and trying not to be shocked.

'You know perfectly well what I'm up to – writing a few books – doing a bit of teaching – sitting on a few committees – going for a few walks . . .'

'You're meant to be a philosopher – you set yourself up as an inquirer after truth. We tried to think of ourselves as a pair of crystallized fruits – but we aren't. We're just a couple of Old Fashioned Humbugs.'

'I'm afraid your metaphors aren't making much sense.'

She stared at him. His pudgy features terrifyingly had become ugly and contorted. She suddenly hated the crinkled gingery hair, the glistening forehead, the heavy thick neck.

'If you don't tell me where Billy is, I shall never speak to you again.'

'OK.' He turned to face her. 'Billy's in hospital, if you must know. She came round here and asked me to arrange it. I knew it was Robby Tulloch's line of country. She'll be home in a day or so.'

She felt herself blushing very deeply, and she once more bit her lips, trying not to cry. 'That seems rather a shame,' was all that she could manage.

The record came to an end.

'Other side, or shall we have something more cheerful?'

'I don't feel cheerful. You don't understand what you've done.'

'You're the one who doesn't understand,' he said fiercely. 'It was nothing to do with you. It was my problem and Billy's, not yours. You are just being absurd and sentimental. You aren't in love with Billy and nor is she with you. You both got caught up with each other, that's all, in the way people do.'

'And what about *you* and Billy?' She felt too shocked to respond fully. What made his words so painful was that, as he said them, they sounded true.

'The same, I suppose. Now, for God's sake don't let's talk about it. Have another drink.'

'I won't thanks, John. For some reason, I feel rather tired. I think if you don't mind I'll go home.'

217

It was the first time for years that they had parted, of an evening, without a kiss.

Confused waves of sorrow enfolded her as she walked home through the dark streets. Light from college gateways pierced the mist. Parties were breaking up. Grey-headed, port-faced men were lurching, gowns tossed over their shoulders, towards their cars. Young people bayed and roared and embraced. Vagrant winoes hovered, clutching cider bottles, accosting the occasional passer-by.

The ghastliness of the evening was none of it, perhaps, John's fault. He had behaved as she would have predicted. So had Tulloch. Even the hateful intertwining of these two men's lives – for she now had no doubt of it – could not in itself explain her mood. She would see John again: she would always love him, perhaps. In the right mood, she would always find him amusing. But it would never be as it had been. From now on, inevitably, the gaps between their meetings would grow longer, the spiritual distance between them more impassable.

Was it Billy? More blatantly, Pamela felt it was love or lust itself which explained it. In an impossibly sad way, it would not have much mattered whether Billy or another had precipitated the crisis. Theirs was a friendship, Pamela's and John's, which had depended on a shared conspiracy never to be serious, never to touch the nebulous areas of life about which others feel intensely. It was this, quite apart from the distinctiveness of their own predilections, which had shaped their destiny to the point where a love affair between them would have been unthinkable; for a love affair would have meant, if only momentarily, an agreement to say what they meant without resorting to irony. Both of them found such emotional restrictiveness necessary in their everyday lives. Both, on the other hand, pined for something different. Both, by a hateful chance, had fled from the delicacies of their shared obliqueness into the arms of the same refuge. Billy's desire to get things straight, to disentangle the jokes and the sarcasms, to have things explained: these, quite as much as her beauty, had made her attractive.

Yet, by their sudden conjunction, Pamela now found both

repellent and embarrassing. She hated herself for having been unable to reconcile these opposites, for needing both Billy and John – or for *having* needed them. Because she loved them both, she regretted their passing. The thought of losing Billy was still too painful to hold in the mind, for she still felt in effect drunk with the girl. Her thoughts were never any more in repose, for every moment was devoted to an aching awareness of Billy's absence, a tearing desire to know where, exactly, she was; what, precisely, she was doing; who, precisely, she was with; who, if anyone, she loved. That old childish set of questions *Who is your best best friend? Who is the person you love most in the whole wide world?* which had tormented Pamela when her hair was in bunches and sticking plasters covered both knees, were the ones which Love raised again. The idea that Billy wanted to spend a single hour with someone other than herself was torture to the imagination. She hated her feelings for Billy because it was so obvious that they could never bring anything but torment and uncertainty.

> *It was begotten by Despair*
> *Upon Impossibility*

and now in her gloom she felt drawn to seek some pillar of fire which could lead her from this wilderness. What was lacking from it all? What was it, that in loving Billy and regretting John she had betrayed in herself? For the cause of her sorrow was self-hatred. She felt let down less by Tulloch and John than by her own departure from something long glimpsed from afar and sought after and loved, but not known.

Fairly certainly, such aspirations for a love beyond herself could be viewed in crudely psychological or theological terms. But while religion perhaps came into it, her longing was broader than that. A love which could be serious – which yet admitted all her own incurable ironies – that was it. A love which was not solemn but which exalted kindness above everything. Could there ever be a justification for unkindness? – either for her own habitual verbal malice or the actual unkindness she had shown to Tulloch, or, in the past, to Slobbering-Myles, or which John had somehow demonstrated towards Billy? Well, yes, surely. Unkindness was justified if it was funny: not if it made others laugh, necessarily, but if it reassured one that the craziness of life was in some nebulous way under control. She found her mind churning into a circle. Funny – well, life was surely funny enough without dragging *humour*, *comedy* into it? It was not humour, really, or even malice that she found herself fleeing. It was the character which had become encrusted about her soul: a thinness of mind which made kindness almost impossible.

She hated the pass to which things had come: the tatters of her emotional and professional life seemed unimpressive trophies to have snatched from the jaws of Death and the Pillock. She knew that life held something different in store for her, something which was worthy of her, not because it was better than anything she had done before but because in an unpredictable way it would be enjoyable. It was not so much the crude social fear of what people would say. Something much more fundamental was at stake, the opportunity to start life again.

Later, drinking Ovaltine in bed, a limp red-leather volume of *Praeterita* and the latest Penguin *Rex Stout Omnibus* open on the covering, neither able to grip her attention, she realized it was a sort of homesickness. Her melancholy very slightly dazed her wits to the point that she imagined it would be half possible to pack her bags and go to see her father in the lovely Archdeacon's lodgings. When she came to herself, however, it was not with bitterness. Two strokes had polished off her mother shortly after her father's lingering death in hospital, and one day she would follow them, but not so soon as she had imagined. She no longer cynically viewed death as a friend; nor did she desperately dread it. She had moved on. The new homesickness, melancholy enough, was shot through with the reassuring conviction that homecoming of a sort could be achieved. This bijou little house was all very well in its way. It had been fun transforming it from a slum into a place of such *chic* elegance.

But it had never been *home*: never pretended to be. Would a baby have made it like home? Now, apparently, the question was not worth asking. Billy would come back; and it would be lovely to see her. But from now on, there would be an awkwardness between them; and they would both be wondering how long they could go on living in the same town, with John hovering in the background. She was not yet strong enough to steel herself for Billy's departure: but it would happen, as her clear, depressed state of mind made obvious to her. And it was not just embarrassment about John and the baby – it was the fact that Billy was simply not her type. Their infatuation with each other would simmer down – as Hereward had predicted – and then what? Pamela knew there would be shrieking rows about the washing-up and conversations at cross-purposes and unlikeable friends brought back to the house; not brought home: for it was not home. And Billy was not, really, domestic. Nor, for all that they had shared so much, was John. It always seemed perfectly appropriate to Pamela that he should lead an institutional life. Home was a shared world: a shared set of little sadnesses; jokes, as well, doubtless, but jokes and irony alone could not sustain it. It was not that she wanted to go all solemn. It was that she wanted a life in which laughter was a natural indulgence, never a retreat.

It was after midnight and so hardly the time you would have expected the telephone to ring. An American voice said: 'I have a call for you: will you hold the line please.' And then a very crackly voice said, 'Billy, sugar, is that you?'

'No,' said Pamela.

'Billy, honey, this is Gale.'

'Billy isn't here. She's gone away for a few days. This is Pamela here, Gale.'

'Billy, speak up, I can't hear you too well – can you speak up – oh, my gosh, operator, what kind of a line is this? Have you put me through or haven't you?'

'I can hear you, Gale!' Pamela could not really raise her voice. She had never in her life had to. But she did her best.

'I got your wire, Billy.'

221

'Gale, it's Pamela here.'

'Oh my gard . . .'

'Gale, can you hear me?'

'Hallo? Who's that speaking?'

'Pamela.'

'Hi Pamela. This line's just awful. Is Billy there?'

'No. She's out.'

'Listen, Pamela, honey, can you tell Billy that I've got her wire and that I've got a flight fixed for the end of the week. Maybe Friday, or Saturday morning if I'm not lucky. I'm sorry it isn't sooner but you'll never believe the trouble I've had getting this show on the road.'

'Friday or Saturday, right.'

'Is Billy all right? Her wire was very worrying.'

'Yes,' she supposed. 'Yes, Billy's perfectly all right.'

'Mel's coming with me. He thought maybe we could look up a few friends. And he wants to go to Lincoln and maybe Barnchurch if we can fit that in. He's never been to Barnchurch.'

'OK, Gale!'

'Look, are you really sure Billy is all right? What was she doing in the hospital, for Godssakes . . .?'

But then the line went dead.

- *19* -

One keyed oneself up for life's big moments, only to find them quieter, less full of incident, than one had expected; not difficult to handle: unnecessary, indeed, to 'handle' at all. Reunion with Billy followed this form. Since Pamela had not been told the girl's movements, she had been unable to collect her from the hospital. By the time she rang up they said that Miss Mac-Namara was coming home in a taxi, and after the elapse of less than an hour, Billy was on the doorstep, pale and unhappy, but at least there. Pamela felt anxious to hold her, but afraid that it would cause pain. During her own experience in the summer, one of the main reasons for keeping her own sojourn in hospital secret had been the dread of embraces from colleagues who were too shocked or embarrassed to know what to say. The last thing she had wanted was sudden haphazard pressing against her more sensitive parts. And although Billy's troubles had not been the same, the fear lingered that she would be in what the medical profession called discomfort. So they leaned forward and kissed each other on the lips with no other physical contact.

'It's eleven o'clock. You probably had lunch hours ago, but let me make you some coffee.'

'Everything in hospital's so *early*,' Billy confirmed. She sat gingerly on the Welsh kitchen chair and drummed her fingers on the table-top.

'Where shall I put my things?' she asked.

No more needed to be said. Both mysteriously knew that their former bedding arrangements had become a thing of the past. The momentous transition from love into friendship seemed to have slipped by without needing to be spelt out. Pamela had feared the need to talk it all through, to ask who had gone wrong and with whom. Billy had dreaded trying to articulate the awkwardness of being torn between John and Pamela, while not wanting, strictly, to be attached to either. She did not know what had happened to her. She felt profoundly depressed, but the depression had no isolable cause or object: regret for the child, sorrow for what had passed between herself and Pamela, or merely a dull low pain, a sense of headache and tiredness; any of these were equally plausible.

'I've made up the little bed in the box-room at the front,' said Pamela. 'Would you like to lie down now?'

This seemed a good plan. Pamela would not have conceived it possible that so much colour could have disappeared from a girl's face. She looked almost grey with exhaustion.

'I think,' Pamela added, 'that we ought to get the doctor. You don't look all that bright to me. Did they look at you today in the hospital?'

'The nurses came round. They were foul – like they were really mad at me.'

'But not the doctors?'

'I haven't seen a doctor since . . .'

While Pamela telephoned, Billy climbed the stairs and flopped on to the little divan in the 'spare room', a Little Ease eight by ten, lined from floor to ceiling with crime fiction. By the time coffee was carried up Billy was in her pyjamas.

'What in God's name have they done to you?' Pamela exclaimed as she surveyed the pile of clothes on the floor. They appeared to be drenched with blood.

Billy merely shook her head on the pillow and felt the tears trickling down her cheeks.

'Poor old Slobbering-Myles is coming,' continued Pamela. 'You really ought to be *seen*, at least.'

'The coffee's great.' She sipped quietly. 'I've missed you.'

'I've missed you, too, darling girl.'

'And you aren't mad?'

'I'm cross with myself for having been so foolish. We don't need to go into it all now, do we?'

'I guess not. So long as you aren't mad at me. All those things you said about you and me and the baby and . . . Oh, Pamela, it wouldn't have worked out, it just wouldn't.'

'I see that, old thing. I see that.'

'Not with John, and you, and me . . . and Christ; oh, I don't know; I feel so unhappy.'

'Gale's coming.'

There was a pause. Billy stared open-eyed and astonished.

'She *is*?'

'She rang last night. It was a bad line, but I think we can expect them by the end of the week. They are going to stay at Barnchurch, wherever that is.'

'They? She's not bringing Mel?'

'So it would appear.'

'What did you want to tell them to come over here for? Isn't there enough chaos already? Do they know what's happened?'

'I don't think so. Gale seemed to know you had been in hospital, but I don't know whether she guessed what for.'

'Maybe we could say I was run down by a truck.'

'A truck? They'll think it's a bit odd you haven't any broken bones or anything.'

'I'll say I was just shook up. But why in hell did you have to tell them?'

The truth was not in her. Neither, Pamela reflected as she went downstairs to answer the doorbell, had it been in any of them, John or herself. The whole episode had been founded on concealments and half-truths and mistakes. How, if Billy had not told them, could Gale have known she was in hospital, unless it was hospital policy to wire the relations of foreign girls . . .

'Look here,' said Swynnerton-Myles elbowing his way through the door, 'is this really as important as you said?'

'She's upstairs,' said Pamela. 'I'll wait for you down here.'

She found, as she wandered up and down it, that she no longer liked her drawing-room: yellow velvet was too much a combination of 'nineties and Trust House and she would be happy if she never saw a Morris wallpaper again in her life.

She hoped that Swynnerton-Myles would not be too offensive to Billy, in the way that RCs so often were about this sort of thing. Pamela felt that no one at that moment could be more passionately hostile than she was herself to that operation, but she was sure Billy was not in a mood for a lecture about the sanctity of life. She patted cushions and cleared the sofa ready for the tweed bum. But when he appeared after ten minutes or so and he had settled with his coffee, she concluded that she had been underestimating him.

'She'll be OK,' he said. There was a tenderness in the genial creases of his face. 'Let's hope to God she'll be OK.'

'You mean she isn't?'

'She seems all right. Don't be too worried by all the bleeding. It's a horrible business – a violent thing. You can't tell all at once whether it will have done any lasting damage.'

'You know who was responsible, I suppose?' she said.

'It's hardly relevant now, is it. If she had been prepared to name the father it would never have happened.'

'I mean, do you know who *aborted* the baby?'

He smiled at her and named the hospital. 'Someone up there. They're doing them every day. People crowd in from all over the world.'

'It was your friend Robby Tulloch.'

He drank some coffee in silence.

'As you might have guessed, I don't like what's happening. A human life is a human life whether it's been born or not.'

Here we go, thought Pamela, but he didn't.

Instead, he said, 'It's not really for me to be anyone else's conscience, though. If Robby thought it was necessary, it was up to him – a matter between him and his patient.'

'I've less trust than you have in what Mr Tulloch thinks is right. If I'd taken his advice my system would have been pumped full of some loathsome drug. As it is – I told you the other week – there's nothing the matter with me.'

'I'll be glad when you've had the tests here all the same. When is it – a fortnight?'

'Obviously, I can't expect you to listen to criticisms of another doctor, but don't you think they're behaving pretty oddly? I mean, on the same day...' And she told him again of her suspicion about her X-rays being muddled.

'It frankly seems to me highly unlikely. No' – he really was being quite human and nice – 'no, I'm not just saying it. I've nothing to gain by covering up other doctors' mistakes, but you ought to be a bit more careful before you go round making accusations like that, you know. Who is the other woman – do you have any suspicions? Have you been to see her? If your theory is correct, she'd be in a pretty bad way by now.'

'It's been awkward. One can't barge into someone's house and ask them if they realize that they are fatally ill. I've kept meaning to call round and see her, but somehow I've been preoccupied with Billy's comings and goings; and other things.'

'What's this woman's name or would you rather not say?'

'Dorothy Higgs. I don't mind saying at all. She lives on that estate up beyond the roundabout. Off your beat, I suppose.'

'No it isn't.' He drained the last of his coffee. 'I have quite a lot of patients up there.' He was staring intently at the carpet.

'Well, my friend is called Dorothy Higgs – 38 Maypole Rise – and her husband is called George and does something at the Press and her son is at the University of Swansea. We got to know each other really quite well in a funny sort of way when we were in hospital. It wasn't the sort of thing you could exactly follow up afterwards – we just weren't the same sort – but you know how these things are –'

'Oh dear,' said Swynnerton-Myles, 'oh dear.'

'She isn't a patient of yours, is she?'

'I can't really discuss my patients with you, can I? Whatever I thought about Mrs Higgs was a matter for her and me and her family. But we'll never know now.'

'Do you mean she's actually . . .' Pamela's mouth fell open with shock. 'You mean she's dead and you still don't believe what I'm saying?'

'She was killed in a car crash a few weeks ago. It was in the local papers. I'm . . .'

She could not believe it. Yet what she said surprised even herself – 'It must have been nice for her to have a family – someone to grieve for her. If it had been me, there would have been no one.'

'I'm sure that's not true. Mrs Higgs was in many ways such a sad person. There was never much you could do for her. She was always so anxious not to give offence, not to cause a fuss – very unlike some people. She seemed to lead a completely self-contained life. You can't know what you are saying by comparing yourself to her. I don't imagine a soul went to the funeral. The son was a sort of yobbo. They did not have any friends . . .'

'Was her husband hurt in the crash?'

'He wasn't with her. It was some young woman. They were in a Mini. Hit a lorry full on.'

'I saw them – we had tea together. Rather a silent, chewing sort of girl. I thought it must be Dorothy's niece.'

227

'She may have been. I forget the details. Look, I must be going.'

'Must you? Please don't. I want someone to talk to.'

Surprisingly, he seemed agreeable to the suggestion.

'You're worried. I can see that. So long as you could convince yourself that Mrs Higgs was dying of cancer you'd come to feel in a superstitious sort of way that you were OK yourself. Now we'll never know and it makes you feel uneasy . . . perhaps a little frightened.'

'Perhaps that's it. Do you remember when you were persuading me to take Tulloch's medicine you said I mustn't expect miracles?'

'Did I?'

'I'm sorry. I was rude to you that day.'

'You were rather. If you've really been cured, or if there was nothing wrong with you, though, it looks as though you had every right to be.'

'I've missed something out of my story. I've told you Mr Tulloch's diagnosis?'

'But I've read it. It wasn't good, you know. I don't want to be alarmist, but this disease does funny things. You can have remissions and feel perfectly all right – sometimes for months, sometimes for years – and then it comes back. It really wasn't very wise to discard all medical advice.'

'And then I went to the States and I was put on a scanner and they said there was nothing the matter with me at all.'

'That, I agree, is wonderfully encouraging. I'm not defending Robby. It's possible there was some kind of mistake. God knows, doctors are only human.'

'But I haven't told you about Walsingham.'

So she did. It was not simply in order to crow over him for belonging to a benighted, erroneous, schismatic branch of the Catholic church; or to do anything so vulgar as to prove to him that she had had an experience which beat Lourdes or Knock any day of the week. She spoke in a tone of genuine inquiry.

'You see,' she said, 'this not knowing about Mrs Higgs throws

228

the ball back in my court, doesn't it? Poor Dorothy. She was such a frightened little thing but I was in a strange way fond of her. Just egotism, I suppose. I felt oddly that our destinies were linked together.'

'Miracles happen – of course they do.' His tone *did* suggest that he'd be pretty surprised to hear of any happening at the hands of a clergyman who wasn't strictly kosher, but the story interested him.

She expected him to elaborate the point, but he didn't. He merely said, 'Hereward's a marvellous man.'

'Yes, yes, he is.'

'People round here think the world of him, of course. Even call him "father". That's what he's become to so many of them.'

'I know that,' she said.

'I'm not High Church myself, as it happens. Go to St Andrew's, always have.' The extraordinary neo-Norman building to which he referred was a bastion of Low Church principle.

She was silenced by this news. He must be teasing her.

'Even so, I have the greatest regard for these High-Church celibates, the greatest regard. Fundamentally, men like Hereward have more in common with Evangelicals like myself than with the wishy-washy brigade.'

'I didn't realize . . . I thought somehow . . .'

She was hardly able to get out a coherent sentence while she ushered him to the front door. There must have been some reason, initially, for supposing him RC. Instead, a wonderful old north-ender. She could have kissed him.

When he was gone, she went upstairs to see Billy.

'He's so nice,' said Billy, '– I had no idea – after all the things you'd said about him being pompous and . . .'

'Oh, he's OK some of the time.'

'He thinks I'm going to be all right. The bleeding's normal – not so frightening as it looks. He asked if I was all right for money and he said if I need any more medical treatment I'm to call him up and not to worry about expenses and everything.

Really, Pamela, you are horrible sometimes' – she said it quite nicely – with something of her old laughter – 'he doesn't slobber – and as for being fat: well, he's really not as fat as John.'

There was coffee to be cleared away, lunch to be thought about, the day to be got through. Billy was right of course about Slobbering-Myles: he was, by his lights, not a bad doctor. It was kind of him not to have *lectured* the girl. And he couldn't help the voice.

The way that he had broken the Dorothy news had shown some delicacy. Billy could scarcely be expected to understand its import and there was no point in discussing it with her. Pamela could not feel grief as for the death of a friend. It was disturbing, not distressing, news. Her first thought had been irritation that the Pillock had been let off the hook. She could scarcely challenge his diagnosis now and, in her own case, one could not very well sue a doctor for suggesting treatment which subsequently turned out to be unnecessary; not if one had refused the treatment anyhow. The further she drifted away from the experiences of the summer the more their mystery would take on the colouring of any interpretation she chose to place on them.

It was not a question of whether Our Lady of Walsingham could or could not perform miracles – for she saw that Hereward had been right: that the thing only bore significance if she was able to feel the whole of life transformed, devoted to truth, not fantasy; kindness, not malice; serenity, not panic. This would all lie ahead. For the moment, there was one thing she could not tolerate, and this was Billy's proposal to lie to Gale. It was not so much the dishonesty itself: that, she had come to swallow. But following so hard on the actual death of Dorothy it seemed tasteless to pretend that one had had a motor accident when one hadn't. She bearded Billy with it later in the day.

'Look, old thing. I don't think you *can* tell the fib about being run over. Wouldn't it be better to tell the truth?'

They were lingering over their tea. The curtains were drawn, the lamps lit.

'Let me do it my way, Pamela, *please*.'

'But why? John was surely the difficult one to face. I just don't see, now he knows about it and the thing is finished, why you have to worry Gale with lies about motor accidents.'

'What's the difference?'

'Motor accidents are horrid: not things to be joked about. That's the difference.'

'I *can't* tell them the truth.'

'Why not? They'd understand: they're not opposed to abortion, I am sure. If you'd asked them, they would probably have put up the money without all the bother of your coming over here.'

'Is that all it's been – a bother?'

'I didn't mean it like that – you know that.'

'I came because I wanted to see Europe, because I wanted to see you . . . Oh, I don't know why I came. But you surely don't think I'm so calculating that I'd get you to help me to come to Europe and then drop you?'

'I don't know what you think.'

'OK, so I probably should never have come, so it's all been one big screw-up. I just really thought it would work out, that's all.'

'It isn't very helpful looking for motives for everything, is it? I just don't see why you think it's essential not to tell Mel and Gale. They'll surely guess.'

'I want to spare them.'

'Spare them what? They aren't fools.'

'I don't want Mel to guess the truth, that's all. I don't want John to guess it either. I know I've done wrong but I couldn't help myself. I was desperate: what else could I do?'

'It was John's responsibility. I can see that.' She recalled with bitterness the acrimonious evening when he had been at pains to make this so clear.

'I made it his responsibility.'

'That's an odd way of looking at it. I should have thought that he made it yours: and you took the only way out you could. I tried to help you, but you didn't want that . . .'

'Everyone's so keen on knowing and telling me how I ought to behave all the time. But I feel bad all the same.'

'I don't see why you should. John's ...'

'Oh, stop saying John's name. I feel so goddammed awful about it I could commit suicide. But I needed the money.'

There was an electrifying pause.

'What money?'

'The money for the operation.'

'And John paid it presumably.'

'Yes, yes. I made John pay for it.'

'Well, wasn't that understandable in the circumstances?'

'It may have been understandable, but it was wrong.'

'I don't see why. If he was the father of your baby ...'

The truth took a little time to dawn.

'Oh,' said Pamela. She felt stupid, naive. Now she had the horrible sensation that she had indeed been tricked. The baby she had promised to rear was not John's at all. The whole thing had been a lie – and to what end?

'John Brocklehurst may think he knows a lot about women but he doesn't,' Billy said.

'Do I really have to hear all this?'

'You've heard so much now I just have to tell you the rest. OK, so he screwed me some.'

'All day every day by an earlier account.'

'We had some great times.' There was a pathetic, almost childish sarcasm in her voice. 'Pamela, do I have to spell it out for you?'

'As I said, I would rather you didn't. But I'm not sure. Are you now telling me that you were really John's mistress?'

'Not everything you do in bed means you're going to get yourself pregnant.'

'Then perhaps I'd rather you didn't spell it out.'

'I've said, he screwed me – some. But most of the time ...'

'Look, old thing, it's better for me not to know, isn't it? Are you telling me that you weren't pregnant?'

'What do you think I've been doing up at that fucking scout

232

camp you call a hospital – not making daisy chains, I can tell you. Oh, yes. I was pregnant OK.'

'Well, then.'

Pamela felt cross. Why drop these lurid hints about unproductive erotic practices if it came to the same thing in the end?

'As I say, he screwed me a little. I'm not denying that. But Pamela, that man's a pervert. Most of the time, I might just as well have been a boy for all the things he wanted...'

'Please don't, Billy. I've told you, I just don't want to know.'

'All right – so you want it all very civilized – you don't want to talk about it – you want it all swept away where you needn't think about it; men only have dicks for watering the garden. OK, if that's the way you want it. Then you can carry on thinking of John as a wonderful civilized, jokey, sophisticated professor.'

'You're mistaken. Can't you see you've poisoned my friendship with John without all this?'

They stared at each other, Pamela beetroot and close to tears, Billy pale and shaking.

'Pamela, I had a period after John left for Mexico.'

It was impossible to reply to all this; it was too worrying, so nauseating.

'I think you ought to know; that's all. That's how I know John wasn't the father of my baby. I told them up at the hospital it was four, maybe five months. They looked at me like I was crazy...'

'You can't mean this.'

'I know. I'm full of shit. I let him think he was the father. I let him pay for the abortion. Do you think it feels good, being full up to the eyeballs with shit?'

'It's hardly a feeling I've ever put into words. I simply can't understand ... why you did it.'

'Why I left Cornell, came here, had an abortion? How I got pregnant – is that what you're wondering?'

'Yes.'

'Mel.'

Billy had told so many lies by now that Pamela could not

discern whether this was another of them. It seemed that every-thing the girl said and did was being calculated to torture and cause pain.

'*Mel* is the father of your child? But . . .'

'How come I was letting him screw me? I've been going with Mel on and off now for five years – since I was fifteen.'

'With Mel?' It still seemed incredible.

'I didn't like it so much at first. It seemed kinda sneaky, with Gale being so kind to me, almost like the mother I never properly had. We never did it often – we'd been so discreet. Then somehow after John left I felt so lonesome I guess I was just less careful than usual, that's all.'

'And that's why you're so anxious that Mel and Gale should never know that you have been pregnant?'

'Can't you see that?'

'Oh, Billy, I can't see anything. It all seems so hopelessly muddled and miserable. I thought you were such a sweet little thing – well, you still are a sweet little thing – but I thought you were an innocent abroad: a little Henry James heroine.'

'And I'm not, huh?'

She seemed actually to take Pamela's sorrow as a compliment. A smile returned to her lips. She added, 'Do we stick to the truck story?'

'You can tell them anything you like,' said Pamela. 'I'm not up to lying any more.'

– 20 –

She found a sort of consolation in the fact that the remaining days with Billy were so painful. It made certain the inkling which had begun to dawn even before her unhappy colloquy with John that the infatuation was over. As Hereward liked to quote,

Surely if each one saw another's heart,
There would be no commerce,
No sale or bargain pass: all would disperse
And live apart.

Their separation – hers and Billy's – would have happened without the cruel revelation that she had simply been 'used' by the girl. Nothing, she knew, could be so simple as the conversation implied. Billy, thrown about in a chaos of self-ignorance, was hardly responsible for her actions. But it helped to be infuriated by her, and to bottle up the fury, and to appear oblivious of the noise and the mess which she brought with her. Billy, the days revealed, was a girl who never closed a door, she slammed it. If she made herself a Welsh rarebit she never cleaned the little drips of melted cheese which had collected in the grill pan and she only occasionally remembered to switch off the gas. She was a girl who did not know the difference between a plate and an ash-tray and if she noticed ash spilt on the carpet she did not bother to sweep it up. Nor was there much place, in her conduct of life, for putting the tops back on jars and bottles after use; and when she borrowed toothpaste without permission the top of *that* mysteriously vanished. The efforts she made to be useful were as maddening as her negligences. It had taken half an hour to find a tin opener put back in the wrong place, and butter, meant for the cupboard, was frozen hard in the fridge. A good Brie had been refrigerated, too, with the eggs (an absurd idea) and, of all things, the sherry. There were smalls hanging up in the bathroom when one wanted to wash one's hair and at night the kitchen window had been left open with the inevitable smells of cat next morning.

The larger shock – the sense of betrayal, the sense of self-reproach, the poignant sense of a lost love – was absorbed into all these smaller shocks of domestic fury. She had glimpsed another's heart, and all had indeed dispersed and vanished.

The effects of the whole Billy episode on relations with John could only be measured much later. When Pamela rang him to say that Mel and Gale would be in town he had been friendly enough and said how sorry he was to miss them. He was off to Dublin to examine a thesis. In term? Apparently. They made no further arrangement to meet, though. She was glad he had not suggested it. It would be no kindness to reveal to him that he, too, had been tricked, as well as she: that the creature destroyed by the Pillock's machinery bore no relation to anyone on this side of the Atlantic. Besides, she no longer knew what to believe. *Mel.* Admittedly, she had hardly given herself much chance to get to know the man. But it was grotesque to imagine this quasi-incestuous union being part of a regular arrangement spanning a number of years. What an odd thing, though, to invent. Either way, it was embarrassing, abhorrent to her. She had seen enough into that particular set of hearts to satisfy herself that she did not want to see more.

Billy probably felt equally disillusioned with her, if the truth were known. How would she see Pamela? It was impossible to guess: over-inhibited, apparently, restrained to the point of neurosis, stuck up, superior, sentimental. Pamela did not give herself the chance to inquire whether this was an accurate guess. The girl was out much of the time, returning only at awkward hours for messy snacks, and slamming the front door without saying where she was going. Silence had descended between them.

Pamela was contented enough, in a miserable way, with the solitude it provided her. She had turned up a few chapters, written years before, about the poetry of Gower, and wondered in a desultory way whether there might not be something there for a book. There were still twelve weeks before she had to start teaching again, and she spent some happy hours one morning recovering the delights of work in an ancient library. The painted ceiling, the bays lined with calf volumes, the misty views of a great dome seen through the low-lying window at her elbow brought peace which set her mind to work again. The obscure pleasures of learning began, after an interval of nearly ten years, to flood back into her brain, as she fingered vellum and resurrected her memories of the great work. Parallels, odd readings, mistranscriptions, eccentricities of syntax in her old author struck her afresh. The Alexander Romances could wait. Gower's English poetry, too, she would save up until she was once more fully the mistress of his magnificent latinity. It amused her that, for once in a while, she was enjoying herself in a manner of which Hovis would have approved.

Libraries offer their own companionship. There were colleagues there whom she had not seen for months, one of whom bought her coffee, another of whom gave her luncheon. Gossip, malice, jokes, the latest fantastic episode thrown up from the lives of the more absurd exhibitionists in the university provided the stuff of some of their conversation. Everyone had something to say about the dreadfulness of the Professor of Poetry. But it was all only punctuation for what she actually wanted to discuss: had Gower read this or that of Isidore, of Seneca, of Ovid; where was he during the Peasants' Revolt? Had anyone noticed parallels between this and that passage of the *Vox Clamantis* in Chaucer's *Parson's Tale*; did anyone know that this figure anticipated a *topos* in Lydgate's *Fall of Princes*; was it not striking that *Vox Clamantis* was quoted in a Trinity manuscript hitherto supposed to be Wycliffite? This was their talk.

By the time she was cycling home after three days spent in such a way she felt the need for companionship of a more personal character and it was almost without thinking that she parked her bike outside Hereward's house.

He had just said evensong and was still in his cassock.

'Let's have some sherry,' he said, closing the study door. 'Frideswide is making my supper.'

Pamela thought it smelt like liver. There were so many things that she had never really asked him – fundamental things, such as his favourite dishes. There had not been enough quiet evenings, when they simply sat together and enjoyed one another's company. Nervous agitation too often took over, the desire to drive things to crisis point or to smoke himself into a fury about theology.

She sipped the cheap Cyprus.

Was it that she had failed to allow herself to notice, or had it been there all along as something she had grown so used to that she scarcely knew it was there? Or was it a new development, arising out of her recent disillusionments? Of one thing she was fairly sure: it was not just a reaction against Billy or John. In so far as they played any part in it at all, it was merely by helping to define by distinction her own nature. Simply, she was not their type. Friendship could only go so far: one saw its limits fairly clearly when the thing had gone on for any length of time, and drew back well before they were reached. The fiasco, as she now termed it in her mind, had forced her beyond No Man's Land in relation to John in a way which was bound to have been intolerable for them both. So much for so long had been so elaborately concealed between them. There were subjects they never discussed: and these, by a series of horrific combinations of fortune, had become their predominant preoccupations. Billy was maddening: at the moment, *maddening*. But although the darkest aspect of the whole affair was the way it looked as though she had engineered it all, the girl could not be thought of as culpable. It was not any of their faults. In ordinary circumstances, perhaps, Pamela would never have met the girl, never found out so much, and so, in turn, never discovered that she herself was fundamentally and deeply *not* John's type, as she had for years supposed she was. But this could not be explained in terms of personal blame or causation.

It was hard to define what *had* caused this epiphany, whether it had a cause at all. It was all set in motion by the discovery – embarrassing to both parties – of a difference in attitude towards sex: a difference so profound that their friendship would probably never survive it. Perhaps, though, there had been more to it than that. Beneath the layers of flippancy and irony which life commanded of one, Pamela believed that there was a bedrock of truth. It seemed that John did not share this opinion. As far as he was concerned, the layers of half-truth could go on for ever. You could dig for ever and still not reach Australia. The ideas in his head were merely tried on for size, like clothes. It would have been no good to pry deeper into the heart of awkwardness. It was the difference between one who considered everything in life to be fluid and changeable and shifting, and one who searched, however fleetingly, for a point inside or outside what we call life where the motion and the half-truth ceased and the truth could be seen in stillness and face to face.

She knew that she put her trust in this notion, even though it was something which any professional philosopher could run rings about. She knew that she believed in right and wrong, beautiful and ugly, as absolute standards which, with taste and conscience as guides, could be referred to in the midst of life's muddle. This belief – the odd and illogical combination of faith in the moral life, and a longing for the stillness at the heart of things – divided her from all those who did not share it. For them, it was all sick hurry and divided aims; but for her, even if the muddle was scarcely less, the attitude to the muddle was different: the difference between a live-wire act with or without a safety net.

How irrational, uncharitable, sad, arrogant, neurotic – or simply boring – this set of convictions made people, she was only too painfully aware. The worst of this kind of arrogance was still found in the Roman church, of course; but Christian smugness was revolting wherever it made itself manifest. Often in company she had felt herself swirling cheerfully back into agnosticism as some self-satisfied, ignorant person pretended to certainty about matters that have always remained veiled this side of eternity. Christian bad taste in moral and aesthetic things caused her equal distress. But however little she liked the designation, she knew, if she had to choose, she was a Believer rather than an Unbeliever. Perhaps it was in the blood: a family habit, the inheritance of a long line of clerical ancestors all professionally engaged in the establishment as an isolable truth of what she only felt as a reassuring hunch. Certainly, many other things went with it: a certain type of humour which, she had discovered, was not quite the same as John's, for all its superficial resemblances. It was much more – why did she need to feel surprised by it? – in tune with Hereward.

She had penetrated the veil which separated him from the rest of the world and found there so many things that she did not know she had been craving: nebulous things which touched memories buried from a lost childhood; specific things, like his hair, his cigarette-holder, his skin, curiously delicate and soft. The neurotic weapons which he used to beat off the approach of unwanted predators on his terrain were largely what had drawn her to him in the first place: affectations of accent, screwed-up eyes, a cleverly timed atmosphere, which he never failed to give off, that he might, at any moment, fly into a rage. Beyond this routine covering of thin skin ('My sister says I'm thin-skinned,' he moaned, one day, 'it makes me feel like a sausage') there was a character who was surprisingly self-assured.

It had occurred to her first ages ago when she had still been trying to view him as a joke. She had tried to explain it to herself in intellectual terms: he's simply too clever for the job. But as she got to know him better she realized that cleverness in strictly academic terms did not come into it. Hereward was clever about people: too clever, which was what made his favourite tag from George Herbert so apposite. He saw other people's hearts by a fast instinct – it made one fear that he would intuit things which were not really there – but it also meant that conversations in which almost nothing had been concluded, still less spelt out or actually *said*, seemed afterwards to have been pregnant with strength and importance.

He had known them already, known them all. He had summed up Billy almost at once; probably intuited John's part in the affair; and, she felt certain, understood Pamela better than she understood herself. It must, she had come to think, be lonely to have quite such sensitive antennae about people. Quite apart from any professional reasons of sacerdotal distance, Pamela felt he was doomed to loneliness: few could expect friendship to flower under such watchful scrutiny as his.

But why, in that case, had her own friendship with him so magnificently blossomed to the point where separation from him seemed almost unthinkable?

'When's Billy off?' he asked.

'Mel and Gale come tomorrow. They're spending three days

here and then they're going off to Lincoln and somewhere else.'

'Which hotel have you booked them into?'

'I hadn't really given the matter any thought. I assume they've done the bookings themselves. But the place isn't crowded at this time of year. It'll be November by the end of next week.'

'They could always stay here – or wouldn't it be grand enough for them? We don't have radiators, etc., but there's a blow heater in one of the bedrooms. It gives off a funny smell, but . . .'

'It would be an absurd imposition on your sister.'

'Nonsense.' He lowered his voice to a whisper and nodded in the direction of the kitchen. 'She rather likes entertaining.'

'Well, let me put it to them,' said Pamela. 'I can't say I'm looking forward to their visit very much. Billy thinks I engineered it all; says she doesn't want them to come. But she'll have to go back with them: she doesn't have any money.'

'These things are never as bad as you fear. They'll spend all their time sight-seeing. There won't be too much embarrassing, You Know . . .'

'I do hope so.'

He had a way of speaking with a smile at the same time as seeming to snap, like a friendly dog.

'I've not told you anything of what's happened, have I?' she said.

'This and that.'

'But I feel you understand everything: it's so wonderful that you do. You don't realize how hard all this would be if you hadn't been around to hold my hand.'

They stood leaning against the chimney-piece and as they did so he took both her hands in his and looked at her.

'You are absurd.'

It almost sounded as if he was going to give her one of his famous tickings off.

'Why?'

'Anyone would think I was some kind of magician; whereas

241

you know, everything that's happened to you has been entirely predictable.'

'Everything?'

'Yes.'

'If you could have predicted it, why did you not move in and stop it?'

'How could I? I decided,' he said suddenly, as he refilled their sherry glasses, 'I decided to let you decide about that country business.'

'What business?'

'The idea of going to live in the country. You're right. It wouldn't do *on my own*. The country can be depressing, don't you think?'

'Almost invariably.'

'Unless you have the right companion.'

'The perfect companion, I suppose,' she conceded.

'I mean, if it didn't work, one might turn to drink, or become one of those, mm-ya, mm-ya, how shall I put it, eccentric clergymen? Terrible bore. You know, model railways, or ghosts; know what I mean?'

'Not really. It's funny.'

'What is?'

'Here we are again, drinking sherry, talking, and last time we had a talk about the country place you said you would have to go there to avoid scandal.'

'Well, we will have to decide.'

'*We* will? What are the parish going to think if we stand round boozing and deciding things?'

'Oh,' he said, throwing his cigarette-end into the hearth, 'bugger the parish.'

'Mel reckons John's not in Dublin at all: he thinks he's kinda shy. He's going to call in on him this afternoon, have him do a guided tour of his college.'

'I'm sure he won't be lucky,' said Pamela.

'You mean you believe he's in Dublin?'

'That's what he said.'

The two women sat together in Pamela's sitting-room. It was, Pamela saw, ungracious of John not to consider meeting them, after all their kindness. She hoped he would give a plausible impression of being out. Perhaps he could hide upstairs with Sir Jorrocks Monteith.

Pamela herself had found it agreeable to renew contact. Mel had found it necessary to spend most of his time in the town on professional business: meeting dum-dums who also worked on 'Alfred'; being very casual, very informal, very intimate; checking things out and sifting through a whole load of crap in the library. Gale had taken a jollier view of the possibilities afforded by their few days' visit, and had insisted on being taken everywhere. Her instamatic had snapped every spire, tower, traffic warden and statue within a twenty-mile radius of the room where they now sat; or so it felt from the way their legs ached and their feet pulsated.

Gale was a good sort – a phrase which recurred in Pamela's mind whenever she contemplated her guest's character. It had manifested itself in all kinds of ways: offers to help about the house; endless letters and postcards scrawled in spindly American copper-plate to a sister who lived on Riverside Drive, Manhattan ('We stayed with her the night before we got on the airplane. She's doing a course at a smoke-end clinic; it made her kinda tetchy; I guess she's feeling sorry she snapped so'); in short, a constant appreciation of the other person's point of view. She was appreciative, too, of the furnishings of Pamela's house and almost made her believe in the sitting-room again.

'You have such really lovely things,' she said with undisguised envy. 'Now, tell me, where did you get that simply gorgeous watercolour over the fireplace?'

'It is nice, isn't it? Hereward gave it me just after I came out of hospital.'

'Isn't he divine? He and Frideswide have been great, just great. We have our own routine, they don't interfere with us, but you know, they just make you feel welcome.'

It was surprising that this was working out so well. How far the Stickleys were really enjoying it was hard to guess, but at least there had been no overt hostility from Frideswide, in spite of Mel's rather unguarded language, and Gale's offer to teach Frideswide how to make a *real* Waldorf salad.

'There's only one thing about Hereward, honey.'

'Oh, what's that?'

'You're handling him wrong. You know, that man adores you. Now what you ought to do is think of getting yourself another boyfriend; some randy post-doc maybe . . .'

'What on earth for?'

'Why, to jack up Herry, of course. I can just see the pair of you hovering on like this until you're both in the sunset home. OK, so you're shy, you're diffident, you're reserved. I like all that. But you aren't characters in Austen. You ought to get him to snap out of it.'

'But I like reserved, diffident men.'

'Oh, you're impossible.' She said it with the air of a connoisseur who had found a particularly rare breed. 'But tell me about the drawing – painting, whatever it is.'

'As I say, Hereward gave it to me when I was ill.'

'Do you think it is *valuable*?'

'It is to me.'

'But who painted it?'

'I've kept asking him. He's vague about things like that. I

244

wondered whether it was one of Ruskin's drawings: but it would surely be signed if it were.'

'It's a willow, huh?'

'No. A weeping ash.'

'I'm going to call him up right now,' Gale announced.

'Oh, please don't. He hates the telephone.'

'So? Who does he think he is: St Simeon Stylites? Do you know, Tennyson wrote a poem about that guy. Mel's been working on it recently. You know, the guy who lived on a pillar in the desert for twenty years or something silly. The question Mel wants to find out is what did they do with the shit?'

'Hereward would probably know.' Pamela had once heard an explanation of this conundrum, but she did not care to repeat it.

A peculiar rapport had grown up between Hereward and Gale. He had even taken her for a solitary drive in the Morris one afternoon when Pamela wanted to pore over Gower in the library, and Billy had put her foot down about any more sightseeing. He had shown her his new parish – the move was arranged, the induction fixed for the Epiphany – and then driven on to the gardens at a neighbouring country house, and a folly on the hill outside the town. There had been time, even, for tea with the nuns at Wantage. On their way out of the town, Gale had been enchanted by the statue of Alfred the Great and asked if it was done from life.

'Herry?' she was saying into the receiver. 'It's me. Gale. I'm just simply enchanted by the lovely painting you gave Pamela a while back ... Uh-huh ... Listen, are you busy this morning, or can I bring her round to see you ... You have? That'll be great ... I wish so, too, honey.'

Pamela gawped in astonishment at the way that Gale had set about the infinitely delicate problem of how to handle the man. Far from causing explosions or total withdrawal her brashness seemed just the ticket.

'He's free any time,' Gale said. 'How'bout you and me going round now while Billy's still out at the stores.'

In the street, they passed Frideswide, a heavy figure cycling furiously, white hair swept back by the wind. She managed a steely smile, but it was only the thing of a moment.

'She rides that thing like it was a broomstick.'

'She's not bad,' Pamela said. 'If you get to know her.' Wondering if she would ever have the chance of verifying the assertion.

'Did you know she wanted to be a nun?'

'No. I never heard that.'

'She spent six months at some place near Windsor. I forget the name of it now. She wanted to stay. They figured it wasn't their idea of a quiet life, I guess.'

'Poor Frideswide. When was that?'

'Forty years ago. She told me last night when we were clearing away the dishes.'

'How bold you are, Gale. I can never imagine extracting such confidences from Hereward's sister.'

But this conversation terminated, because they had reached the front gate and he had thrown open the door exuberantly to greet them.

Coffee was on the boil: a few shortbread biscuits laid out on a plate. He was wearing his check shirt and brown corduroy trousers, and sandals on his feet. He ushered the two women in with shameless amusement.

Pamela's initial explanation for all this bonhomie was that Hereward perhaps believed Gale – all Americans – to have come to Europe for the sole purpose of unloading surplus cash and that the splendid edifice for which he took responsibility might in consequence hope to benefit. But there was more to it than that. He was evidently, simply, charmed by Gale. She was animated, beautiful, uninhibited, big-hearted, amusing.

'You know,' he said. 'You're going to discover my guilty secret. Let's have coffee in the garage.'

'Isn't this exciting!' Gale exclaimed, and Pamela could not help feeling excited too, even though she felt mildly jealous that, if he had a mind to start disclosing secrets, it should be to Gale rather than to herself. She wondered what the garage could contain. Although he had often mocked at it in other members of his profession, Pamela strongly suspected that it was a model railway. She had met at least three clergymen who had this harmless dissipation and although it had not struck her before as Hereward's kind of thing, perhaps he had protested a little too much. This was, in any event, going to be a day of discoveries.

The smell of turpentine soon proved her speculations false. He had led the way through a tiny patch of garden and it was not long before she saw that the garage was being used as a highly cramped artist's studio. At one end, a large drawing-board supported jars of brushes, pencils, knives and quills. At the other, an easel supported a bare canvas, recently stretched and primed. All over the floor, the walls, the benches, were paintings and drawings. There were flower paintings, landscapes, sketches of trees, all, obviously, belonging to the same school as the *Weeping Ash* already in Pamela's possession. There were Mediterranean buildings – oils evidently 'worked up' from sketches of Nice, Bologna, Cadiz. There were, moreover (and however hard she tried not to make the connection, it seemed unavoidable), about thirty oil sketches of a much romanticized thin, elegant woman, pale as marble, sometimes with blonde hair in a bun, sometimes with it loose and abundant, covering face, shoulders and whatever torso would have been painted were the works complete. Was it pure vanity which made her feel that these studies stood out from all the rest: that there was a freedom and near brilliance of execution, particularly in his handling of the *hair*, which made one freeze and stare?

'I was going to ask you who painted that adorable little tree you gave to Pamela. Now I guess it's unnecessary to put that particular question . . .'

'Why did you never *say*?' Pamela asked. He was clearly, in a sheepish way, delighted by the surprise occasioned by the scene.

'Do you have exhibitions of all this stuff?' Gale was asking.

'Lord, no. Who would want to buy it? You see, my trouble is that I was taught to paint by a great-uncle who was practically a contemporary of Lord Leighton's: a painter, I might add, whom he regarded as lamentably "modern". I have tried the other stuff and I just can't do it.'

'But this is simply so *good*,' said Pamela. Before, she had always felt the need to consciously bolster his self-confidence; now, the praise flowed spontaneously. She was so surprised that she could not really believe that the paintings and drawings were real.

'Not good,' he corrected her, handing round the biscuit tray, an unlit Gold Flake dangling in the holder between his lips. 'It is totally secondary, academic, flat. It's *competent*,' he corrected her faltering interruption. 'I'm not being falsely modest. There is probably no one in England more technically competent.'

'I just didn't think people painted this way any more,' said Gale. She was surveying a glossily handled piazza. In the foreground, a young man in a suit and a girl in sunglasses were sipping with a straw from a single glass. Behind the café tables, the west front of a baroque church caught the mid-day sun. Every detail, from the glistening Coca-Cola in the tumbler to the glazed relief of the Madonna in the architrave of the main porch, was rendered with Pre-Raphaelite exactitude. A bicycle, beer mats, a little boy in a T-shirt and shorts, the shadowy plane trees, the thick blue of the Italian sky – created a curious impression of temporal dislocation. It was a scene of the last ten years: faded posters, half torn from the stucco on the side of the café, alluded to the World Cup, Andreotti, strikes, cigarettes. But it was a scene surveyed by a disciple of Millais: its detailed assembled evidences of modernity did nothing to dispel the impression. The young lovers, perfectly proportioned, their fingertips half touching as they drank, were plainly in disguise. The 'flip-flop' shoes, the sunglasses, the short sleeves did nothing to hide the fact that they were Victorian ghosts.

'It's beautiful,' Gale said. 'I'll buy it. Please, please, let me buy it.'

'It isn't worth anything,' he said. 'Can't you see? You have said yourself. One just doesn't paint pictures like that any more.

There have been other ways of manifesting that sort of exactitude – Magritte's way, Hockney's – whom I admire inordinately. But not this way any more. It would be money down the drain if you bought that.'

'Even so. I want it. How much do you want for it?'

'I don't want anything for it. If you're serious you can give some money to the poor old church which one of these days is going to need a new roof.'

'OK. How much d'you suggest?'

He lit the cigarette.

'Oh, I should think about a thousand.' The shocked pause allowed him to add – 'I don't know how much things are worth. But give what you like.'

She was producing a cheque book.

'Mel's going to kill me,' she said. 'Not only for buying the picture – because I think he'll like it – but for giving you money for your church. With all respect, Herry, Mel thinks religion stinks.'

'He's very probably right,' said Hereward smiling triumphantly. 'In general. Mine doesn't. It merely costs a great deal of money.'

Pamela watched the negotiation with a mixture of admiration and embarrassment. She had just reached the point of convincing herself that he was not going to milk Gale for a contribution to his parish funds, and the manner in which he had done so was so unexpected that she could only incredulously stare. Her eye fell back to a perusal of the sketches – none of them quite right – of herself. For, the more she looked at them, the more convinced she became that they could not be anything else. There were so many that they reflected something amounting to an obsession.

'I started them when you were in hospital,' he said, in answer to her unspoken query. He and Gale had finished their trade. The cheque had been pocketed – arrangements had been agreed about packing up the painting and sending it across the Atlantic; he had whined something about generosity.

'Perhaps,' Pamela said boldly, 'I ought to sit for you properly.'

Gale seemed curiously unaware of the Pamela pictures. She was wandering round at the other end of the garage rummaging among the drawings.

'You can take a handful of those since you've been stung so handsomely for the painting,' he said.

'I can? That's just wonderful. Can I take any of them? Don't you have any favourites?'

'Not particularly.'

'Didn't you ever think of being an artist?'

'I am an artist – in a part-time sort of way.'

'Gale meant, not in a part-time sort of way.'

'Not really,' he said. 'I've already explained. I haven't really got a *style*. Anyone can learn to draw.'

'Not as well as this.' Gale was holding up a pen and ink sketch of a dead elm. 'It's absolutely fantastic.'

'I could have been a forger,' he said archly. 'No, no. I'm perfectly serious. When I was in my late teens, early twenties, I realized that I had this knack. I had fun playing about with it. I stuck to Victorians. I don't know if I could do an earlier period. I did a whole series: an Arthur Hughes, a couple of Hopleys, a Henry Wallis, a Mulready. Then I tried a Rossetti. Easier, you would think, his style was more idiosyncratic than any of the others, and he was less competent. I had difficulty with the first attempt, though. It was a caricature – like one of the thousand Rossetti imitators. Strudwick or someone. Then, one day, the thing took off. It was like spirit-writing – spirit-painting. I was alarmed. Somehow, although I was pleased by the result, I did not feel comfortable with the thing in the room.'

'What did you do?'

'This was thirty, no, thirty-five years ago. I didn't have a lot of ecclesiastical real estate to keep up. I hadn't even been ordained.'

'You mean, you didn't sell it?'

'No. I gave it away. The mother of a friend of mine took a fancy to it. Thought it was a Medici print and then realized it was a cut above. I signed it for her – a really flamboyant

250

D.G.R – and we put the thing in an old gilt frame that she bought from a junk shop and I painted the title at the bottom: *Paolo and Francesca*. It was pastiche; not a copy. A scene based on the two lovers in the *Inferno*, you know.'

'What happened to it after that?'

'I saw it again about twenty years ago in Bond Street. I went into the gallery where it was being given pride of place and asked about it. A private owner had decided to sell it. I asked them if they realized that they were selling a fake. It was up for sale as the genuine article, of course. Admittedly, Victorian painters were less absurdly expensive than they have become since, but they were asking a pretty penny. They asked me *why* I thought it was a fake and I stupidly told them. Well, you can imagine the reaction. Lunatic clergyman. They'd bought it under the impression it was genuine. They weren't going to change their minds. It made me glad I hadn't gone into the thing professionally.'

'Perhaps it was genuine,' Pamela said.

'I remember painting the bloody thing.'

'But perhaps things can become real even if they started out as fakes. I mean, if everyone believed the painting to be a Rossetti – except you, and perhaps the person who sold it – what's the difference?'

'That's a very religious question,' Gale interposed. 'Mel would say that Herry'd just gone into confidence tricks of a different kind since he turned his collar round.'

'Would he indeed?' His face had reddened immediately. The lips became tight and, reassuringly, an atmosphere of fury was resumed. 'I hate that sort of arrogant agnosticism,' he spat out. 'What in God's name does Mel know about it?'

'Nothing, I guess.' She had not meant to spark off this eruption. 'Don't be mad.'

'Why shouldn't I be mad?'

'Don't quarrel,' Pamela interposed. 'Gale's been very generous to you, Hereward. She wasn't meaning to hurt your feelings. Besides, you don't want to part on bad terms. She's going home tomorrow, remember.'

He was still simmering – in spite of his, 'Perhaps you didn't mean it offensively. I didn't mean to snap. Let's have some gin.'

– 22 –

It was absurd to have become Firework Fellow.

John stared at the fantastic armoury which littered his carpet. A large catherine wheel had been whimsically suspended from the key in the door of his grandfather clock. Around, lay boxes of sparklers, rockets, Roman candles, squibs, bangers.

The celebration of Gunpowder Treason was a College Tradition. Some imagined that it dated back to the seventeenth century itself, but it had actually been initiated for an Armistice festivity in the 1920s by Sir Jorrocks Monteith. Until recently, the old man had supervised the arrangements himself, but the responsibility now passed in rotation among the younger fellows, together with a manual, compiled by Sir Jorrocks himself, which insured that an identical rubric was followed each year.

Yesterday, John had supervised the erection of the huge bonfire behind the college pavilion. The explosives themselves, on Sir Jorrocks's insistence, were stored with the Fireworks Fellow until the afternoon of November 5th, when they were transported by college servants to the playing fields. It was not known whether there was a specific reason for this over-elaborate precaution. Some people dimly remembered a nasty incident when an undergraduate let off a rocket in the quad in 1937 or 8. But it was probably a manifestation of Monteith's delight in creating childish surprises. He loved secrets. He had hobbled down the stairs several times that morning to make sure that John was checking through the supply as directed in the rubric.

'I usually put the smaller Roman candles flat down under my bed,' he had said, hovering near the window on his good foot. 'And the rockets I stow on the north side of the room. Cooler. And switch off that gas fire.'

It had meant, by the time he had finished his directions, that explosive devices had been laid down at points all over the room.

'Mind how you go,' the old man had barked. 'It would be a nuisance if we had a fire. I've got diaries upstairs spanning half a century and more.'

John had cancelled or postponed that morning's tutorials. The intrusion of so many brightly coloured parcels all over the furniture and carpets made it somehow impossible to concentrate on his books, and there was still, besides, much to be done. Even had he wanted to see them, there would not have been much time to fit in Mel or Gale. He hoped that the claim to be in Dublin would go unchallenged. It was not that he did not like them: rather, that he liked them both too much, and found the way in which the Billy fiasco had poisoned relations in that area too painful to face squarely.

He had noticed more and more with the passing of the weeks that he was actively missing America. It had been hard to settle down to anything since his return. His long mornings in a bright air-conditioned library glowed in the memory; so did the evenings in the company of bright garrulous people whose low standards of conversation meant that talk always flowed. That ghastly sensation of 'drying up' at dinner: not knowing in the slightest degree what to say to your neighbour: allowing the moment to pass, the silence to deepen and thicken, until speech became almost physically impossible: this familiar pattern of English life had reasserted itself since he came back, and he pined nostalgically for the atmosphere which had enabled him to chatter in a natural way about his poetry, about politics, about food, films, friends. Perhaps it had been a mistake when, after two semesters at Cornell, he had turned down the chance of a permanent job there. The pay had been good, the appointment honorific. Moreover, the Americans were simply more *appreciative* of merit than the English. He did not think this in a spirit of total self-conceit. He knew that he was developing a reputation in England as well as on the Eastern sea-board and up-state New York. His books sold well in England, as such books go. His lectures were well attended. But it often took years for an English colleague to get round to saying they *liked* a book, article or lecture. Even Pamela, to whom he had sent his volume of verse, had said almost nothing about it. He had felt forced to ask if it had actually reached her, since her silence on the matter seemed eerie; and all she had said was, 'Yes, yes it has. Thank you, John, so much.' And gone on to talk about why people liked gnomes in their gardens.

It was hard to *keep on* without encouragement. Perhaps this was what had been wrong, from the beginning, with his friendship with Pamela. He had, without allowing himself to admit the fact, expected too much: all the emotional advantages of a marital intimacy without any of its risks or responsibilities. Conversely, with Billy, he had merely wanted the risks and thrills, with none of the reassurances of companionship in a spiritual or unseen sense. It was odd that, in spite of all that had happened, he could not think of *her*, personally. He had a sinking sense of dread which he associated with her. He knew when he had this feeling that she was near or that business to do with her was to hand: a mixture of the criminal's fear of being found out and simple animal lust. But he had never got it right, this difficulty of women. Either he should have left women alone altogether, or he should have taken the risk once more and sought a wife. He saw the force of this strongly. The sad thing was that Billy was so strongly and obviously the wrong sort of girl; and Pamela, who had seemed more or less as close as you were likely to get to Miss Right, had now irrevocably slipped from his reach. He should have played that card much earlier – years before, in an hotel in Pembrokeshire, had been the moment – if anything were to have come of it.

He sat at his desk checking Sir Jorrocks's rubric and writing notes of his own. At three o'clock the porters would come to take away the fireworks. The bonfire was already in place. He ticked those two items on his list. Instructions about chestnuts, cocoa, toddy, had been confirmed with the college kitchens.

It is advisable that the Fireworks Fellow sports his oak until the arrival of the porters. Visitors should not be given the chance of

seeing (*or appropriating!*) *any of the fireworks . . . In general, follow
the dictates of Common-Sense.*

He smoked his pipe as he read the irritating bossy sentences. He was taking some pleasure in minute infringements of the
regulations. When the old bore had departed, for instance, he
had moved the Roman candles from under his bed and put them
in his wardrobe. He did not intend to freeze for the rest of the day,
so the gas fire remained lit. But he supposed that if he did
not close the outer of his two doors, there would only be
complaints next time Monteith waddled down to badger secre-
taries in the Bursary.

As he went to close the door, he almost bumped into Billy.

'So much for your being away,' she said.

'Come in. I'm very busy. I must shut this outer door.'

'Oh-oh. *No*, John. Not this time.'

But he closed it, ignoring her imputation.

'Security,' he assured her.

'I came to leave you a note. Now I guess I can say good-bye
person to person.'

'Yes you can.'

'It'd've been better to write. It's kinda hard to know what
to say . . .'

She began to tear her envelope in half.

'I wanted to thank you. I guess I wanted to say sorry. And
then again I wanted to make you feel lousy.'

'You've already done those things.'

'Convenient for you, isn't it?'

'What?'

'Mel and Gale just descending like this to take me away. Now
you and Pamela can get on with your wonderful lives just as
happily as if neither of you had ever met me.'

'Don't be like that.'

'Just lucky the hospital – fuck them – sent a wire to Gale.
She thought I'd sent it. She's crazy. Poor Gale . . . ?'

He was staring at her with incomprehension in his face.

'But I sent the wire.'

'Pardon me?'

'The wire. I sent it.'

He realized as soon as he spoke that he should never have admitted it. He had not realized fully that there was anything wrong with having done so. Someone had to take responsibility for the girl, and in recent years, this task had fallen on Gale. John did not feel equal to shouldering it himself.

'You really hate me, don't you? You really want to screw me up. Just when I was starting a new life, independent of Mel and Gale, you screw me up all over again.'

'I was trying to help.'

She replied quietly, but hysterically.

'No, John. You were trying to wipe me off the slate, trying to destroy me. You weren't trying to help me at all. It's like I said, you just wanted to carry on as nice as if you'd never, either of you, fallen in with me. Don't you see I needed a break from Mel, for God's sake.'

'Mel?'

'The whole thing is so sick and you and Pamela are so stupid. So fucking stupid. Mel's just crazy about me. It's tearing *me* apart. It's not doing him much good either. We're lovers . . .'

'Don't do that!'

She had leant forward to the gas fire and ignited the corner of the envelope which she held in her hand. He did not really take in what she was talking about. The sight of naked flame in the room suddenly caused him to panic.

'It's the letter I wrote you,' she said. 'Like I said, you don't need to read it any more. I've come to say good-bye person to person.'

'Blow it out, stamp on it, no, NOT in the waste-paper basket.'

'What's eating you? You some sort of pyrophobic nut or something?'

'Haven't you *noticed*, or are you too busy telling me about the infinitely tedious and predictable state of your trivial little soul, we are in a room surrounded by FIREWORKS.'

'Firecrackers?'

'Yes. Bloody firecrackers. Put that flame out at once. Here. Let me have it.'

He grabbed forward impulsively towards the burning enve-lope and she started back in fear. The flaming charred paper fluttered from her grasp as if it had life of its own, hovering for a moment like a grotesque butterfly and landing eventually in a box of rockets on the writing table.

'Say!' said a voice outside. 'What's going on in there? I can hear you, John. I'm just going to stand here till you open the door.'

'Oh Christ! Don't you realize never to knock if someone has sported his oak?' John shouted back through the keyhole.

'Pardon me?'

'If the door's shut, you aren't supposed to knock.'

'How does someone know you're here if the door's locked and you aren't supposed to knock?' persisted the voice. 'It's Mel here. Quit the play-acting.'

Billy was screaming. The wrapping paper round the box of rockets had already caught fire. Was John crazy? Why didn't he do something instead of bellowing at someone through the door? In the split second during which he opened the door and ran back to the table brandishing a cushion, it was too late.

Mel stood in the doorway grinning, on his head a pork-pie hat purchased at an old-fashioned outfitters in the High Street that morning.

There was a thunderous explosion which threw John side-ways. Six or seven rockets flew off simultaneously into opposite corners of the room. Billy knelt down on the sofa and screamed. Mel ran towards her, calling out, 'I'm here, honey.'

John could see that. He wondered why. Sir Jorrocks Monteith was already at the door as the catherine wheel on the grand-father clock, ignited by a passing rocket, started to revolve.

'What the devil's going on?' he barked. 'Precisely what we wanted to avoid. Here, Brocklehurst, we must start a line of volunteers with buckets.'

He rattled the handle of the large red pail on the landing. Undergraduates were coming out of their rooms. Vi had run down to tell the Head Porter to telephone the fire brigade. There were now little pockets of flame all over the room. John's great-grandfather over the mantelpiece was encircled with fire, like a performing poodle jumping through a burning hoop. Squibs were sizzling across the carpet. Billy remained on the sofa, where Mel vainly tried to comfort her.

'Watch out!'

'Let's get the hell out of here.'

'Oh, Mel, be careful! Oh John, *do* something.'

John was on the landing with Blundy, S. T. and Kominski, F. X., throwing sand and water about in a fairly undisciplined way. It was then that Mel made his mistake.

'Let's get out through here,' he said, dragging Billy into the bedroom. They were no sooner in there than the case of the grandfather clock, ablaze with orange, crashed against the lintel, forbidding exit, imprisoning them between bed and wardrobe.

They could hear voices in the other room, but by now the smoke was so thick, and the muddle so intense that it was hard to know where any individual screams were coming from.

Below, in the quadrangle, a crowd had collected. The smoke was belching not only from John's window but from the windows of Monteith above. The old man stood on the grass, hoarse with fury. Fanned by breeze, helped by an uncommonly dry, crisp November morning, the fire was racing its way through and along the roof. Firemen with no equipment appeared in helmets, only to realize that they had driven their engine to the wrong side of the college. It was twenty minutes or more before they had their hoses trained on John's windows.

By then, crowds had been cleared well back into the garden, and it was obvious that the conflagration was to be enormous. Staircase servants and dons were detailed to make sure that no one was left indoors. There was a complete evacuation. Leaping along the crenellations as if following a fuse, the flame had now reached the Founder's Library, the Old Bursary, the Conduit Room, and was spreading to the roof of the hall. It was all far too much for the pair of fire engines which had been initially summoned.

'There are still people up there!' John was shrieking, while

Jorrocks Monteith and Vi confirmed that everyone on their staircase was answered for. 'Where in hell are they?'

'Guests, d'you mean?'

'Guests, you silly old goat, of course I mean guests.'

'Well, look here. Something must be done. Fireman! Fireman!'

Sir Jorrocks had already given the firemen so many instructions (and had actually managed to organize Blundy and Kominski into hurling trunksful of his private papers out into the quad) that the men took no notice of him.

With murderous terrifying speed the fire was defeating them. The roof of the hall and the chapel was ablaze. The vast spread of buildings groaned and howled like a monster in pain. Masonry began to crumble. It was the noise, and the blackness of the smoke, which arrested John's attention, the infernal energy of the flames themselves, licking cloisters, bell-tower and Warden's Lodgings. It was so terrible, and yet so beautiful in its terribleness, that he stood like a man transfixed in the crowd on the lawn staring at the disaster in an attitude of dumb worship. Afterwards he was treated for shock. By afternoon, they managed to get the fire under control, but the rubble was still smouldering many hours later. Somewhere in the middle of it all, Mel and Billy lay, clutched to each other, but charred to cinders.

Envoy

Midnight. New Jersey snuggles beneath five inches of snow. Inside the apartment, the lights are off. The thermostat clicks, the boiler hums; the electric clock on the Teasmade in the bedroom registers the passing of a minute or two. His arm round Gale's waist, his knees tucked snuggly against her calves, his lips almost touching the nape of her neck, John lies awake, conscious that sleep is not far away and that he is, in a fashion, happy.

The years have proved that Gale is a woman you can live with; row with; make love to; rely upon: a wife. Every night he clings to her in this foetal position, grateful in some new way for the day that has passed. His hair, what there is of it, is cut the way Gale likes it, brushed forward like a Caesar. The beard, too, which tickles her shoulders as she sleeps, is her idea. The shirts and socks and suits and ties hung in the closet were all bought under her supervision. Even the short scarlet nightsmock he now wears, stretching only to his navel and the small of his back by the time he is comfortable in bed, was Gale's purchase. There is a jaunty nightcap which goes with it, which John says makes him look like he was Santa Claus, and which hangs up above the headboard over the bolster. What freedom it all brings. Oh, so they bicker from morning to night about their domestic arrangements: he's forgotten to switch on the dishwasher, or she's smashed up the near-side wing of the car, or how d'you give a party if your husband has forgotten to buy pretzels and cashew nuts and gherkins, or how d'you write a book if your wife comes into your study every ten goddam minutes with her hang-ups about Paul and Maxine's marriage, or her wanting you to zip her up behind or her needing sour cream in a hurry and can you drive down-town and get some at the delicatessen store. Your *husband*; your *wife*. It felt good making these complaints;

they were words John and Gale often used. It isn't bickering that gets you down. John scarcely notices it happening any more. Rows – like screaming, getting mad, feeling sore – they never have rows. And, oh, those tender long happy hours beneath the duvet when at last, and again and again, he discovers what long ago he had given up any hope of finding. The music of their bodies makes a harmony. It seems to happen without any special effort on his part or on hers: there is no special trick that he has not 'used' with other women and found at last satisfactory. It is not a mechanical thing. The mystery simply happens, time and again, and brings them joy, and heals up all the wounds that he has so prided himself on keeping open, like a child picking the scabs on his knee.

Gale teaches him that you have to keep pressing on. If they steal your shirt, press on without your shirt; if they rip the pants off you, press on without your pants. His attitude was less progressive at first: it had all been, in his view, a matter of digging in his heels: thus far and no further. It is she who has shown him that there is nothing to be fighting *against*, that the battle has all been fought with images of himself that he can happily and easily discard.

The bare outlines of his biography now have a feeling of inevitability about them: the fire, the terrible day of the fire; the collapse which followed – a nervous breakdown they could call it if they liked – the long days in the bin when depression was so intense that he could scarcely move: the inanities of his fellow-patients, the dull sense that he had sunk into a dark hole of melancholy from which nothing could release him. And then, the unpredictable break in the clouds: the sense of freedom which came from knowing that, because he had lost EVERY-THING, the slate was by the same token wiped clean: the way forward was the only way, because all the doors had banged shut behind him.

The nightmares had abated after that. He had come off the drugs, started to talk a little, to read, to plan, to think. From the purely external view, from the professional angle, there was nothing for it but to go. The fire had been his responsibility and his alone. The Warden had been regular in his visits, urged him not to resign his fellowship, assured him that life was getting back to normal; there was not much hope of saving any of the old college buildings, except the bell-tower, but architects had been approached, plans were in motion, other colleges were being very hospitable, and it was rather fun eating in the gymnasium of the choir school instead of in that gloomy, vast hall. It was even mooted at the last meeting of Governing Body that John might consider becoming next Senior Tutor ... It all made the future clear enough to him. Physical strength returned when he had been granted this insight. The abrasive effect of disappointment when he discovered that there was nothing for him at Cornell was merely a spur to action. The Princeton offer had come a few weeks later. Not very prestigious, this appointment: it had been a 'move sideways'. But it was at least a move. He had written the letter to Gale; they had been reunited, and all that had happened since.

He knew (they told him about it when he was 'better') that Pamela had visited him when he was at his worst. He had a dim memory of staring silently ahead while she sat with him and tried to talk, and how her blushes and tears had only increased the black cloud which hung so heavily upon him: made the muscles in his neck and arms stiffen, the horrible blankness of his mind become deader, the pain in his heart more scorchingly acute.

He misses her now. Sometimes she writes to him. The scarcely legible scrawl on the envelope stirs regrets too deep to be felt. He leaves the letters a week or two before answering them and they are less frequent now than they once were. Perhaps their correspondence will one day peter out altogether. He hopes so. Then he will be fully weaned. She is the one he loves. It is this fact which throbbed through his brain in the bin and made him mad. The turbulent fantasies which held him at that time in their power made it hard enough to separate truth from falsehood when the head cleared. There were moments when he believed that the whole episode of Billy had been a product of his diseased imagination; and there were other moments when he wished it had been. The appalling grossness of the sexual images fed into his brain by that particular phase of the madness made actual and fantastic interludes equally real: a bedroom in Mexico, in Shepherd Market; down-town Manhattan and up-state New York: they were all the same obsessive, tormented place which he would have escaped, or so his inner demon cruelly asserted, had he thrown in his lot with Pamela, long ago, in Wales, in a blue and white hotel bedroom, where the damp salt air seeped through the lace curtains. Pamela, since the madness, had become idealized out of all recognition: her skin softer, her eyes brighter, her heart more expansive than he knew from memory to be the case. He began a journal in which he spoke to her, poured out all the fears and horrors which had been buried since childhood, declared himself, as he had long ago wanted to do.

(*After the difficulty over bedrooms had been cleared up – the hotel had inadvertently booked them in as man and wife, and there was a momentary flicker when they both had wondered: should they tell, or should they take the chance? – after the suitcases had been heaved along landings, and they were both established in their single bedrooms, they had walked on the cliffs, looking out towards Caldey. It was there that he could have declared himself. After that moment, he had clammed up, piled on the jokes and funny voices, and let it pass.*)

Then dreams would come and they would find themselves together in that Welsh hotel bedroom. Sometimes the dream-phantom would lull him into believing that she loved him, and he would wake with a sense of absurd relief and happiness which the gradual dawning of his conscious self made intolerably poignant. At other times the dreams were cruel: he was in the room with her, but she did not notice he was there. She was with another – her arms round the shoulders of an old man – while she spoke of John in the savage terms she reserved for the joke gallery. He was one of the men with nicknames – had been all along – he could hear her mocking him and taunting him, but she could never see him there, and had she done, he would have felt afraid. After those dreams he woke up frightened, black, low.

Even now, in the warm cosy security of his marriage to Gale, he is not quite safe from the Pamela nightmare. It will throw him off course for a day or two. He will maybe even sit down and pen a long emotional letter. Usually he has the sense to tear them up straight away. Sometimes he lugubriously stores them in his desk drawer, and will take them out to read a week or two later with a mixture of self-disgust and fascination at the power of his own emotions. Sometimes – once or twice a year perhaps – he will post them. He never has any acknowledgement of these emotional outpourings when she next writes. The phantom Pamela, the cruel nightmare Pamela, perhaps enjoys knowing that she has precipitated so much inner torment. But, with the part of himself that is still capable of feeling embarrassment, he does not allow himself to think about it. Whatever Pamela was to him – and she will always remain in one part of his mind the most important person – she is not his wife: she is not the woman who stopped him going crazy by her constant goodness of heart and commonsense. Now that the ocean divides them, she can become less and less real to him: a religion, a creed, a lost figure from a past he has never been able to puzzle out for himself: the quintessence of all that he was in love with in that past – but now firmly, he is thankful to feel, a phantom.

The soft spongy belly beneath his fingers pulsates steadily in a balanced breathing rhythm. He kisses her fleshy shoulder. She stirs slightly, tickled by his beard. In a moment, they are both possessed by the velvety oblivion of sleep.

February howls and hovers over the grey Atlantic. The night brings snow from the west, sweeping over England. It is six o'clock in Berkshire, and it is still dark, but the thick white blanket over the downs gives off its own eerie light, so that, lying awake, Pamela wonders whether the dawn has risen.

On her dressing-table she can make out the shape of the hideous figurine – a glazed china crinoline lady. She has had it over two years now. How sad it was when the boy appeared on the doorstep of her funny little house – shortly before it was sold. At first, she thought he had come to read the meter. He was unprepossessing, spotty, pale, miserable. 'I brought you this.' Not a gas-man, but a supplementary Christmas postman. Yet the parcel had no stamp, and was only wrapped round with newspaper. 'My mum – we found she'd left like a will. Well, it was a little letter, more like, with instructions, see. She wanted Miss Cowper to have this. You are Miss Cowper?' He was agitated, partly by plain embarrassment, partly by distress. 'She said that she knew you'd appreciate it: in the letter. My dad's never liked it anyway. Always said it was a horrible thing.' The boy had come in; he watched her unwrap it, watched her puzzled intelligent face evidently trying to piece together who he was. Then she said, 'Are you Barry?' He had not stayed long – Christmas shopping – had to get back . . . She was left holding the little china object in her hand, her eyes full of tears. This was Dorothy's idea of Pamela herself: for all its hideous, cheapened, glossy unnecessary vulgarity: a *lady*; a crinoline *lady*. *Most highly favoured lady* . . . Nothing before had emphasized to Pamela so strongly that Dorothy was dead, dead (she could still not stop thinking of it in this way), dead in *her* place. The figurine would follow her about now like a tutelary idol, an emblem of her deliverance. When, all those months, years, ago, she had been told that her own number was up, she had not thought about drawing up a will or settling her affairs. Perhaps as the end approached she would have wondered how to distribute her possessions: between church, college and, presumably, John Brocklehurst. It would never have crossed her mind to remember poor Dorothy in this way. Their time together in the ward had been important, but not *that* important. It could, she felt, equally have been anyone. Only the arbitrariness of things had made it Dorothy; and it had not in any strong sense thrown them *together*.

Now, as she lies still, that time seems impossibly far away: the self of those days vanished and changed: almost hateful to her now. She is embarrassed when she has encountered it, in notes, letters, diaries of the period: its archness, its intolerance, its brittleness. *Swich fyn hath false worldes brotelnesse.* John, poor old thing, still remembers that self. She thinks he has shaken off the absurd delusion of being in love with it, but some of his letters still have to be read lightly, for fear that they will have embarrassing declarations slipped in when you aren't expecting them. *Oh Pamela, why didn't we marry years ago? Why didn't we?* That was a sentence in his last. He seems obsessed by that holiday they once had in Wales when the hotel thought they were married. From Pamela's recollection of the event, he had been only too glad to get the suitcases in separate bedrooms as soon as possible. She had given him all the facial indication that she could that she *was* rather lonely, *would* rather like a more intimate arrangement. But the moment had passed. He was not remotely interested then. Why did it crop up now? She still suffers little stabs of embarrassment when she remembers it all, even though the letter was immediately destroyed, stuffed in the Aga with the other burnable rubbish: eggshells, cereal packets, potato skins, cones from the surrounding cedars. The Aga is meant to heat the radiators and the bath water. But you grow used to feeling cold. The large house would be spoilt without its draughts, its badly fitted windows. Austerity improves the mind and makes you work harder. Her thick volume on Gower is to be published in the summer by the University Press.

She has learnt how to be happy. It is an art. For her, it consists in having plenty of things to cram into the day: research and teaching, which used to occupy so much of her consciousness, are now pushed to the borders of life. Cooking has become a delight: so has the garden (three acres); a little carpentry; a little visiting of the aged. The day is structured: early rising, early bed, hardly an hour which feels 'free'. She has learnt not to be touchy: one person in a household being touchy is quite enough. Others probably ask how *can* she be married to a man who loses his temper at such slight provocation? Others do not know that he worships her, and that living with a devotee is the greatest of life's compensations. Others have no sense of what he was like before. The outbursts of anger now merely punctuate life, they do not infuse the whole of it. He is dedicated to his job, as popular in the village as he needs to be. But he is no longer fussed by it. 'There are more things in life than church,' he says to people: and this truth brings him peace. Most days he paints. His paintings are changing: now less disciplined, in many ways more turbulent, they have lost none of their stylish competence. He has had a one-man show locally; they were nearly all sold. There is talk of an exhibition in London. Last year he was hung in the Academy. As for the fury when his toast burns or the boiled eggs are hard or the car won't start: well, he would not be Hereward without them. Such tempests do not disrupt the tranquillity of her happiness. He has given point to existence. He has not interrupted her old life. She retains her old job, motors into college from the country three or four days a week during term, and at last has started to enjoy it. She even feels a soft spot for Professor Garfield – why had she once called him Hovis? Since his slight stroke, she visits him once a fortnight with a fresh supply of Rex Stouts and sometimes he asks her to read aloud from, of all people, Andrew Lang.

The sky, almost imperceptibly, is growing lighter. She sees it through the gap between her bedroom curtains: a vast pale grey, snow-covered beech and cedar silhouetted against it; beyond the garden gate, the boxy tower of the church. The skinny form, lying in pyjamas beside her, is still deeply asleep. He will not wake until half past seven. He has been so happy – she knows, so happy, since they had the good news confirmed. Sparrows, in spite of the winter darkness, have started to sing. Within the womb, she feels the mysterious stirrings of a new life.